I0597530

BY FORTHRIGHT

FORTHWRITES.COM

Amaranthine Saga, Book 7
Rhomiko and the Confirmed Bachelor

Copyright © 2024 by FORTHRIGHT
ISBN: 978-1-63123-085-1

TWINKLE PRESS

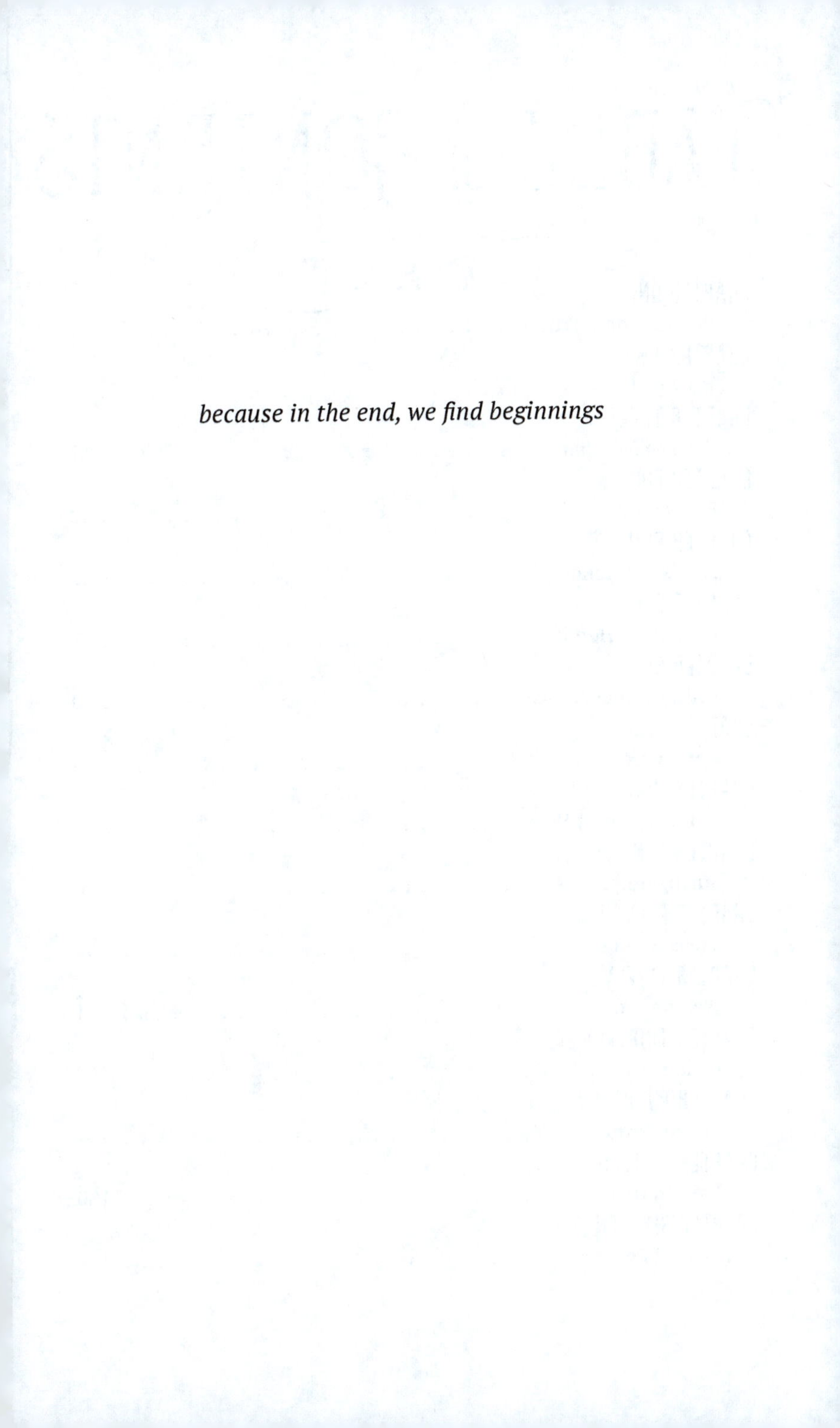

because in the end, we find beginnings

Table of Contents

A MESSAGE FROM FORTHRIGHT

RECOMMENDED READING

*Over the course of their writing, the books in the **Amaranthine Saga** and the short stories in the **Songs of the Amaranthine** collection have been overlapping in interesting ways. Each informs the others, and new details are always coming to light. The same can be said of **Lord Mettlebright's Man** (Amaranthine Interludes, #1), a serial (in 100-word chapters) runs behind the scenes of the Amaranthine Saga, beginning after the events of Book 1, all from the perspective of Jacques Smythe.*

*And now we have **Suuzu and the Nine Nippets of Legend** (Amaranthine Interludes, #2), a short story set during those few weeks between the end of Bk5, when Suuzu finds the golden seed and is sent to Stately House by his brother … and the end of the rescue mission at the end of Bk6. Necessary reading? I have two words for you. Boniface Smythe.*

If you want to catch the significance of all the allusions in this book, I suggest brushing up on the Saga & Songs before you proceed. If you haven't yet explored the option, reading (and rereading) is truly a pleasure with the audio editions, narrated by Travis Baldree.

*And if you aren't ready for the stories to end, I invite you to seek out my blog at **ForthWrites.com** and my account on Patreon, where serials are underway & where new stories will be announced.*

RHOMIKO

AND THE CONFIRMED BACHELOR

1

WISHES COME TRUE

Hisoka opened his eyes and found Argent hovering at the side of the bed. Nothing in the fox's expression gave away how much he'd overheard, but ... probably everything. Argent would want to know about Hisoka's past, probably *needed* to know, but he wasn't ready to face the kinds of questions that would drag splinters of truth out of the wound in his heart.

Argent's brows lifted, but all he said was, "I will bring food."

And so the fox retreated, leaving Hisoka alone to face Nemi's legacy.

Rhomiko stirred and opened eyes unlike ... anything. Their irises might have been carved from dull gray stone, without a hint of shine. The only thing that spared them from lifelessness was the glitter of black pupils that widened, then tightened down as they focused on him.

Recognition livened Rhomiko's whole expression. The hand Hisoka had been holding pulled free, and Rhomiko sat up. Blankets fell away, baring pale skin freckled by innumerable tiny facets. Hisoka couldn't say for certain if these were reflecting the ambient light or if Nemi's child had inherited some of her shine.

Hisoka was already reaching for a bare shoulder to check, but maybe he shouldn't?

Rhomiko didn't shy away from his claws. Indeed, Nemi's child pivoted toward him. Permission.

Warm skin felt ordinary enough. But visually, it was wholly unique. Pretty.

Rhomiko bent nearer, and the hacked ends of long hair slipped forward, framing a face with pronounced cheekbones. She ... he ... *they* looked undernourished. Propping up on an elbow, Hisoka ran a cautious hand over the jut of a shoulder, then gaunt ribs. Concerned, he mumbled, "You must be starving."

"Do you think so?"

"Argent is bringing food."

Rhomiko traced one of Hisoka's eyebrows with a fingertip. "Are *you* hungry?"

"I can't remember the last time I ate."

"Will you teach me?"

"You don't know how to eat?"

"I have never had the pleasure," Rhomiko said, sounding as if they were quoting someone. Nemi. Yes, the inflection was pure Nemi. "You will teach me."

Hisoka should have realized. Rhomiko had never been outside the chrysalis that had also protected Nemi. A whole life spent in captivity, safely kept in their mother's arms, awaiting rescue. Awaiting *him*.

He asked, "Do you even *need* food?"

"I wonder. My father consumed sigils, and my mother took strength from songs."

Neither sounded particularly filling. "I know a moonbeam who likes custard."

"Teach me that, then."

"I don't know what Argent might bring."

"Neither do I," said Rhomiko, sounding delighted that they had something in common.

Hisoka was finding this half-star, half-stone person increasingly confusing. Hannick Alpenglow had explained that Nemi's child was without gender, that Impressions could choose either. Or choose to do without. The imps Hisoka had met before had either presented as male or female, but Rhomiko's scent and what he could see of their physiognomy ... nothing was definitive.

Felines embodied curiosity, and new things were inherently interesting. But Hisoka's instincts had him second-guessing every response. He hadn't realized how much of his clan's culture and how many feline courtesies *relied* on gender. Averting his gaze, he mumbled, "Do you have any idea what you might need?"

"Only that I need you." So serene, so pleased. "And you are here."

Hisoka eased back onto his pillow, wanting to put more distance between them. "I don't know what to do."

"I do not mind." Rhomiko scooted closer, pushing up onto hands and knees, looming over Hisoka, trapping him. Their hair curtained the rest of the world from view.

Hisoka wondered if there was impish allure at play. He couldn't bring himself to look away, even though some part of him was anxious for escape. What was Rhomiko after? But then he caught the briefest sparkle of green within the liquid black, like fireflies dancing in the distance. He watched intently, hoping it would happen again, noticing too late that the space between them had diminished considerably.

With a smile that set off another spiral of green sparks, Rhomiko kissed the tip of his nose.

An old memory flowed back. Of Nemi drawing Hoshiko into her arms and bestowing kisses, some light, some lingering, and one bright enough for any to see. His sister may have had Hiroki for a twin, but it was Nemi's mark that shone upon her brow.

Rhomiko next pressed a soft kiss to Hisoka's forehead, as if trying to bestow the mark shining in his memories.

And still, Hisoka didn't know what to do. Should he rebuff as he would any advance? Should he reciprocate as a form of greeting? Rhomiko was not a child, but they may as well be newborn. And so he took up the same refrain, even though it made him sound petulant. "I don't know what to do."

"You have never kissed someone before?"

"I … have."

"Am I mistaken?"

Hisoka finally managed to lower his gaze. "I would hardly criticize a courtesy."

"The first was from Mother. She asked me to give it, and I have kept my promise."

A kiss from Nemi? But why? Affection? Gratitude? Forgiveness?

"The second was from me. I thought it would shine. In Mother's stories, a kiss to claim would shine."

Hisoka's gaze was pulled back, then drawn deep, for that fizz of green sparkles kindled his curiosity, held him rapt. Rhomiko's eyes held something like the fire in a gemstone, dancing just out of reach. Akin to the whisper-light touch of Michael's soul whenever he coaxed for a tending session. Teasing. Alluring. Perfect.

"Why would you ...?" Hisoka began. But he was already shying away from the answer his question might bring. He'd lived too long with starry portents not to be wary of truths. Especially those he didn't want to hear. So instead, he asked, "Why *Rhomiko*?"

"My name?"

"Yes. It's not a star's name. Rhomi, perhaps. But *miko*?"

"For you."

Hisoka hesitated. "I don't understand."

"You have watched over others called miko."

"That's true. But how did you know?"

Rhomiko went on. "You oversaw their happiness, and you envied their happiness. You wished for a miko of your own. Or a ... a Michael of your own?"

"I ... I *never* ...!" At least, not in so many words.

"Mother must have known what you wished for." With all the confidence of stars, who know the truth simply because it is true, Rhomiko declared, "I am the answer."

2
WASHED UP

The sea had nearly doused the sun when Sinder dragged himself wearily onto the beach below Stately House. Cold seas and bitter winds had him curling tight atop snowy sand. He might like swimming, but crossing the ocean twice in a matter of days had stolen the last of his reserves.

"Shit, it's cold." He tried to think who to call for help.

"I knew you'd be back."

Dunce and double dunce. "Heyyy, Fend. Here to do me in?"

"That would hardly be sporting. Not when you've already half-killed yourself."

Sinder had been expecting teeth. Or perhaps claws. Instead a tongue rasped across his shoulder, and a velveted paw rolled him onto his back. He stared with mute misery into mocking eyes.

"Come along, Damsel."

"Not going anywhere with you," he muttered, jaw clenched to

keep his teeth from chattering.

"Wrong. I found you, and I intend to keep you."

The big cat lowered himself over Sinder, which may have been some kind of feline posturing, but all that really mattered was that Fend's fur was warm. Sinder grabbed hold with numbed fingers, burying them deeper, seeking heat.

"Unless you want to be scruffed like a kitten, you'll need to get on my back."

"Can't."

"You should be honored that I'd offer."

"I'm serious. Body's shutting down." Sinder was helpless, and he was too tired to care.

"Rouse yourself, and I'll bring you to Timur."

"Michaelson?"

"You want him, don't you? Fan that ember of desire so we can get on with it." Fend lifted off him, moved alongside. *"All you need to do is climb on."*

"Can't," he repeated weakly. Sinder wasn't being stubborn. "Bring help? That's a good kitty."

"I don't like *having my hand forced."*

Those words fanned against Sinder's ear, and there were hands tugging, arms lifting. Sinder guessed that meant he was rescued, but ... by whom? Heavy eyelids dragged upward enough to give a glimpse of a stranger looming near. Sinder managed a quizzical trill.

"Hush. I'd rather not draw attention at this juncture. There's a good dragon."

Sinder tensed, though there wasn't much strength to coil.

"Don't struggle against the inevitable. I have you, and I will keep you."

That voice. He knew it. Sinder whispered, "Fend?"

It had to be. The mocking gaze was much the same, but the Kith had taken speaking form. Sinder wasn't sure which part surprised him more. That Fend *could* take speaking form, meaning he had to be Kith-kin. Or that the cat who'd only ever tormented him was being so gentle.

Shaking his head, Sinder asked, "Since when?"

"That's a secret you can barter for later." Lips brushed Sinder's eyebrow. "Don't expire, lovely one. You're integral to my plans."

Sinder faded in and out of consciousness, but each time he revived enough to take note of his surroundings, Fend's whispers brushed his ear, plying for more trust, promising him safety. So far, Sinder's trust had been richly rewarded, because he was clean and warm and dry, and the scent of spikenard was slowly gaining strength. A homey touch.

Fend's voice filtered through the haze. "I'm keeping him. He'll let me. See how he clings?"

"All dragons cling when they're cold. And really, you can't lay claim to someone without their consent."

"I can because he'll *let* me. My reasons are as excellent as my inducements." Claws lightly scraped the nape of Sinder's neck.

"Don't pretend you dislike the idea. A dragon is just the thing for *your* plans, too."

"Not that way. Like this." And then a larger, surer hand was plucking and adding pressure, working its way down Sinder's back.

A groan slipped out. "More of that, Michaelson, and I probably *would* let you keep me."

"See?" The damned cat sounded far too smug. "Pass me the gruel."

Sinder tried to pull away, but he and Fend were all tangled up. And though Sinder was awake enough to track with the conversation going on over him, he was beyond weary and oddly muzzy. Which could only mean one thing. "You pollinated me?"

"A *whisper* of huddlebud. Timur insisted we skimp, but it definitely went to your head," said Fend. "Do you remember the bath?"

"Nooo."

"I kept you from drowning."

"Okay. Thanks for that. I guess." He squinted in the low light. "Where is this?"

"My old room. We're crowding in for now." This time, Timur's voice came from a little way off. "Fend left you on my doormat, figuratively speaking. There *was* a bath. You're terribly depleted, and I needed to warm you." Timur came back to the bed and passed something to Fend. "There's tea cooling, but first, eat."

Then Fend was spooning something custardy past his lips, which was awkward in bed. "Let me sit up, at least." Sinder tried to pull away, and some dribbled down his chin.

"No need to panic." With a soft tut, Fend swooped in and lapped it up. "Not poisoned. See?"

Before Sinder could summon words, another spoonful arrived.

"Warm enough?" Fend murmured solicitously. A furred leg rubbed Sinder's skin.

He searched the feline's unfamiliar face, needing to reconcile new facts against old assumptions. When he took more gruel, Fend purred over him. It was probably patronization, but Sinder was starving, and it'd been a hot minute since his last taste of Sonnet's cooking. How long had it been now? Eight years?

"You're surprisingly docile. I suppose Juuyu's recent match left you ripe for the picking. I'll make a much better partner."

Sinder rebelled against the suggestion with a soft hiss.

"Oooh, I hit a nerve. Don't be sad. I'll value you properly." Fend chased the final spoonful of gruel with a kiss.

"You little shit."

"You'd be more convincing if you weren't so comfortable in my arms." And raising his voice slightly, Fend said, "Reward our captive, Timur. Welcome him with a kiss, as is his due."

Sinder stilled. Okay, yeah. A kiss was technically traditional, and Timur was classically trained. But he didn't like that Fend was toying with him. And while pollinated? "This is coercion."

Fend countered, "Only if the pact is sealed while you're under the influence."

"*What* pact?" Sinder was beginning to be angry, but ... it was such a fuzzy, listless thing.

Fend brought a cup to Sinder's lips.

"Tea," said Timur. "Take all of it. And don't let Fend get to you."

This time, the cat let Sinder up enough to drink. He grumbled and gagged, but he downed the lot. He knew from experience it'd clear his head. And possibly clarify his predicament.

Fend slipped an arm around his waist. "I'll lay out every detail once you're lucid. For now, rest. I need you at full strength, with all your wits about you."

This was quite the turnabout from past aggressions. Sinder accused, "You hate me."

"Do I? That would be incredibly shortsighted."

He asked, "What's changed?"

"Quite a lot." Fend flopped against fat pillows and smiled up at him. "First and foremost, you've turned out to be a reach. Very convenient. I need someone who could take orders without my having to shift."

"No. Just, no. Why would you even think I'd take orders from you?"

"Because Hisoka is weak right now. Washed up. Next to useless. And *you* hold all his secrets."

Sinder blinked. "I'm not telling you anything."

"Your lot had their chance, and you did well enough. But you left the job half done. That's where *we* come in." Fend nodded toward his partner. "Timur's a dragon slayer. He's going to kill the Rogue. And I have vixens to outfox."

"Uh-huh. Pretty sure Argent'll take issue with your trying to take over."

"Should Lord Mettlebright ever notice the asset that exists right under his pointy muzzle, I have little doubt he'll recognize my value. In the meantime, you and I will hold the world together. Carefully. Quietly. Which is why I cannot afford for you to sicken. There's too much at stake."

Sinder frowned. "I haven't agreed to anything."

Ignoring him, Fend continued, "We'll triumph, and in the

peaceful years to come, you can help us train Gregor and the rest. All Timur's progeny will need practice."

"I don't wanna fight baby battlers."

"Not *fight*," said Fend. "Most dragon lore is about prettying and pampering. Timur's sons and daughters will adore and adorn you."

"I don't like kids."

"But you'd do it for Timur," he coyly countered.

"You're not listening," Sinder grumbled.

"To a pollinated youngling who's too tired to see the sense I speak? No. I refuse to dignify your protests. At *this* point." Fend was back to petting his hair. "We'll revisit any valid concerns at a later date."

Sinder scowled. "The tea's working just fine. My head's clear. And leave off with that youngling business. *I* have the years."

"Sure about that?"

"I remember when you were born. Added you and your littermates to the file myself."

Fend flashed fangs. "Years are not maturity."

"Maturation isn't experience."

"I don't mind if you underestimate me, but don't dismiss me just to be petty." Fend rubbed their cheeks together and whispered, "Want me to remind Timur that you're waiting for a kiss?"

"What did I ever do to deserve this?"

Fend said, "You're perfect."

"Look, you helped me out. Maybe even saved my life. But I'm not joining a new taskforce." Sinder grimly added, "Stop patronizing me."

"Sway won't work. On either of us. And this isn't patronization. It's peacemaking."

"Because I'm perfect," he said flatly.

"Mmm. Intelligent. Informed. Connected. Capable. And becoming increasingly attached to both me and my plans for you. Or at the very least, to the place they'll create for you." His next words slipped unspoken into Sinder's mind. *"Timur moped for days when you abandoned him. Retake your place. Come and abide at my hearth."*

As a reach, Sinder was able to counter in kind, speaking without words so Timur couldn't overhear. *"A hearth, huh? Wasn't last summer all about my needing a* harem?*"*

"Semantics." And then Fend adopted an entirely too innocent expression as he tugged Sinder's head down onto his shoulder. "Make room for your hearthmate. Timur, help me warm him."

The mattress dipped as Timur eased onto the bed with them. "All right there, Damsel?"

This time when Sinder twisted away from Fend, the feline let him go. In fact, he gave a little push so that Sinder rolled straight into Timur, putting his nose firmly in the center of Michaelson's hairy chest.

Sinder looked up into brown eyes that shone with happiness. Had Timur really missed him? He announced, "Your cat is a megalomaniac."

"If you can tell, then you're definitely thinking clearly." Timur's smile was apologetic. "Feline presumption and all that."

"I intend to resist capture."

"You're not a prisoner."

"You're home," interjected Fend, who plastered himself against Sinder's back.

"I don't have a home."

"Says you."

"Yes, I *do* say so. I would know."

"Fend only means that you could consider *this* home. If you wanted. Though the room's temporary. We're going to build a house." Timur's free hand sought the back of Sinder's neck and began to knead. "You could join the enclave. Bunk with us. I have far too many special skills and no one to appreciate them."

Sinder wilted into the man, biting his lip to hold back a too-hasty reply.

"We're really just glad to see you. And that you're safe." Timur quietly pointed out, "Crossing the ocean at low ebb was *dangerous*, Sinder."

"I just wanted ...." Sinder tensed when Fend's tongue made a slow swipe across his shoulder blade. Would teeth be next?

"Hmm?" invited Timur. "What did you want so badly that you'd risk yourself?"

Sinder tried to come up with an answer that made sense. All he really had was a pocketful of yellow seashells, vague worries about Hisoka's state of mind, and ... this. He'd wanted to get to where Timur was. "Maybe it *was* stupid," he mumbled.

"It's all right now," the man soothed. "Sleep. We'll guard your rest."

Sinder really should protest.

"Stop pretending to resist," ordered Fend. "This is a mutually beneficial arrangement for all three of us. An unassailable alliance—brains, brawn, and beauty."

Sinder frowned. "Which of those am I meant to be?"

Timur's voice held a smile. "Admit it, Fend. He's smarter, stronger, and prettier than either of us."

"Mmm. All the more reason to woo him to our side."

"Time enough for that later." And then Timur asked, "Do you want tending?"

Oh, Sinder wanted it. Probably needed it, too. "Sure. Okay. Yeah."

"Thank you for your trust." Nobody could fault Timur's manners.

"Yeah, yeah. Duty and delight, yadda, yadda." But the first splash of tending curled his toes. Sinder was dragon enough to believe himself smarter, stronger, and prettier. But the way things had piled up and played out, he was also needier. And the damnable cat knew it.

A velvety tail came up to lightly boff Sinder's nose, then quiver under his chin.

Sinder muttered, "I'm going to be so pissed with you in the morning."

"Morning?" Fend's amusement had a superior quality. "You'll sleep a week. And by the time you wake, you'll be so used to my softness and my scent and my voice in your ear, you won't even question why you're willing to take your first meal from my hand, morsel by tender morsel."

"Not happening." And to Timur, "Don't let him mess with me."

"I have you." Timur reached around, and it felt like he was playing with Fend's hair when he amended, "Both of you."

"Lucky us," said Fend, a peevish edge to his tone, though a moment later, his happy sigh fanned Sinder's neck.

Sinder still thought he'd be angry later. Or ... annoyed. Or at least embarrassed.

Because—dunce and double dunce—the space between Timur's tending and Fend's purrs felt warm and safe and homey and *his*. Which was definitely going to bite him in the ass. In about a week. Because Fend was right. Possibly about everything.

Normally, he liked that about cats.

3
FAR TOO FAMILIAR

Hisoka was in no position to refuse another visit from Canarian. His nephew needed to confer with him on several points, ostensibly because he was filling in as acting Spokesperson while Hisoka was on sabbatical. His text had mentioned a summit, several constitutional amendments, and upcoming Dichotomy Day appearances. He *hadn't* mentioned bringing along Catalan. The snoop.

Cat was barely through the door when he spied Rhomiko. "So it's true? Our perpetually solitary uncle is a bachelor no longer? But look at you! What is this luster? Canary spoke of shine, but … ah, you are exquisite!"

Hisoka shot a look at Canarian.

His nephew shrugged. "I can understand wanting to keep them to yourself, but that isn't our way. Rhomiko is yours, and that makes us kin."

"Yes, let us dote." And showing his hands to Rhomiko, Cat begged, "May I touch?"

Rhomiko stepped lightly into the jaguar clansman's embrace, expression going blissful the moment Cat began to purr.

"I think you're misunderstanding …!" Hisoka protested.

Cat went right on, speaking to Rhomiko. "You are his, yes? And he is yours? What could be simpler?"

"Hisoka has not decided what he wants." And a softer confession. "My kisses fade."

"Say it isn't so! What kind of fool flees from an imp's regard?"

Canarian mildly posed, "Someone who doesn't value himself enough? Really, uncle, when did you last sleep? You're woefully depleted."

He may have hissed. A little. But Cat was being far too familiar, and Rhomiko had no context for feline courtesies. Perhaps worse, Rhomiko was being entirely too candid.

They said, "Once he decides, I will know."

Catalan's next glance cut. "Leaving your partner in suspense of your intentions? That is easily as despicable as leaving such lovely hair in this state. For shame. I need scissors!" And to Rhomiko, "Have you not yet seen the inside of a bathtub? Terrible manners. You must forgive Uncle's rudeness. Here, now. Trust us. Cat and Canary will make things right."

Hisoka knew he'd been remiss and slouched into an apologetic posture.

Canarian did give a mild warning to his partner. "Curiosity is natural, but don't impose."

"Where is the imposition?" Cat countered, nuzzling a glittering cheek. "We're kindred, and with cats that means closeness. Come, Rho-Rho. I must even out your hair before Canarian washes it."

Rho-Rho? Hisoka hissed anew at his nephew's presumption, casually claiming an imp by bestowing a nickname.

Yet Rhomiko let it pass, seemingly more interested in something else. "Kindred …?"

"It's true," Cat assured. "If you are Uncle's, then you are ours."

"Close, but not closest," interjected Canarian. "Stop trying to rile Uncle."

Cat simply laughed, wholly unrepentant.

Canarian left Hisoka's side to offer his own embrace. "I don't show it as much as some of my brothers, but I also have an impish legacy. If the gossip is true, my father's mother had a daring streak. She chased storms until she caught one, and so Petros was born. My father is very beautiful."

Hisoka had known, of course. Himeko had chosen Petros for the unique coloring that was a quirk of his heritage. But Hisoka hadn't thought to mention it to Rhomiko. Perhaps because he didn't want to contemplate impish flings just now.

Cat came to Hisoka then, expression suddenly serious. He softly asked, "Why are you being shy about this? Rhomiko is an innocent, and you are a teacher at heart. Or do you need a go-between? Will I do?"

"This isn't that kind of arrangement."

"I can see that. Be plain. Are you struggling to adjust to this bond? Or are you truly rejecting it?"

Hisoka whispered, "I don't know what to do."

"You're *here*, where no lady mistress can meddle, so you're free to choose for yourself." Cat pulled him into a loose embrace. "Is it not best to give Rhomiko that same freedom? Let me take them around, introduce them to those who consider this their home. There are other crossers. Other imps. You need not be Rhomiko's whole world."

"I wasn't trying to impose restrictions."

"Yet I don't think they'll leave your side unless you encourage it. Let them go, and they can come back to you with news of how their world is growing wider. Distance is the beginning of closeness."

Felines loved paradoxes.

A push to pull.

A snub to snare.

A lie to trust.

Cat promised, "I'll speak with Deece and his boys. They'll keep watch for your sake. But for now, let us give proper welcome. Your charming imp should be pampered and purred over."

Hisoka threw a rebellious thought at his nephews. *"Why does everyone insist Rhomiko is mine?"*

Canarian's answering thought lilted with amusement. *"Because they are not feline?"*

That surprised Hisoka. And worried him enough to silently demand, *"Why would that matter?"*

Cat's eyes sparkled. *"Because you're a* tom. *Rhomiko is the one who will rule over you."*

Hisoka protested aloud. "Rhomiko isn't a lady mistress."

"Neither is Canarian, and yet ...!" Cat winked broadly. "What you see from the house rarely betrays what's happening backstage. Spokesperson is a role you took on for all our sakes. A leader in the limelight. But the tom beneath the trappings? Ah, I can see it already. Our uncle will tremble in starlight, with living stone for his hearth."

4

RECOGNITION

Not many people could find the upper hall that led to Lord and Lady Mettlebright's rooms, so Ginkgo was more than a little surprised to find someone he didn't know crouched there, petting the leaf-patterned carpet. "Hey. You."

The fair-haired stranger startled and slowly straightened.

They were a full head taller than Ginkgo, and he didn't think he was imagining the shimmer to their complexion. Relaxing into a smile, he showed his palms. "Sorry about that. You're Rhomiko, yeah? I'm one of Argent's sons. Ginkgo."

Bypassing his hands, Rhomiko stooped to rub their cheeks together, kitty style.

With a soft laugh, Ginkgo patted their back. "Nice. *Someone's* been hanging out with Catalan."

Rhomiko straightened but stayed in the circle of Ginkgo's arms. "Yes. Did he speak of me?"

"Oh, I can tell by scent. And I recognize the shirt."

"He gave me his. And these were in a cupboard." Rhomiko lifted their shirt enough to show that the waist of pale green silk pants had been cinched tight above slim hips.

"Those must belong to Jacques, since he sometimes stays in Sensei's room. He won't mind sharing, but he'd insist on hauling you across to his tailor. You'll need things that fit better."

"Jacques Smythe."

"That's the guy. You've met already?"

"Nooo, but his name was often woven into songs. Mother said he was foretold."

"That's probably something we should mention to Dad. Argent, I mean. He'll want to know anything you can tell him about Jacques."

"He protects those he loves."

"Dad? Or Jacques? It's true either way."

"Will he love me?"

Ginkgo's heart went out to their newcomer, whose tone was so wistful. "I don't make a habit of speaking for others, so you'll have to ask them and see. In the meantime, if I'll do, I'm an affectionate guy. Plenty of love to spare."

"Thank you," Rhomiko murmured, pulling Ginkgo closer.

After a few minutes ticked slowly by and Rhomiko showed no signs of letting go, Ginkgo decided to redirect the impish crosser. "Say, are you busy?"

"Is this busy?"

"Nah, this is just *hello*. But I was thinking you could give me a hand."

Rhomiko eased back a smidge and slowly let go, offering both hands.

"What I mean is … I could use your help."

"Is that so?"

"I'd be really grateful. You see, I'm officially Stately House's gardener, but I'm also on call as a nanny. But I only have two arms. Stick with me, and we'll be doubly effective." Ginkgo hooked Rhomiko's elbow and got them moving.

Rhomiko didn't resist. Only asked, "What is a nanny?"

"Someone who takes care of children. Do you like little ones?"

"I have never had the pleasure."

"It's not hard. You like hugs, yeah?"

"I do."

"You'll be a natural," Ginkgo promised.

He steadied Rhomiko down the stairway. It hadn't really occurred to him just how many simple things were totally new to someone who'd spent their whole life hidden away, just … waiting.

"Take your time," he urged. "Enjoy the experience."

Rhomiko flashed a shy smile. "I would be lost without you."

"You'll be fine. You've got good people to guide you—Hisoka, Catalan, Tsumiko. She's Lady Mettlebright."

"And you?"

"Sure. Me, too. And plenty of others." They reached the foot of the stairs, and Gingko let Rhomiko set their pace. "Most of the kids are busy someplace else right now, otherwise you'd be gathering a crowd. There's bathtime with Cat and Deece and Nonny. And storytime with Michael. But even after a week, some of the newest members of the family are still getting used to this place. And us."

Rhomiko's expression slowly shifted. "I hear sadness."

Ginkgo angled his ears toward the hall leading to the kitchen. "Me, too. Should we see if we can help?"

Rhomiko caught his hand and led the way, straight to his winter garden. On the worn couch tucked under a bay window, Perse and Twosies huddled together. It was plain that Twosies had been crying. Perse's arm tightened protectively around the younger boy, and wary red eyes locked onto Rhomiko.

"Hey, guys. Thanks for looking after Mercy for me." Ginkgo leaned over the warded bassinette where the little girl slept. "Is there room for two more? This is Rhomiko, and they need training in. Can you believe they've never held a baby before? Maybe you could give them some pointers." And to Rhomiko, "Perse and Twosies are pros. Very dependable."

Twosies sulkily said, "Babies are *easy*. Especially Mercy."

"Yeah, she's a good baby. That's why I thought Rhomiko should start with her." And scooping her up, Ginkgo nodded at the couch. "Sit here, and I'll pass Mercy to you. See how I have her? Just like this."

Rhomiko plunked right down next to Perse, arms open, expression eager. "I want to try."

"I like your enthusiasm. Gently, yeah?"

"I will do no harm."

"That's the stuff." Ginkgo had the strongest sense that Mercy would be safe, so without any further words of caution, he placed his sister in Rhomiko's keeping.

Darned if the imp wasn't already making little crooning noises.

And Mercy, who adored attention, opened her eyes.

Rhomiko murmured, "Mother would sing for me. Do you think Mercy would like that?"

"Go for it," urged Ginkgo, dropping to a seat beside them.

They began by humming, and words soon followed in a language Ginkgo didn't recognize. But Twosies gasped, and Perse began humming along.

Twosies exclaimed, "You know our star's song!"

Rhomiko left off in order to answer. "My mother is that same star."

"She sang for us, too!"

"I remember." With another of those shy glances, Rhomiko said, "I was there, too, but in a different kind of cage."

Twosies hopped down and came to sit on Ginkgo's lap in order to get closer to Rhomiko. He said, "Sing more. I miss her song."

Rhomiko began again, singing with a smile on their face.

Ginkgo wasn't surprised when, a few minutes later, Opulence Windlore drifted into the kitchen, a sleeping child draped against his shoulder. Only a dragon could look graceful flopping to the floor—opalescent robes billowing, white hair pooling, blue-eyed gaze unwavering. As Rhomiko's song continued, Ginkgo could see the bard's questions piling up, but he made no effort to interrupt. In fact, Ginkgo thought he was trying to fade from notice. Probably so he wouldn't alarm any of the children who were still dragon-shy. That included Twosies.

But then Opal began to hum along.

Rhomiko noticed and sort of ... brightened.

And then the song became a duet, and Opal harmonized with such confidence that Ginkgo guessed he already knew the song.

Rhomiko sang out with more strength, and the whole household took notice. Sonnet appeared and began to putter at the counter, her tail swaying in time to the music. Sansa eased into one of the big rockers across from the couch and propped up her feet, hands folding over her swollen belly, a restful expression on her face.

Leeuwen Withershanks, who looked very like his illustrious mother, led four little girls, fresh from their evening baths, hair neatly braided. Then Michael arrived with Gilen and the six smallest boys, barely bigger than toddlers. Cat escorted four more, then Lilya and Elara arrived with six of the older girls. More came, all in clusters, since Tsumiko and the mares had set up a buddy system. Every child knew who to turn to if they needed their hand held.

Ginkgo didn't have any official assignment. Neither did Timur, Akira, Suuzu, or Nonny. Mostly because the children who'd been with them the longest didn't think it would be fair. They were *everyone*'s big brothers. In much the same way, the kids had somehow already begun sorting out which of the ladies of the household they'd look to as a mother.

If this evening's impromptu concert was any indication, Rhomiko would be a huge comfort, and Ginkgo kind of hoped that Hisoka decided to stay instead of returning to Keishi. Totally selfish. Probably impractical. But judging by the hush in a room packed with little ones … yeah. It was something worth hoping for.

Kyrie stole up on him and joined Twosies on Ginkgo's lap.

The littler boy's eyes were brighter now, and a smile teased at the corners of his mouth. In a proud whisper, he announced, "I'm part star, too."

"You are," Kyrie acknowledged.

Twosies wove their fingers together and mumbled, "I wish Try could hear."

Kyrie quietly asked, "May I call Zuzu?"

"Sure, little bro. Should be fine."

Kyrie scrolled through Ginkgo's contacts, searching for the chatty tree who could probably make Twosies' wish come true.

Tsumiko finally turned up, Dad in her wake. They stopped just inside the kitchen door, staying on the edge of a crowd that had grown to include their Kith and several nearby Kindred. Oblivious to their audience, Rhomiko and Opal sang on. But Dad? He was watching their audience with care, noting every nuance of response, especially in the kids he'd helped rescue.

Most people wouldn't notice, but Ginkgo had a lot of practice reading Dad's moods. And nowadays, they shared a bond of trust, so he saw the flicker of surprise and the subtle wash of relief, then gratitude, then ... yeah, there was just a hint of smug.

Foxes didn't trust easily, and Dad was warier than most. It was already a miracle that Opulence Windlore, a.k.a. Opal the Sage, had been brought through Stately House's doors and given access to the children. So Ginkgo knew how rare it was when, with a single song, Opal managed to rise in Dad's estimation.

5

NO USE PRETENDING

Hisoka wasn't ready to leave his room. He couldn't have said why he needed to stay. It wasn't as if he had any particular attachment to the suite, unless the simple act of sleeping safely here had turned it into a sanctuary. One he clung to, even though this wasn't his rightful place. Home had always been in Keishi, where he owned land that had once supported an eldermost grove.

Gone now.

Long dead.

He poked through piles on the bureau without much interest. He'd read all these books, but he didn't like to complain. Jacques would have noticed. He'd have refreshed the piles and filled the empty biscuit tins. He'd have brought tea trays and household gossip and Michael. Because Jacques had always known what Hisoka liked and wanted and needed.

Alone in the suite, Hisoka paced to the window and gazed out at a gray sea under gray skies. Mournful hues. Lifeless. Lonesome.

A voice filtered through the emptiness, tentative. *"Uncle?"*

"Deece."

"Am I interrupting?"

Hisoka balled his fists at his sides. "Not especially."

"May I bring Rhomiko outside?"

"I am not that child's keeper."

His nephew hesitantly contradicted him. *"Rhomiko is not a child."*

Too tired for debate, Hisoka waved listlessly, pointlessly. "Where will you take them?"

"Nonny wants to introduce Rhomiko to Randolla. They'll be measured for clothes."

"I see."

"Is that all right with you?"

"Rhomiko is free to do as they wish."

Another pause, and then Deece promised, *"I will keep them safe for you."*

Reassuring. Frustrating. Because with the star-child gone, Hisoka was stranded alone in a room that echoed with memories of better days ... and into which the gray world was creeping.

Wait. Better? Were they really *better* days?

Hisoka slunk to the bed and hid under the covers, ashamed for wanting to go back, to abandon Nemi. To betray his vow and bury a truth that wouldn't change.

The door opened, and Hisoka tensed. A teacup clattered faintly against a saucer, and steam carried the first whisper of steeping tea. His favorite blend. *Jacques*.

Hisoka quickly pushed aside his blankets, but ... no. It was Rhomiko. They shuffled awkwardly forward, bumping the door shut with one hip. They were resplendent in a new tunic and wearing—of all things—embroidered hearth slippers.

"They are a gift from Catalan," Rhomiko announced happily. "He asked a friend to make them for me."

"Very nice."

"There is a pair for you as well. Since your hearth is my home."

Hisoka couldn't argue, but matching hearth slippers implied ... ah, well, they could imply any number of things. However, the underlying meaning *was* one of belonging, and Rhomiko had stated it plainly enough. The two of them shared a home.

"Thank you."

Rhomiko came forward, cup and saucer in both hands, focused on not spilling a drop.

Hisoka reached out with both hands, thinking to rescue the cup.

But then Rhomiko said, "I met your Michael."

Hisoka flinched backward, and cup and saucer jumbled to the floor, bouncing upon the rug, staining it with splashed tea.

"He is beautiful," Rhomiko said, dropping to their knees on the rug, blotting at the spilled tea with their sleeve.

"He is not mine."

They hummed in a way that begged to differ. "You say that about me, too."

Hisoka felt chastised. But also stubborn.

Rhomiko looked up, their expression serene. "I asked your Michael to visit. He was glad to agree."

"I ... why would you do that?"

"Because you will let in *his* brightness."

A point Hisoka wished he could argue, but he'd never been able to resist Michael. Or refuse him. Taking the boy for his apprentice at Ingress Academy had been a shocking departure after centuries without an apprentice. An embarrassingly selfish impulse, especially at a time when he should have been fully devoting himself to carrying off the Emergence.

Back then, he'd been intrigued by some of Michael's little habits, especially his sigilcraft. He'd suspected there was another mentor, but he hadn't pressed for details lest he lose Michael's trust. Only in hindsight had the foxy overtones come into focus. And then Argent's need had become Hisoka's concern. For Michael's sake.

"He will be here for your sake," Rhomiko said, as if they knew Hisoka's thoughts.

Because Hisoka's needs had become their concern?

And yet here Hisoka sat, pretending not to see. Like a small child who believes that closing their eyes makes them safe from discovery.

Michael would never know how much Hisoka might have sacrificed to keep him.

Conversely, Michael's good opinion had buoyed Hisoka during those last, worst years, when the Emergence kept hitting roadblocks and snagging in red tape. After long weeks of special sessions and treaty talks, he'd tumble into his student's waiting arms, to be scolded and tended and tucked in.

"He probably saved the world."

Rhomiko stood and reached with both hands, framing Hisoka's face. "I do not think he is finished. Let him scold you and tend you and tuck you in?"

Hisoka wondered if the reason he couldn't refuse was because he wanted so badly to see Michael. Or because Rhomiko had also become someone else Hisoka couldn't refuse.

Rhomiko was unusually quiet during Michael's visit—posture respectful, expression thoughtful. Hisoka wasn't sure why he'd expected traces of jealousy or resentment. Had he wanted to inspire some sort of posturing? That possibility was both unexpected and ... frankly embarrassing. People generally assumed he liked being in charge. In all areas.

Hisoka rather wanted Jacques' opinion, but in the meantime, it was clear that Rhomiko both liked Michael and loved the puzzle he'd brought.

"I wanted your perspective, Sensei. I understand you already had some contact with these?" Michael patted the green crystal in Rhomiko's arms. "While I'm humbled by the trust everyone has placed in me, I'm honestly baffled."

"There are four," Rhomiko said eagerly. "All four were found?"

"Yes. We've been sharing them around, taking turns inter-acting with them. It's haphazard, but until I can sort out what they need ...." Michael ended with a shrug.

"Do you know what you need, little sibling?" Rhomiko crooned.

Michael brightened. "That's right. These would be your half-siblings. On your father's side."

"Dayith. Yes." They had shed their shirt in order to press the flat of the chrysalis to their belly. The top of the glittering stone came nearly to Rhomiko's chin. They cuddled it close and rocked from side to side, humming softly.

Michael quietly asked, "Do you hear that?"

Hisoka found his voice. "The wardstone is tuning its song to Rhomiko's."

"They're definitely responsive to singing, humming, instrumental music. Even wolfsong. But once the music ends, they lapse into silence. It's like they're waiting for something. And I have no idea *what*."

"Whom," Rhomiko quietly corrected.

"Is that so?" Michael looked to Hisoka for confirmation.

With unaccustomed vulnerability, Hisoka said more than he needed to. "I have considerable experience with trees and with stars, but I know next to nothing about the mountain clans. We will have to learn together."

Eyes alight over the prospect, Michael bumped shoulders with Rhomiko. "We'll be relying on you, Rhomiko-sensei."

"I will only know what they tell me."

"Ah, but you hear more than we do. Perhaps in the same manner as Kindred who are attuned to the voices of their clan's Kith."

Rhomiko clarified. "I hear a song."

Michael raised a finger. "I hear a song, too. What I'm asking is … does the song you hear have words?"

Rhomiko's head tipped to one side, then the other. Then with a small smile, they gently pointed out, "These are *babies*. I do not think they have words for what they need. Only understanding."

"So they may not be able to speak until they, well, we've been assuming they'll hatch or emerge somehow. But until they find their words, they can't tell us how to help them."

"A mystery that has protected them for many years."

Michael's brows drew together. "I suppose so. But how did you know that?"

"I was in a similar state." Rhomiko's gaze sought Hisoka's. "Sometimes, the only way to be safe is to hide."

Hisoka tensed. Did Rhomiko mean him?

Michael cheerfully took their words at face value. "I do hope they can somehow sense that they're safe with us. And that we'll do all we can for them, both now and after their emergence."

Rhomiko asked, "Do you love them?"

"Mmm, I wonder. It's a little like waiting for a baby. Or babies, this time around. My wife is expecting, and the twins should arrive soon. I've never seen those little ones, but I know without a shadow of doubt that I *will* love them. I suppose I do already. Only there's a part of me that's holding back until I can hold them in my arms and tell them their names and make every foolish promise I can think of."

"And once they know your embrace and learn their names and trust your foolish promises … they will love you, too?"

Michael beamed. "That's the usual way of such things."

Hisoka caught Rhomiko watching him again and averted his face. But deep down, he wanted to know what kind of foolish promises Rhomiko might make. And if he could trust them to teach him what he needed. Because right now, Hisoka wanted to hide. From everything. Even Michael.

6

FIRST DRAFT HEROINE

Lapis hated Isla's favorite sweater.

The shapeless old thing bunched and pilled and sagged in shades of gray that did nothing for her complexion. Once upon a time, it had belonged to Hisoka Twineshaft. Lapis remembered the first time she'd worn the cast-off—several sizes too large and steeped in her mentor's scent. He'd been shocked enough to corner her. At barely fourteen, she'd been much too young for the claim such a gift implied.

Blushing to the roots of dark blonde ringlets, Isla had confessed. Culled from his closet, consigned for destruction— she'd pilfered the sweater from a rag bag destined for Dimity- blest demise, to be twisted into lamp wicks or pulped for paper, no doubt. But the way Isla treasured it, you'd have thought the thing was a courting gift, loomed from Twineshaft's own fur. It was neither.

Lapis had advised getting rid of it. For the sake of Hisoka's reputation.

She'd listened. Or so he'd thought. Years later, the sweater reappeared, and its further dilapidation showed just how often she'd wrapped herself up in wishful thinking. The most frustrating part was knowing that she wore the storm-cursed wreck of a garment in front of *him* because she trusted him with her secrets. Proof of a bond that had changed shape more than once, deepening from affection to alliance and collusion.

Even so, Lapis hated that sweater.

So when Isla strolled through the door to the Blue Parlor in bunched, pilled, and sagging gray, he went back to staring into the fire crackling upon the hearth. But he did wave in her general direction with the stack of papers he was meant to be reading.

"Is that our manuscript?" she asked sharply.

"Let's call it a first draft. But yes, it has manuscript-worthy aspirations."

Lowering a box of books onto an already-crowded table, Isla asked, "Should you be reading it *here*, where just anyone could walk in?"

He had to smile at that. "Really, my dear. You've laced these pages with so many sigils, I doubt anyone else would notice them in my hands, let alone catch a glimpse of what's printed on them."

"Yes, well. It's important to be *careful*. There are a lot more people hanging about these days."

Hanging about? Not the most generous choice of words. Not for a consummate diplomat like Isla. Lapis eyed her closely and casually asked, "What has you so fretful?"

"Oh, it's nothing important." Isla pushed a stray curl out of her face. "I took issue with a scene in one of the books we're reviewing, and Kimi just … smiled."

"What variety of smile?"

"The knowing sort." Isla grumbled, "I may not be as *experienced* as she is, but I do *know* things."

"May I read the scene in question?"

"I *did* just have it here." She passed along her phone.

He read the passage twice before meeting her gaze.

"It's impossible, isn't it?" she demanded.

"With respect, my dear, I *do* think it could be accomplished. Especially since most Amaranthine can defy gravity."

"You can't."

Always so blunt. He inclined his head. "I cannot."

"Could you do it?"

"With cooperation? Yes, I think so."

Isla's frown turned into a pout. "Show me."

Lapis missed a beat as the players in the scenario were recast in his imagination. Unwise. *So* unwise. Offering up her phone, he shook his head. "This isn't a point that needs to be proved. Or disproved. It's an enticing bit of fiction, nothing more."

"We've done staging before!"

"From time to time. For our own books. Which we agreed would never dip into such hackneyed territory."

"They say that the classics are classic for good reason." Isla shot a guilty look over her shoulder and lowered her voice. "Do let's try? I want to know why Kimi's smile was so superior."

"Bondmates and babies don't equal superiority. And Kimiko

is your friend, not a rival in matters of … connubial bliss.”

Isla wasn't satisfied. Lapis could tell. They'd been connected for years now, and they *did* occasionally explore possibilities for scenes together. Usually during walks. Never in closets.

Lapis set aside papers and flung a hasty sigil at the door to improve their privacy. “We don't write these sorts of scenes.”

She wavered for a moment. Facts were facts. But she countered, “Could we call it academic interest?”

The truth, then. “You're curious.”

“Aren't you?”

“That is entirely beside the point.” Lapis supposed he only had himself to blame for this muddle. “You're trusting me, and that's gratifying. But aren't you forgetting something? I'm male.”

She rolled her eyes. “I'm aware.”

Rather than quibble—because that assertion was dubious at best—he brought up another salient point. “Dalliance can lead to accidental bond-building. What if your little experiment left you with an unintended bondmate?”

“I'm warded.”

“Do you really think that would stop me?” Lapis was more than capable of dismantling every defense that veiled her soul. Except, perhaps, blindness.

She waved that aside. “Even if you could, you never would. It would be un-Amaranthine!”

“Such conviction is admirable where the nobility of my people is concerned, but we're shockingly selfish, dragons. And you are terribly beautiful, my dear.”

Isla heard him, but she didn't listen. Not really. “You don't trust yourself? That's absurd! Oh, *do* just give in like usual. I don't have anyone else to go to with these sorts of questions."

Questions he could deal with. Dragons were good with words. He could weave them like sigils and shape them into barriers to hide behind.

But if he did this, if he allowed it ... no, that was shading the truth. Phrasing things in a way that swept aside his part in such a scheme. He wouldn't be *allowing* her advances. He'd be encouraging them. A willing participant in the breaking of his own heart. Because first love had taken Lapis entirely by surprise. Especially all the parts that pained him.

"I *will* give in," he acknowledged. "But only if you oblige me as well."

She shifted into a more neutral posture. "We couldn't collaborate if you and I weren't willing to compromise."

He blandly countered, "There is compromise and then there are compromising positions."

Isla relaxed into a smile. "What's my part in the give-and-take?"

"About the manuscript. Let me rewrite the heroine."

Wilting somewhat, Isla asked, "Again? You didn't like her?"

"Unfair, my dear. How could I possibly dislike her? She is you."

"But she's nothing like the others."

"A different name, a different face. New backstory, new goals. But her hopes are your hopes, and she approaches the world much as you do."

Curiosity sparked in green eyes. "I'd like your perspective, please. How do you think I approach the world? That might help me, moving forward. Wait. Should I write this down?"

Lapis reached for her hand. "Our first-draft heroines are

universally intelligent, aspirational, outspoken, and ambitious. But when it comes to love, they wait to be noticed."

"Too passive?"

"I suspect you adhere to an underlying belief that patience will have its reward. And that perfection is achievable." He posed it another way. "If you can just get it right, then you'll get him, too."

"Oh." Isla looked away.

She'd set her heart on a confirmed bachelor, so she never noticed the entirely available, hopelessly smitten bachelor right in front of her. Lapis had to concede that it was a classic trope. Really, the only saving grace in his situation was that it would never develop into a love triangle. Tiresome things.

He gave her hand a squeeze. "Did you want an authentic armoire? Or will any old closet do?"

And just like that, her smile was back. "Authenticity is a must!"

"I believe there's an armoire in the Rosewood Parlor. The children don't venture much into this section, so it should be quiet enough."

"Then let us repair to the parlor!"

Lapis banished sigils and pocketed stones, the better to ensure privacy for Isla's fact-finding tour. They moved a few rooms along the hushed hallway, both contributing sigils to make sure they didn't draw attention. All the while, Lapis paid close attention to Isla's posture and scent.

Happy. She did like getting her way.

Curious. Probably in a general sense.

Relaxed. Because her interests lay elsewhere.

Once the room was secure, they faced the appointed armoire,

and he offered a mild complaint. "I have no great fondness for cramped spaces."

Isla said, "It's *such* a popular trope."

He swung open the double doors. "Behold, our first plausibility issue."

"No such thing as an empty closet?"

"If we're both going in, then most of that has to come out."

"Right, then." Isla pushed up over-long sweater sleeves and set to work. "I wonder why people think it's romantic to be trapped together? I suppose it *is* a convenient catalyst, since it forces two people to face each other without distraction."

"Closets are probably the kindest variation on the theme. No plane crashes. No cave-ins. No prison cells." Lapis set aside the last of the boxes and surveyed the hanging garments. "It would simplify matters if these were gone, but the book mentioned clothes."

Isla grimaced. "Out with the rain gear, keep the winter cloaks?"

"How very Narnia of us."

She beamed. "At least it'll be warm."

"I *was* beginning to miss my fireside spot."

"This promises to be snug." She jauntily waved him forward. "After you, sir!"

Lapis lowered himself to the closet floor, swung his feet inside, and braced them against the opposite wall. Then Isla was pushing at cloaks and stepping between his legs and pulling shut the doors with a firm *click*. He gave a cautious push, and the latch held. Still, he murmured, "A barrier, I think. There may be some ... jostling."

"It would be a shame to damage such a lovely old piece." Isla sank to her knees, shimmying her hips to push his legs further apart.

He traced an unnecessarily intricate sigil on the door's interior. Mostly to distract himself.

Isla, being Isla, began unpacking the trope. "In some cultures, this is a children's dare. Two people are sent into the closet where they're meant to trade intimacies."

"Mmm."

"In the romance genre, two people are locked in together. Usually by accident. Often overnight. And in the books *we* review, one of those people is most certainly Amaranthine. Instincts come into play. Simmering passions surface. In some stories, common fears are addressed and allayed. *Those* books are usually the most helpful in correcting misinformation where the clans are concerned." She paused to ask, "Ready to begin?"

"No. I'm sitting on my hair."

"Here. Let me."

"Isla," he groaned, because he had to lift and lean forward, which thrust his face into the vicinity of her bosom.

"Put up with it," she briskly countered. "Won't take a moment."

At least the sweater mashed against his nose was no longer redolent of Hisoka. The dreadful thing had become hers in every sense ... and scent. He inhaled slowly, deeply, and somehow his hands found their way to her hips.

"You have so much hair," she grumbled.

"I'm a dragon. It's expected."

"From what I've read, it's more of a birthright. Beauty, I mean."

If he'd been some silly romantic lead, he'd have asked Isla

if she thought him beautiful. But Lapis wasn't in the mood for drivel. He was a dragon. Beauty went without saying.

"That's done it," she muttered. "Can you move freely now?"

"That's debatable."

"And disprovable," she said smugly. "Oh, drat. Should I be facing the other way?"

"I believe that maneuver is meant to occur mid-scene."

After a pause, Isla asked, "Should we … skip ahead?"

"Feeling claustrophobic?"

"Not at all. In fact, this is interesting. Darkness means relying on other senses, which can make you aware of someone in new ways."

She was speaking in generalities, unaware as ever. He blandly reminded, "While true for humans, I can see you just fine."

Her eyes widened. "Oh! That's unsettling in a way. Couldn't we use that sometime?"

"Probably."

"Though as a reaver, I'm not *entirely* blind. I can sense the remnant stones in your jewelry, and that makes it easy to orient myself. Which we could *also* use. Umm … Lapis, what's *that* sigil for?"

"Which one?"

"The one on your midriff."

"It anchors a shield array." Isla may have been at the forefront of the diplomatic division, but she was an accomplished ward in her own right. "Fairly recent. Purportedly subtle."

"Well, I'm practically sitting on it. Or I should be. Depending on where we start." She frowned blindly in his direction. "Why haven't we started?"

Lapis sighed. "How sturdy is that rod?"

Isla reached up and gave an experimental tug, then wrapped both hands around it and did a partial pull-up. Vintage cedar creaked ominously. "*Not* sturdy enough."

"Then I'll have to improvise. Give me as much space as you can. I need to ...." Deciding he wouldn't mention the adjustments he needed to make to the drape of his clothing, Lapis simply braced his feet, flexed, and wriggled. Then offered a tentative, "Beg pardon."

When his tail looped around her waist, Isla squeaked in obvious delight. "Partial shift? But that's wonderful! How much control does this take?"

"I am exercising restraint." And when she began stroking his scales, he grimly added, "That tickles, my dear."

"Right. Sorry. So what did we need a tail for?"

He lifted her off her knees, and she squeaked again. "Prehensile? Oh, that's an untapped trove of ... oh, my! Well, yes, that'll do." She was nearly as tall as he, and it took a few moments to sort out their limbs. Barely containing her laughter, she asked, "Where should I put my hands?"

"Isn't accidental fumbling a mainstay?"

She found his shoulders and braced herself. "Why do you wear such light fabrics, even in winter?"

"I'm a dragon," he repeated. "It's expected."

"But you're not in front of a camera here. You could wear something warmer."

"Like you?" he inquired, plucking at the gray sweater. "This is hideous."

"It's cozy!"

"It itches you, and you know it." Sliding his hands underneath, he let his fingers skate up the tight-fitting second shirt she wore as protection against rough fibers. "I'd offer to lend you something appropriately sumptuous, but that would be hypocritical."

She muttered, "I know you don't think I'm good enough for him."

"I've never said that, Isla."

"You've thought it."

"You have no idea what I think."

"Nonsense. We've been friends for ages. We're confidantes."

In point of fact, she was the one always spilling secrets. But he wasn't planning to part with any of his, so he asked, "Ready?"

They maneuvered their way through the scene, puzzling out each transition with a seriousness that kept titillating thoughts at bay. Lapis proved that an Amaranthine partner was more than capable of feats that might otherwise have been impossible. Isla went limp and sulky in his grasp, and Lapis let their noses bump together. "You're flushed. Get rid of the sweater."

"Why are you so set against my wearing Sensei's sweater?"

"It's ugly, and at this range, it's making *me* itch."

To his surprise, she wrestled out of it, letting the thing drop.

He trilled a pleased note. "How shall I reward your sacrifice?"

Isla lifted her head, and their noses bumped again. He nuzzled toward her ear, and she angled toward him, as if encouraging secrets. But Lapis held his tongue and kissed her cheek, making sure the caress lingered long enough that it couldn't be explained away. She stilled. He nudged along her jawline, and her heartbeat quickened.

Oh, this was unwise. *So* unwise.

"What are we doing?" she whispered.

"Skipping ahead ...?"

Would she listen if he told her? Would she understand if he showed her?

Then came a light knock on the armoire door that banished their combined sigilcraft. "Isla? You're in there, yes?"

They froze guiltily.

She cautiously answered, "Yes, Papka."

"Normally, I wouldn't dream of intruding but ... well, the rock imps are resonating, and Rhomiko is quite certain that you're somehow the source. It's our first brush with success, and I didn't realize you were ... ahh ... busy. I'm really very sorry to interrupt. You, too, Lord Mossberne."

Isla tensed. "This isn't ...! You're not *interrupting*."

People didn't get far in debates with Isla, but these weren't Council chambers. Michael said, "I've interrupted *something*. The resonance fell away when I knocked."

"We're only ...! This is for a book, Papka!"

Isla had been sixteen when their first book debuted, and Lapis had insisted that at least one of Isla's parents be informed of the nature of their collaboration. He'd half-expected her to choose Ginkgo, since fostering gave her the loophole, but Isla had wanted Michael.

Sounding just a little too bland, Michael asked, "Shall I open the door, then?"

"No!"

Lapis's ears were sharp enough to catch the man's muttered, "We'll be having a chat, Lapis."

Which was fair. *The fathers are strong*, and all that.

"More importantly, Papka." Isla's curiosity now warred with her embarrassment. "The baby rock imps were responding? To which part? We've remnant stones, sigils ... and there *was* a barrier. It's *rude* to banish someone else's barrier, Papka. But did you mean to say Rhomiko called *me* the source of the resonance? Or was it Lapis?"

"Ah. Both of you, actually." Michael sounded genuinely puzzled. "I'm not sure how they know all the things they do. Probably a quirk of impish heritage that remains to be explored. But when the four chrysalises took up a new song, completely out of the blue, Rhomiko announced that the source was Chastity Landis."

7

UNTIL FURTHER NOTICE

Really, my lord. I do know the way."

Argent thought it a token protest. Oh, his man was as poised and presentable as he could make himself, but a whisper of uneasiness slipped past wards that couldn't quite contain ... whatever it was Jacques had become. "We have added additional wards along this hall."

"Are we pretending they're set against me? You *do* realize I can see them now. Very friendly seeming." Jacques' smile was the same as always. He was really too good at keeping up appearances.

"Then the sigils are working."

Jacques studied the palm of one hand, which Argent had labored over for the better part of an hour, Suuzu looking on the whole time. "Don't you usually use crystals for tuning wards?"

"I was in a hurry."

"Because Hisoka asked for me?"

"Not precisely." Hisoka's doors were barred to all visitors, but Argent was hoping that the cat would consider Jacques an exception. He wasn't sure what else—or who else—to try. Perhaps Sinder?

"I've lost all track of the calendar. Is Hisoka due for a long sleep?"

"Past due."

Jacques stopped walking. "What aren't you telling me? Lord, he wasn't injured, was he?"

"No."

Rounding on him, Jacques searched his face. "I don't need the fact that I'm a Smythe to tell that you're hiding something. Is it awful?"

Argent sighed. "Hisoka is ... in retreat. We are calling it a sabbatical. He has not left his rooms this whole time. Not even for Blessing's whelping feast."

"I was sorry to miss it myself. Akira and Nonny sent pictures, so I wasn't totally left out."

"Until we know more about the consequences of your inheritance, I cannot have you gadding about."

Jacques shrugged that off, even though Argent's restrictions were making him increasingly restless. "Why has Hisoka gone into seclusion?"

"I cannot speak for him." Argent admitted, "I am hoping he will confide in you."

"He might. But isn't this disastrous? I've been confined to quarters—nay, confined to *bed*—by a fussy bird and his beautiful boy, so forgive me for being entirely out of whatever loop this is, but ... who's holding the world together if not Hisoka?"

"Canarian Evernhold is acting spokesperson."

"Ah. That's all right, then."

Argent tended to agree. Hisoka's nephew had been working closely with his uncle from the beginning, and Canary hadn't hesitated to step into his new role. Even if he was only an understudy, all the world was his stage. But that was the political arena, and this was home.

It had been an all-around awful week, and the past two months had left much of Argent's personal life in unaccustomed disarray. He wanted his man properly back, handling things in ways that were impossible to take for granted anymore. Especially with Tsumiko gently reminding him how much Jacques usually took on.

Argent touched Jacques' elbow and tried to get him moving again, but a few tails slipped into the open. Traitorous tells.

"My lord?" Jacques prompted.

"I thought you found overprotectiveness adorable."

A blank look. "Do I?"

"You even expressed an interest in seeing the whole process from the beginning."

Recognition dawned. A conversation from more than a year ago, back when Eloquence Starmark was hovering over his pregnant bondmate's every step. "Oh, lord. I *did* say that. But I meant Tsumiko!"

"Word your prayers with care, supplicant. Sometimes, the Maker gives you precisely what you ask for."

Jacques' gaze went soft and solemn. "I wouldn't take any of it back, even if I could."

"Apologies. I did not intend to make light of your … condition."

"*Non*. You were trying to divert me. It hasn't worked. Tell me what I'll be facing."

Argent felt more tails slipping free. "You are not the only one who came away from the recent ordeal with an impish legacy."

"*Mon dieu*. Him, too?"

"No. Hisoka's circumstances are entirely different than yours. I need to introduce you to Rhomiko."

"Who is his …?"

"Yes. His."

That earned a flat look. "If that was calculated to intrigue, your aim was off."

"When Hisoka fled that island, it was with Rhomiko in his arms. That person is a unique existence, and we are uncertain about the nature of their relationship. Again, I have been hoping that Hisoka will confide in you."

This time, when Argent indicated the way forward, Jacques matched him stride for brisk stride.

Officially, Spokesperson Twineshaft was unreachable. That hadn't stopped either Harmonious or Lapis, and it certainly didn't stop Argent. However, when he attempted to usher Jacques into Hisoka's rooms, Rhomiko barred the way.

"Lord," breathed Jacques. "You're a star!"

"My mother is a star."

Jacques belatedly offered his palms, and Rhomiko took him by the hands and drew him inside. Argent followed, swiftly scanning the room. Hisoka was abed, but the blankets stirred. Crossing to the stool that Rhomiko must have abandoned, Argent murmured, "I brought Jacques."

"Did you? Why?"

There was so much suspicion in his tone, so much confusion, that Argent wasn't sure how to answer. Hisoka wasn't himself. Or perhaps he'd been changed. Either way, Argent was doing his best to sort out what his friend needed. "I thought Jacques might be a comfort to you. He has been your usual companion for so long ...?"

"Will you use him to compel me?"

The low question startled Argent into silence.

Meanwhile, Jacques was being his charming self. "An impish crosser? You definitely present as a star, but I'm not certain ... lord, I'll just ask. What are your preferred pronouns?"

Their heads were together, and then Rhomiko slipped both arms around Jacques' waist in order to lay their ear over his heart. Jacques was so good at inspiring trust. Argent watched closely and soon decided that Jacques wasn't flirting. He was treating Rhomiko with the same care he showed to any of their children. Which was telling, in a way. Rhomiko was physically an adult, and they often made remarks that carried the weight of centuries. But there was an innocence in their manner that stirred Argent to protectiveness.

It would be interesting to hear Jacques' opinion later.

He was saying, "So if your mother is a star, then your other parent ... *mon dieu*. You're another one of Dayith's!"

"You met my father?"

"Briefly. Intensely. And with lingering consequences." Jacques turned toward Argent, wonder in his eyes. "I can *tell* he's one of Dayith's. And here I thought his legacy would be more lonesome."

Argent really needed to get Jacques to Michael—or vice versa—to see if the island's former wardstones responded to him in any way.

"I did not meet the father who helped to protect me. Not even in dreams. I am not certain why." Rhomiko's hands trailed down to Jacques' midriff. "Oh? Ohhh."

"Long story. Did you know you have a half-brother named Solace? Both impish parents, as well. But tree instead of star." With the slightest quaver, Jacques said, "You're going to be ... lord, is there a non-gendered version of aunt and uncle?"

Argent hadn't told Hisoka about Jacques for the same reasons he hadn't betrayed any of Hisoka's confidences to Jacques. Their stories weren't his to tell. But he'd brought them together, and Jacques wasn't exactly being coy. But neither had he stated matters plainly. Argent glanced at Hisoka, curious if he'd caught on.

The cat spoke in an uneasy undertone. "That's not Jacques."

"It is." Argent would have explained further, but Hisoka's expression halted him. Low, urgent, Argent repeated, "It *is*."

Jacques, newly attuned to such things, glanced Hisoka's way, then calmly, pointedly took a step back. That put Rhomiko between him and Hisoka. And with just as much deliberation, Jacques took an apologetic posture. Even though he was innocent of any wrongdoing.

"So much has happened. For both of you." Argent hesitated, hoping Jacques would jump in. "Should we take the time t–"

"I'll go," Jacques interrupted. He backed to the door, gaze still averted, voice carefully neutral. "It's all right, Hisoka. I'll go."

The door clicked shut behind him.

Argent leveled a glare on Hisoka. "That *is* the man you have always trusted."

Hisoka lowered his own gaze. "What happened to him?"

"What happened?" Argent echoed gruffly. "You *hurt* him."

With a curt nod for Rhomiko, he hurried after Jacques, who'd stopped in front of a window partway along the hall. His perfunctory smile barely reached his eyes.

"He was afraid of me, Argent. I could feel it. Hisoka took one look at me and recoiled." Jacques quietly asked, "Have I become something ugly?"

"No." Far from it. Argent caught Jacques' sleeve. "I handled that poorly. It never occurred to me that Hisoka might not accept the alteration to your soul."

Jacques eased into an unnecessarily submissive posture. "Perhaps I shouldn't be entering any more rooms unannounced."

Argent admitted, "I have been reluctant to shutter you along-side Tsumiko. Who knows what the consequences of the proximity of two such souls might be? But to seal you away, simply because you are an unknown existence? Unthinkable."

"I would prefer a caged soul to a caged self."

"We only want to be sure you are safe."

"Good intentions on every side." With a small shake of his head, Jacques asked, "May I go to my own rooms for a while? I'll stay put. I just need a change of view."

Argent took his elbow again, then sighed and claimed his hand instead, leading him along. "I *am* sorry."

"I know," Jacques murmured. "I can feel that, too. Don't worry overmuch on my account. More importantly, how are the children adjusting?"

"Their trust is in tatters. Most are wary of me."

"Foxes again."

"Yes. They are somewhat more receptive to dragons. Lapis is preoccupied with Council business, but Opulence is a welcome surprise."

"The dragon bard."

"Mmm. And despite Hisoka's qualms where you are concerned, I am holding out hope that you will prove as popular as ever with the children."

"Even though I've gone all reaver-ish?"

"You are brimming with your inheritances from Dayith and Solace, and that has left you with an impish allure. It really is quite affecting."

Jacques laughed wearily. "Alluring, am I?"

Argent blandly pointed out, "You can tell."

"I can. But for you to admit it out loud ...? I'm touched."

Outside the door to Jacques' rooms, Argent asked, "Do you want me to stay?"

"*Non.* Leave me to potter in peace. I'll call for Nonny if I need anything."

Argent wasn't quite ready to let go. "How much can you tell about me?"

Jacques hedged. "Usually, you want my opinion of other people."

"I need to know."

The man gave his fingers a light squeeze, then pulled away. "I know you're fascinated and frustrated by turns. I know there's a ... a sort of greediness. And that you're holding it back. Far less unsettling are the possessiveness and protectiveness. I think they're your brand of caring. I'm also sure I was missed, and I feel needed. As more than a cog in necessary machinations."

Argent went so far as to say, "I did not wish to lose you."

"And so I am found." Jacques quietly asked, "How much can you tell about me?"

Turnabout was fair. Argent answered, "You are uneasy and unhappy by turns, and I do not know how to make reparation for all you endured."

Jacques smiled crookedly. "You aren't very good at this, my lord. I was meant to be in the limelight, but partway through, you slipped into talking about yourself."

Argent growled softly. "You are simplicity itself, yet impossible to define. Tell me what to do."

"Trust Suuzu. At least, that's what I'm doing. Although hiding in my own room might count as an act of rebellion."

"Shall I ward the door against him?"

Jacques looked tempted, but he shook his head. "If he sweeps in and scolds me, he's within his rights. Did you know he's gone and made me a nestmate? I fear Suuzu will come to regret taking responsibility for his beloved's erstwhile paramour."

Argent frowned. "Avians do not usually share."

"Suuzu did try to explain. Some of it boils down to his duty as a tribute, but Akira complicates things. He refuses to think of me as an uncle any longer. And in trying to sort out Akira's less-than-familial attachment to me ... well, I've apparently received special dispensation because I remind Suuzu of a tree."

A supporting role. Needful cooperation. Argent grumbled, "You deserve better."

Not for the first time, Jacques replied, "I know."

8

BONHOMIE

Anjou was counting hearths. Stately House had more than its fair share, and it seemed an appropriate enough pastime for a hearthcat left to his own devices.

Oh, he could have volunteered himself for any number of odd jobs. His upbringing in a rural enclave meant he was used to reporting to the kitchen or the creamery or the laundry or the nursery. Anjou had let it be known that he was a tribute, but more than a week had passed, and nobody had found a use for him. Which left him in an awkward position. Young toms waited to be called.

Keeping busy might have helped to pass the time, but Anjou didn't like to show a sad face. So even though he'd tell any who asked that he was counting hearths, Anjou was mostly searching for quiet corners. Someplace to work up the courage to be happy for his friend. Because he'd seen Eiji's face—

surprised and delighted and exquisitely happy.

After all they'd been through, Eiji deserved every happiness. Anjou wasn't jealous, exactly. But neither had he been chosen.

His hopes had been up. He would have loved to be of use to Hisoka Twineshaft, even if only peripherally. But despite arriving at Stately House amidst the triumphal songs of dragons and having helped with a mass rescue, Anjou hadn't once met the illustrious spokesperson, let alone been added to his cortege.

In the back of his mind, the lilt of his former mentor's voice coached him to be patient. *Await, await, await.*

Someday, perhaps, a mistress would single him out, and he would devote himself to her. But his someday wasn't *this* day, and he was beginning to fear that his someplace wasn't here either. What if Lord Mettlebright suddenly recalled the stray cat within his boundaries and put Anjou out?

"*You there. Lend me your hands.*" One of Stately House's feline Kith.

Care of and communication with Kith fell solidly within a tribute's duties. Anjou adjusted his posture even as he turned, already asking, "How may I ...?" But he left off, lunging to rescue the toddler dangling by the back of his pajamas from the black panther's jaws.

This Kith was one of Minx's many cubs, an adult male with his father's eyes. Anjou sat on the floor, cradling the cheerful boy-child while he waited to see if there would be more orders.

"*Anjou Bonhomie. Clan tribute. Prospective consort.*" The Kith sprawled languidly beside him. "*Mother passed you over in favor of your friend.*"

"Eiji is a fine tom."

"And you are a sorry one?"

"I'm alone."

"No, you're not. Do stop moping."

But of course that's when tears sprang to Anjou's eyes.

The Kith scooted closer, rubbing their cheeks together, whisking away each drop as it fell. *"Are all toms this eager to live at the whim of another?"*

Anjou lowered his gaze. *"Non."*

"Your friend surprised me." The black panther rested his jaw upon Anjou's thigh, his upturned gaze searching. *"Kith-sire is an unusual aspiration for those not born to it. Are you sulking because Mother stole your other half?"*

"I never aspired to anything. And I knew Eiji and I weren't likely to be placed together."

"He is *a crystal adept."*

"Mm-hmm. We were thrown together, and we enjoyed each other. Neither of us expected much, but … I will miss him."

"You're being overly tragic, considering how near he'll be. My father's hearth is wide. Indeed, all of this enclave's felines are generous."

Anjou knew he was being unreasonable, but he couldn't help pining. Not for Eiji specifically. Just for something that could be his. He tried to change the subject. "This child …?"

"Mine to mind." He sounded supremely bored, but he nuzzled the toddler until the boy giggled. *"Gregor is son to Timur, who shares a pact with me."*

"The battler from the Order of Spomenka."

"The very one, though he keeps his ties to dragonkind a secret."

Anjou adjusted his posture, promising discretion. But he had to ask, "Why is it secret?"

"Who can say? Maybe they like a touch of mystery? It's a solemn vow shared by all members, yet they traipse about with banners flying. Secrets should be better kept." Tone shifting to something less sarcastic, he said, *"Ah. She found us."*

To Anjou's amazement, a serpentine creature rounded the corner, spied them, and broke into a series of pretty trills that were probably scolding. She glided to Gregor, who lifted his hands and lapsed into excited baby talk.

"Is she some variety of Ephemera?"

"No. I'm told she has a full set of wits as well as a voice. Wind dragons are being brought back from the edge of extinction. This one decided she belongs to Gregor." Sounding smug, he added, *"I lured her here. I'm making her our accomplice."*

Anjou wasn't sure he liked the sound of that.

"She has a useful knack. Breezes right past barriers. And there are certain wards that allow me through if I'm carrying Gregor. We'll be using these two to open a path for you."

"For ... me?" Anjou had assumed their meeting was coincidence. With the stirrings of hope, he ventured, "Did someone ask for me?"

"This is more sent *than* sent *for."* The Kith looked away. *"I agreed to lead you to the place you are most needed. Shall we?"*

"But wait. I'm not clear. Who is sending me?"

The Kith's tail flicked. *"What if I said it was an angel?"*

Anjou needed several moments to gather a response. "If so ... if that is true ... then I would be a fool not to listen."

The Kith left Anjou stranded behind barriers formidable enough to curl his whiskers. If Lord Mettlebright caught him so near the heart of his den, banishment was the least of his worries. Even so, Anjou hurried deeper into danger. A familiar scent beckoned and lent him bravery, and when he reached the appointed door, Anjou gladly knocked.

A muffled answer came from within, and then the door opened. "Anjou? How did you find your way here? Is anything the matter?"

At a glance, Anjou could tell that Jacques Smythe had been crying. So he flung his arms around his neck and clung. "Am I still welcome at your hearth?"

"Lord, of course you are. Come inside." Jacques drew him into a steadying embrace.

When the door shut behind them, Anjou shamelessly pleaded for comfort.

Perhaps Jacques needed comfort, too. Hadn't he somehow, unthinkably lost Akira to another? Anjou pressed little kisses on Jacques, who petted his hair and whispered to him in French. He warmed to a new idea. Maybe *this* could become Anjou's place?

"I can tell you're in a melancholy mood," said Jacques. "Where's Eiji?"

"Busy elsewhere." And because he felt safe confessing it here, Anjou added, "He's found a place. He was chosen by a lady mistress."

"Oh? I'd heard Pim Moonprowl was somewhere hereabouts. You mean her?"

"*Non*. Pim is a wolf of the packs. Eiji has moved in with Deece."

"Minx? Well, that's a twist." He tucked Anjou under his chin and stroked his back. "I hadn't realized Kith could accumulate consorts."

"Most don't. This Minx, she is ambitious."

"Mmm. How does Eiji feel about being acquired?"

"He's *pleased*. He'll protect this place and these children."

"And what about you?"

"I'm left wanting." He dared to ask, "Did you truly yield Akira to another?"

"He was never mine."

"You love him," Anjou protested. "You wooed him so patiently. Only a little longer, a little more, and he would have given himself to you."

"I ran out of time, and there'll be no more chances." Jacques admitted, "I knew from the beginning that I'd have to give him back. It's for the best. Watch, and you'll see for yourself. Suuzu adores him."

"I could adore you." As soon as it was out of his mouth, Anjou regretted opening himself up to fresh rejection. Still, he pressed, "You have no reason to rebuff me this time."

"So hasty." It was a chiding tone. Or perhaps a cautioning one. Either way, Jacques softened his words with a kiss. "We're barely acquainted, you and I. And the person you promised yourself to at the resort was mostly pretense."

"*Non*. You held my life in your hands." Anjou meant it when he said, "I'd withhold nothing. I'd entrust everything."

Jacques gave the low tail of Anjou's hair a tug, urging him away in order to study his heating face. "What's made you so desperate? You have all the time in the world. And ... I've become something mysterious. Trepidation seems to be the order of the day."

"Cats are curious." Pressing closer again, sighing against Jacques' throat, he whispered, "May I explore your new splendor?"

"A bit risky. Even his lordship keeps me at arm's length."

"Foxes embody caution. Felines are freer. Trust me?"

"I wouldn't want to harm you," Jacques murmured.

A token resistance. Anjou touched his tongue to warm skin and tasted victory. "You couldn't harm me. Not you. But if it would ease your fears, touch here. I have fine crystals. They can become safeguards."

Jacques' fingers found the remnant stone in one of Anjou's earrings. "Before I ... just, *before*. There's something you need to know. I came back from our adventure with a souvenir of sorts. Something unforeseen, yet also foretold. And exceedingly precious. I think it's why Argent is being so circumspect. As tempting as your offer may be, I need to ensure that the things I carry are safe."

Anjou took a longer look at Jacques and felt stupid. "You're freshly warded. Show me your palms."

The sigilcraft was as delicate as it was devious, and Anjou wondered if the fox responsible ever took apprentices. He smoothed over the artistry, all admiring, then pressed a kiss to each palm. Lifting his gaze to Jacques, he awaited an explanation.

"I've been sprigged. Are you familiar with the term?"

He gasped, for a tribute's lessons included tales of lorefolk.

A gentle quaver brushed against Anjou, setting his proverbial whiskers aquiver. Then Jacques was unbuttoning his vest, and Anjou's heart leapt for eagerness. He reached for the knot of silk at his collar, helping him disrobe.

Jacques laughed softly. "Lord, you do know how to boost a chap's ego."

The man's hands fell away, and Anjou took that for permission to proceed. So he was the one to uncover Jacques' secret ... and stood transfixed. A gem-green coil, like the tendril of a plant, curled snug against the skin surrounding Jacques' navel.

"Every warning you've ever heard about Amaranthine trees is true," said Jacques.

Anjou knew the lullabies of trees, but they were cradle songs to beguile children. To think that such lore sprang from a true seed. A golden one. He bent in order to sniff and nuzzle and kiss and croon.

Again, Jacques laughed, and this time it was warmer, and Anjou felt welcome.

"I will not harm your child." He looked up and confessed, "I want to be part of this, to ready your hearth for this kitten. Give me a place, and I would give any vow."

"Don't be so reckless with your vows." Jacques quietly added, "Thank you, Anjou. For accepting this. I'm still getting used to the idea."

"You're afraid?"

"Does it show? Yes, a little. And perhaps a little more as things progress." He gruffly admitted, "I'm good with babies, but I'm less confident about carrying one."

"You will be perfection!" Anjou promised. "I will see to every little thing."

"Are you offering to be my consort? I'm not a lady, you know."

"But males who share a hearth share everything. I want a share in this." Eager to prove himself, he peered around the room. "I can unpack your trunk. And oversee your sleep. Are you hungry? I could bring a tray. Or even cook for you. I'm sure the wolf in the kitchen would allow it if I explained."

If the previous emotion Anjou had sensed from Jacques had been a tremor, this was a quake.

Jacques asked, "There's a wolf? In the kitchen."

"Yes. She is unusual. She intrigues me."

"Sable fur? Eyes like whiskey? No doubt apron-clad and foisting bowls of gruel on orphans?"

Anjou was astonished. "What is this? *Non*, I know what this is! You are radiant, and it is beautiful." He rubbed their cheeks together and wondered aloud. "Is this why I was sent? To unlock a star? Oh, I am jealous. Who is this wolf, my rival for your heart?"

Jacques looked almost frightened when he whispered, "Sonnet."

9
COMMANDING A HEARTH

Anjou loitered in the kitchen until Sonnet dismissed her young helpers, then he hurried to catch at her sleeve. "We must speak," he begged.

Her surprise, like her very manner, was mild. "I'm listening, Kindred."

"This is a private matter." And taking her hand, Anjou drew her toward the butler's pantry.

She permitted his audacity, her expression quizzical, her tail slowly swaying. Pleased that all was proceeding smoothly, he closed the door behind them, warded it against interruption, and pushed himself up to sit on one of the counters, feet dangling.

Sonnet took a receptive posture. "What is it, love? Can I help you somehow?"

"Yes, but first ... if you'll forgive a touch of trickery?" And he banished the simple sigil he'd used to gain the impact he might need to secure this lady's good opinion. "Help me to understand why someone I care about trembled to learn there was a wolf in the kitchen."

She blinked and breathed deeply, then deeper still. Eyes wide, she whispered, "*Jacques*. You have been with Jacques?"

Anjou had always liked the little games that lovers played, and he smiled over finding two so startled and so smitten. More and more, he wanted a part in their future. But would a wolf tolerate the sorts of affections that were common to consorts? All he could do was try.

Beckoning her closer, Anjou murmured, "Don't be shy, lady. Wolves like scents, yes?"

To his delight, she didn't hold back, murmuring apologies as she pressed her nose to his neck. He tugged her closer, turned his head, and purred to encourage more nuzzling. Oh, he liked this lady. If such a mistress were to rule over him, he would be so free. Hadn't the lovely Elara been similarly tempting? He'd allowed himself to imagine it ... without much hope of finding such a one for his own. Yet here was Sonnet, and she was stealing a taste.

She muttered a husky, "Oh, I do beg your pardon."

"*Non*. I will beg *more*." He drew back, searched her face. "I came to you straight from his embrace. He sent a kiss. Do you want it?"

"You kissed him?"

"How could I help it?" Anjou readily confessed, "He called me reckless and put me off. Perhaps because his heart belongs to another? To you, yes?"

Sonnet's cheeks bloomed with color. "He sent a kiss?"

"These are the games that consorts play. You will find me an amenable tom."

"A kiss … for *me*," she said wonderingly.

"Mmm. Take it." He carefully drew her down, marveling when she allowed it. And then her lips were on his, and a growl bade him submit, and he shivered in surprised ecstasy. Even though he knew she was chasing after traces of another, he met her and matched her and mewed in disappointment when she finally drew back.

"Oh, love. I shouldn't be kissing you."

"You *should*." Anjou clung as he pulled his scattered thoughts back into order. He'd come here with a plan, and he mustn't abandon it. Brushing his lips against her rosy cheek, he earnestly said, "You should take me as your consort."

"Anjou," she said, gently putting him off.

He loved her voice. He loved her scent.

And more softly, "Anjou, wait. Not me. You can't want me. I'm a wolf."

"Mmm. You are dangerous in the nicest way." He knew his tone, his scent, his everything was betraying him. "Oh, lady. Will you listen?"

She was a little warier now, but she repeated, "I'm listening, Kindred."

"A star sent me. Or so I was told. A star sent me to Jacques."

"Where is he?" Sonnet begged.

"His promise to Lord Mettlebright is the only thing that is keeping him from you. He must remain behind wards until … ah, who can say? The fox is cautious, but his reasons are good."

"Is Jacques hurt?"

"No, lady. But turn your thoughts to *my* plight for a little longer? Or do you not care for the sending of stars?"

Sonnet bowed her head. "I do. My mother was born a Starmark. I've always caught the strains of starsong, even after becoming a wolf. Stars tell the truth."

Anjou let himself hope. "Eiji has become consort to Minx. He was chosen, and he is happy with his new place and his good lady. I want a place, and I am begging for it. Be my lady mistress? Choose me."

"*Jacques* is my choice."

"Take me, too?"

"For ... employment?" Her gaze slipped sideways. "You want a place in the kitchen?"

"You know that's not it," he chided. "For a tom like me, there must be a lady mistress. Choose me, and I'll devote myself to you and to him. I'll make *such* a hearth for you! And I'll be grateful and gentle and generous." He caressed her cheek. "You care for so many, but who cares for you? Be my lady, and I'll be his man, and I will honor your wishes in all things."

"We all belong to Stately House. Isn't that enough?"

"Stately House is an enclave. Many are her households. Ours will be *magnifique*."

"Anjou," she sighed. "Do not run ahead."

"I am too eager, perhaps. I want you."

"Why?" she countered. "I'm not a cat to command you."

"Is that not better?" he asked. "A tom can only await a lady's whim. With you, I can freely choose. Is that not a truer love?"

"You don't want a female?"

"*Non*! I do! I've always wanted a lady. Be mine?"

"Anjou," she said again.

"*Oui?*" He loved hearing his name on her lips.

"You have to know I'm not ...." Sonnet gestured vaguely at herself. "I'm male for Jacques. His preference is for ... well. He never kisses females."

"Then this is perfect, no? Your first consort is peerless—your favorite, dearest to your heart. But in commanding a wider hearth, you have secured another ardent admirer. One who longs for his lady's favor. Oh, the kisses we will share." And stretching up, he brushed his lips across hers. "A lady *must* be adored."

"Anjou," she said again. But there was hesitation there. Confusion, as if startled by his suggestion. Or at herself. Then she shook her head. "I have responsibilities. My granddaughter, for one. Linnea is here for school."

"I would accept any children at your hearth into my heart."

"A cat and a mouse?" she asked, mild again in her amusement. Softening?

"Jacques will find it funny. Let us make him smile. He has been so sad." Ah, his timing was good. He'd always been skilled at persuasion.

"I want to see him," she confessed.

"Then we must apply to Suuzu Farroost. Let me? I could act as your go-between, if you will only trust me. A little now. More as you come to know me."

Sonnet surprised him anew by touching his silver hair and murmuring, "You're like a moonbeam."

"A favorite of wolves?"

"What are your years? You must be young if no mistress has spoken for you."

"No longer a child. But ... that autumn voyage was my first consort call." He wasn't sure if moving on to ordinary things meant he was being considered ... or dismissed. Anjou blurted the same thing he'd said to Jacques. "Give me a place, and I would give any vow."

"Oh, love." She enfolded him, and the embrace worried him.

"Please, lady. I'm not a child."

"No, you are not. But you're afraid." She nuzzled his hair, stealing every secret in his scent. "You said Jacques is someone you care for. That you speak for him. That he sent you to me. How did you gain his trust?"

"He saved me."

"You were in the place where all these little ones were captive?"

"Yes. I was captive, as well." And realizing that he could spare Jacques the necessity, Anjou offered, "Will you hear this story? Jacques ... he was courageous."

"I want to hear *everything*. Nobody ever says enough. Tell me now, and then ...." She paused, lost in thought, then brightened. "And then you will bring Jacques a tray. And my return message."

Jacques tipped his head to the side, trying to catch Suuzu's eye. "Why so shy? You're meant to be leading, yet your posture is meek at best."

The phoenix's gaze lifted to his, then slid away. "Is it not enough to learn the steps?"

"*Non.* You must never neglect your partner."

"Akira is meant to be my partner."

"I'm only taking his part in order to teach you yours. You *wanted* dance lessons." He cautiously asked, "What is this? You're protesting, but it's token at best. Argent mentioned an allure. Am I affecting you?"

"You ... are."

"I see. I do apologize." He let his hands fall to his sides. "Unforeseen consequences abound."

Suuzu huddled there, practically hugging himself. "This is confusing."

"So it does bother you? I thought ...." But Jacques closed his mouth and took a step back. The young phoenix didn't want him, had *never* wanted him. But he'd never rejected him. "Are the seals no longer working properly?"

A startled glance. A soft cluck. Suuzu stepped closer. "What is this?" he muttered.

Jacques wasn't sure if he'd asked the same question on purpose. But having lived cheek by jowl with each other since his return, it was almost impossible not to catch each other's moods.

Suuzu asked, "What has happened?"

"I confuse you. I confuse myself. I haven't changed at all, yet everything is different. And then ... well. Today's been rather much."

"I will clarify. You confuse my instincts. I do not want to share courting dances with you. You are not Akira." Suuzu was so earnest, so honest. "But when we move together, it is ... hmm. I know it is only your new nature, but I am surprised at myself. You are *not* the one I want."

"But you want me anyhow."

"How do I keep you close and guard against you? It is ... confusing."

Jacques considered the floor. "At least you're not afraid of me."

Another soft cluck. Suuzu's gaze was soft with concern when he repeated, "What has happened?"

"Hisoka. He rejected me. He was utterly paralyzed, yet on the verge of crashing out the nearest window. Like I was some kind of monster."

Suuzu simply stepped up off the floor, gaining the height advantage he needed to pull Jacques against his chest. Tutting and clucking, he encouraged Jacques to lay his head over his heart, then began an unhurried preening session.

Jacques turned his face into Suuzu's tunic, wrapped both arms around the phoenix's slender waist, and confessed, "It was ... it felt .... It hurt."

His self-proclaimed nestmate didn't say anything, but he proved he was near.

"Suuzu?"

"Hmm?"

Trying for an even, un-hurt tone, Jacques asked, "How long has Sonnet been back?"

"Mmm." He took forever to think it through. "While I was last sleeping. Nearly a month ...? She arrived with ...." He trailed off.

Jacques glanced up. "Lord, what's wrong?"

"I ... *forgot.*"

Jacques had to adjust his hold to bear up under the sudden weight of Suuzu slipping from midair. He quickstepped to the settee at the foot of the bed, and they ended in a graceless tangle upon its cushions. "I suspect it's impolite for me to be privy to so many of your emotions. Why are you suddenly so flustered? I can tell it's not me."

Suuzu whispered, "Boniface."

He hesitated in honest confusion. "There can't be many of *those* lying about. Do you mean Bon-Bon? You met my brother?"

"I ... I *hired* your brother. I think." They stared at each other for several moments, and then Suuzu called, "Hajime?"

"Leafling," warmly greeted the tree. "I knew you would not forget our friend."

Jacques righted himself, but he still felt knocked sideways. "Did you just call Bon-Bon a friend? That's as ridiculous as it is traitorous. Lord. *How*?"

Suuzu seemed to take the accusation of betrayal to heart, because he was on his knees in a moment, framing Jacques' face with his hands, then pressing an urgent kiss to his lips. "I should have considered your feelings. Nonny *did* say you and this brother were at odds, but I was alone, and he was frightened. So when Argent made him my responsibility ...!"

"Bon-Bon was *here*."

"Yes. For a few weeks." Suuzu shot a pleading look at Hajime.

"At that time, Suuzu was newly exposed to my pollen. Many conversations occurred while the three of us were together, and so he has forgotten." The tree beamed at the phoenix. "You called for me. You remember me."

"I do." Suuzu touched Hajime's hand. "Many of us do."

Jacques knew there had been little time to compare notes with Argent, but a visit from Boniface seemed at least as important as Sonnet's return.

"Including Jacques." The tree admitted, "Naoki is curious why you and your brother are unaffected by my pollen."

"I wouldn't say *unaffected*." Jacques let his fingertips trail over the nearest cluster of silken petals that festooned Hajime's hair. "Your scent is decidedly ... invigorating. Have I never forgotten you? I wouldn't remember if I had. Did we ever test that theory?"

"I did not notice at the time of our meeting, but you knew me upon your return. That is beyond rare. Boniface distinguished himself in much the same way. Canarian wanted him for Hisoka, but Suuzu gained a greater portion of your brother's trust. And so Stately House will claim him."

Jacques couldn't think of a single nice thing to say.

Suuzu was worried enough to bestow a pleading peck.

"Lord, I just ... well, I mean ... it's Bon-Bon. He's a prissy, self-important prig."

To his surprise, the phoenix laughed. "He was no kinder in his assessment of you."

"What did he call me?"

"Exhausting. Eccentric. Expensive." With the hint of merriment in his eyes, Suuzu added, "He thinks you have the whole Amaranthine Council in your pocket."

"Lord, that's basically flattery." A new thought occurred. "Did he actually come to see *me*?"

"Is that surprising?" Suuzu asked. "He is your brother."

"It's unprecedented. I've lived here for more than a decade." At the phoenix's slow blink, Jacques helpfully reminded, "In human terms, we're estranged."

"By choice or by consequence?"

Jacques had to ponder that. "Boniface doesn't approve of me, but I think that's more public stance than personal opinion. Maman dictates that sort of thing. But really, in those few times and places where she couldn't intrude, it was us against her."

Suuzu's attention swerved, and Jacques knew what it meant.

A familiar rap preceded Akira through the door. "Look who I found!"

Anjou breezed inside, a tray held high and a carpet bag swinging from his other hand. "May I beg entry, good phoenix? I have things for Jacques."

The tom looked brighter, happier. *Joie de vivre* had replaced his earlier desperation. Things must have gone well, and Anjou looked eager to share what he'd learned. So as soon as Suuzu abandoned him for Akira, Jacques patted the place at his side. "What have you brought me?"

With a swoop that somehow failed to rattle the cups and saucers, Anjou proffered the tray. Jacques accepted it, a smile on his face as he poked through the contents. Tea—his favorite blend. Teacups—her clan's colors. A beribboned bud vase held a bouquet of paperwhites. And peeking under a tea towel, he found a basket of hot, fresh muffins.

"*This* seems out of place," Jacques remarked, indicating the baby bottle.

"*Non*. All is as it should be," Anjou assured, placing a kiss upon his cheek.

Grinning foolishly, Akira dragged over a footstool and moved the tray onto it. With similar radiance, Anjou set the carpet bag across Jacques' knees.

"Lord, she didn't."

"The lady mistress, she sends good gifts."

Jacques braced the baggage with extreme care, then pointed. "There's a sigil just here. I can tell. Can you dispatch it?"

"The pleasure is mine."

Suuzu drifted closer, looking increasingly mystified. Jacques undid fastenings and eased the bag open. From the center of the soft nest within, Ella blinked worriedly.

Akira laughed. "Somebody knows *exactly* what Jacques needs."

He'd definitely been missing the children. Reaching for her, Jacques hesitated. "Will she be afraid? I've changed."

"Don't be silly," countered Akira. "Ella loves you."

The tiny crosser had noticed Anjou and began making the little whimpers that always led to a full-on squall. Jacques interrupted by scooping her up. "Ah, *mon petit chou*! Did you miss your Uncle Jackie?"

He stood, swaying with her toward the window, putting a little distance between her and those she didn't realize she could trust. Murmuring to her in French, he praised her courage and Sonnet's cleverness.

Her answering smile eased something in his heart.

And made him take a longer look at Anjou.

10

SURROGATE

Isla knew Papka was getting in to see Sensei, which was understandable, what with him being Hisoka's former apprentice and First of Wards and everything. But Isla was Sensei's *current* apprentice, which meant he should rely on her more. Well ... he *was* relying on her, but not in all the ways he *could*.

She and her staff were making certain that Canarian Evernhold was properly supported and that all council members and their people knew what to say and how to say it. They couldn't stop *all* the murmurs, of course. It would be enormously helpful if Sensei would just make a showing. A press conference was probably too much to hope for, but they could put him on a panel, for instance. Let Harmonious and Argent do most of the talking. Even a stroll through Kikusawa in Keishi would make a world of difference. Unofficial. Casual. But effective in reassuring the general populace. People needed to see that he was okay. *She* needed to see that he was okay.

Instead, she shuffled two upcoming interviews to later dates and offered to supply an article in his stead. She cancelled a photoshoot and redirected several appearance requests to different Council members. Eyeing the calendar unhappily, she acknowledged that if Sensei didn't budge soon, she'd be spending Christmas alone. And New Years. Even though she'd worked it so they could attend Cyril Sunfletch's holiday gala together, then follow local tradition by returning to Kikusawa for the first shrine visit of the new year.

It would have been *perfect*.

This was so frustrating. Isla needed to know when Hisoka-sensei would be back. Back to normal. Back to her.

Maybe Lapis was right. She was being too passive about this. Patience wasn't getting her any closer to Sensei's side. She needed to be proactive ... persistent ... present. And once his eyes were on her, she'd make him see.

Right.

Fine.

She might not be on Sensei's approved list, but Papka was, and *his* door was always open. She'd bring him around to her way of thinking, and he'd escort her past Argent's wards. Not the most detailed of plans, but Kimi was always saying she didn't need to map out every little thing. This was improvisation. This was reckless. This was love.

By the time she reached Papka's office, she'd worked out a rationale.

The moment she leaned through the door, he brightened.

"Isla! Perfect timing. Lend me a hand?" His gaze flicked past her, and he added, "Even better if Lord Mossberne is here …?"

"No. Sorry. Lapis needed to make several appearances and oversee preparations for an event he's hosting over the weekend."

Papka indicated a pair of green crystals that took up most of his desktop. "You haven't had the chance to interact directly with these. Lend me your expertise?"

"I doubt any but the eldermost recall the mountain clans, and they're notoriously stingy with facts."

"But there are *stories*. And you've read your way through most of Kimiko's family's archive."

"Well, yes."

Papka patiently prompted, "Were any of them about the mountain clans."

"Certainly." She could feel her cheeks warming. "But you must know that those records—if you can call them records—tend toward romance."

"I think that's understating it."

So he *did* know. "Papka, I don't think ancient erotica will help you with your baby imps."

"Still, as someone who's more … ah … broadly read …? Perhaps there are details in those tales that could point us in the right direction."

Us. She liked that *us*. Never once had Papka ignored her input simply because she was young.

"Right, then. Mountain clans, also sometimes called the earthbound folk. They're the embodiments of hills, valleys, mountains, monoliths, volcanoes, and any number of other geological formations. Many people believe that the deifying of certain mountains or stones have a basis in ancient realities. However, the mountain clans purportedly left the Widelands behind, but not before Cadmiel guided them in sowing the earth with precious metals, jewels, and *most* notably, remnant stones."

Papka simply nodded. And waited for more.

She thought back, trying to summon up any useful tidbit of information. "Some of the rarest references are about meadow imps. I read an article once that suggested they were actually a plant form, like Amaranthine trees. That a field of flowers could waylay passersby in the same way a grove of trees could. But others say it's the ground itself that's an Impression. On a related note, many preservationists believe that the earliest Song Circles—I suppose *eldermost* would be a more accurate term—were actually sentient!"

That rabbit trail distracted them for the better part of an hour, but it didn't get them any closer to solving the riddle of their sentient wardstones.

"Setting that aside!" Isla sat a little straighter in her chair. "Why haven't you asked Dr. Naoki about them? Wasn't he involved in caring for them or … something?"

"I *have* asked, and his input has been invaluable, but I wanted a fresh perspective. One colored by narratives instead of by scientific methods. I suppose you could say I'm looking for inspiration."

"If so, why not ask the new bard-in-residence? Or Lapis for that matter?"

"Oh, I'll be relying on them as well." Gaze sharpening, Papka said, "Speaking of Lapis …."

She winced at his tone. "If you mean that thing, I really do wish you'd let it go. It's been a week, and it really wasn't anything."

"It was only four days ago," Papka corrected.

"Well, it feels like forever. And I hope you didn't take him to task. The whole thing was my idea, and it really was for a book." She sternly added, "I trust him *implicitly*. He wouldn't do anything. I can't even imagine it!"

To her surprise, her father looked put out. "I'm certain of Lord Mossberne's integrity, but what were you thinking, putting him in such a difficult position?"

"He didn't have any difficulty proving me wrong." She huffily added, "I was quite vexed."

"Isla, you're missing the point. He's male."

"Yes, yes. I'm aware. But he's a dragon of the heights. They're chaste."

Papka snapped into a dominant posture so fast, Isla blinked in surprise.

"Is that the excuse you're hiding behind?"

"I'm not making excuses. Neither of us did anything wrong!"

"So he explained."

"Then you *did* confront him?" she exclaimed, indignant. "Papka, I told you …!"

"I heard him out, and then I *apologized* to him." His expression went soft and sad. "*Think*, Isla. Are you properly considering *his* feelings?"

Isla could only be incredulous. She and Lapis were great friends, and the dragon knew she had no interest in him, not in that way. He was her confidante, so of course he knew that *Sensei* was the one for her. The only one. Which reminded her of why she'd come to Papka in the first place. She was meant to be coaxing for information. Or better yet, an escort.

And then the office door opened.

Someone lovely and luminous leaned in, spied Papka, and—despite a certain gangliness—glided gracefully into his arms.

"This is a pleasant surprise!" Papka exclaimed warmly. "Is everything all right?"

"All is as well as he will allow."

"And you?"

"I was curious, and so I am here."

Isla was beginning to be giddy. She may have been informed about Impressions, but it wasn't every day you met an imp. But she was honestly confused. "Papka ...? You have a new acquaintance ...?"

"Ah! I suppose you wouldn't have met, since Rhomiko kept to Sensei's room until recently."

She recognized the name from the other day. Papka hadn't explained then. So *this* was the person he'd been referring to?

Papka was in the midst of a rambling introduction, offering the sorts of details only a parent would think important. So Isla raised a hand and interrupted. "Sensei's room? Hisoka-sensei's?"

"Canarian didn't mention ...? Ah, well. Not surprising, really. Sensei brought Rhomiko back from that island."

"What for?"

"I suppose the simplest answer is ... rescue. That applies to everyone Argent and the others brought home."

"But ... why wasn't I told?"

"Probably just an oversight." He smiled at Rhomiko. "You've been making yourself at home, I hope?"

"My home is his hearth."

Isla was growing increasingly uneasy. She'd heard something about a small child that Sensei had come across. A toddler who was part Ephemera. It was a fine thing that Sensei had rescued that little one, but he hadn't *kept* them.

She switched up her stance, asserting dominance. "I'm Hisoka-sensei's apprentice."

Rhomiko slowly inclined their head, acknowledging her statement without seeming to understand its import.

"What are you to Sensei?" she pressed.

Rhomiko simply gazed at her from within the circle of Papka's arms.

Her father stepped in, nodding significantly at the chrysalises on his desk. "Perhaps *more* importantly, what is Rhomiko to *them*? Can you sense the shift in their tone?"

Isla let herself be diverted. For now.

Crossing to the desk, she rested a hand on a silken-smooth crystal. A trill found its way into her soul, and she couldn't help smiling. "Is this the same one that resonated with me earlier?"

"No." Rhomiko had slipped to her side. They reached for her hand, fingers sliding between hers. Lifting it to the other crystal, they pressed her palm into firm contact and murmured, "Here is your part in the song."

She stared into strange eyes sand knew amazement.

Rhomiko's expression was so peaceful, so patient. Ancient. Isla didn't realize she'd been edging closer until they bumped together. An arm slipped around her waist, steadying her, and

Rhomiko whispered, "Do you like to sing?"

"No. I'm awful." Isla whispered, "Are you shining?"

"A little, yes." And with a knowing sort of smile—the kind that Isla hated most—they softly asked, "Are you captivated?"

"Impish allure," interjected Papka.

An imp. Of course. Isla nodded vaguely.

Rhomiko nuzzled her cheeks in a very proper feline greeting. "I am similarly intrigued. May I touch your hair?"

"What ...? Oh! Err ... yes, you may." And because the simplest way to carry a conversation forward was to turn a question back, Isla asked, "Do *you* like to sing?"

"I yearn to sing, but not every moment can hold a song." Rhomiko became increasingly distracted with petting and rearranging her hair. "I live in anticipation."

Papka's voice came from quite close, right behind her. "Isla, may I adjust your personal wards? You're clearly susceptible."

She hummed vaguely, intrigued by the softness of Rhomiko's skin.

They leaned their cheek into her hand and blinked contentedly.

"That's done it. I think. Isla?" Her father gripped her shoulder. "Fascinating, isn't it? I can't say for sure if the allure is from the star part of Rhomiko's heritage. Nobody seems to be affected by Twosies, and he's part star. But Naoki pointed out that they have different parents. Also, Twosies was sprigged, which technically makes him tree-kin. Isla ...?"

"I'm thinking clearly enough to be embarrassed." She tried to pull away from Rhomiko's face, but their hand covered hers, and again their fingers tangled. She stiffly said, "I have no desire to impose."

Rhomiko's smile faded. "I am imposing?"

"Well, I rarely get this close to people I don't know well. Unless they're children."

"I am no child."

She did have to look up, but not much. Isla was taller than most of the human women in her acquaintance, even Kimi. But she'd picked up on her father's careful use of neutral pronouns, so Rhomiko probably wasn't female. Was Sensei susceptible to allure? She was trying to puzzle out feline proclivities and impish influences when Rhomiko's lips brushed her eyebrow.

"That was an apology," they murmured. "Not a claiming sort of kiss."

Had they been claiming Sensei with kisses? Surely not. He wouldn't allow it.

Isla rummaged up a smile. "You can't help being you. And it's interesting, in a way. I mean ... I've always been immune to undue influences. I'm not swayed by dragons."

"*Yet*," Rhomiko said softly. They pulled her close, wrapping both arms around her shoulders.

She didn't resist. Maybe she couldn't? It was more fascinating than frightening, and then Papka's arms were around both of them, like he was giving their friendship his blessing. Or ... no. His attention was on the chrysalises. With a laugh, Isla asked, "Are you trying to make them jealous?"

"In my experience, children don't like being left out. Maybe some form of contact is key? You were certainly close to Lapis when they began resonating before."

"Since we collaborate, our schedules do intersect with more

frequency than all the others, but we each have our own agendas." As an example, she rattled off, "I'm leaving for Keishi tomorrow, meetings in Belgium on the fifth and sixth, then straight on to Lapis's for a soiree. It's his turn to host. I'll take an extra day there, catch up on some reading, but I'll probably only see him for an hour or two here and there. Then it's back-to-back interviews and appearances and events straight through Dichotomy Day."

"So there's no time for the two of you to cuddle a rock baby."

"No. I mean ... unless he fills in for Hisoka-sensei for the holidays. He'd be sacrificing a few days of sleep, but he'd be a good choice. Americans are so in love with dragons right now." She shook her head. "It's still small snatches, though. Even if I can get our schedules to mesh, it's not as if we can carry one of these babies away from here."

"Argent would never allow it."

Rhomiko hummed a few notes, then suddenly said, "Carry them. Yes. They want to be carried."

"Really?" Papka left their huddle to heft one of the chrysalises. "So you *have* been feeling left out. Up you come, there's a brave little love."

Isla covered a smile.

He admitted, "If they need to snug up to someone, I'll certainly volunteer. Perhaps they need access? Something like cosseting. We could create an atmosphere that fosters peace and maturation." With a soft grunt, he added, "You're a bit heavy. Toting you around all the time will throw off my balance."

"Tell that to Mum!"

"Oh, I'll get no sympathy from that quarter." And to the baby rock imp, he affected Mum's brusque kindness. "What is hard is good, yes?"

"Isla Ward." Rhomiko spoke slowly, softly. "You must learn your part in the song."

She didn't like being told what to do, especially by someone who didn't know anything about her. And it was ten times worse when that person was preening about knowing something she didn't. "I have a place," she asserted. "I know my part."

"Isla Ward," Rhomiko repeated. "You cannot learn another's lyric."

She grimaced. "Look, I know stars are meant to be oracles or good omens or something. At least that's how it is in stories. But could you drop the affectation and say what you mean plainly."

"The words are not my own."

"Surely you're capable of paraphrase."

"Certainly. I have already translated the song into a language you know."

"Interpretation, then," she muttered, pulling free and standing apart.

Rhomiko slowly inclined their head, then spoke with surprising authority. "Hisoka was never meant for you."

Isla shot a look at Papka, who showed no sign of having heard. "That's not for you to say."

Rhomiko solemnly repeated, "The words are not my own."

"So you can't speak for yourself?" she challenged, suddenly keenly aware that she was in the same room as her two greatest rivals for Hisoka-sensei's time and attention.

"I can."

"And…?" she prompted, ready with a thousand counter arguments.

Voice low with urgency, Rhomiko said, "Hisoka will never call you to his side."

Isla turned on her heel and walked out.

11

TREASURE ROOM

Kyrie expected no trouble slipping past the barriers protecting the treasure room at Kikusawa Shrine. This was the final hurdle. It had been *far* more difficult to get permission for a trip to Keishi in the first place. Ginkgo had offered to bring him, but Dad wouldn't hear of it. Too many dangers lurked beyond the safe haven of home. Crossers gone missing. Spirited away by foxes.

It was Mother who suggested someone else for his bodyguard, and Dad couldn't deny that Kyrie would be safe in a wolf's keeping. Not when that wolf was Boonmar-fen Elderbough.

Of course, that meant Kyrie had a whole new problem.

"Going somewhere, kid?"

"Just … around …?" he tried. Boon was surprisingly difficult to elude.

The tracker crouched in front of him, peering into his face.

"May as well level with me."

Kyrie tentatively offered, "I will not lie."

"Wouldn't matter if you did." He gave Kyrie's nose an affectionate tap, then touched his own. "You can't fool this. Or me. So bring the rest of your team up to speed. What's the plan?"

"I want to check something."

The wolf beckoned with both hands. "You're skimping on details I need. Increase my trust."

Kyrie asked, "Are you going to try to stop me?"

"Not necessarily. I've been known to bend a rule or two for a good cause. Good at keeping secrets, too. Even better at teamwork." He pointed a finger. "Also, I like your attitude. You don't think I *can* stop you, do you?"

"No," he admitted.

"We're gonna revisit that notion another time. But for now ...?"

"The winds who followed the ships home from that island have been whispering. If I understand correctly, then there is something I must do."

"Here at Kikusawa."

"Yes. I will not leave the shrine."

Boon's brows rose. "I heard the rumors. Sinder mostly, but Moon chimed in. You really do chat with wind imps?"

Kyrie shyly admitted, "They like me."

"I like you, too, kid. What else can you tell me?"

"What I plan to do is not dangerous, nor is it specifically forbidden. And I want to do it myself."

"I can understand that. All right. Sure." Boon pointed to one of the shrine buildings. "I'll grab a seat in the sun, do a little basking. And you holler if you need a hand.”

“I will.”

Reaching slowly, in case Boon wouldn't like it, Kyrie touched the wolf's face, tracing the scars that ran in ragged lines down his cheek. Boon held Kyrie's gaze the whole time, his posture relaxed, even receptive. There *were* questions Kyrie wanted to ask, but his errand was more interesting right now. Maybe that meant he was selfish?

Lowering his gaze, Kyrie murmured, “Thank you, Boon.”

“Not a problem.”

So Kyrie turned and jogged away, taking the first corner in order to slip out of sight. A leap put him on a tile rooftop where trackless snow heaped. Even if he was light on his feet, he'd leave prints, but would anyone notice? Deciding to minimize any evidence, he ran away from his destination and gathered himself for a leap into Kusunoki's branches.

He'd played in the shrine's sacred tree many times, but it had taken a while for him to properly remember him. The tree had stirred from a centuries-long sleep around the same time that Kimiko had begun courting Ever's older brother. By the time Kyrie's best friend had moved to the shrine from the Starmark compound across town, Kyrie already counted Kusunoki among his friends, albeit a secret friend. Not many people outside the Miyabe family knew that the Keishi landmark was a person.

Kyrie dropped onto the treasure room's roof, crouched in the shadows long enough to be certain the building was empty, then befriended one of the crystals anchoring its wards. A minute is all it took, and he slipped inside.

Moving with care, he found the cabinet and opened it.

Wait. No. It was filled with nice things, but they were so ordinary. Nothing like the tales brought to him by anxious winds. Confused, he quietly closed the double doors and peered around the room for another cupboard. But ... surely not? Had someone moved the bottles?

"What are you doing in here, Merciful Dragon?"

Kyrie ducked his head guiltily. "Hello, Kusunoki."

The tree lightly rested a hand atop his head. "You are here without permission. Sakiko will not like it."

"I thought something was here." He indicated the cabinet. "Did you know that someone long ago trapped four wind imps? I was looking for their bottles."

"I know where they are."

Kyrie asked, "Show me?"

"What do you plan to do?"

"Break the seals."

The tree took a long time to respond. "There would be consequences, I think."

He doubted Kusunoki meant Aunt Sakiko's scolding. "Good ones, I hope. Winds should be free."

"Hmm." Finally, Kusunoki admitted, "You chose the correct cupboard, but it has a secret."

Kyrie watched closely while the tree demonstrated the trick to opening a recess where many precious items were secured. His heart leapt at the sight of four bottles. He took the first with both hands and marveled at the weight of it. Then marveled anew at how skimpily the prison was warded. *Anyone* could open these. It would be as simple as pulling a cork.

He murmured, "This will be easier than I thought."

"Not in here," Kusunoki cautioned.

"Help me carry them outside?"

"Certainly." The tree showed no qualms over taking the remaining three bottles from their hiding place. Scooping Kyrie into his other arm, Kusunoki stood and said, "My way is faster."

Kyrie blinked when the dimness of the treasure room was replaced by daylight. Kusunoki lowered him to the sturdy boards of a treehouse that Kyrie and Ever had built with help from his Uncle Laud. Lashed among Kusunoki's branches, it was well-hidden even in winter because the tree was evergreen.

Sitting down, Kyrie inspected the simple tag on the bottle he held. It said, **SOUTH**, and its simple seal had been broken. That meant this had once been Tzefira's prison.

Kusunoki knelt opposite and carefully arrayed the remaining bottles between them. They also had labels—**EAST**, **WEST**, and **NORTH**.

"Do you remember when this bottle was opened?" Kyrie asked, tapping the deep green bottle with the tip of one painted claw.

"No. It was while I was sleeping."

Kyrie said, "So you do not know what will happen when I open the others?"

The tree imp tipped his head to one side, then the other. "Only that there will be consequences. This is very reckless of you."

"Do you think so?" He ran his fingertips across the rippling surface of a bottle that was the deepening blue of a twilit sky. "It seems the right thing to do."

"I agree. But why *you*?" Kusunoki solemnly added, "Why in haste? Why in secret?"

"Winds have always liked me. They are friendly and even helpful, but they never stay." He really was being selfish. "I think these winds will be different."

Kusunoki frowned. "Little dragon, do you want to woo them to your side? Because in all the stories I know, wind imps are tempestuous. Think of the trouble they gave Persiflage Beckonthrall."

Kyrie brightened. "I have met Lord Beckonthrall. He is happy with his wives."

"*Now*." The tree imp looked half-ready to snatch back the collection of bottles. "Consider instead the beginning of his story. It is meant to keep other dragons from making his mistakes."

"I am not wooing winds. I want to release them. They may be grateful."

Kusunoki hesitated. "Your heart is set?"

"It is."

"Then ... I will do what I can to keep you safe."

Kyrie reached again for the tall, blue bottle. Its tag claimed that it held the west wind. He'd looked up all the stories he could, but none of them ever explained which wind came from which direction. Nor had he been able to find their given names. All he really knew from Bethiel's lore were the types of winds that he'd supposedly tamed.

A summer breeze.

A typhoon.

A whirlwind.

A thunderstorm.

If true, then it was probably a good thing that Kusunoki had brought him outside before opening the bottles. With little more than a fleeting prayer that all would be well, Kyrie braced the blue bottle against his chest and worked free its stopper.

Nothing happened.

Kyrie traded a look with Kusunoki, who wore an uneasy expression.

But then ... a faint scent ...? That's when Kyrie realized that all the other winds in the vicinity had gone still. Worried the trapped wind was too weak to escape, he offered a soft warble of encouragement and tipped, as if to pour the imp out. Still nothing.

He risked a sniff at the bottle's opening.

Kusunoki covered his mouth with his hand, eyes wide.

Kyrie ducked his head, chastised. But he *was* sure the new scent had come from the bottle. Perhaps an imp had been there and gone? Escaped. That was good. It wasn't as if Kyrie had been expecting thanks. He should get on with it.

Setting the blue bottle next to the green, he reached for the one with a rich purple hue that wasn't much different than the color of his hair. This one's tag boldly declared **EAST**. He pushed at the stopper, then dug in his clawtips. The seal came free with a hiss that blew his hair into immediate disarray.

"That ... worked ...?" he whispered to Kusunoki.

The tree peered upward. He still looked worried. "That was *not* a happy imp."

"Can you blame them?"

The final bottle was also blue, but a lighter, brighter shade. Not quite sky blue. Or perhaps it was the color of the sky in some distant land. This one's tag read **NORTH**, and Kyrie coaxed the stopper free.

Something sort of ... gasped.

"Do not be afraid," Kyrie urged.

All at once, wind buffeted him from all sides, and he yelped in surprise when the tumult threw him from the platform. He was falling. But then he collided with Kusunoki's broad chest, and there were strong arms around him, and they were safe atop the roof of the Miyabe house. Kyrie meant to thank the tree, but he was startled by a loud crash and the tinkle of breaking glass.

An instant later, he and Kusunoki were on a different rooftop. One of the storehouses this time.

"What happened?" Kyrie asked, only to flinch when glass exploded against the snowy tiles at Kusunoki's feet, sending purple shards flying.

The tree imp rushed him to another corner of the shrine courtyard, on the ground this time, near a row of stone lanterns.

"Those were two of the bottles," Kusunoki calmly answered.

"They are breaking their prisons."

Something whipped past, crashing against stone pavers. The green bottle this time. Again, the tree took him to a new place, back up among his branches. "Merciful Dragon, they are aiming for you."

"But ...!" There was a rattling in the tree's branches as foliage was stripped from limbs, torn into a whirlwind of confusion. The scent of bruised leaves and spilled sap drove a spike of guilt into Kyrie's heart. He exclaimed, "Are you hurt?"

Kusunoki didn't answer, only ducked as the fourth bottle whizzed past to plummet down. Kyrie could hear the bottle smacking against leaves and bouncing off limbs. Far below, it shattered.

When the tinkling stopped, silence reigned for two beats. Then Boon's voice carried. "You okay, kid?"

"I am uninjured."

"Need that hand yet?" the wolf blandly inquired.

Kyrie listened to the stillness, then offered the only answer he could. "I ... I may need a broom ...?"

To his surprise, all Boon said was, "On it."

12

WEATHER FORECAST

Tsumiko took Akira by the arm and guided him upstairs, explaining, "While Lady Starmark was visiting, there were *four* beacons in the house, and Vanya isn't far behind in brilliance. Argent did what he could, but Ella's been inconsolable ever since Boniface left."

"Who?" asked Akira.

She bit her lip, then breezed on. "Twosies is sulking, and he wouldn't say why. Thankfully, Dad knew the reason right away, and Elara confirmed it. I feel just *terrible*, but how could any of us have known? We put an ocean between two best friends."

"Sis, slow down." He pulled her to a standstill on a landing. "I mean, I can sympathize, but it's not up to you to make sure everyone's happy."

"Except it *is*."

"Not entirely. I'll call Fumiko. Maybe even talk to Juuyu. If they have a sad tree on their hands, they're going to be just as ready as us to make it right." He searched her face. "Let me help more. This is my family, too."

"Thank you. I'll be relying on you. In a way, I already have been." She really should have asked sooner. "How's Uncle Jackie?"

"Jacques has pretty bad nightmares, and his appetite's kind of pitiful. But he's mostly bored. I've been enduring more than my fair share of facials, and this morning, he threatened to resume my dance lessons."

"I think I want to hear more about your trip. The parts that make you smile like this." She reached up to touch his face. "You and Uncle Jackie came back different."

"We got to know each other pretty well." This time, *he* took *her* arm, guiding her up the final flight of stairs. With a crooked smile, he quietly added, "Suuzu and I will make sure Jacques is okay. And I'll happily take a turn holding Ella, but Jacques is still her favorite. Couldn't he rejoin the naproom rotation?"

"If Argent and Suuzu can agree ...?"

"Guess I'll have to talk to Argent when he gets back."

They'd almost reached the naproom when Sibley hurtled out the door, colliding with Akira's legs and wrapping both arms around his waist. The boy—her new son—was almost combative in his affections, as if daring anyone to try to come between him and the people he cared about.

"You came! Can you stay? Perse likes you, so that'd be good." And in a gentler tone, Sibley added, "Hi, Lady. Hey, do you know where Kyrie is?"

"He had an errand to run, but he should be on his way home."

Sibley pulled away from Akira, looking uncertain, maybe even uneasy. "He left?"

"Yes. Quite early this morning."

"He didn't say nothing." Sibley shuffled forward and lowered his voice. "Why'd you let him go? It's not safe."

"Boon is with him."

"Oh, yeah?" Sibley gave a grudging nod. "Guess that's all right."

The same day two windships' worth of dazed children arrived at Stately House, Sibley had proven to be a very brave boy, willing to take on Lord Mettlebright himself if it meant keeping the other crossers safe. He'd been everywhere. Counting heads and checking in. Grumping at the mares and whispering promises to the little ones. Overseeing bed assignments and dragging Kyrie around to make sure each child met their biggest brother.

Sibley's belligerent pronouncements carried more weight than her father's—they all knew Dr. Naoki—and even Elara's. So when Sibley told them all, *this is a good place*, they'd believed him. And calmed.

Tsumiko had reason to be grateful, but she also saw how Sibley sagged into Kyrie, glad to share a burden no child should have ever had to carry. Even now, he was sacrificing himself. Given the chance, she was certain Sibley would have barged past barriers and claimed a spot in Kyrie's room. Instead, he'd put himself in charge of the four children who seemed to think that the long rows of beds in their dormitories were a little too much like long rows of cages. So instead, they'd taken up residence in the naproom.

Twosies, the sulky boy-child who was part star.

Hotaru, a little girl with antennae who shone with a light all her own.

Perse, an older boy whose inheritances included both hooves and scales.

And the as-yet-unnamed girl who was somehow part Ephemera. Apparently, the closest thing she had to a name was Bother, which wouldn't do for one so lovely.

Tsumiko reached out, silently offering to take Sibley's hand.

As had happened before, he tucked both hands behind his back. "No offense, Lady, but I wouldn't want these claws of mine to … well, y'know. Safer this way. But don't feel bad. When you're close, it's already like a hug." Cheeks ruddy, Sibley escaped into the naproom.

Akira slipped his arm around her shoulders and gave a squeeze. "Seems like little half-dragons *also* have a way with words."

Tsumiko whispered, "I need someone to ward a pair of mittens so I can hug that boy without worrying him."

"Sounds good. And … sounds quiet. Ella's not crying?"

"You're right." She led the way into the naproom. The padded flooring lent a spring to her step as she navigated around pillow piles to the oasis of firm flooring in the corner. Rhomiko had claimed one of the rockers, where they swayed with little Ella. Tsumiko smiled. "This is a nice surprise. She took to you?"

"She was calling, and I answered," said Rhomiko.

"Thank you. Is Sensei all right?"

"Not *all*, no." Rhomiko's gaze shifted to Akira, who slid into the rocker next to theirs. "Hello, Akira."

They hadn't met yet. At least, not that Tsumiko knew.

Akira raised a hand in greeting. "Rhomiko, right? It's good to meet you. I'm ... well, I'm Tsumiko's brother."

"You are the phoenix's boy."

"That, too," he replied easily. "Is that how someone described me?"

Rhomiko said, "Stars sing almost as much as wolves. But I would like to know you by more than the lyrics you have inspired."

"I'm not sure you should trust rumors, even nice ones. It'd be better if we hang out. Like this." Akira crooked his fingers at Twosies, who leaned against the arm of Rhomiko's chair. "We can all be friends."

Tsumiko sat on the floor nearby and shifted two pillows, uncovering their half-midivar child's hiding place. "Come to Lady?"

With a slither of turquoise scales, the girl coiled around Tsumiko, hiding her face against her sweater, then trying to swarm inside it.

Sibley bustled over with one of the fur blankets. "It's colder here," he muttered. "She doesn't like that. But everything else's really good. Bother's always liked exploring, and this place is full of rooms."

"Will you help me choose a better name for her?"

"Me?"

"Why not?" She said, "I let Kyrie name one of his other sisters. Have you met Mercy?"

"Yeah, of course." Sibley scooted closer on his knees and twitched the blanket up over the little girl's shoulder. "You ... you're adopting Bother, too? She's not a dragon-crosser. Not *kin* or whatever."

"This may have started with the hope that we could reunite Kyrie with as many of his siblings as possible, but we're welcoming *all* of you, no matter your heritage. Argent and I want each and every one of you. You're home."

Sibley scooted closer. "There's a lot of us. Could be there's more out there."

"Like you said, we have a lot of rooms."

"Umm ... Sis?" Akira looked vaguely worried. "Rhomiko has a question, and I think it might be important."

"Yes?"

"Are storms terrible?" asked Rhomiko.

"Some people find them unsettling. Are you afraid of lightning and thunder?"

"I do not know." They glanced between her and Sibley. "Could I befriend them rather than fear them?"

"That would be interesting. I'm not sure if there are thunder imps or lightning imps specifically. But there certainly could be. As part of a sky clan." Tsumiko wasn't sure she was answering the question. "We do *get* storms. There are shutters and gutters and lightning rods. But this time of year, we expect snowstorms."

Rhomiko asked, "What about rain? I think there will be rain."

"In winter, we *sometimes* get rain, but it freezes as it falls, coating everything in ice. It can cause damage, especially to trees. And in the gardens."

"Then you should warn the trees. And prepare your shutters and gutters."

Akira stood, clearly ready to play messenger. "I'll talk to Ginkgo. He'll know what to do. We can check the weather forecast and notify the rest of the enclave."

Tsumiko checked her phone. "Today. Tomorrow. All week. The forecast is for sunny skies."

Rhomiko said, "Imps are unpredictable. They cannot be forecast."

"Wind imps caused a lot of damage on that island," said Akira. "Maybe I should talk to Lapis, too? Dragons are supposed to know all about winds, yeah?"

"He isn't here. Council business. Maybe Opulence?"

"There is a storm coming." Rhomiko's tone was portentous, though with a small shake of their head, they amended, "Storms. Three of them. And they are angry."

13

INCLEMENT

"Hey, kid."

Kyrie had been waiting for Boon to speak up, but he still winced when it happened. They'd left Keishi on foot, and normally, Kyrie liked running with wolves. The speed. The freedom. But it was becoming increasingly difficult to ignore the whispered warnings of passing winds.

Running had become *out*running, and Kyrie was going to lose the race.

Boon stopped on the edge of a thicket, and Kyrie halted before him, head bowed.

"Maybe you should have a look," the wolf said.

A rough gust blew Kyrie's hair forward. Tucking straying locks behind his ear, he turned so the next burst of wind cleared his face. In the distance, Keishi was buried under an ominous cloud. And nearer to them, a smaller smudge of black scudded their way—slow but determined.

Boon said, "Funny weather. Unseasonable."

"Yes."

"Those are imps, aren't they? We had a close brush with their sort in the tropics."

"Yes."

"And that pile-up of—how would you put it—inclement weather? It's looking for you. And that littler one's got a fix on you."

"Yes."

Boon grunted. "Gonna make me quiz you into a corner? Come clean, Kyrie. What are we facing?"

"Do you know stories of the Changing Winds?"

"Sure. Bethiel's buddies."

"They were trapped in bottles. I set them free."

"No kidding?" Boon lifted his head, partially baring his fangs as he tasted scents. "They don't seem particularly thankful."

Kyrie watched unhappily as the smaller cloud spat a lightning bolt at a pole that carried power lines. "No. They do not."

"For starters, let's check back. You know how to get ahold of your bestie?"

"Yes."

Boon passed him his phone. "Make sure they're all right."

Moments later, Kyrie was talking to Ever. "Is it raining there?"

"Pouring!"

"When did it begin?"

"Right after you left. Just ... crash, bang! Thunder and lightning. And it doesn't smell like a normal storm."

"Are you all right? Boon wants to know if you need help."

"Nope. We'll be fine. Uncle Laud says it's moving off."

"Which way?" asked Kyrie, glancing at his companion.

"Not sure. Lemme check." A few beats later, he was back. *"Quen says north. Which is also weird. Not the usual path for a storm to take."*

"I thought so. Yes. I will lead it away."

"What?" Ever sounded worried. *"What's going on?"*

"That storm is looking for me. But do not worry. I will also be fine. Boon is here. We will work together."

"But how do you lead a storm? Are you singing to it?"

"No. But that is a good idea. Thank you."

When he passed the phone back to Boon, the wolf placed his own call. "Got a question, little bro. Can Michael's barriers hold out weather? Okay, I get that. But *can* they? Because I've got *your* little bro here, and we're pulling a pissed-off storm. Find out? Yeah, we'll give you some time. Scenic route. Sure."

And he offered the phone to Kyrie.

Ginkgo sounded the same as always. *"Having fun, little bro?"*

"I have not decided. This is certainly … interesting. But I do not want my curiosity to make trouble for everyone."

"What's caught your interest?"

"Captive wind imps. Only they are free now. And they are following me."

"Isn't that natural? They'd be interested in you, too."

"I … hope so? I would like to befriend them, but their approach is ominous. I do not think they are entirely safe."

"Gotcha. Well, you've got Boon right there, and Michael and I will support you from here. Keep us posted?"

Kyrie glanced at Boon, who bent close to promise, "Regular updates."

Ginkgo asked, *"Need us to send anyone?"*

"Not likely," said the wolf. "But if that changes, you'll get word."

The call ended, and Kyrie turned to look at the sky. That small, black cloud was rolling nearer. Kyrie frowned. "Is it getting smaller?"

"Yeah. Definitely losing strength."

"Should I try talking to it?" Already making up his mind, Kyrie said, "I will try talking."

"You *did* want to make a friend. Let's see if that's possible."

They began walking toward the oncoming cloud, which seemed to be wisping away at the edges. Worried now, Kyrie picked up his pace. "Help me reach them in time?"

"You got it, kid."

Boon scooped and set Kyrie astride broad shoulders, then leapt into the sky.

Ever had suggested singing, and that made a sort of sense. While Kyrie didn't want a bride or anything, he did want to woo this wind to his side. To make friends. So he stretched out his hands and warbled a welcome.

"Good plan. Keep it up," urged Boon.

They stopped near the smudge of darkness, and Kyrie listened, hoping for some whisper of response.

Boon warned, "That is one unhappy cloud."

It also looked unhealthy. Kyrie did the only thing he could think of. He used sway. "Come to me. I will shelter you. I will lead you to a safe place. Please, believe me."

The cloud swirled and sank, and Boon moved up, as if to catch it. Then there was a cool mist all around Kyrie's head and shoulders, and a masculine voice filtered into his thoughts—weary as a sigh and decidedly out-of-sorts. *"Drown you ... rattle your bones ... throw bolts until you're ... burning. Traitorous wretch. Where's my ... my friend ...?"*

Kyrie gasped in surprise, then choked on the thickened air.

"Serves you right ... little terror." And then with a shift in tone. *"Little. You're only little. A child ...? Who sends a child against ... an eldermost storm?"*

Immediately, Kyrie could breathe again, so he whispered, "I tried to help. Let me help?"

"Where's Haizea and Tzefira? What've you done to Dima?" And in a plaintive whine, *"Bethiel?"*

Kyrie tried again, coaxing, "Come to me, and I will shelter you. I will lead you to a safe place."

"You? You!" And with traces of disdain, *"I don't want you."*

Even so, the cloud curled into a tight ball and sank into his outstretched arms. But trying to hold a storm proved impossible. It dissipated with a puff, and all was silent.

"You okay, kid?" asked Boon. "Seems like you got through."

"I could hear his voice, but it was very weak."

"Cloud's gone, but the air's thick with the scent of him. Like there's a storm coming." Boon quietly added, "He's still here, yeah?"

"I cannot tell where he went, yet I do not think he has gone far."

"Little terror," muttered the voice.

"Oh." Kyrie placed a hand over his heart. "He is with me. Somehow ...?"

"Are they taking from you?" Boon sounded worried. "Would you know if you're being depleted?"

"I would know. And I am not." Kyrie gave the wolf's hair a soothing pat, then immediately felt silly for doing so. "It is as if I have become his bottle. Should I try tending him?"

"You know how?"

"Not officially."

"Let's not rush into any bond-building without Argent's say-so." Boon circled there in midair to stare off toward the south. "And I'm not eager to find out if you can contain something bigger. Because if the stories are true, that'll be Dima. And she's got a whole lot more in the way of staying power."

Kyrie had been playing with passing winds all his life, but this felt both different ... and dangerous. "Can we lead her out to sea?"

"Better for everyone if we do." Boon handed up his phone. "I'm gonna shift, so hold tight. Update Ginkgo. Tell him we'll take a seaside approach to Stately House. And to expect a typhoon."

14

IMPISH PROTOCOLS

When Michael jogged through the kitchen, cloak billowing, Tsumiko happened to be between him and the door, which forced him to face her. She asked, "Has something happened?"

He did a terrible job trying to hide his crystal-topped staff behind his back. "Ah! Well, not ... precisely ...?"

She gestured to the staff, which she knew had come to him when he'd been granted status as First of Wards. While its remnant stone wasn't Stately House's anchor, it acted as a key of sorts. Michael had explained its function to Kyrie back when he was still quite small. Six? Maybe seven? Now that she was thinking on it, Tsumiko recalled that her son hadn't asked *about* the stone. No, he'd asked Michael to introduce him *to* the stone. Because the little boy had winnowed out its remnant song from among the myriad voices that only he seemed able to hear. The resulting lecture had been incidental.

"Is there a problem with the wards?" she pressed.

"As it happens, Kyrie called. He and Boon are on their way, and they need a ... well, a back door." With a tentative smile, Michael added, "I'm sure it's nothing to worry about."

Tsumiko stepped aside, and the moment he was gone, Tsumiko softly called, "Sonnet?"

"I'm here, Lady." The wolf dropped a cardigan around Tsumiko's shoulders before scooping Mercy from her arms. "Button up, love. The weather's turning."

On her way across the snow-drifted garden, Tsumiko pushed her arms into thick woolen sleeves and fumbled with fastenings, but most of her attention was on the sky. A storm wheeled out over the water.

Michael was already up on the wall overlooking the drop-off to the beach, his staff held ready. Deece was at his side, along with a few of their Kith, and Ginkgo was on his phone, his expression unusually grim.

She hung back, not wanting to interrupt. Perhaps he was talking to Kyrie? Michael said he'd called ahead, asking for help. Because of a storm. No. Rhomiko had said there were *three* storms. Was Kyrie bringing them home? It didn't take much of a stretch of the imagination to believe he could.

Kyrie, who heard the songs of stone and the whispers of wind.

Kyrie, who beguiled strong wills with swaying words.

Kyrie, who slipped out of notice, simply by holding still.

Tsumiko hadn't been surprised when Sinder gave his assessment of Kyrie's reaver qualities—crystal adept. Michael had formalized matters, inviting the boy to become his apprentice, even though it was obvious in hindsight that he'd been guiding their son all along. Only the ambuscade part had baffled her. Kyrie was such a gentle soul.

And yet ... she thought he didn't confide in her as much as he once had. Not that he was hiding anything. He simply didn't share every little thing. Their interests overlapped, for they both loved books. But Kyrie had a way of taking the things she found academically fascinating and putting them to immediate use. He stole from every saga and song, arming himself with lore, winning the aid of lorefolk.

Kyrie had always been sweet-natured, compassionate, and kind. Yet Sinder had so eagerly asked that they recast him as a battler. An unforeseen shift. She'd hoped for peace. Kyrie seemed more disposed to fight for that peace ... and to defend it.

She could tell whenever his sly little sigils settled on her, whisper-light and hopeful as prayers. When the truth of his parentage had come out, he'd changed. Maybe it had been a loss of innocence. Maybe he'd caught a glimpse of purpose, much as she'd done when he'd been placed in her arms. If Tsumiko had to put it into words, she's have said that Kyrie was the self-appointed guardian angel of every crosser at Stately House.

The only thing that saddened her was that they needed guarding at all.

Something teased at her, an awareness honed by years of raising a dragon's child. Despite her concerns, she found herself smiling. Because Kyrie had a guardian angel of his own. "Sibley, are you close by?"

"Hi, Lady. You noticed me? That's pretty good."

Tsumiko offered her hand. "Your ears are better than mine. Can you tell me what they've been saying?"

The boy came forward, boots crunching in snow. His deep red eyes only lifted briefly to hers. "My claws. I wouldn't want to hurt you any."

"Where are the gloves I asked Randolla to make for you?"

He pulled his hands from his pockets, showing them.

"Come here, Sibley. Will you tell me what they've been saying? I don't want to interrupt."

Gaze full of a heartbreakingly wary sort of hope, he let himself be swayed.

He was sweet, but this was so silly. Sibley definitely got close to others—Uncle Jackie, Ginkgo, Boon, Akira. She didn't like being an exception, even though it proved he cared. Giving Sibley her full attention, Tsumiko promised, "You won't hurt me just by being close. If I hug you, will you hug me back?"

"Okay, I guess. If you're sure ...?"

She slipped her arms around sturdy shoulders and pulled him into contact. He hid his face against her thick sweater. Slowly, cautiously, he put his arms around her waist and proceeded to cling. She smoothed wavy hair and quietly asked, "If I love you, will you love me back?"

His hold tightened, and he nodded, nuzzling closer.

Tsumiko let everything else fall away, as if the two of them were a world unto themselves. She went right on petting his hair, giving him time to get used to the idea that *this* was his place just as much as Stately House was. Argent did this with the children, too, urging them to take in his scent, to learn his voice, to find reasons to trust.

Sibley lifted his face in order to meet her waiting gaze. He said, "There's a storm coming. It's chasing Kyrie. Him and Boon will outrun it, and … umm … P-papka's gonna open the way. Only Deece is worried about what else might get in if they do."

He was a good communicator, this boy. She knew Michael was encouraging all their new children to simply call him Papka. Sibley was shy about it, though.

"Chased by a storm?" she echoed, turning to peer at the sky again. "Kyrie usually gets along very well with winds."

"This one's pissed. Oh. Sorry, Lady. It's … uhh … incensed. That's a word I learned from Uncle Jackie. It's a good one, yeah?"

"Uncle Jackie knows many fine words," she murmured. He was the one person Sibley wasn't shy about owning. Jacques had been his Uncle Jackie right from the start. It was too bad Argent's protective streak was keeping everyone from their favorite uncle.

Ginkgo turned then. Possibly to spare her from questions about whether or not Uncle Jackie could have visitors yet. Dropping from the low wall, he asked, "Need a boost?"

"Please."

Sibley stepped back, and Deece took her hand, steadying her upon this new vantage point, which offered an unparalleled view of sea and sky.

"You, too, little bro." Ginkgo urged, and Sibley reclaimed his place.

This time, Tsumiko could tell that he wasn't clinging for comfort. His arms around her waist were an anchor, lest she fall.

She saw Ginkgo's approving nod and held her peace. According to what Jacques and Boon had shared with her, Sibley had gone out of his way to protect the children at the lab where they'd been found. He would be a leader, this boy.

Michael murmured under his breath, a lilting string of words in another language. Not for the first time, she thought it sounded like he was casting a spell. But now she knew that the incantation was Old Amaranthine poetry, and that the verses were a traditional invitation to any willing winds. Their cooperation made sigilcraft possible, or so the stories went.

She added silent prayers for Kyrie's safe return.

Ginkgo's ears twitched her way, and he smiled. "Lousy time for Dad to be gone, but Boon's more than a match for most things. And so's his backup."

Following his nod, Tsumiko spied several wolves striding their way, confidence in their swaggers and in the easy sway of their tails. Whatever was coming, the Elderboughs were ready. Ninook, who was Adoona-soh's bondmate, was in the lead, and Pim Moonprowl, one of Boon's bondmates, was at his flank.

Ginkgo said, "The barrier's only going to be down for a few moments, but just in case someone's been lurking in the area, waiting for an opening ...." He trailed off with a shrug.

"Is that the only danger?" Tsumiko didn't like the look of the sky.

"Probably. Kyrie's stirred up trouble, but I think Dad'll be proud of him. He freed some captive wind imps, so all that? The storm's just one big, worked-up Impression, and it's chasing our guys home."

"The storm's attacking?"

"Mmm. I think that's overstating things. What's that story? *The Boy and the Thundercloud*? Like that."

She was surprised into laughing. "But that's a love story."

"I know. And little bro is three-timing it. Not bad for a crosser!" Ginkgo cheerfully added, "One more imp, and he'll be the only dragon to ever match Lord Beckonthrall's good fortune."

Michael warned, "I'll be lowering the first few sections now, so … guard up."

Deece traded a look with Ninook, who calmly readied a bow that was nearly his own height. Tsumiko had time to register the crystal glittering at the point of the arrow he nocked. Then Ninook signaled to his packmates, and they leapt into the sky, taking up what must have been a defensive formation out over the water.

"So it *is* him. I *am* glad I came."

Tsumiko turned. Opulence Windlore had arrived without a sound.

His gaze was on the sky, but his words were for her. "It would seem I have another confluence of destinies to weather. Ah. No pun intended."

Tsumiko had reason to be grateful for the dragon bard's arrival in their household. His lullabies had a calming effect, and his breezy manner helped to offset the current mood at Stately House. She might be the heart of their home, but emotions were running high, and that made setting a peaceful tone especially challenging.

Unrequited loves.

Unfinished business.

Unexpected bonds.

Unhappy children.

"A confluence of destinies?" she echoed with a smile, appreciating the allusion to an angel whose stories were popular with the children. "Are you embracing Fandriel's foresight? Or his faith?"

"I fear my situation resembles one of Fandriel's misadventures at this point." There was an uneasiness to Opal's smile when he sought her gaze. "Something more along the lines of ... be sure your sins will find you out."

Kyrie had never approached home from the direction of the sea, and he was having trouble picking out the right section of shoreline. Only once they were near enough for him to catch the resonance of Sinder's underwater array did he realize that there were illusions at play, masking the view. "I have not been tuned to these barriers."

"Sinder and Argent might be the only ones." Boon checked his speed, then pulled up short. "Uhh ... uh-oh. Seems we have another contender for your attention."

Following the wolf's gaze, Kyrie gasped.

"I'm not due for any visitations that I know of. Not sure these guys ever make appointments, though." Boon blandly said, "Given this and that, it's probably for you, yeah?"

"I do not know that star."

"Neither do I. Want to say hey?"

"I would. Very much."

Boon redirected, but he kept to a much slower pace. "I'm not totally unfamiliar with protocols here. Want me to do the talking?"

"Please." Kyrie swiftly created two small sigils to protect them from a star's unique allure. He'd just patted Boon's into place when they came even with the gleaming person who'd caught the wolf's eye.

Boon said, "Do you have a message for one of us? Or … maybe a personal stake in the proceedings?"

"As it happens … both."

Kyrie knew two stars. Novi, who had spoken to him at Wardenclave. And Eri, who had quietly joined their enclave when Andor Skypact had accepted the place—and privacy—Dad had offered. Apparently, the bear clansman's former home had become popular with tourists, which hadn't been good for Andor's mood. Or for his precious bumbers.

Like those two stars, this one was luminous, with a cascade of creamy hair. But Kyrie was intrigued that this star's eyes had been artfully adorned. Surrounded by sharp lines of red paint, with rosy hues blended outward in a fashion that appealed to the dragon in Kyrie. Would Mother let him try it? In addition, the star wore a carved stone pendant. Pure white. Coiling scales. A dragon, beautiful in its intricacy.

"I am Zeriel, and I only wanted to make certain that Haizea does not succumb to exhaustion." A solemn gaze sought his. "She needs you, Kyrie. Go to her, and call her by name. She will be glad to find that Anan is already with you."

Boon pivoted. "Aww, hell. Poor thing's running out of steam." And he shot back the way they'd come.

Kyrie's conscience pricked. "Should we have thanked him?"

"Angel says *go*, you go. We can thank him for the heads-up sometime else." Boon pulled Kyrie snug against his chest and dropped, only making small adjustments as they plunged toward a waterspout wavering in advance of the larger storm.

The controlled fall was like nothing Kyrie had experienced before. Exhilaration bubbled over in a delighted laugh that probably wasn't appropriate under the circumstances. He glanced guiltily at Boon, who grinned. "Nothing strange about a dragon finding pleasure in flight. You probably crave the sky as much as the next drake."

"I ... yes. I believe I do."

"You know what? I'll bet you'd love surfing. Once summer's here, lessons. And more airtime." With an intensity that came on suddenly, Boon asked, "Ever ride a wolf before today?"

"Only Torloo."

Boon held his gaze for a long moment, and in that brief space, a choice was made. "In the old days, ambuscades were always partnered by wolves."

Kyrie considered the trail at his feet and made an oblique statement of his own. "I want to become my clan's tribute."

"Music to my ears. But I'll have to wait my turn." Slowing to a stop above low-rolling waves, Boon boosted Kyrie back onto his shoulders. Giving his calves a squeeze, he rumbled, "Okay, kid. Do your thing."

Kyrie composed himself and sang a few lines, and the waterspout veered their way. He quietly said, "Anan? Haizea is here. Help me?"

The thunderstorm grumbled, *"What are you on about? Why are you so pretty?"*

Feeling foolish, Kyrie ventured, "Dragons *are* pretty?"

"There is that. Yes, that is a point in your favor. But you have shine!" It sounded like an accusation.

"The kind you need?"

"Well, it's better than a bottle," the thunderstorm grumped. But then he seemed to catch up with what Kyrie had said. *"Haizea? She's here?"*

"And she is growing weaker. She needs a safe place? Can I do that? Is there … is there room?"

"Get me closer!" demanded Anan. *"Don't you dare let her fade!"*

Kyrie renewed his song, and this time, he threaded it with more than sway. For he *did* have shine—carefully kept, secretly nurtured.

Boon's grip tightened. "That's …! Hell and hellions, kid, that's a dangerous combination."

Oh, it was. Or it *could* be. But Kyrie only ever used it to soothe away nightmares, to sweettalk wardstones, and now, to woo another wind to his side. Because Zeriel has sent him. Because Anan had asked it. Because Haizea needed the haven he could become.

Kyrie wasn't sure how much—or even how—Anan could see, but his voice came again, rough with urgency. *"More of that, dragonling. I can't … quite … reach."*

"Closer, Boon!"

"Not a problem. I gotchu." With the audacity of a surfer who doesn't fear the curl of a wave overhead, Boon dropped into the eye of Haizea's dwindling storm.

Immediately, Kyrie could feel a vibration coming up through his heels. Boon was trying to soothe the storm in his own way, with a wolvish rumble. Worried it might frighten their wind, Kyrie tuned his voice, truing it to that note, and from within came Anan's voice.

"A wolf. Always did like a wolf. Never fears a storm. Knows how to howl."

So winds could appreciate the songs of wolves? All the better. Kyrie added a cadence he'd learned from Torloo, high and sweet, a promise of peace.

Haizea showed far less reluctance than Anan had done. Maybe she was simply too weary to resist. Maybe it was the exasperated orders coming from the thunderstorm. Whatever her reasons, Kyrie felt a definite shift in her mood. Water sheeted back into the sea, leaving a swirl of wind that lifted his hair and explored his scales with whispery little touches. When he drew breath for the next lyric of his song, it caught in his throat.

A sudden well of heat startled him into stillness.

"Kyrie?" checked Boon. "Everything good?"

"Is she safe?" he whispered.

"So weak," Anan complained. *"She needs to borrow. Is there more?"*

"They want more." Kyrie leaned down, seeking Boon's gaze. "Anan says she needs it. *They* need it."

"Planning to tend them?" The wolf pulled him down and cradled him close. "That's real generous and all. But are you sure that's the best course? I'm in no place to criticize, but I speak from experience when I say … you'll be bond-building. Possibly in triplicate."

"If I release them again, once they are stronger …?"

Boon cracked a smile despite the worry in his gaze. "I'm probably not the best one to advise you on this. Because I'm the kind of guy who'd love to add a wind-wielding, barrier-wrecking, wolf-riding, sway-capable ambuscade to my team."

"Ohhh," Kyrie breathed, and Anan shared in his delight, for he'd let some of his reserves spill over.

"Your parents are gonna skin me for this."

"I will protect you."

"What're you ...? Kid, those were binding words." Boon eyed him keenly. "Why vow it?"

"Because you are one of mine now."

"Huh." As Boon turned toward home, he bluntly asked, "Did you know Sinder thinks you're our best weapon against your sire?"

"Yes."

"Argent isn't likely to let you test that theory."

Kyrie decided to be honest. Brutally so. "Dad could *try* to stop me."

"There's that attitude again." Boon frowned. "You don't think he can?"

"No."

"I hope you don't plan to go off on your own ...." Boon gruffly said, "Tell me you're smarter than that."

"I am." Kyrie knew it was the truth when he added, "I will not be alone."

Ginkgo lifted Tsumiko to the ground and urged her to back up. She listened, if only because she knew Argent expected him to protect her. She hugged Sibley to her side as barriers fell and the wind whipped up.

Boon dropped through the opening Michael made. Already, the barrier was reforming. Perfectly coordinated. No signs of trouble.

Then Kyrie stood in the snow, and Ginkgo was kneeling before him, hands roaming, nose working, words welcoming.

"Okay if I go, too, Lady?" asked Sibley.

She hadn't realized how tight her hold had been. Patting his shoulder, she smiled and nodded.

Ninook and the Elderboughs were still in the air, but Pim had followed Boon to the ground. While she didn't fuss over him, her tail puffed wide, and there was a definite twitch.

Boon hauled his bonded into a one-armed hug and said, "Easy does it. That was more excitement than danger. And it's not over. I don't doubt we'll be seeing some unseasonable rain."

Ginkgo spoke up. "Michael says he *can* block the weather but he'd rather not."

"It's all good. I'm pretty sure we should let the typhoon get to the kid."

"How do you figure?" Ginkgo challenged.

"Angelic say-so."

"*Which* angel?" asked Opal.

Tsumiko wasn't sure when the bard had slipped behind her. When she tried to step aside to stand with him, he edged backward, as if trying to hide.

Boon said, "Nice enough guy. Real considerate. Gave the name Zeriel."

"Well, that could become awkward," muttered Opal. "Or perhaps ironic? Definite hints of poetic justice. We disagreed, you see. On whether I took the right course. But I stand by my interpretation, not that I am the sort to say, 'I told you so.'"

Tsumiko tried to sort through what he'd said. "You and Zeriel?"

"Yes, yes. Zeri and I."

And putting the pieces together, she lowered her voice. "*You're Zeriel's dragon?*"

"Oh! You are familiar with our story? That ballad is quite obscure. Stopped performing it ages ago. Yes, I am Zeri's dragon. Though it is equally accurate to say he is my star."

"We must tell Suuzu," she said warmly. "On account of the nippets."

"Charming tradition. But dear lady," Opal inclined his head to where Kyrie stood hand-in-hand with Sibley. "You are wanted."

"I am home, Mother."

"Welcome back," she murmured. "I'll want the whole story eventually, but for now ... are your new friends safe? Do they need anything we can provide? Or send for?"

"I would like Papka to check on them, please. And ... Grandfather Naoki has considerable experience with lorefolk." He looked as if he were about to ask for something more, but his expression shifted to surprise, and he looked up.

Over his head, a storm cloud billowed into existence, small and black and surly.

Kyrie asked, "Are you really going to ...?"

And with a fizzling pop that might have been meant for thunder, the cloud began to drizzle on him and Sibley. Murmuring an apology, Kyrie took two quick strides to one side, which put a slack-jawed Sibley in the clear.

Tsumiko could only stare.

Everyone was staring.

"Sorry." Kyrie hunched his shoulders and glanced sheepishly at his cloud cover. "Anan must be feeling a little better, since he is strong enough to disapprove."

Tsumiko thought her son looked quite happy with this new development. He lifted his face, letting the rain wash it. She said, "You must be *freezing*."

"It *is* cold, but I do not think I should bring a thunderstorm into the kitchen."

Gingko said, "Sibley, help me get a fire going?"

Tsumiko took a step closer. "You really are just like *The Boy and the Thundercloud*."

Kyrie blinked a few times before saying, "That might be interesting, but I do not think Anan is flirting with me. He believes I am abandoning Dima, even though I will not. She is the typhoon I must next sing to my side."

Every head turned to consider the oncoming storm.

"And ... he thinks I have betrayed them to an old enemy." Kyrie's gaze turned cool as he considered a point just above Tsumiko's head. "What did you *do*, Opulence Windlore?"

15
TRENDSETTER

The whole world knew about Lord Mossberne's mountaintop retreat. Television tours. Magazine spreads. Countless snapshots and selfies on social media. Everybody who was anybody seemed to find their way to the glittering castle meant to give credence to Lapis's token lordship. Though the view of the night sky was exquisite, Lapis was only in residence when he was expected to entertain.

Isla found her way to his side. "Did you speak with Ambassador Sorenson yet?"

"Should I?" His gaze drifted briefly to the pale green crystals glittering in her hair. Each was a remnant, and they formed a discreet defensive array. He wanted to inspect them further, but a single touch to Isla's artfully arranged curls would send the gossipmongers into a tizzy of speculation.

Heedless of his need to remain aloof, Isla let her fingertips graze bare skin at the small of his back. "He has good news, and I know he'll want you to hear it from him."

"I am all aflutter."

She laughed lightly. "I need to introduce myself to the newest members of Tenna Silverprong's cortege. And … soon-to-be First Lady Sunfletch has just arrived. Shall I welcome her on your behalf?"

"Please."

"Done!" And she sailed off, positively sparkling with purpose.

Lapis averted his face, feigning indifference, lest the snap of a shutter capture any hint of a lingering gaze or a longing look. Instead, he strolled in the general direction of the ambassador. However, a familiar face on the far edge of the crowd thoroughly distracted him. Changing course, Lapis hastened to greet someone who couldn't have been on the guestlist. "Boniface? Welcome to my humble home."

Jacques Smythe's elder brother blinked in obvious surprise. "Lapis. Lord, you *live* here? My sympathies."

The staffer at his side winced. In an aggrieved tone, he said, "Boniface, this is *Lord Mossberne.*"

"Clearly." With a puzzled glance between them, he added, "We're acquainted. I've permission to use Lapis's given name."

"At home, certainly. But during official functions, where every other person in the room is a reporter, influencer, or pundit, please address members of the Amaranthine Council by their proper titles." The avian adjusted his glasses. Their darkened lenses mostly hid cloudy eyes. "Ideally *spokesperson,* since each clan adheres to differing terms. I'll make certain the full and annotated list makes it onto your desk upon our return to Keishi."

Lapis both knew and liked Magarr Oathbide, a genial magpie clansman who hadn't balked at serving under Suuzu, whose years were scanty by comparison.

"Right. Yes. Noted." And with a faint smile, Boniface blandly started over. "Good of you to remember me, Spokesperson Mossberne. Thank you for so generously opening your home to this madding, glittering crowd. Nothing to criticize, but *lord*, doesn't rattling about this place make you homesick?"

Lapis reached for his hand and took Magarr's elbow as well. "The allure of Stately House cannot be denied, but ... Boniface, I'm confused. How did you come to be wearing Spokesperson Farroost's crest?"

"He hired me."

"Suuzu never said!" Lapis felt sure he would have.

"It's probably slipped his mind." Boniface shoved his free hand into his trouser pocket. "Doesn't matter, really. I'm worse than useless."

Magarr whistled a mild protest. "Mister Smythe's position is unique but not unprecedented."

"Your brother," Lapis realized aloud.

With a sulky glance that he quickly averted, Boniface said, "I suppose the comparison is inevitable."

Somehow, Magarr knew and with a series of gentle touches, he corrected the man's posture. "Sylphon and I have undertaken Boniface's ... acclimation. Hence our attendance this evening. Please, don't let us keep you from your other guests."

A gentle reminder that Lapis was drawing attention with his interest. "I'm surprised, but pleasantly so. Ah. Does Argent know?"

Boniface fussed with his orange armband. "I'd be shocked if he didn't. Why ...? Oh, bloody hell, was he invited?" And quickly lowering his voice, he asked, "Is *Jackie* here?"

"Your brother is ...." Lapis trailed off, for there wasn't much he could say. "Judging by the state of Argent's tie, no. He is not."

The man's eyes slowly widened. "Do you mean to say that Argent bloody Lord Mettlebright is in the vicinity?"

Magarr clucked and pressed a warning finger to Boniface's lips.

Lapis stepped back, yielding his place as Argent revealed himself. "Language, Bon-Bon."

Far from cowed, the man exclaimed, "*Mon dieu*, your tie! Why hasn't Jackie put you to rights?"

Argent mildly asked, "Would you be so good?"

"R-really?" And with ill-concealed concern, he repeated, "Why *hasn't* Jackie put you to rights?"

"He is resting at home."

Boniface attacked Argent's tie, muttering, "While you're being slovenly in public? Totally unacceptable. I know Catalan said Jackie was safe, but he'd *never* let this slide. Something's wrong."

Ignoring his statement, Argent softly inquired, "Why are you here, Bon-Bon?"

"I'm embarking on a new career. Apparently, spare lordlings are the next best thing to cossets when it comes to recruiting a cortege." Easing into a cautiously receptive posture, he added, "You can hardly cast stones. You started the trend."

Argent indicated Boniface's armband. "Suuzu would have mentioned."

"He'll remember. Eventually. It's not my fault you lot are taking forever to acclimate to Hajime's pollen."

Lapis said, "That *would* explain the memory lapse."

"But not Boniface's lack of one." Argent coolly addressed himself to Magarr. "Will you require a personal meeting with Spokesperson Farroost in the near future?"

"So far, we are managing all communication by call or by courier."

"Is your Mister Smythe capable of acting as courier?"

"Lord, give me *some* credit," grumbled Boniface.

Magarr placed a hand on the man's shoulder. "I have every confidence in his abilities."

"Then I'll expect him in time for the solstice." And arching a brow at Boniface, Argent added, "Kyrie wants you home for Christmas. Do not disappoint him."

He strode off, leaving behind a dumbstruck Boniface.

"Oh, I *am* envious," Magarr said cheerfully. "A personal invitation from Lord Mettlebright? He is famously selective. Quite an honor. Unless … did you have other plans?"

"I … hadn't really." Boniface sought Lapis's gaze. "There's hardly any time. Barely more than a fortnight, and …! *Mon dieu,* how many children even are there now?"

That wasn't a detail to be bandied about in public, so Lapis only asked, "Does it matter?"

"*Rather*! It's Christmas, isn't it?"

Only after the man turned to Magarr to inquire after appropriate shops did Lapis realize that Boniface intended to bring gifts for everyone at Stately House. And quite possibly the enclave as well. Because to do any less would be unforgivably rude.

Lovely man.

Definitely a Smythe.

After everyone had either been seen off or guided to guest quarters to await departures on the morrow, Lapis retreated up a certain stairway. Dazzling crystals anchored the heavy wards that ensured the sanctity of a traditional, cross-shaped suite. Four chambers stood in readiness for the four brides Lapis would never accumulate.

A light shone under the door to the Eastern Bride's quarters, and he rapped lightly.

"It's fine. Come in," Isla answered. She'd already abandoned her evening's finery. Flannel pajama pants. An oversized Wardenclave hoodie. And the bewitching scents of soap and self.

Lapis crossed to where she sprawled, stockinged feet propped before the fireplace, book open on her knee, phone in hand, a smile already brightening her countenance. Feeling a little like a supplicant, he knelt before her and propped his chin upon his palm. "Am I interrupting?"

"Uncle Jackie texted. We've been catching up. See?" She scrolled up, then held out her phone so he could read from the beginning.

O, font of knowledge, I beseech thee!

I'm hardly an oracle

Closest thing to!
And in the know
So it's safe to ask

Discretion for discretion

I have an unaccountable craving
For lamb, of all things
Do you think it a consequence of
the delicate condition in which I
find myself? #Sprigged

What a coincidence!
Lamb was on the menu this evening
We brought in a chef especially

You've been noshing on
the very thing I crave
Very mean of you
Send takeaway by herald

The two had gone back and forth for some minutes, indulging in the fond chit-chat that marked their relationship. Jacques actually sounded like himself. He couldn't be, of course, but he was making an effort.

"Why unaccountable?" Lapis asked, returning the phone. "Do they never have the stuff at Stately House?"

Isla was already tapping.

Why would you find lamb concerning?

Never really cared for it
More Bon-Bon's thing, come to think

Isla hesitated over an answer. "Does Uncle Jackie know about Boniface's visit?"

"If not, are we the ones who should be breaking that news?"

"No. I think not." Isla began a response. "Aunt Tsumiko is the one with closest ties to them. Or Kyrie. Maybe it simply hasn't come up? A lot has happened over the last few weeks."

Again, she angled the screen for him to see.

> **I'll ask Revic about cravings**
> **Dr. Naoki may have insight**
> **He has firsthand experience as well**

> **I don't like borrowing Naoki too often**
> **The children cling to him**
> **And he clings right back**
> **But I'll have a quick word with Hajime**

Who is that, please?

Which sparked a swift exchange of information, including a selfie in which Jacques beamed up at the camera, cheek-to-cheek with a tree-imp, red flowers cascading.

When Lapis only reacted with mild amusement, Isla squeaked in indignation. "You knew?"

"So did you, though you've since forgotten."

"Why haven't you?"

"Prolonged exposure. You don't frequent Stately House with the same regularity."

"I visit when I can!"

"I'm not criticizing, my dear. Merely pointing out that I've spent more time sleeping under trees."

"Right. Sorry. It's just … I feel left out!" As a peace offering, she budged over, making room for him on the wide chair. "Or foolish. I definitely remembered that Dr. Naoki had firsthand experience carrying children, but it never occurred to me that the father was in the picture. Tsumiko must be so happy. And Akira, too. Oh, do come up here. It's grown chilly."

Lapis stood and stepped back. "I should change out of these things."

"Swapping silk for more silk isn't much of a change. Come where it's warm."

He let her have her way, insinuating himself into the offered space.

With artless affection, she turned her body into his, slouching down so her head rested against his shoulder. He wondered what Michael would think if he saw them like this. The man had been understandably concerned about Lapis's handling of his daughter. But not concerned enough to bring in Sansa.

Reassurances had come easily. Yes, Isla was often alone with him, just as they were now, but to her, Lapis was nothing more than a piece of home. A source of comfort. A comrade in whose arms she felt safe. But his intentions? Unwilling to lie, Lapis could only abase himself and admit that he'd beguile her if he could. If anything, Michael had seemed relieved.

Lapis still wasn't entirely sure why. He didn't really like the idea of being on reserve if Isla's plans fell through. No dragon should be thought of as a consolation prize. And he might be annoyed if it turned out that Michael was trying to protect his former mentor, sparing him from a needful confrontation. Yet Hisoka continued to pretend Isla's feelings weren't fixed upon him, and Isla seemed equally unwilling to speak for fear of rejection.

Idiots, both of them.

But him most of all.

Lapis rested his cheek against her hair and asked, "Where are my other brides?"

"Tenma turned in already. He and Inti are in the western suite. And Revic wanted a flit, so he slipped out. I think he misses mountains, so he's having an especially nice time."

"Mmm. And what are you reading?" He touched a long finger to the book she wasn't *quite* hiding from him. "Something you'll recommend?"

"Oh, it's fine, but it's not really holding my attention." She lifted her face to pout. "I can't imagine why I'm so distracted."

"Should I be redirecting you onto wiser courses? Or distracting you further?"

"The latter, please. And begin with this!" Her fingers trailed up his arm, stopping at a bangle he'd added to his evening's attire.

"You noticed!"

"Couldn't miss it." She touched the milky blue remnant, an ancient thing, and asked, "Does it have a nice song?"

"A trifle wistful, but I think that's part of its appeal. Did you want to hear?"

She turned further into him, eyes bright.

Heart light, he urged, "Slide it free so I can reach."

Then the bangle was in her hands, and his framed hers, and he knew a teensy thrill of triumph. He'd always arrayed himself with unusual stones that he happened across, but these past few years, he'd sought more of them, intent on acquiring unique specimens. Because they attracted Isla's interest. Because they pleased her.

Humming lightly, he unlocked the remnant, and they shared the visions hidden within.

She sighed and dabbed at her eyes, and her tone was subdued when she asked, "Why have we never had a story with a crystal adept?"

"Too close for comfort?" he suggested.

"Maybe at first, but now ...?"

"All right. Would the adept be the human? Or the Amaranthine partner?"

Isla said, "Maybe they share an affinity, and that's what brings them together. Initially."

This is how their stories always started. Tossing an idea back and forth, from his hand to hers and back again. Each suggesting and amending until a story's potential shone with enough clarity to begin.

The hour had grown exceedingly late when Lapis stole her glass and set it aside. "You need sleep."

"Mmm. When will you need sleep?"

"I'll find time next month."

"Are you pushing your limits?"

"Usually," he admitted. "I'm hoping that if I wait, Jacques will be allowed to watch over my rest."

"What if Argent forbids it?" Isla's brows drew down. "You can't have always gone to Uncle Jackie. Who did you trust before?"

"I would go to Harmonious." With a small frown, he said,

"I *could* apply to Canarian and Catalan Evernhold. They step in from time to time."

"What about me?" she asked.

"*Isla.*"

"What? I could watch over your long sleep."

"Hardly appropriate."

"Why not?"

"You're female."

"So?" She pointed out, "Uncle Jackie is gay."

"I am not." Merciful skies, she was serious. And on the verge of being stubborn. "And I talk in my sleep."

Isla rolled her eyes. "I'm impervious to sway."

"But not to curiosity."

She bristled. "You don't trust me?"

He warbled wearily. "Think. Your father would undoubtedly object to our spending a week in bed."

"I don't see why." Which went hand-in-hand with not seeing *him*.

"*Isla*," he protested.

"Think!" she urged, turning his own admonition back on him. "Papka will love the idea, since he'll be able to tuck us in with a baby rock imp and monitor the resonances."

Unwise. So unwise.

But she beamed at him and promised, "I'll clear my schedule."

16

GIFTS OF PEACE

Ginkgo tried to gauge how much Kyrie needed him. At nearly thirteen, his younger brother was plenty mature, but that'd never stopped anyone from needing a hug. However, the boy's gaze was calm as he indicated that Ginkgo should precede him to the beach. Times like this, Kyrie really resembled Dad. Maybe more than Ginkgo ever would. Honestly, it was pretty cute.

Scooping up Sibley, who definitely needed as many hugs as they could sneak in, Ginkgo caught Deece's eye. "Bring kindling?" he asked.

Deece signaled his support.

So Ginkgo jumped to the top of the wall and jogged along it, aiming for the stairs that clung to the cliff face. "Is our brother following?"

Sibley looked startled, then stunned. Brotherhood was taking some getting used to, but only because the kid seemed worried that it was too good to be true.

"He's walking slow, but yeah. Kyrie's on his way."

"Good. We could use the head start." When Ginkgo skipped a few dozen stairs on his first jump, Sibley throttled him. Landing in a crouch, he checked, "You okay, little bro?"

Eyes wide, he asked, "Can you fly?"

"Nope. But I'm fast and … kind of bouncy, I guess. Like it?"

Sibley mumbled, "Just wasn't ready for it, is all. Do it again?"

"Anytime you want," he promised, vaulting over the next rail into another giddying plunge.

He was absolutely positive that Sibley was hiding his face to cover his smile. *Cute* clearly ran in the family.

On the beach, they walked side-by-side past the lineup of festival booths toward Ginkgo's driftwood pile. "We'll dig up this way, far enough from the water that the tide won't be a problem. Actually, the storm might kick up some waves, too, so let's hug the cliff."

They dug together, creating a shallow pit, and Gingko showed him where he stashed a pile of blackened stones that the swim club used for ringing fires.

"Looks like the wolves are satisfied." He nodded to where Ninook and the rest were breaking formation. "The barrier's back in place. What do you think? Seem good?"

Sibley asked, "Wouldn't you know better than me?"

"You'd think so. I have access to more sigilcraft than you can see, and I didn't notice anything. But you're a dragon crosser with a whole different set of experiences. You know what we're up against better than most, and you might be sensitive to a clansman if he happened to be nearby."

"You think I can help?"

"I *know* you can." Ginkgo sat in the sandy bowl they'd been creating. "I'll be asking Kyrie the same thing."

Sibley nodded once, scrutinized the sky and sea, then shrugged. "I don't see nothing, and I don't feel them."

"You can feel … what?"

"Those foxes."

"The vixens?"

"Yeah." Sibley shrugged again. "They were hard to spot, but I could always feel their eyes on me. I got good at getting around them. It was the only way to avoid the meanness."

Ginkgo asked, "What kind of meanness?" It was so hard to get any of the children to talk about the things that had happened. But Sibley had a way of jumping in and speaking up, letting them know about everything from food allergies to bed wetting.

"Different things," he said vaguely. "Lots of nasty smiles. And being all glad that they'd tricked you in the first place."

"They're the ones who kidnapped you?"

"Me, yeah. And about half of the others." Sibley went back to shoving sand. "The rest were born there. Kodoku liked making strange matches."

"You're here now."

"Yeah. This is a good place."

"Let's keep it that way. Let me know if you see any problems, and I'll step in."

Sibley looked at him sharpish. "There's people here you don't trust?"

"No, not at all. But … what if it turns out that one of our little sisters is afraid of bears. Or what if a little brother needs to eat more than he's taking? I'd want to know, and I'd be glad if they told me. But maybe they don't trust me enough yet." Ginkgo dropped another rock into place. "They trust you, Sibley."

"Well, yeah."

"So help me help our family."

"I can do that, yeah."

Deece arrived with reinforcements. Gilen and Jarrah and Sho each carried an armload of kindling. The boys picked through the driftwood pile, and Deece oversaw the fire-lighting while Ginkgo backtracked to the water's edge where Kyrie stood apart, looking out to sea.

Boon crouched just beyond the range of the thundercloud, the picture of patience despite everything.

A fine drizzle had turned Kyrie's hair lank, but he had a secretive smile, like something was turning out even better than he'd hoped.

Ginkgo ignored the rain in order to hug his brother. "You okay?"

"Yes."

"You're gonna need to start at the beginning for me. Eventually. More importantly, you did great, letting us know what was important. But I'd still appreciate hearing everything from the start."

Kyrie said, "For that, Opal will need to go first."

"Want me to find him?"

His brother's gaze drifted to one side. "He is already here."

"Yes, yes. I am here," the dragon bard announced. "To be thanked or blamed, whichever you deem best."

Kyrie asked, "Why do my winds consider you their enemy?"

"It is a long story."

"I do want the whole story, but for now … what is the most important thing?"

Opal shivered in the winds preceding Dima. "I am the one who lured and sealed the Changing Winds. Their captivity was my doing."

Ginkgo *really* wished Dad was home. "Okay, that's a lot, but I'd like a little more detail. Why would you do that?"

"It has to do with the Junzi and their remnant songs. I don't suppose you ever heard of them?"

"Yeah." Ginkgo traded a look with Boon. "As it happens, I'm pretty familiar."

"The crafters who created them did so by listening to the songs of stars. I was there—helping refine their purpose, helping test their strength, helping shape their lore. I always did work closely with reavers, especially battlers." With a sidelong look at Kyrie, he added, "Especially ambuscades. Anna Green—now Lady Starmark—is my most recent association. She is descended from the first to wield the Bamboo Stave."

Kyrie asked, "What do the Junzi have to do with the Changing Winds?"

"They are meant to wield them. Or that was my interpretation. Zeri disagreed at the time, but I could not in good conscience ignore what I felt was my duty. The current confluence suggests that I was either correct or, at the very least, I forced this outcome."

Ginkgo could tell details were getting away from them, but he wanted to see where this was headed before backtracking. "Can you be more specific? What outcome are you talking about?"

Opal fluttered his fingers at Kyrie. "You summoned the Four Storms."

"I only brought three, but I have met the fourth. She is very nice." To Ginkgo's amusement, his brother paused, then spoke with his voice pitched for his passengers. "I was there for her descent and for her wedding. Tzefira is well and happy."

Boon casually lifted a hand. "This is the first I've heard of anyone but reavers wielding the Four Storms."

Opal said, "They were gifts of peace, initially given to reavers. But they were always meant to be entrusted to imps, should any be found. The Changing Winds were ideal for the job: companions of stars, shepherds of winds, tuners of stones. If ever an Amaranthine—especially a dragon—succumbed to the allure of the shine newly born in the descendants of wind and tree and sea, then the Four Storms would take up their weapons."

Kyrie announced, "There *is* such a dragon."

"Alas, the Junzi were lost."

"Yeah, about that," said Ginkgo. "We have them. Well, we know where they all are. And we could probably get them here pretty quick, if necessary."

Opulence Windlore gasped softly, then teared up. Finally he whispered, "Fandriel's foresight, I was right."

Kyrie took a step closer to the dragon bard. "I want to know—*we* want to know—how is any wind, even an eldermost storm, supposed to hold a weapon?"

"It's no small matter, and yet … simplicity itself." Opal twirled a finger at the ominous cloud over Kyrie's head. "They will have to descend."

17

SKYWATCHING

Argent might be obligated by international law to submit to the rigors of human travel, but he now had free rein within Japan. So once he re-entered the country and passed through customs, Argent was able to take to the sky.

After several high-profile sightings were caught on film, Caleb and Josheb Dare had done a special episode of *Dare Together* to reveal that avians weren't the only flight-capable clans. They'd carefully spun things to imply that Amaranthine needed to be in truest form to fly, but ... responses were largely favorable.

According to Sinder, skywatching was becoming a favorite pastime in rural Japan. Similar to birdwatching or plane-spotting, there were even school clubs dedicated to catching glimpses of Amaranthine in flight.

Charmed by this news, Harmonious made certain that the Starmark clan was well-represented. His staff publicized upcoming romps, which drove picnickers and photographers into the parks and fields along their flight path.

Other clans were taking to the sky as well. Most surprising, perhaps, was how quickly the custom had won hearts in America. Werewolves were barely a blip on anyone's radar anymore. Instead, dragons were trending. Lord Beckonthrall and his sons had become media darlings by touring national parks and natural wonders via dragon barge.

Fox sightings were harder to come by, but Argent wasn't stingy. He varied his route to and from Keishi, diverting when he happened across skywatchers, often circling back when those groups included youngsters. He hated to disappoint the hopes of children.

Night had long-since fallen, so Argent wasn't expecting an audience. Still, he didn't take the most direct path home. For a fox, zigzags and double-backs were a way of life. He touched lightly upon a winter-white field, frisked around a lighthouse, and skimmed past sleepy fishing villages as his course turned northward.

And then … blood.

He slowed and lifted his muzzle.

Argent wasn't immune to fox magic, but illusions lost their power if you knew how they were accomplished. He'd learned a few things from other clans who excelled at the illusory arts. Some of those tricks he'd stolen, for that was how certain clans passed down their knowledge. Some had been freely given— trust for trust, discretion for discretion. Which is how Argent came to realize that Senna and Nona Hightip were shockingly unimaginative. As if there was some inherent superiority to the unsullied foxiness of their patterns.

Borrowing from tanuki tricks and monkey mischief, Argent slipped from view and moved with painstaking stealth toward a lonesome spit of land that he always passed on his homeward treks.

He knew it was a trap. Of course it was a trap, and not a particularly subtle one. But Senna and Nona knew him well enough to make it an effective one. Argent couldn't very well leave when the fluting cries of a dragon-child carried on the wind.

They'd tried this same thing before. Had Mercy's mother been a trial run?

Only this child wasn't an infant. Maker have mercy, there were words mixed in with the cries. Argent had missed them at first because of the language. Sobbing pleas in French lanced through his heart.

Although their maternal inheritances varied widely, all of Kyrie's half-siblings were bound to Argent by an inviolable vow. That meant the vixens had taken and toyed with his child. *His.*

He stayed utterly still until his anger cooled to steel.

For months, there had been signs that the Hightip sisters were mapping his travels, marking his homebound trail. That's how they'd learned of this obscure seaside tract. He passed it without fail. Not because it held any great beauty or personal significance. It wasn't even a landmark on the true route home. But it was his habit. One they'd finally pinpointed.

Their trap had always been his.

Waves rolled, obscuring scents with damp and brine. He stalked along the shore in the shadow of a silver fox, a doppelganger for a decoy.

Nona wasn't fooled. This time.

She sauntered forward, the full sleeves of her tunic fluttering. "I know your weakness," she announced by way of greeting. "I know *all* of your weaknesses."

"Hardly a secret. I take in many children."

She cocked a hip, propping her hand on it. "Compensating for something?"

He sidestepped, avoiding Senna's attempt to ambush him from behind. Gaze still fixed on Nona, he coolly inquired, "Did you have a complaint for your spokesperson? Or perhaps a confession? I will hear you out."

"He's withered by the Waning," taunted Senna. "Unable to rise in a mating flight."

"Perhaps his interest has already cooled for the woman in his den," Nona said sweetly.

"I hear it's the manservant he keeps closest. Some do develop a taste for squandering."

"More likely he's bound to that woman's will." Nona took a step forward. "Is she cowed in some corner, leaving you free to ... *roam*?"

Their postures slipped into salacious territory.

Did they actually think he could be seduced?

He calmly inquired, "Are you cuckolding your patron?"

Senna flushed, and her gaze promised death. Interesting.

Nona's chin went up, eyes glittering. "We could free you."

"Why would *you* have the means to unfetter my soul?"

With a jab of her finger, Senna triumphantly exclaimed, "I *told* you he wasn't free! He's a kept lord!"

Nona's lip curled. "*Well* kept. His flourish certainly points to regular feasting. Why are you not among the Broken, Argent?”

“Maybe the rest of the Five supp with him. It’s what draws them to his den over and again.”

Argent attempted to redirect them in a more pertinent direction. “Are you claiming to be responsible for my captivity?”

Senna shrugged. “You were too unreasonable. You deserved what you got.”

“Did I, now?”

“You wanted to hear our complaints, didn’t you, *Spokesperson*? You spurned us.”

Argent asked, “Which of you was I meant to take?”

They exchanged a look.

“Both of you? That’s not our way. Ah, but you have had other influences.” He tried for the gossipy tone Jacques employed with great effect. “Which of you was the dragon bedding in his boredom? Or should I be asking *which* dragon? I understand the elder twin was quite the philanderer. Or was it their sire? Did you veil yourselves in illusions, letting him think he was visited by willing winds?”

“I think he’s jealous,” Senna smugly whispered.

“I think he should mind his own business.” Nona’s eyes flicked to a point just past Argent’s shoulder. “I want him dead.”

Then came the ambush. Argent’s defensive array gleamed into sharp focus when it stopped the swipe of claws that sizzled faintly against his sigilcraft. With an unhurried pivot, he faced his third attacker.

“Hold still.” Anger and sway and confidence.

Argent strolled in a circle around the Rogue, mostly to prove he wasn't taking orders. Honestly, he was underwhelmed. Oh, the colors were correct—purple hair, red eyes. But without the vibrant scales and speckling that so many of his progeny had inherited, the Rogue didn't make much of an impression. Bland. Insipid. But a dragon was a dragon, and Argent wasn't fool enough to ignore the two vixens in striking distance.

"My father is dead. Are you the one who killed him?"

"Alas, no." Argent wasn't volunteering anything further. "Shisoku, I presume?"

The dragon scowled at Nona. "You promised revenge."

She said, "Even if the final blow wasn't his, the scheme was."

Senna added, "Don't forget the children. He's been snatching them up."

The Rogue's gaze turned shrewd. "You are the reason for survivors? How many of my offspring have you stolen?"

"How many of them have you abandoned?"

"I never bothered to count. Too many failed attempts." His smile was tight, humorless. "I liked trying, though."

Argent felt several tails slip free, fanning around him in a warning display.

"Nona and Senna were finding them for me, but the lab was flattened. The guards all said you took them. Where is Stately House?"

Looking to Nona, Argent inquired, "Are you having trouble finding the place? How frustrating for you. Especially since you visited once before."

She seethed in silence.

Shisoku tried again. "Lead us there. I want those children."

"Why?" asked Argent, curious what they thought they could do.

"It is my turn to be Father, and I will be better at it. I am founding a clan." He breezily announced, "They are mine. If they do not come when I call, I will kill them."

"I am afraid their true father would never allow such a thing." More tails flashed into the open, causing Senna to give a little gasp and shimmy.

Shisoku frowned. "What do you mean *true father*? There is only me. They bred true. They have my eyes, do they not? They have my hair and my horns, my strength and my speed?" He flexed his claws. "Some even have my sting."

Nona said, "Argent is referring to himself. He adopts them."

"Children are his weakness." Senna's gaze flicked briefly in the direction from which the whimpers of a child still came at intervals.

And with that one glance, Argent swiftly rearranged his priorities. There was nothing to be gained from questioning these three. So he deployed another series of sigils and left them quizzing an illusion.

He didn't make it far before Nona barked, "He's running!"

Argent sent a silver fox racing out to sea and paused long enough to mark the features of the dragon that leapt into the sky after it, dark and dangerous and reeking of poison.

"Waste of time," muttered Nona. "He'll have gone for the child."

Before the vixens could act on that entirely accurate assumption, Argent darted away, intent on plucking the bait from tonight's trap.

They'd stranded a child near the end of the spit, and if the litter of pebbles on the sand was any indication, Shisoku had been tormenting the child by pitching things at him. It made so little sense, claiming to want his children enough to reclaim them, all while abusing the one in his grasp.

Argent swept up a boy who couldn't have been more than three years old, offering words of comfort in French, using the very same baby talk that Jackie crooned over their youngsters. "Hush, child. You are safe from the monsters. Breathe, little one. No one will hurt you. You are safe."

Wide eyes lifted to his—red, further reddened by tears.

"I heard you, and I came for you. Can you trust me?" He caressed matted hair, his thumb bumping over tiny horns. "We must fly fast. Hold on."

The little boy didn't struggle, even when Argent took the time to banish every tracer and tether the vixens had plastered to pale skin. He tutted over one sigil whose only purpose was to inflict pain if he made any sound. Which meant that this boy's cries for help had cost him.

"I apologize for taking so long to find you. All will be well."

Swinging in a long, low arc, Argent chose a course. Before long, a sigil on his thigh warmed slightly, alerting him to the fact that the call for support he'd triggered earlier had done its good work.

"Help is on the way," he murmured. "Have you ever met a wolf? Ours are wild and strong and loyal and good."

Just then, a dragon's roar came rolling from far out over the water. No doubt Argent's illusion had faded, frustrating its pursuer. Not entirely unexpected, but the noise startled the boy, and Argent winced at the sudden push of claws through cloth.

"Easy, now. He is noisy, but he cannot find us." Pressing a kiss to the child's forehead, Argent added, "Your Uncle Jackie will be noisy, too, once he sees the state of my suit. He is *very* particular about clothes. You shall have better ones. He will insist."

Argent flew as fast as he dared, aiming in the direction from which the Elderboughs would be coming. There was nothing in this part of the countryside but orchards and paddies and pastures. Was that a storm cloud piled up in the distance? He listed sideways and blinked hard. The stars had begun to double and blur.

"Sting, hmm? Perhaps I will give you to Sibley. Your brother was very brave, just as you have been … very brave. Mmm." Argent tightened his hold on his small passenger. "This might be bad. I hope they hurry."

A small eternity later, when a howl split the night, Argent wobbled toward it.

"All right, child. Nothing to fear now."

But Argent's sinking flight turned to falling. He registered a streak of light fur, bright as lightning, and then he was swept up and carried aloft.

"Argent! What's wrong?"

"Pim," he managed as more wolves surrounded them. "He did not mean to poison me."

18
BUILDING UP A RESISTANCE

Tsumiko woke knowing that Argent was near, and in the next moment, she was sure something was wrong. *What* was a mystery. The sense was unprecedented, but it drove her from their bed. She was just knotting her robe when Hajime arrived in her room with a cluster of hangers-on. She didn't know who to go to first. Argent hung limp in Pim's arms, and Boon was trying to soothe a weeping toddler. All of them were soaked to the skin.

Boon gruffly announced, "Argent's poisoned. Any chance Lapis is here?"

"No, he's not. Argent was coming from his place. What happened?"

"A kid. This kid."

Tsumiko moved to take the child, whose coloring clearly marked them as another of Kyrie's siblings.

"Hold up. This little guy is the source of the poison. I'm immune. Say, is Sibley nearby?"

"Still on the beach with Kyrie, I think."

"On it."

But Pim stepped into Boon's path. "Were you planning on going for Sibley or for Lapis?"

"Both. In that order. I'll leave the little guy with his big brother, then get along. Lapis is the one who saved my life when *this* happened." He pointed to the scarring on his face. "Something about an antidote. Huh. Do you think *I* have the means to help? The details are a little fuzzy, but I could call Penny."

"Wait a moment. Let me think." Then Tsumiko turned to Hajime, and asked, "Bring Dad?"

In a trifling, Naoki was there, hair rumpled, glasses askew. Hajime must have shared the basics, because he immediately took charge. "Get him out of that coat. Goodness, why is he wet? Rain? That's right. Young Withershanks did say something about a storm."

He was rambling, but his hands stayed busy. Tsumiko hurried to help him peel Argent out of his suitcoat, revealing the bloodied shirt beneath. Prayers didn't quite still the shaking of her hands as she pushed wet hair from his brow. Argent turned his head toward her, and he raised his eyelids with obvious effort.

"O, ye of little faith," he muttered. "I will be fine."

Despite everyone looking on, she kissed him lightly.

Her father addressed Pim. "Set Argent on the bed, please? I'm quite familiar with this poison and its potency. Boon or I could do *some* good—I've also built up a resistance—but it would be better if Sibley were to do it."

"I'll bring him," Pim said, moving toward the balcony doors.

Hajime appeared in front of her, hands outstretched. "If I may? There are so many barriers between you and the boy."

Meanwhile, Tsumiko moved to a perch on the edge of the mattress, sure that Argent would want her in reach.

He offered a faint smile before acknowledging his doctor. "Naoki. There was a small ... mishap."

"Help is on the way," he promised.

"Mmm. Boon? A word."

The wolf stepped forward. "Right here. What do you need?"

"To update you and yours." Argent's voice held an edge of pain. "I have met the Rogue. Every suspicion ... confirmed. He *is* colluding. The Hightip sisters. This poor child was bait for their trap. Give him here."

Boon arched his brows, but he complied. "Your daddy wants you, runt."

Argent gestured limply to the side opposite Tsumiko, and Boon carefully lowered the little one so Argent could pull him snug. He murmured endearments and encouragement in French. It was little more than baby talk, so Tsumiko understood most of it. The child calmed, then wriggled close, lisping apologies. Argent curled around their new boy, a faint smile on his lips despite signs of discomfort.

Then Hajime returned with Pim and Sibley.

Naoki waved Sibley over. "It's poison. Help me help him?"

"Aww, geez," Sibley muttered, pulling off mittens and coat and dropping them. "This is kinda not good, you know? What is it this time? A scratch? A bite? Gouge?"

"Shallow puncture marks. Barely pricked."

"Okay, yeah. Should be fine if we're quick. But … umm … D-dad? It'll hurt some."

Argent murmured, "Understood. I trust you, Sibley."

"'Scuse me, Lady. I needta be where you are."

She gave up her place. "You've done this before."

"Lotsa times." Sibley crawled onto the bed and prodded at Argent's bare shoulder, then brightened at the sight of the toddler in his arms. "Hey, little bro. Umm. Say, Dr. Naoki? I don't wanna bite if I don't gotta."

"Hajime knows where my kit is." Moments later, Naoki located a scalpel.

Tsumiko thought to ask, "Why are *you* immune to the poison, Dad?"

"Oh, well. Let's just say that Dr. Kodoku had a short temper." He kept his gaze on Argent, making small incisions.

Sibley sighed and began to lick at them, muttering apologies as he went. "I know it stings. Trust me, though. Could be worse. Lots worse."

Tsumiko's father didn't seem like he was going to expand on his answer, but Hajime stepped in, gently pushing up one of Dad's sleeves. Tsumiko's heart clenched at the sheer number of scars revealed there.

Her father quickly pulled the sleeve back down. "It's not as bad as it looks. Not really. I was in that dragon's keeping for many, many years. These were inflicted at odd intervals, often with centuries between."

Centuries? Tsumiko stared at her father, who seemed barely

older than Akira. How long had he been borrowing years from Haji-oji? Or ... were there other factors at play? She couldn't tell, and this didn't seem the right time or place to ask.

Naoki was still trying to soothe her fears. "Believe it or not, the poison is less devastating for humans, at least in small doses. Our resilience works in our favor. Amaranthine heal so much more slowly. They suffer longer, although ... yes, I think we have been quick enough to spare Argent the worst."

Everyone fell silent while Sibley did his part. Rain battered against the windowpanes, and Tsumiko guessed that meant Kyrie hadn't yet tamed his typhoon. Pim came to her side and guided her into her usual chair, tucking a blanket around her.

Then came a short rap and the familiar thump of hooves on rug. Nonny wavered just past the threshold, then hurried to Tsumiko, shooting worried glances at the bed the whole while. "Sorry to barge in, but Sonnet sent me to check on you. Seemed to think something was up. Which it *is*. Need anything from the kitchen? Or anywhere, really."

Tsumiko's thoughts turned to practical things, like hot tea and warm towels.

But from the bed, Argent spoke up. "Bring Jacques."

Bad dreams had been plaguing Jacques ever since the debacle with Kyoko. Dragons were a recurring theme, made worse now that he had a name and face. Kodoku's demise hadn't stopped him from sauntering into Jacques' dreams and making them hellish.

Equally terrible were the nightmare storms that loomed, then lunged, shattering every window in the small cathedral that had somehow appeared in Stately House's garden. Winds tore at gray stone and green glass, which crumbled to sand and sifted to the ground at his feet, leaving him alone with a heavy bundle in his arms.

In a new twist, Boniface appeared, warily picking his way through the rubble in order to offer him an embroidered handkerchief. He asked to see the baby, which didn't make any sense since there wasn't any baby yet. But then Bon-Bon tweaked back the blankets covering the bundle Jacques held, and they stared uselessly at a chrysalis of green stone.

"Keep it safe from the foxes," Bon-Bon urged.

And then there was a thump and rattle, and the rain was trying to get in.

Jacques gasped and reached blindly, fumbling for help and bumping into Akira. Because Akira was his talisman against nightmares. Because Akira had kept his promise. Because he didn't shy away from all the things Jacques had done in an effort to protect him. Like falling in love.

Akira hummed and reached for him, his voice slurred by sleep. "M'here. S'all right. Just a dream."

The nightmare was fading, and the sharpness of Jacques' fears gradually gave way to fondness. Jacques knew Akira in intimate ways—the scent of him and the sleepy sounds he made. Little details that anchored Jacques. Maybe if he'd ever had a long-term lover, he would have learned these things about other men. But … *non*. Flings were shockingly impersonal. Two people chasing similar satisfaction without lingering in loving ways.

For weeks—no, it was months now—Akira had been closer than any lover. Satisfying in a sense, but Jacques was keenly aware that he was trespassing.

Akira patted Jacques' shoulder, mussed his hair, and checked for tears with the swipe of a thumb. Sounding more awake, he quietly said, "Hey, we're here. You okay?"

Suuzu warbled a soothing note, a reminder that a nestmate was near. Something that should have kept Jacques from trying to get closer to the comfort Akira represented. He edged forward anyhow, but a hand found his hip.

Anjou nuzzled at his nape, kissing the flower-shaped blaze Dayith had placed there. The cat murmured, "You'll wake the baby."

Ella. Of course. They'd tucked the baby between him and Akira.

Then Anjou raised his voice slightly. "Who is there?"

It dredged up a bad memory. Of a knock in the night. Of a dragon at the door.

Suuzu softly said, "It is only Nonny."

Which left Jacques feeling foolish. And peevish. "What are you doing, traipsing about at this hour?"

Nonny lit the lamp on Suuzu's desk and came closer to the bed. "I was in the naproom. My turn on the rotation, but then Sonnet suddenly got it into her head th–"

"*Sonnet*," Jacques interrupted bitterly. "You might have mentioned."

"Well, yeah. I might've." Nonny frowned. "Are you getting pissy with me?"

"You of all people ...! Yes, I'm enormously annoyed. *Sonnet's* back, and you never said."

"Bloody hell," Nonny grumbled. "When exactly was I supposed to mention it? You and your daft plan—no offense, Akira—and your being up the duff and under lock and key. Plus, the guv said *no drama*, but I'm pretty sure he meant no ... uhh ... seductions— no offense, Anjou."

Anjou began to purr, and his fingers began questing.

Jacques caught the wandering hand and murmured, "Not in front of the baby." Which immediately made him feel wistful and fraught and hopeful and ... no longer annoyed. "I have no plans for grand seductions."

"Who needs plans?" inquired Anjou. "Improvisation is its own pleasure."

"Why's it always *cats*?" Nonny complained, then swore. "Jacques, I came to get you. The rest of you lot, let him up. He's wanted."

"*Sonnet ...?*" Jacques whispered.

"The guv." Nonny tensed. "I was starting to tell you. The guv's hurt."

"Argent is?" Akira quickly sat up, forcing Suuzu from the bed. "What happened? Should I come?"

"Not sure on particulars, but it might be better if you stayed here. With Ella. Lady's riled. Well, as riled as she gets, but it'd probably set Ella off."

Anjou was already out of bed and across the room, selecting

a clean shirt from the armoire that Akira had insisted Jacques needed. Nonny hurried to help, nixing the cashmere in favor of something less precious.

A telling detail. And yet ... Nonny fended off further questions with orders to hurry.

Jacques let Anjou buckle his belt and tie his shoes. Nonny bustled him into a vest and buttoned it, but Jacques went to the mirror to knot his own tie. Suuzu appeared behind him, looking young and earnest and determined as he set to preening. Jacques turned, bowed his head, then dropped a kiss on the phoenix's nose.

That earned him a chiding sort of chirp.

But also a fleeting smile.

Still fiddling cufflinks into place, Jacques strode out the door, close on Nonny's hooves. The hall was dark, and rain washed up against the short row of windows they passed. "Were you holding anything back?"

"Usually am." Nonny slowed and hooked his arm, lowering his voice. "I only got a quick look around, but ... damn it all, there was blood. Dr. Naoki was there, and so were Boon and Pim, so ... there's that. Should be fine ...? But everyone's on edge."

"Right then. Making an entrance." And Jacques burst through the door.

"Arse," Nonny accused, leaving him to saunter ahead.

Of course, Jacques' saunter was checked the moment he spied the crumpled suit on the floor. "*Mon dieu*. What's the meaning of this? Argent, this is the vicuna! And it's torn? Randolla will be heartsick."

From the bed, which Jacques was studiously ignoring, came a rusty chuckle. "Really, Jackie? Where are your priorities?"

"Good lord, is this blood? You're a menace."

Sibley spoke up. "What's vicuna?"

"Friendly folk. An absolute treasure of a clan off in South America. Dainty creatures with *exquisite* fibers. Very hard to come by, and yielding very expensive cloth. Making this travesty especially tragic." And finally turning his head, Jacques quietly added, "I hope it's the only loss we suffered ...?"

"I believe we have come out ahead in the exchange. Come here, Jacques. Meet Etienne. At least, that is what I think he has been trying to say. There is some stuffiness about the nose and a slight lisp."

"Are you Etienne?" Jacques inquired, wanting to be sure.

The boy turned his way and fluttered damp lashes. He had ragged hair, all hacked ends and limp strands, and freckles ran rampant across the bridge of a pert nose.

"Your daddy is magnifique, but Uncle Jackie is prepared to adore you. Come, my fine lad."

"Hold up." Sibley patted at Argent's shoulder with the flat of his hand. "Ettie—or whatever—could scratch Uncle Jackie."

Argent said, "You should make an effort to learn your brother's name."

"Sorry. Say it again?"

"Etienne."

Sibley repeated it enough times to draw the littler boy's attention. Etienne spurned Jacques' offer and tried to climb over Argent to get at Sibley instead. With a laugh, he said, "Hey, little bro. Seems like you and me have something in common. Lemme see your claws."

Naoki interjected, "Have you finished?"

"Think so."

"My turn then. I'll bandage Argent while you teach your brother how to be gentle."

"Come on. I gotcha." Sibley hefted the boy and crossed to a settee, working his way into its corner with Etienne on his lap. "Only problem is, I dunno French."

Jacques came to sit with them, sliding his arm around Sibley's back. The boy leaned into him, sniffing and scowling. "How come Uncle Akira and Anjou get to see you, but I can't?"

"Precautions."

"What's that?"

"Argent is careful with the people he cares about. Precautions are the rules he makes to keep us safe."

"Not sure I like rules," Sibley grumbled. "But it's a good word."

"A rebel after my own heart." Jacques whispered, "My man can get you in. Ask any time."

"You've got a man?"

"*Oui*, since I can't bring myself to turn him out. Anjou is a good sort." Jacques would have gone into more detail, mostly for Argent's sake, but just then, the door swung wide.

Nonny must have been sent to fetch things while Jacques was distracted, because he'd returned—clearly from the kitchen—preceding Sonnet into the room.

Jacques would have liked a little more warning before facing the wolf, and Sonnet must have been equally surprised. Her tray would have hit the floor if not for Anjou's reflexes. The feline caught it, sliding it safely onto a nearby table before backtracking to Sonnet, who stood transfixed. Without a trace of apology, Anjou said, "Please excuse us, Lord and Lady Mettlebright. Matters of the hearth."

And with a hand at her elbow, he guided his lady mistress from the room. But not before giving Jacques a look that was pure *come hither*.

Jacques kissed Sibley's forehead, chucked Etienne's chin, and gamely echoed, "Matters of the hearth."

He moved to follow, but hesitated at the foot of the bed.

Argent blandly said, "You hardly need my blessing."

Boon piped up then, from his post beside a rain-slicked window. "Mine either, but he's got it. The trail's at your feet, Devotion. You gonna give chase?"

Jacques had been left wanting for so long, he'd hardly let this chance get away from him. But Argent's opinion mattered. How often had his lord and master complained that he deserved better?

Expression softening, Argent waved him off. "You have always chosen well for yourself."

19

ELDERMOST STORM

Kyrie hunched inside the extra-big waterproof parka Ginkgo had brought, trying to reason with Anan. Which felt a whole lot like talking to himself. Because ever since Opal's last revelation, the thundercloud had stopped responding. He'd also stopped drizzling, but that was probably only because Hurricane Dima more than made up for his efforts. He was probably cheering her on.

Shortly after Grandfather Hajime brought Pim to fetch Sibley, Ginkgo excused himself to check on things at the house. So for the moment, Kyrie had the beach and three winds all to himself.

"Nobody can make you descend," he reasoned. "It would be your choice."

"Choice," Anan scoffed back. *"I was tricked once. I won't listen to any dragons."*

"What about half-dragons?"

After a longish pause, the thunderstorm asked, *"Is that what you are?"*

"Yes. My sire is a dragon, but my biological mother is human. An unregistered reaver."

"Reaver?"

"People with bright souls …?"

"Those descended from stars and hills and trees and tides."

"Yes. We have stars and trees here. And beacons and baby rock imps. And now you."

"I'm not someone you can simply have.*"*

Kyrie didn't really want to sit in the rain, quibbling terms, but this was so much better than silence. "Do you have me, then? Because I can tell there is a connection."

"A small connection. Barely worth mentioning. A stringy, stingy link. It could be better. It could give more. Haizea needs more."

"I wonder if that is wise. Boon says that would mean bond-building."

"We need more, and that's the truth, dragonling. I can't help it if you happen to be unusually pretty."

Kyrie was curious. "Am I tempting?"

"You're a little terror. Do these others know you're a storm unto yourself?"

Heat briefly suffused Kyrie's face, for that felt like a compliment. "Most people do not see me from the inside. And I try not to show the parts that make me a terror."

It was the strangest feeling, that Anan was rummaging through his secrets.

"Better you than that bard. He's a menace. All those pretty words.

All his pretty songs. But ...." Anan's next words came more slowly. "*But becoming music was ... yes, that was tempting.*"

The imp's shiver of delight surprised Kyrie. "You like music?"

"*Not just any music. The wind instrument. That's how I was caught and kept. I couldn't resist its song. I couldn't resist becoming a song.*"

The Bamboo Stave was a wind instrument. A flute as long as a man's arm. Kyrie could imagine a wind wanting to pass through it, coming out as notes. He thought maybe it was a little like tuning a whole forest full of remnant stones to carry his song.

"So you were lured by the flute? By the Bamboo Stave?"

"*How would a child know about something so rare?*"

"I am a rare child." Stray raindrops slipped under the tarp and smacked Kyrie's face. "My family says I am loved by winds."

"*I do not love you.*"

"Are you certain?"

"*If I did, I cannot imagine admitting it.*"

"That, at least, is honest."

"*I'm no liar. I'm not even clear about how lies work.*"

Kyrie laughed. "I like you, Anan."

"*Nooo. You shouldn't like me. You should tremble before an eldermost storm. You should cower in awe before my might.*"

"I know how you could impress me."

"*I may have been stranded for half of forever in a bottle with nothing but the memory of a melody for company, but that doesn't mean I'm a fool. Spare me your attempts at trickery.*"

Kyrie wasn't done. "Do you like challenges?"

"*I don't recall. And I said no tricks. Are you defying me? That's asking for trouble, little terror. Inviting disaster.*"

"Yes. I want to invite disaster."

Anan missed a beat, then asked, *"Is this about Dima?"*

"Yes. I would be impressed if you could help me woo her to our side."

"Our side? Ours?"

"Mine, then. I am not trying to trick you. I am trying to make peace with Dima. But she only rages." Kyrie quietly admitted, "I am cold and wet and willing to admit that I need help. Can you help? Or do I need to ask Mother to call Lord Beckonthrall? He might have advice, since he has wooed winds before."

"I have half a mind to descend, simply so I can throttle you."

"If you were to join me here, I would send for the Bamboo Stave." Kyrie didn't have the authority to do that, but Dad did. So he went further, lacing all his wheedling with vows. "I will give you the stave, and I will sit at your feet. I will listen as every breath you draw becomes the melody that was your only company for too long, and I will be glad for you."

"Do you know what it would mean for an eldermost storm to hold one of the Four Storms?"

"Tell me."

"Do you understand the Bamboo Stave's purpose?" Anan pressed.

"Music?"

"The four storms are weapons, little terror. You should tremble more, or aren't you part dragon?"

"Dragons *do* fear the Four Storms." That had been interesting to Kyrie, but he didn't find them ominous. "What was the Bamboo Stave made to do?"

"Steal voices."

Kyrie sat up a little straighter. "It silences people?"

"Not that. I should have said disarm. *These weapons are intended to disarm a dragon's voice."*

"Swaying words!"

"If the Bamboo Stave is singing, all those who can hear it are safe."

Kyrie laughed again, happy to have made such an important discovery. "The Four Storms are not *weapons.* They are defenses!"

"All depends which side of the conflict you're on."

"Do you know what the others do?"

"No. I'm not even sure how I know what the Bamboo Stave does."

"Maybe you know because it was always meant for you." Kyrie firmed his resolve. "I will get it for you."

"Swear it."

"I promise. It may take some time, but Father will surely see the necessity. Yes. I promise, Anan. I will set the Bamboo Stave into your hands myself."

There was the faintest scrunch of snow and sand. "I believe you."

Kyrie turned to stare for several moments at an angular man with ebony skin and an unruly cloud of curls. Then he jumped to his feet, surrendering his borrowed parka. "Anan ...?" he asked, even though he knew.

The imp's eyes flashed silver-bright with amusement. "Surprised you, did I?"

"You descended."

"I made room for Dima."

Kyrie pondered this while he fastened the parka, which didn't suit Anan at all, but at least it covered his nakedness. "Was there no room for another storm?"

"You are bursting with potential, but you are still a boy. And she is a tempest like no other."

"She does seem very strong. She has not stopped storming, even though it has been hours."

"This?" Anan scoffed. "This is nothing. Dima is weak as a naked hatchling, quivering in its nest. At her best, she could raze cities, then wash away their rubble. The world drowned once, you know."

Kyrie whispered, "The Flood?"

"But in this state? I doubt she could manage four days and four nights." Anan slowly reached out, setting his fingertips against Kyrie's cold cheek. "Are you afraid, little terror?"

He shook his head. "I think ... is it foolish to say I would be honored to make her acquaintance?"

A crooked smile flashed—there and gone—as if Anan didn't want to let on that Kyrie's answer had pleased him. He turned his face into the rain. "I hope you appreciate my sacrifice!"

"You have lost the sky." Kyrie was shivering without the second coat, but he left the shelter of the fire and its covering to stand at Anan's side. "If I gain it one day, I could carry you."

The imp favored him with a sidelong look, then pressed the flat of his hand to Kyrie's back. "Do you mean these wings?"

"*Are* they wings? Nobody c-could say for c-certain." His teeth were beginning to chatter.

"I was a ruler of those skies, gliding effortlessly through the firmament, darkening lands and lashing them with lightning. The sound of my approach sent humanity burrowing for cover, and none could withstand my strikes." His eyes crinkled at the corners. Just a little. "I know the shape and feel of wings. Yours are not fully formed, but isn't that how it is with dragonkind? Cursed, they were, to cling to the earth."

"I remember the story."

Anan warned, "I'm going to test you, little terror."

"All right. How, please?"

"A kiss."

Kyrie brightened. "Oh, I know about that sort of kiss. An imp's regard shines brightly on the one they love … unless their love is not wholeheartedly returned."

"A rare child, indeed," Anan grumbled, bending closer.

"Wait. C-could … could it be in a s-secret place?"

"Choose," Anan ordered.

"S-s-someplace I c-can see, but others will n-not notice." Kyrie really was very cold. "Even if they are a f-fox. Or the F-first of Wards. Or … or another imp."

"Why?"

"I want to share a secret with you. Th-th-that is another k-kind of b-bond."

Anan frowned, but then he said, "Show me your hand."

Kyrie lifted both.

With another flicker of a smile, Anan pressed warm lips to each palm. They watched together as filigree sparkled across Kyrie's skin, twirling into patterns that reminded him of the work of spiders. It was so beautiful, he gasped in dismay when Anan rubbed at them with his thumbs.

"Now I'll know the truth," Anan said ominously.

Kyrie couldn't have been happier. "You *want* me to love you."

"You are allowed to love Haizea and Dima. I need very little.

Hardly anything. Except … perhaps a bit more of that pretty soul of yours."

His teeth were chattering worse, so he simply nodded.

Anan straightened, faced the storm, and shouted, "Dima! He believed me!"

Kyrie's brows drew down, and he wanted to ask Anan what he meant. But he was too distracted by the fact that the typhoon, with a final patter of raindrops, simply … stopped.

20

TWINESHAFT'S DRAGON

Sinder had been drifting in that pleasant haze of relaxation that means you're coming off a good long sleep. There's this little window of cozy comfort, when your stomach hasn't begun rioting yet, driving you from bed in search of food. But something had changed, and it was concerning enough to push Sinder closer to the waking world. What ... was ... wrong?

Someone was petting his hair, but that was fine. Totally normal.

Except that when he burrowed closer to the warmth and scent of safety, it wasn't Juuyu.

Sinder wove his fingers more snugly into thick fur and knew it would be black, but he didn't really want to think about *why*. And just like that, he realized where he was ... and what was wrong.

"The rain stopped." He stirred, trying to orient himself, looking for a window.

His companion kept right on playing with his hair—methodical, maybe even meditative.

Sinder cleared his throat, and said, "Hey, Fend."

Utterly relaxed, the feline silently searched his face. There was a hint of amusement in orange eyes that reminded Sinder eerily of Hisoka's. It was a look that usually meant he'd done something silly. Or betrayed secret knowledge. Or rambled on about things his boss was too ancient to get.

Belatedly, Sinder caught on. Because he'd been clutching it for who knew how long. "Oh, shit. Sorry about your tail."

He tried to disentangle himself, but Fend didn't let him get away. Wriggling down until their noses were bumping, he pressed their cheeks together—one side, then the other. Sinder figured it was forgiveness. Or maybe courtesy? Fend wanted to make peace, but his motives weren't exactly pure. All kinds of warning flags were waving because Timur's beast was bent on world domination. Or ... well, on saving the world, at least.

"Ohhh, lovely one," Fend murmured. "I wanted you for Timur, but you are too distracting."

Sinder wasn't sure what he might have done to deserve criticism, but then Fend was nudging and nuzzling and ... okay, this was new. Fend was kissing him, unhurried and sorta ... soft. It was certainly nicer than being chomped on, but it was also vastly more confusing.

When Fend stopped, Sinder braced himself for mockery or some kind of *I told you so*.

Best he could tell, the cat was waiting for something, too. A complaint? A rebuff? Swearing was probably called for, but

Sinder wasn't inclined. Honestly, that worried him a little.

Fend seemed at least as surprised as he was. A barely audible purr revved up between them, and Sinder began to wonder if Fend was going to kiss him again. Sinder had always been sort of curious about things like this.

"Too distracting by far," the cat decreed.

"Sorry ...?"

"You needn't be. Dragons are said to inspire reckless devotion."

Sinder rolled his eyes. "Whoever said that was probably a dragon."

Fend's eyes took on fresh shine. "You're probably right. Wily beasts, dragons. Nearly impossible to tame."

"Are you calling me tame?"

"You're Twineshaft's dragon. Culled from the heights despite your youth. Given reach and sway and access to every secret. I'd call you intelligent, intuitive, even impetuous. But tame? Not you."

Sinder wasn't immune to compliments. One problem with working among other elites was ... nobody was ever really impressed. Amazing was expected. All part of the elite brand.

Fend said, "Not *tame*, but I know both your strength and your weakness, and that gives me sway over you."

Reality reasserted itself. "You want to use me."

"I want to give you purpose. To shift your understanding of what it means to be Twineshaft's dragon. And then I want you to become Timur's dragon." Fend nosed his way toward Sinder's throat, which was all kinds of disconcerting, but after a lengthy perusal of Sinder's scent, the only damage Fend did was a tiny nip to Sinder's earlobe. The feline whispered, "Let me have my way."

"I don't know how you know how much I know, but ... look. I

won't betray Hisoka's trust, no matter what you say. Or do."

Fend apparently took that as a challenge. Or maybe an invitation. Because he laid gentle kisses on Sinder's face, each punctuating brief remarks that added up to a report. "You slept for eight days. This is the first of December. Twineshaft remains a recluse. Rhomiko sings like an angel and speaks like an oracle. Kyrie returned from Keishi with the Changing Winds in tow. Argent has been poisoned. Opal's star is Zeriel of the Beckoning Sky. Also, Juuyu has been summoned."

Sinder's heart leapt and lurched and panged and pounded, for each piece of news was monumental. He needed more information, but Fend pressed into his mouth, and Sinder had a deepening kiss to navigate. He was beginning to see what all the fuss was about.

Then Fend drew back with a soft oath. "No. You are meant for Timur." And swiftly touching his lips to Sinder's mouth, jaw, and throat, he gruffly warned, "And he has returned."

A warning rap preceded Michaelson into the room. Dishes made a faint clatter, which suggested a tray, but Sinder couldn't bring himself to turn ... or even to look away from Fend. In the privacy afforded by a Reach's ability, he flung his words in thought-form. *"I don't want to be used, but I like being trusted."*

Fend's responding thought had a bitter tone. *"I have little choice but to trust you, lovely one. You've found me out."*

"I know your strength and your weakness, too. Is that it? So you're under my sway as well?"

The feline's heart leapt to a quicker beat, and his lips parted. *"Are you challenging me?"*

"Somebody has to."

Oblivious to the silent conversation underway, Michaelson lowered himself onto the mattress at Sinder's back and touched his shoulder. "All right there, Damsel?"

"Sure. I'm good. Never better." Not until Fend lowered his gaze and melted from the bed did Sinder turn. And frown. "Uhh ... interesting fashion statement. I'm no expert, but I don't think that's a good look for you."

Timur laughed. "This is a wolvish baby carrier. Ideal for skin-to-skin contact. Or skin-to-stone, in this case. I did have Gregor in here earlier, though, while Ninook was teaching me how to rig myself. *This* little guy's a bit heavier. I might put him to good use and do some squats."

Sinder pushed onto his knees, noticing for the first time that he was drowning in a too-large Camp Wardenclave T-shirt. But most of his attention was on the green crystal strapped to Timur's bare chest. "Hello again," he murmured, touching living stone. "I know Argent wanted to get these to Michael. Did your dad foist this one on you?"

"In a roundabout way, it's Rhomiko's fault."

Fend had dropped that name earlier. Something about angels and oracles. "Who's this Rhomiko person?"

"One of our newbies. I guess Hisoka-sensei brought them home, but nobody's really explained how they're connected. Only that they're definitely connected." Slipping into that teasing tone where he let more Russian into his accent, Timur suggested, "Shall we find out? You be Fend's spy. Uncover Sensei's secrets for him. And I will tell you about the typhoon you slept through. Is good, yes?"

Sinder remembered then. "The rain stopped! Which means it was raining. Hold up. Fend said something about Changing Winds, and ... a typhoon? Are we talking eldermost storms, here?"

"Very good. Papka explained while he was fitting me out." Timur patted his crystalline passenger. Then his gaze sharpened, and he carefully cupped Sinder's cheek, sliding a thumb across his lower lip.

Sinder stopped breathing.

Timur softly asked, "Do I need to take my partner to task?"

"Uhh ... what for?"

"You look very kissed." And with obvious concern, he asked, "Did Fend overstep?"

"I'm pretty sure this was just *good morning* in cat."

"And you're conversant in cat?"

"Well, nooo. Unless you count Twineshaft. But he's not a very catty cat."

Timur hesitated a moment longer, but he nodded and moved on. "Do you have an affinity for crystal?"

"Sure. Nothing extraordinary, but better than basic. I mean ... dragon." Tapping the stone, he said, "I helped collect these four."

"Well, this one's ours."

"Excuse me?"

"Yours and mine. According to Rhomiko, we're the key to helping this little guy hatch. Or emerge. Or whatever it is baby rock imps do."

Okay. So a lot had apparently happened while Sinder had been doubling down on the trans-oceanic crossings and sleeping late-ish. "I feel like we need to back up and start over. Because I missed the memo or the meeting or whatever. Since when am I this rock's daddy?"

"Maybe you're the mommy," suggested Fend from across the room.

"Do I *look* like Sonnet?" And locking eyes with Timur, Sinder said, "I can think of a dozen people more qualified. No, *two* dozen! In fact, just go to Sonnet. He's one hell of a mother."

"Easy does it." Timur's soothing tone held an undercurrent of amusement. "Nobody's forcing you into anything. I won't obligate you, but ... can't you feel it?"

Sinder looked between the man and the wardstone and even risked a glance at Fend. "Not sure what you mean. What do you think I should be feeling?"

"There's a resonance whenever I ... well ... ahh." Timur looked vaguely sheepish. "I noticed something when I was treating your abrasions. There was a lot of salve. I used spikenard, since you favor it. And I suppose there was a bit of tending involved."

"Okay ... so you took care of me. It's no different than last summer. Except this time it was sand. Took off a layer or two of skin. Hurt like you wouldn't believe in salt water, but less so with scales, so I mostly stuck to ... truest ... form ...." Sinder cocked his head to one side. "Is that you?"

Timur turned toward him. "Yes. Let me in?"

"For tending? Sure. Why not? It's not like we've never ... uhh. Okay, that's new. I see what you mean. Definitely picking up some resonance." Resting both hands on the swaddled stone, Sinder scooted closer. "You like that, huh? But why? And why's it gotta be us?"

"Not really clear on that," Timur said with obvious caution.

Sinder wanted more info. "Who has the other wardstones?"

Timur said, "Papka has one, and one's apparently meant for Isla."

He frowned. "One each? But we're supposed to be in this together."

"Oh, they're paired off, too. In a manner of speaking. Isla and Lapis Mossberne. And Papka is going to have to talk to Hisoka-sensei."

"Huh." Sinder cut a look in Fend's direction.

Timur said, "So each duo includes an Amaranthine and a reaver with some level of crystal affinity."

"Okay, yeah. There's that."

The cat shot him a private aside. *"He can be so dense."*

"Does the fourth wardstone follow the pattern?"

"No. Or not yet. Rhomiko hadn't assigned it to anyone, but we have plenty of crystal adepts hereabouts. Kyrie, for example." Timur leaned forward. "Would you be willing to stay with us while Papka sorts out what to do?"

"This is perfect." Fend's thoughts held the snap of authority. *"Agree. Now."*

"I travel a lot for work." Not that Sinder wanted to go anywhere.

Fend spoke up then so Timur could hear. "Hisoka probably needs you close. And he's in a similar position. So stay. I'll tuck you in with Timur every night."

"That *would* give us time to interact with our imp." Timur looked so hopeful.

Sinder wanted to agree, but was that the best course of action? It was difficult to think clearly when the things he wanted most were giving a baby impression reasons to sing.

Timur set his hand over Sinder's and smiled. "At least one of us likes the idea."

Fend stole up, draping himself over Timur's shoulders. "Do as you're told, lovely one. You were meant for this. You're ours now."

"Look, you …!" But Sinder's protest fizzled before he could give it form. In more subdued tones, he said, "Look, I'll talk to Hisoka first. After that? We'll see."

Nuzzling Timur's cheek, Fend said, "He means *yes*."

Tugging at the Kith-kin's ear, Timur grumbled, "Give him room to decide for himself."

"Why should I?" argued Fend. "He's perfect."

Timur gave Sinder's hand a small squeeze and let go, but not before saying, "I think so, too."

21
SHELTERING

Ginkgo had enough sigilcraft in place to know that Kyrie had moved from the beach, so he cut short his meeting with Michael. What hadn't been obvious from the inner room became plain when he passed a window. *Clear* skies. They were still pre-dawn, but not by much. And the rain had stopped.

He reached the kitchen at the same time a stranger burst through the door, an unconscious Kyrie in his arms. He wore the parka Ginkgo had zipped his brother into earlier, and he radiated an alarming mix of peevishness and power.

Silvery eyes locked onto him, and Ginkgo knew his tail puffed, but he managed a level tone. "Hey, there. Were the two of you able to work out your differences?"

"The brother."

"One of them." Ginkgo took a step forward. "Need me to take him off your hands."

The imp took a step back. "This boy carries people precious to me."

"Okay, I get that. It's why the rain stopped, yeah?"

"I can summon up more if you weren't sufficiently drenched earlier."

"I'd really rather you didn't." Ginkgo took another step forward, palms open for courtesy. Mostly. He was also hoping to get Kyrie away from a guy who felt wilder than wolves. "Peace, friend."

"You and I aren't friends, but peace would be convenient."

Ginkgo's senses were straining. He took some comfort from the gentleness of the storm's hold on Kyrie ... and on the fact that he'd done the exact right thing by bringing him to the house. "You know what? There's a parlor along this hall with a fireplace already going. We can warm him up in there."

Kyrie stirred and opened his eyes. He remained utterly relaxed in the imp's arms when he murmured, "This is Anan. He tamed me."

"Thought it was supposed to be the other way around."

"I do not mind being wrong."

Ginkgo said, "We need to get you warm."

"That would be appreciated." Closing his eyes, Kyrie softly called, "I am *fine*, Sibley. Do not blame a storm for storming. He cannot help raining when he is so sad."

Anan's eyes widened, and Ginkgo sighed. "Come here, Sibley."

The younger boy skulked out of striking range and shuffled to Ginkgo's side. With a firm hand on the boy's shoulder, Ginkgo said, "Get these two to the fireside, then go for towels and blankets. Stuff like that. I'll follow in a few minutes with food. Got it?"

"Yeah, I guess. If you're sure."

"Increasingly certain. You can trust Kyrie to know what's best."

Sibley nodded once, marched up to the imp, and grabbed Kyrie's hand. Immediately Sibley's face changed. "Hey! You're cold as snow. Come on, storm guy. Stop standing around. My brother'll get sick like this! I'll show you where."

He dragged them off, and Gingko turned to the kitchen. Usually at this hour, Sonnet was preparing the morning meal. Left to his own devices, Ginkgo was caught between raiding and reheating when hooves sounded along the hall. Nonny's brows shot up. "Need help?"

"Probably. Where's Sonnet?"

"Kinda busy. What needs doing?"

"Not entirely sure. This is a first. We have an eldermost storm in the Rosewood Parlor."

"How do you suppose he takes his tea?"

Ginkgo laughed. And couldn't stop laughing. Flinging an arm around Nonny's shoulders, he accepted some much-needed support.

Nonny elbowed him and repeated, "What needs doing?"

"Kyrie's chilled through and probably half-starved. I was thinking tea and a couple of trays. I have no idea what wind imps eat."

"You keep that up. I'll do some of that custard dragons like. Timur showed me how."

For a while, they worked in silence. Just the clatter of pans and scrape of a whisk. Ginkgo was pretty distracted by everything, but he finally picked up on the goat-crosser's mood. "Anything the matter?"

"You mean besides the guv being poisoned, the bad guys lurking nearby, and an eldermost storm in the Rosewood Parlor?"

"Yeah. Aside from those."

"I mighta made a mistake." Nonny briefly met his gaze. "I didn't tell Jacques that Sonnet was back. He was angry about it. Maybe ... betrayed. Like I was keeping things from him to hurt him."

"Why blame you?"

"I'm probably the one who shoulda clued him in. I knew how much it'd mean."

"I knew," said Ginkgo. "Dad knew."

"Well, yeah. But him and Sonnet, they were ... umm." Nonny shuffled his hooves and stole another look.

"They totally were." Ginkgo shrugged and repeated, "I knew. Dad knew."

"Right. Well. I just thought ... Jacques is the kind of guy who likes to look his best. And since he came home, he's not really been tip-top, you know? And what with everything else ...." He switched off the burner and stirred in a glug of something from an amber bottle. "Everything's been mad, so I was waiting for it to calm down a bit. But it's getting madder by the minute. Why did I ever think things would go back to normal?"

"Lack of experience." Ginko laughed and shook his head. "Normal is this myth, and ordinary days are a miracle straight from the Maker."

Nonny made a face. "That's not how I remember it. When I came here, it was nothing but good days."

"You were a kid. You had good days because we adults sheltered you from the kinds of things kids shouldn't have to worry about." Ginkgo stole a taste of Nonny's cookery. "Now, you're one of the guys who's doing the sheltering."

Nonny poured off the custard, his brows still furrowed. "Which side of that line is Kyrie on?"

"Honestly? I think Kyrie's been on the grownup side of things since last summer, when he found out about his sire." After a moment's thought, he added, "Mercy's arrival changed him again. He's determined. Almost ... obsessed. Tsumiko prefers words like *zeal* and *fervor*, though."

"Nobody ever says it, but ...." Nonny grimaced. "The Rogue seems like a zeal and fervor kind of guy."

"You're not wrong."

"And you're not worried ...?"

"Nope. Not even a little bit."

Nonny swore. "I'm not talking about Kyrie, you know. What about all these kids who didn't start out having the guv and Lady and you and Jacques."

"You mean kids like you?" Ginkgo lightly patted Nonny's back. "If I remember right, *you* started out in a cage."

"I never said so."

"And I never told." With a small shrug, Ginkgo admitted, "Fox dreams can cancel out bad ones. But pulling you out of scary places meant catching glimpses of them."

Nonny swore softly, then muttered, "Thanks."

"Opal's lullabies are even better. He doesn't give nightmares the chance to take hold."

"Dragons and foxes. You're not all bad."

Ginkgo stacked his trays and picked them up. "Here's hoping eldermost storms aren't all bad."

"They have a bad reputation?"

"You could say that, but I'll leave the storytelling to our bard and focus on being a good host."

Nonny grabbed the third tray and vowed, "I'll make sure our kids have plenty of good days. As many as possible."

"Well, I think Kyrie's had a rough day. And a long night."

"This'll set him right." And Nonny sailed along the hall, head held high, exuding the very same self-assurance that made his mentor so easy to trust. Jacques would've been proud.

Ginkgo caught up outside the door to the Rosewood Parlor. "You know, Jacques probably isn't actually angry with you."

"Nah. He's probably in love with the whole world right now."

Which could only mean one thing. "Sonnet got to him?"

"Anjou made sure of it." Rolling his eyes, Nonny added, "Cats. Y'know?"

"Mmm. Wolves, though." And because he wasn't sure if Nonny knew how much he knew, he cheerfully added, "To each their own, yeah?"

Nonny called him something rude, smiled sweetly, and sauntered into the parlor.

Kyrie sat on the hearth rug, head bowed. Sibley must have gone and returned, because he stood behind his brother, toweling his hair. Anan was there, too, keeping a close watch over the proceedings.

"Anan, do you eat?" Ginkgo slid his trays onto the low table in front of a sofa.

"How would I know?"

Nonny, having stashed his tray on a desk, propped his hands on his hips. "Want to find out?"

Anan considered them both, then angled his body into something close to a receptive posture. He beckoned to Nonny with long fingers. "What do you have to tempt an eldermost storm?"

Immediately brightening, Nonny replied, "Let's find out how you take your tea."

The imp's brow furrowed.

Nonny wasn't put off. "I've had to sit through a hell of a lot of tea tastings over the years. My mentor's strict about temperature and timing."

While he arrayed his tea implements, Ginkgo snagged the custardy stuff and dropped to the floor beside Kyrie. "Nonny's got you covered."

Sibley peered over Kyrie's shoulder. "Oh, nice. That stuff's the best. Get it in you."

Kyrie, who'd been stripped of wet clothes and swaddled in blankets, spooned and sighed, his eyes going half-lidded. Sibley hummed encouragement, his fingers busy neatening Kyrie's drying hair. Meanwhile, Nonny narrated his way through a tea tasting involving half a dozen cups.

"You want a full-on tea ceremony, you'll have to wait for Lady Starmark's next visit. I'm just giving you a splash, and while it's not fussy, it's plenty of fancy. I'm using the good tea."

Ginkgo wondered if it was wise to be giving anything caffeinated to someone whose scent reminded him of gathering storms and lightning strikes. But Nonny was good with people, and his irreverence was hitting just the right note. Anan was probably used to more in the way of awe and intimidation, but Nonny was more interested in other things.

"Honey over sugar, then. I like it better, too. But how about milk?"

As Nonny directed him through more sips, Anan's mood mellowed. Sibley joined Kyrie, and Ginkgo helped rearrange the blankets so they were snug. Only after Nonny proudly placed a cup in Anan's hands—honey and lemon having been sussed out as his favorite—did Ginkgo make another attempt at basic courtesies.

"I'm Ginkgo Mettlebright. Welcome to Stately House." And when the imp didn't respond, he asked, "How would you like to be called?"

Kyrie spoke up. "Anan Eldermost—ruler of skies, darkener of lands, harrower of hearts, and stealer of voices. He was and is and shall become music incarnate."

"No kidding?" Ginkgo made his most dignified gesture of greeting. "We're honored."

Nonny said, "I'll stand on formality if you make me, but can I just go with Anan? Simpler than juggling titles. Oh, and I should probably ask. You okay if the little ones end up calling you Uncle Anan. I think that's inevitable, really."

"Anan likes children," murmured Kyrie.

The imp snorted. "You are *all* children."

Sibley had been fading from notice, but he drew attention to himself again by speaking up. "Hey. Hey, Kyrie? Something wrong?"

"Not exactly." Tucking a lock of hair behind his ear, Kyrie admitted, "Dima is loud."

"Let me talk to her." Anan set aside his teacup and beckoned with both hands.

To Ginkgo's amazement, Kyrie wriggled free of his blankets and crawled straight into the imp's arms. While Sibley and Nonny rearranged the bedding, Ginkgo searched Anan's impassive face.

"You don't actually have to be in contact to speak with the other wind imps, do you?"

Anan simply firmed his grasp, practically curling around Kyrie.

"He was worried," said Kyrie. "So was Dima. That is why she started shouting."

"What're they worried about?" asked Sibley.

With a sigh, Kyrie raised his voice and called, "You may as well come in, Opal. They know you are there, and there will be no peace unless we make it."

Leaning through the doorway, Opal the Sage offered a small wave. "In the interest of peace, I did have an idea. Perhaps your winds would be willing to trade with me in the manner of friends?"

"You are no friend of ours," Anan growled.

"But I *could* be." When this was met with stony silence, the dragon bard cleared his throat. "As I was saying … in the interest of peace … a friend of mine could reach out to a friend of yours. Invite them to arbitrate between us, since he is famous for truth-telling."

"Ohhh," breathed Kyrie. "That is a good idea."

Ginkgo asked, "Who's this friend of a friend?"

Anan's expression wavered, and he tentatively asked, "Bethiel?"

"The very fellow!" assured Opal. "As a token of my good intentions, allow me to reunite you."

Nonny broke the sudden silence to ask, "An angel, huh? Wonder how he takes his tea?"

22

CANNY AS TREES

Hisoka held still, rooted in place as surely as if he were a tree. He didn't understand his persistent need to stay at Stately House. Perhaps the compulsion was simply another sign that he was, in truth, a bereft tree-kin. With no seed and no sibling, he'd buried himself instead.

He didn't know what to do, so he did nothing.

Or ....

A new idea niggled at him. Was it possible that like most trees and their kin, he was canny enough to know what he needed? And the thing he needed most was here at Stately House.

He shied away from the possibility. It would be selfish to abandon his post. A leader mustn't be self-serving. The needs of others came first. Should be foremost. Must rule the ruler. Because to lead was to serve others.

These were things he'd always believed.

Or … had come to believe …?

Hisoka hugged a pillow, trying to remember why he'd ever been sure that the future of the Amaranthine clans had been his to secure. Why had the Emergence been the answer to every question anyone raised? How had he convinced so many to risk everything for peace?

Had it worked because he'd secured their trust? Or was he only trusted because his plan worked? Two centuries of preparation. Decades of wondering if cooperation was possible for the clans, then if they'd see eye-to-eye with the reavers of the In-between. And finally, peace with a planet full of humans busy with their own struggles and disputes.

How could anyone have guessed that their unveiling would sweep across the world, changing the landscape on a scale that hadn't been seen since the Maker answered Veliel's restless longing with a single word—*bloom*.

"Leaf and twig before flower and fruit," Hisoka murmured.

All at once, at the faintest of sounds, his heart gave a feeble leap.

He knew that step in the hall, knew the rhythm of the knock before it ever touched the door. Hisoka curled more tightly under the blankets, embarrassed for Michael to see him like this.

The man paused on the threshold, no doubt sensing Hisoka's mood. With a more cautious tone that usual, Michael said, "Good morning, Sensei. Do you have time for me?"

"You should not have to ask." Hisoka winced at the creak in his voice. How long since he'd last spoken? Or bothered to drink? He was parched as sand, and he'd let the tea Rhomiko poured earlier go cold. A vague apology died on his lips when he uncurled enough to see past his blankets.

Michael sat rather heavily on the edge of the bed and held out his hand.

Hisoka poked his own out from under the covers, all the while eyeing the crisscrossing bands of cloth that bound one of the wardstones to Michael's upper body. "I already knew your affection for crystal was unrivaled the whole world over." He sat up, rubbing wearily at his hair. "I suppose it was only a matter of time before you began doting on them as you would your children."

With a light laugh, Michael said, "Babies need a healthy amount of doting. Would you like to help me pamper this one?"

Hisoka touched the topmost curve of the stone, the green shining prettily against the dark blue of Michael's tunic, setting sparkles into eyes that held concern. The man's soul was all lightness and luster, starry enough to dazzle, soft enough to do no harm, even as it looped around Hisoka in intangible ways.

Not because he was special. Well, no more special than anyone else in Michael's circle of friends. Because as he was always saying, Michael always got attached.

Hisoka was far less trusting. Even less so, given recent betrayals.

And yet he longed for this man, for his Michael.

According to Rhomiko, Nemi had known what he needed, wanted him to trade his Michael for a miko. For Rhomiko. Let go *this* starry soul and embrace a half-star.

Hisoka had always thought that trees and stars were meant for each other. History was repeating itself, or perhaps themes were recurring. For Hoshiko, there had been Nemi, and on some level,

Hisoka had wanted Michael to be his star. In a sudden flash of clarity, Hisoka realized that if he pushed the analogy further, he'd essentially chosen Jacques for his tree. The safest of companions. Seductive yet chaste. His place to return. The arms in which he slept.

His mortification intensified. A tom of his years, playing house like a child. Makeshifting bonds that were doomed to be both unrequited and ephemeral.

"Sensei?" Michael tugged him into an embrace made clumsy by the chrysalis, humming in the funny approximation of purring he'd developed as a child. An endearing quirk.

Michael also wordlessly opened himself up for tending, oblique permission for Hisoka to take what he wanted. Not that he ever did. He'd gotten good at polite evasion. Timely distraction. Gracious refusal.

Well, there had been that *one* time when he'd allowed himself to take comfort in the manner of felines. But that had been Jacques, whose soul had posed no temptation and who understood cats and their ways. This was Michael. Like the fox who'd raised him, he'd chosen once and well. That was yet another thing Hisoka found charming about Michael. He was the sort of man who believed in true love.

"Sensei, please don't put me off. You *need* this."

"I can't." Hisoka was too tired to deflect. Too weary to be wise. "It's not my way."

Michael, being Michael, actually listened. "No? But you want to. I can tell that much. Or did you mean ... oh. I wonder why I never considered ...? Ah, yes, I think I see."

Hisoka didn't believe him.

"Well, then," Michael said gamely. "Shall I?"

Little reavers with stellar lineages were taught to let an Amaranthine set the pace in a tending session. As a courtesy. By the same token, they were sigiled and warded and sealed and trained that generosity could be dangerous. Strictly portioning their soul kept both parties safe.

Restraint had long been the hallmark of Michael's tending, so Hisoka wasn't in any way ready for the sudden tide that stole his breath and left him dizzy. Vaguely, he was aware that he'd pushed up onto his knees, that his hands were on Michael's shoulders, that he'd pressed his face to the man's neck in silent plea, teeth gritted for fear of what he might beg for.

"All right, Sensei. Trust me."

Slowly, Hisoka eased away, retreating to a more polite distance. Sitting back on his heels, he took Michael's hands. Handholding had always been Michael's way when it came to tending, so Hisoka was startled when the man gently pulled free.

"Right then. Lie back against the pillows." A firm push at Hisoka's shoulder reinforced the order.

He did as he was told.

Michael worked at the sling, loosening until he freed the chrysalis. "Your turn," he announced, carefully lowering the crystal onto Hisoka's bare chest.

The stone was warm, smooth, and heavy. Fleetingly, he worried that Michael would hurt himself, lugging so much weight around.

"Hold still. Keep them steady."

Again, Hisoka obeyed, bracing the chrysalis with both hands.

Michael folded away the carrying cloth, then straightened the blankets. Next, he crossed to the table, raided one of the trays abandoned there, and returned with water. All while maintaining the giddying tumult of tending that stole Hisoka's ability to protest.

"Drink."

Hisoka did.

"When did you last eat?"

He could only shake his head.

With a small nod, Michael returned to the trays, and after much rattling through their contents, brought something that smelled savory. "Open your mouth."

Startled by this entirely unprecedented turn of events, Hisoka parted his lips to receive a morsel of food. His stomach immediately rumbled for more.

Michael smiled crookedly. Still, his tone was firm when he said, "All of this then. It'll do you as much good as the tending."

Hisoka knew he should protest. He didn't. Mostly because Michael didn't give him the chance. All Hisoka could do was yield, allowing Michael to dictate their pace, pressing more on him than Hisoka ever would have let himself take. Utterly awash, he basked without burning and felt safe.

Even though Michael was close enough to notice.

Even though there were no secrets left to hide.

"Sensei?"

When had he closed his eyes? Hisoka stirred himself enough to open them and blinked to focus. Michael's expression was difficult to read, but they were connected deeply enough for

Hisoka to catch moods. Michael was happy about something. Hardly surprising. Michael was always happy about something.

"Hmm?"

Michael quietly asked, "Can you feel that?"

He was feeling a great many things, but Hisoka shook his head.

"This resonance. It's pleasant, don't you think?"

Hisoka smoothed his hands up over the wardstone. When had it begun to sing? Surely this wasn't the first time. Because this melody had been reeling through his mind for days.

"I think they're making a bid for attention." Michael smiled approvingly at the stone. "Argent expects me to sort out what these little ones need, but I'm mostly at a loss. So far, the only things I've discovered are that they resonate with certain people ... and that Rhomiko seems to know when the rock imps have chosen them."

"And this one chose you?"

"Us," Michael gently corrected. "You and I. So you see, I really *do* need your cooperation."

Hisoka's curiosity stirred. "Is it always two people?"

"So far, yes. I'm pleased to have been singled out, or perhaps it's more accurate to say *paired off*. Experiencing the phenomenon firsthand is bound to help me understand what's going on. I don't have any answers, though." Michael peered thoughtfully at the chrysalis. "I would expect there to be instincts at work, but I'm not sure if there's something you and I are meant to provide ...? Or if they're drawn to something that exists between two people ...?"

Hisoka cautiously asked, "Who else do they resonate with?"

"They first fixed upon Isla and Lapis."

"Oh."

"Mmm. But before we leap to conclusions, the other duo is Timur and Sinder."

"That's ... unexpected." Hisoka searched his memory for mentions of Michael's son in Sinder's reports. "I know they became acquainted last summer."

"Timur's never mentioned Sinder to me. Then again, we mostly talk about Gregor. I didn't even realize Sinder was here until Rhomiko pinpointed him as Timur's other half. So there must *be* a bond."

"Or there *will* be. Did you ask him?"

"Certainly, but much of what Order members do with dragons is held in the strictest of confidence. So Timur only said they worked closely for a short time." A smile played at the corners of Michael's mouth. "Sinder is more likely to let something slip. Or ... Jacques might know. He inspires confidences."

Hisoka winced.

The concern was back in Michael's gaze. "Argent didn't go into any particular detail, but I got the impression that you and Jacques ...? Was there a falling out?"

"I didn't recognize him."

Michael didn't question his excuse. Only asked, "Did anyone explain why?"

"Perhaps. I don't know. I haven't been listening."

"Will you listen to me?"

Hisoka fidgeted. After the last bombshell, discovering that Kodoku and his twin were Nemi's children, he was honestly afraid of what he might hear.

Michael's tone shifted, and he firmly said, "Listen carefully."

So Hisoka did.

When Michael finished filling in parts of the rescue mission to which Hisoka hadn't been privy, one question remained unanswered. Feeling peevish, he asked it. Again. "What am I supposed to do?"

"What do you want to do?"

"I have no idea." Because Michael had served as his confessor, Hisoka grumbled, "I've always had a star to ask."

Gaze searching, the man posed, "Has that changed?"

Hisoka hesitated, unsure how to answer. Rhomiko might have a star's legacy, but they'd spent their whole life in captivity.

"Rhomiko *knows* things. I cannot imagine they would mislead you."

Michael didn't say it, but there was weight to his implication. Hisoka—leader of the Emergence, orchestrator of the New Saga, the one everyone looked to for guidance—liked for someone else to be in charge.

"Have I made your life more difficult by needing you?"

Evasion was reflexive. "*Do* you need me?"

"Sensei!" Michael exclaimed in disappointed tones.

Hisoka averted his face.

"Do you know what I think?"

He gestured mutely for Michael to continue.

"Rhomiko is learning as much as they can as quickly as they can, and they're making a place for themself here at Stately House. I think it's for your sake. And … I think that means your place is here, too." Michael betrayed a hope that was as true as it was tempting. "At heart, you've always been a teacher. Stay, Sensei. Teach at Stately House."

23

CHOICES AND THEIR CONSEQUENCES

Suuzu's truant nestmate not only stayed out all night, he turned up the next morning around mid-high with a hitching gait, a brave smile, and an entourage.

"I'm trying not to panic. Last night, I wasn't thinking straight—lord, that's almost funny—but this morning, when Anjou was—ah, I'll spare you the details—but it dawned on all of us that we were too reckless and there might be out-of-the-way consequences. So they rushed me here. Can you check? Will you be able to tell?" Jacques fumbled with the ties of his dressing gown.

Suuzu quickly dropped to his knees, anxious for a look at the sprig, but he was keenly aware of Sonnet, whose skirts rustled when she joined him on the floor.

"Ignore the scratches. The bruises are similarly incidental. I know I'm redolent, but ... lord, don't swoon." Jacques took a pleading tone. "Steady on. *Please*, Suuzu. I haven't harmed this little one, have I?"

Suuzu had been looking after Jacques ever since his return, but now, with a wolf looming at his side, he trembled to touch.

Sonnet leaned close and reinforced Jacques' request. "Please, love. We're on tenterhooks."

That *we* seemed to include Anjou, who'd taken possession of Jacques' hand.

Suuzu knew he was blushing badly, but he pressed his hands to Jacques' belly, already sure that he could allay their fears. Warbling soothing notes, he performed a careful inspection of the tendril that had coiled further around Jacques' navel.

"I don't know what came over me," Sonnet whispered, all contrition. "His scent's changed, and it's really very affecting."

"Hmm." Suuzu had taken Jacques into his nest, and that came with responsibility. "Are you using his allure to excuse your behavior?"

Sonnet's eyes widened. "Oh. Oh, my. *No*, Suuzu. I know this seems precipitous, but last night was the culmination of a long-standing attachment."

Suuzu angled his head toward Anjou.

"An admittedly recent adaptation. You see, our den has a hearth." Sonnet tugged at his sleeve. "I *like* how that sounds. Don't you? It's homey."

The feline quietly complained, "This is bad for my heart. Please, good phoenix. How is our baby?"

"Safe," Suuzu quickly promised, meeting Sonnet's gaze, then Anjou's. "Jacques carries a tree's blessing. I can show you what your bondmate needs, but perhaps we should visit Dr.

Naoki. He and Dr. Perrine are monitoring our progress. They will want to know that you have taken responsibility."

"*Bondmate*," murmured Sonnet, clearly pleased.

Anjou began purring.

Jacques ruffled Suuzu's hair. "Glad to be rid of me?"

"Indeed no." Suuzu stood and pulled Jacques' free hand until it was pressed over his heart. "A nestmate is here and always will be."

"Lord, you're cute." Jacques gathered him close, even going so far as to pull his dressing gown around Suuzu's shoulders. In avian terms, it was shockingly possessive. "I love you. I do. And I'm not done needing you."

Jacques' breezy confidence and charisma had always been fascinating from a safe distance. Up close, with the recent addition of impish allure, the radiance of his happiness was putting a wobble in Suuzu's knees. He managed a faint peep.

"He's awash," warned Anjou.

"Give him to me," said Sonnet.

Jacques steered Suuzu into the wolf's motherly embrace. Her sniffing and crooning had him relaxing. And a little relieved. Wolves weren't the sort who liked others meddling with their mate. But Sonnet radiated so much contentment, there was more than enough to share.

"You and Akira are precious to Jacques," she said. "May I consider you family?"

"Such generosity." Suuzu wasn't sure he deserved it. He'd been an awkward nestmate at best. "I was supposed to make any suitors woo Jacques away from me, but he flew to your side without a backward glance."

"I am willing to court him."

"Unnecessary. Although you may yet answer to Lord Mettlebright for taking his man to your heart and to your hearth."

Jacques said, "I'll want a word with Akira."

"You shall have it." Suuzu reminded, "He will insist on attending our exam."

"I need a wash." Jacques hurried to his armoire, and Anjou slipped into the *en suite*. The sound of running water came a moment later.

Sonnet cupped Suuzu's cheek, lifting his face. "You're carrying, too, aren't you, love?"

"Yes."

"Glad news."

"Hmm."

Sonnet was quite prepared to go on. "Akira must be beside himself. To think! A baby phoenix will certainly brighten things up."

Suuzu leaned into her touch. "Akira is like your Anjou, calling this child *our* baby."

"*My* Anjou," she echoed shyly.

Again, she sounded so pleased. Full of delight and properly possessive. It made Suuzu restless to belong to Akira in the same way. To share a nest, yes. But also its delights.

Suuzu's gaze drifted to where Jacques sat on one of the other examination tables in the healers' suite. The man was totally surrounded—Sonnet and Anjou, Elara and Akira. Even Nonny had barged in partway through his checkup, demanding details.

"Feeling left out?" asked Naoki, who eased up onto the cushioned table beside Suuzu, letting his legs swing.

"No." Suuzu admitted, "In some ways, it is a relief not to be the center of attention."

"Well, you have mine. How are you feeling?"

"Well enough."

"Appetite?"

"Mmm. I do forget to eat. But I am often reminded to try." He curved a hand over his abdomen. "Are there signs of malnourishment?"

"No, no. Nothing like that. But you really do need to eat more." Nodding toward his son, he said, "Akira will make sure of it."

"Yes. He has been very attentive."

Naoki eyed him closely. "And yet ...?"

Suuzu tucked his chin.

"I am willing to listen, even if it means learning that my son has been remiss in some way." Letting his shoulder gently bump Suuzu's arm, Naoki added, "Why so despondent?"

"Are you and Hajime ...?"

Naoki waited patiently for Suuzu to fill in the blank, but Suuzu wasn't sure how to ask if Naoki was like Akira. It was indelicate to ask, yet ... who else would know?

Finally, Suuzu asked, "Are you Hajime's brother?"

"That is not my role, no."

"Yet you share a bond."

Naoki inclined his head. "Are you curious about our story? Or perhaps my years? Or about the children we loved and left behind?"

Suuzu blinked.

"Or are you hoping that the nature of our relationship will give you insight into the bond you want to share with my son …?"

That was closer to the truth, but Suuzu found himself asking, "Other children?"

"Akira is the youngest of many."

Which begged a very important question. "What became of Lady Mettlebright's seed?"

"Ah, yes. You of all people would think of that." With a sheepish look in his son's direction, Naoki said, "I don't think you'll judge me *too* harshly. You see, we were on the run, so putting down roots wasn't an option. But Keishi was a good place, and raising a family there sounded nice. So we risked it, and Tsumiko was born. And because I've always believed siblings are important, I wanted to give her one. *Akira* is what became of Tsumiko's seed."

"You took her seed?"

"Yes. I took it and I swallowed it and I carried another child. We had done it before. Many times. We think that is part of the reason why I stopped aging, although it is only a guess." Naoki solemnly said, "That seed Akira holds now, the tree that springs from it will finally take root and flourish and know their brother's love."

"How many times?" Suuzu whispered.

"Ah. I've always loved children." Which wasn't a number. "A long while back, when it became important, we established a family registry. Older siblings would quietly bring in younger ones so they wouldn't simply spring from nowhere." He waved vaguely. "And with sons and daughters starting their own families, Hajime's legacy spread. Human children. Tree children. Akira's siblings are scattered throughout the world."

Suuzu was staggered by the enormity of Naoki's transgression. And yet …! As he said, Suuzu couldn't bring himself to criticize, since Akira was the result.

"Argent knows." Naoki smiled faintly. "He not only applauded the choices that led to Tsumiko's birth, he's encouraging me to try again. Since it's safe to do so."

Suuzu didn't really mean to hiss.

Sonnet turned his way, brows rising, and he lifted his hand in apology. Only after her tail began to sway again and her attention returned to Elara did Suuzu give Naoki a sheepish look.

"With a *new* seed," the man clarified. "Hajime is happy, and that always leads to fruiting. Who can say? If you or Akira decided to add to your family …?"

Suuzu allowed himself to imagine such a future. He whispered, "Truly?"

Naoki laughed and said, "Trees do love to be generous."

24

LATE BLOOMER

Everyone scattered after the exam, but Suuzu caught Akira's hand, needing … more. Only he couldn't think what to say. He wavered into a posture he'd learned from Juuyu, something from one of the phoenix courting dances, something Akira wouldn't even understand. Which was painfully frustrating.

Akira stepped closer, face upturned, expression open. "Yeah? What's up, Suuzu."

"I am so … confused."

"About what?"

Suuzu glanced up and down the hall, grabbed Akira's hand, and hurried him through the nearest door, which happened to lead to a second-floor laundry room. Nobody was using it at the moment, but if the stacks on the folding table were any indicator, this was where the mares washed bed linens and bath towels for the dormitories.

"Say, Suuzu? It's dark."

In a way, that made it easier to speak. Because even though Suuzu had no trouble seeing Akira's expression, Suuzu could hide his embarrassment. "I am not sure how to wait for what I want."

"Umm ... is this a tribute problem? Like you're not allowed to initiate any kind of courting behavior. Or is it a species thing? I'm human, so I'm missing a bunch of nuances that another avian would have picked up on? Or ... is it just a *me* problem, since I'm the latest blooming tree-kin that ever lived." Akira reached blindly, but he quickly found Suuzu. "If you're waiting for me to figure out what you need, I'll probably just disappoint you."

Suuzu sifted through Akira's hair and sighed. "You are *not* a problem. I apologize for making you think I am disappointed in *any* way."

Silence took over.

"Hey, now. Come on. Keep talking. This is important. We've always faced our differences before. We're just curious about different things now. At least, that's what I keep telling myself." Akira looped his arms loosely around Suuzu's waist. "We were brave, so we got closer. Best friends. Only now, we're figuring out a new kind of close. Because we're more than friends."

So Akira *had* been thinking about all of this.

Akira asked, "Remember when I was curious about your blaze?"

"I do." That conversation—and the cautious explorations that accompanied it—had deepened Suuzu's trust in Akira a hundredfold.

Smiling crookedly, Akira said, "And there was that whole body hair thing."

Suuzu hung his head. "I *am* sorry."

"You don't have to keep apologizing."

"Deeply, abjectly sorry."

"Oh, come on. Sure, it was awkward, and I'm never telling anyone. Ever. But it's kind of funny now." Akira eased a little closer. "We chalked it up to cultural exchange. No big deal."

But it had been. For Suuzu.

Akira went right on. "Looking back, when we were still in school, there were lots of times when I didn't know I was messing with your feelings. I was thoughtless. So I need to know. Am I being thoughtless now?"

"No." Suuzu's warble was too melancholy to be much of a bluff. "Seeing Jacques today …? I envy his happiness."

"Okay if I'm blunt? We can say it's in the interest of further cultural exchange."

"Please."

"I'm not … what did Jacques call it? I'm not *averse*."

"You confided in Jacques?"

"He's someone I trust, and he knows stuff." He gently reminded, "You asked him to bring us together. He wanted to help."

"Hmm."

"So … intimacy doesn't frighten me or disgust me, it just doesn't *occur* to me. Or it didn't. Now that I know how you feel …." Akira's eyes closed, and he muttered, "It's right there, whenever you look at me."

Suuzu ventured, "I … apologize?"

"No. Don't. What I'm trying to say is that you can get closer. You could kiss me again. I mean, I want to be the one you kiss.

The only one.”

Suuzu managed a weak, “Oh?”

“I need to see your face. Can I turn on the light? Or do you have any of those nightlight crystals?”

“One.”

Suuzu fumbled for it, and a soft golden glow warmed the space between them. As always, Akira’s expression brightened, as if he was perpetually glad to set eyes on him. Such a small thing. Such a heartening thing. Suuzu liked being the only thing Akira could see.

“Hey,” Akira said, gaze serious. “I’m not upsetting you?”

A small headshake. A sheepish smile.

“Good. So here’s the thing. I know I’m technically supposed to be the suitor. Maybe it’s not fair, but it would help me a lot if you took the lead with this stuff. I think I’ll be comfortable with anything you might want.”

Anything? Suuzu wanted everything.

“You’re still holding back.” Akira reached up, took hold of Suuzu’s hair, and pulled until he could reach. The kiss was as straightforward as its giver. “Haven’t you waited long enough?”

Suuzu had been rushed the first time he kissed Akira, and the only one since had been a stolen peck. This time, he wasn’t taking his nestmate by surprise. Akira was calmer than Suuzu by a longshot, but there was an expectancy to his posture. He was facing their differences. He was willing to explore them.

So Suuzu stopped holding back. A little.

With whispery tuts and murmurs, he pressed kisses to Akira’s lips.

To his amazement, Akira coaxed him deeper, which was *good*. And distracting enough that Suuzu found himself contemplating the tidy stacks of linens and towels as nesting material. "Wait," he managed.

Akira, who'd gone up on tiptoe, was practically beaming. "How come? This is nice."

"Oh. Well … yes."

Then his nestmate's hands were in his hair, and he was exploring Suuzu's fangs, and suddenly, there was a nibble, and Suuzu's knees gave out. He sank to the floor.

Akira knelt in front of him, eyes alight. "More?"

Suuzu nodded, then shook his head. "Perhaps not just now. I would prefer not to establish our nest in a communal space."

"Very sensible." And with startling composure, Akira said, "Hey, I know."

Then without any real fuss, Akira carefully unpinned his courting gift from Suuzu's tunic. He smiled at the circlet of nine nippet eggs, turning it this way and that in the soft light. And making up his mind, he repinned it against swagging pleats with the vert nippet egg topmost.

"A gift," Akira said simply. "From me to you. For keeps this time. Okay?"

Suuzu managed a strangled warble.

He hadn't expected this, even though he'd been waiting for it … wanting it.

Akira showed no trace of impatience, his gaze soft. Like he knew—because of course he knew—that Suuzu would need time to compose himself.

"Yes," he finally managed.

Nodding once, Akira moved on. "Did I get it right? The color matters, doesn't it? Something about secret messages. Kyrie said this would please you, but he wouldn't tell me why."

Suuzu looked down at the tiny green eggshell that carried a message he'd learned only recently. "In avian courting games, the vert nippet egg may be the most appropriate for a tree-kin. It is an invitation. You are asking me to help you bloom."

"Oh! That *is* pretty perfect." Akira turned around, taking his usual spot, using Suuzu as a backrest.

"Hmm." Suuzu began toying with Akira's hair, which would help calm him down.

"So secret messages, huh? Do you want me to ask for help? Or would you rather teach your suitor about courting games?"

"No need."

"Really?" Akira tipped his head back, trying to see Suuzu's face. "It seems like something I could learn. I mean, it's gotta be easier than dance lessons with Jacques."

Suuzu supposed it was appropriate that this, like everything else that had gone before, had been accidental. "You are no longer my suitor. Your suit is wholeheartedly accepted. I am yours."

"Really?"

"Truly."

"Okay, that was *much* simpler than a three-year courtship with a full-time staff and publicity campaign."

"Much."

"So ... we're bondmates?"

"We are."

Akira sat there, totally relaxed. His calm was catching, and Suuzu returned to preening.

Finally, Akira tipped his head back, once more seeking Suuzu's gaze. "Are you disappointed? I didn't do anything to make this special. I mean, you deserve better than an ultra-private non-ceremony in a laundry room. Weddings should be memorable."

"The founding of a nest does not require ceremony. Only … love."

"Yeah? We're set then." And with the simple acceptance that had first drawn Suuzu to him, Akira said, "I love you, too."

25

BRIEF AND DEBRIEF

Hisoka didn't budge when someone knocked. From what he could tell, Argent had rigged things so that anyone who could *find* his door was also able to open it.

Moments later, Sinder tentatively asked, "Hisoka? Are you … decent?"

He pushed an arm out and waved blindly.

"Oookay, we'll call that good." There was a cautious shifting of layers, and Sinder's face appeared. "Hey, boss. You're looking … well, you kind of look like crap. Rough week? Or … a couple weeks, I guess."

"What do you want?"

Sinder's face registered surprise. "There's this thing we do. Standard routine. I report in, and you send me out again."

"I'm not in charge at the moment."

"So I gathered, since Canarian's been sending end-of-day

summaries. I caught up with those last night, so I figured I should see what you need. Oh, and uhh ... before you reveal any deep, dark secrets, is it okay that I have a plus one? I kind of picked up a tagalong."

Hisoka hadn't realized the scent Sinder was sporting was quite so *fresh*. "Fend ...?"

"Uncle."

Propping up on an elbow, he considered the Kith. "Did you need something?"

"I've taken a liking to your reach. So I'm keeping him on a short leash."

His attention bounced briefly to Sinder. *"You already have a reaver partner."*

"Timur is a man of good sense." The big cat curled his tail around his feet and remained in a studiously neutral posture. One that implied polite respect. Between equals.

Hisoka wasn't sure how to react. "Sinder, is Fend making a nuisance of himself?"

The dragon hesitated. "He's not so bad when he's not sinking his teeth in. Did I show you my scars from last summer?"

"So you've made peace?"

"More like he's got plans for me." Sinder grumpily added, "He wants me put out to pasture so Timur's wee ickle Spomenka hoarde can rough me up."

Hisoka's brows arched. "Remind me. How many children did he sire?"

"Counting Gregor? Twenty-five."

Looking to Fend, Hisoka asked, "Is Timur hoping to lead their summer courses?"

"Far better to offer a full scholarship to Stately House. Let the grandparents sort the battlers from the wards, then initiate a dynasty-class mentoring program."

Hisoka sat up, rearranging blankets and pillows before conceding, "That's a good idea."

"Very well. Suggest it to Argent. Timur will be entirely grateful." Fend blinked placidly. *"Michael, too."*

Hisoka acquiesced with a slow nod.

Sinder asked, "Is he ordering *you* around now?"

"I wouldn't go that far." Surely this matter was the reason for Fend's visit. It was only natural for him to want Timur's happiness, even if he resorted to roundabout methods.

The big cat rose, his gaze unwavering as he stalked forward.

"Yeah, yeah," muttered Sinder, backing away so Fend had a clear path.

"Following orders?" Hisoka asked, mystified by the traces of deference in Sinder's posture.

"Sure. Why not? I usually do what *you* say. Maybe by now, it's reflexive." In wry tones, he added, "I remember when he was *this* big. Much cuter when all he could manage was baby talk."

"Uncle." Fend leapt onto the bed and prowled closer, planting his front paws on Hisoka's thighs. Then he proceeded to rub their cheeks together, the barest rumble of a purr building between them. *"Grab hold since I cannot."*

Hisoka wrapped his arms as far as they would go, burying his fingers in plush fur.

"Tell me the truth."

"What did you want to know?"

"Are you able to leave this room?"

Hisoka flinched. *"It's not as if I'm locked in."*

"Will you leave if I give you a reason to do so?"

"I can't imagine what …?"

"Hunt with me." Fend wasn't pleading. That had been an order. *"Come hunting, Uncle. Tonight, we'll have a nice, long prowl."*

"Ah."

"You have no reason to refuse, do you?" Still nuzzling and purring, Fend smugly said, *"I will hold you to your word."*

"I did not give my word."

"You need this, Uncle. You need me." Fend licked Hisoka's ear and rumbled, *"Yield."*

With a snort and a smile, Hisoka said, *"All right. Yes. I yield."* There was no harm in humoring a kinsman.

Fend placed a dainty lick upon his brow, then flopped languorously across Hisoka's lap, purring in noisy contentment.

A short distance away, Sinder sat on the floor, slouched against a small sofa, wrists on knees, hands hanging loosely. For once, there was no technology in evidence. All of the young dragon's attention was pinned on him and Fend.

"How much of that did you hear?" asked Hisoka.

"None of it. Reaches can't eavesdrop, so it's up to you if we're included or excluded. But it looks to me like Fend got his way."

"He did."

When he volunteered nothing else, Sinder moved on. "Sooo, post-mission debrief time? Any interesting aftermath stuff? Persons of interest?"

When Hisoka didn't immediately answer, Sinder rolled his eyes.

"I'm assuming Rhomiko isn't a state secret since I spotted him in the garden with Deece. What gives?"

"Not *him*. Them. And there's very little I can tell you."

"Because you don't know? Or because you won't say?"

Hisoka had no idea what expression he made, but Sinder reacted by angling his head to communicate apology.

"You know what? That's fine. I can do the legwork. Firsthand information's best anyhow. So I'll settle for *that*. Or ... I guess they'd be another *them*." He pointed at the wad of bedding from which Hisoka had emerged earlier. "Tell me about them."

"Ah. You noticed."

"I'm a dragon. Crystal affinity for days. You're warming a wardstone." Sinder made a helpless gesture with his hands. "Timur has ours."

"Ah." Did that make this simpler? Or more revealing?

"You've got to be thrilled to the tips of your whiskers. These guys are curiosities and mysteries and bundles of possibility. Exactly your sort of thing."

"Which is why I urged Michael to leave this one with me. That and ... these crystals really are too heavy for a human to be carrying around."

"Someone should tell that to *my* baby-buddy. Our imp is being used as a free weight, contributing to Michaelson's muscle mass. It's leg day."

"I see."

"So did you and the illustrious First of Wards figure out anything? I assume the goal is hatching. Or ... what's the right lingo? Emerging? Jacques is going to be all kinds of happy if we can increase the population of Widelands rock-folk."

Hisoka nodded, hoping that Sinder's rambling wouldn't circle back. But dragons were wily, and Sinder had proven exceptional at his job. Which mostly involved collecting secrets.

"This has 'confluence of destinies' written all over it. These wardstones came to us for good reason. Orchestrator of the Emergence, First of Wards, two from his dynasty, a couple of dragons. Extrapolating the runt of the litter's pick could involve hours of fun for me, but it'd probably be quicker to ask your oracle. Or you. You and Michael … you have a theory." It wasn't even a question.

"You have it all wrong, lovely one. This isn't about power or influence."

Both Hisoka and Sinder looked to Fend.

"Selections from Michael's dynasty are incidental. A necessity of location."

Sinder sighed. "Look, you. I started with the obvious stuff. It's called brainstorming."

"I'd say you're too close to the problem, but in reality, I want you to get even closer. The imp is reinforcing my earlier point." And with a sly lick to Hisoka's chin, Fend purred, "Tell *him,* Uncle."

Hisoka couldn't seem to meet Sinder's keen gaze. "Michael speculated that the rock imps are drawn to a preexisting bond. Strong feelings or perhaps even … ah … attachment …?"

"Okay, sure. I'll buy that. Michaelson kept me on my feet while we were at Wardenclave together, and when the time came …." Sinder flattened a palm over his own heart. "He was the one who helped me regain the sky. That kind of thing? It means a lot.

When you pulled me off the training detail? That was hard."

"Because you missed Timur."

"Yeah. Waaseyaa, too. And Zisa. But Timur? I dunno. I wrote it off as the memorability of a potent soul. And he knows his way around dragons. Found spikenard for me. Redecorated the whole cabin in my comfort colors. He was great."

"*He may as well have been courting,*" interjected Fend.

"It wasn't like that!"

Hisoka casually asked, "Were you bond-building?"

"No! It was just ...." Sinder whispered, "Shit, I don't know. I *did* want to get here. To see him again."

Fend asked, "*Why is everyone shying away from the obvious? The rock babies are responding to a strong emotion they associate with their parent. You're suitable because you're similarly tragic in your pining.*"

Sinder said, "A captive rock imp, last of his kind, longing for ... well, it could be any number of things. Freedom. Lost love. All these kids they took from him. The promised Smythe."

Hisoka slid a hand under the covers to touch the wardstone. "You think we're also in impossible situations? That we exhibit an unrequited longing."

"*Just call it* love *and move on to the more important question.*"

Sinder said, "I admit nothing, you pushy conniver. But I do want to know what you think is the more important question."

"*Why do they resonate?*"

Hisoka considered the question, then started with the obvious. "Because crystals resonate."

"Not for no reason," rejoined Sinder. "And these don't just resonate. They *respond.* They're sentient."

Hisoka reviewed his conversation with Michael. "They're sentient, yes. But they're in their infancy. They're resonating because they don't have words yet."

Sinder's trill had an impatient quality. "Why me? Why not Tsumiko or Sonnet or Catalan or Elara. Plenty of people around here are way better at being parents."

Fend butted in. *"Everyone you just volunteered as a replacement is in an established, settled, flourishing bond. Your imp has a taste for unresolved feelings."*

"Why are you so set on shoving me into Michaelson's lap? We're friends, okay?"

"If you prefer, I could push Timur into your lap." Fend's tail flicked playfully. *"You do interesting things to his scent. With a little encouragement …!"*

Sinder grumbled, "Back off already."

"No." Fend drawled, *"You'll come around. I'll see to it."*

Hisoka chose not to remark upon the interesting things happening with Fend's and Sinder's scents. Felines did so love to toy, and dragons craved attention. These two seemed to be enjoying themselves, after a fashion. Perhaps he should have a word with Timur, though. Make certain the man wasn't caught in the middle.

Ah.

Well, now.

It would seem Hisoka had plans. Plural. A welcome turn of events, thanks to these two. These two *children*. Hisoka had always enjoyed teaching children.

"You little shit!"

"Haven't you tired yet of this token resistance?"

"Give it up. I won't cooperate!"

"Sway doesn't work on Kith."

"Yeah, well what abou–"

Sinder's exclamation cut off when Fend sprang from the bed, knocking Sinder sideways and bathing his face. The dragon wriggled and pushed and broadcast a tirade of dire oaths that soon petered into apologies, grumbles, and an undignified squeak.

"Hey. That tickles!"

"Hmm? Show me where."

"You're the absolute worst!"

"Nonsense. I am your best outcome."

"Can't be," Sinder exclaimed, though he didn't sound entirely sure on that score.

Hisoka raised his voice, much as he would if calling a classroom to order. "There is another possibility, I think. Rather than parents, we may be functioning as midwives. Once the children are here, they may gravitate toward more suitable minders."

"No. No way. Maybe the rock imps won't care, but for us—for Amaranthine—birthing is a bond. If I coddle that rock alongside Timur for however long it takes, and they hatch into my hands …? That's a trigger for *my* instincts. That kid will own a part of me." Sinder wriggled up onto his elbows, though his lower body was still pinned by Fend. "I'm not one of the fathers, and I'm no good at this crap. But I know that's how it works because of Kyrie."

"You consider him yours?" Fend asked. *"How endearingly paternal."*

"What? No! It's the other way around. I'm one of his." And more gruffly, "We're incredibly selfish, dragons."

"The fathers are strong, but the brothers are not weak," intoned Hisoka.

"*If we're bandying about dragon proverbs, another is more appropriate,*" Fend said crisply. "*Rest, regard, and revenge cannot be rushed.*"

Hisoka balked. "I hardly think *revenge* is the appropriate term."

"*No?*" Fend turned to look at him. "*This is as personal for you as it is for Kyrie.*"

"Kyrie could not help how he came into this world."

The big cat's eyes narrowed. "*Nor could you help how Shisoku came into this world. Or Doku and Kodoku before him.*"

"How ... did you ...?"

"*I pay attention.*" And in a gentler tone, "*Stop blaming yourself.*"

Hisoka felt sick.

Sinder gave Fend another useless shove. "You know, I still say they're the key. The Rogue's kids might be young, but if they're anything like Kyrie ...? He's the right kind of scary."

"Even so." A growl slipped under Hisoka's next words. "We are not sending children to war."

"Yyyeah, you're totally right. Sorry. That was the wrong kind of scary."

"*If you're done being* heinous," interjected Fend. "*Why are you afraid of Kyrie?*"

"Ever seen him in action?"

"*I really couldn't say.*" Fend dragged his tongue up the side of Sinder's throat. "*Tell me what you think you know.*"

"The only person who scares me more is Juuyu, but some of that's instinctual."

Hisoka lifted a hand. "When you say Kyrie scares you, are you pinpointing him as a potential threat?"

"No, not like that. *Scary* as in … healthy respect. Kyrie's a sweet kid, but when he gets serious? Let's just say he'll win. No matter his opponent, my money's on Kyrie."

"Are you being literal?" asked Hisoka. "*Any* opponent?"

"Juuyu and Boon have more experience. Argent … fewer scruples. But sure. In battler games or a tracker challenge, I think Kyrie would come out on top."

"*He is* mostly *correct,*" Fend said with calm authority. "*Impressions are a factor.*"

Of course. Trees. Hisoka hadn't realized the subtle import of surrounding Stately House with a grove. If any trouble arose with the dragon crossers, an Amaranthine tree could intervene. Better still to surround the Rogue's children with good influences. Which Argent had already done. And if Michael had his way, Hisoka could become one of those influences.

Maker bless.

How had he missed it?

It was so obvious now.

If Hisoka agreed, he would be teaching Nemi's descendants. He could do that much for Nemi. Hoshiko and Hiroki would have wanted it.

Something frantic inside of Hisoka calmed.

He would have to speak to Argent.

Because Hisoka finally knew what he wanted to do.

"Uhh … Hisoka? Did you hear what Fend just said?" Sinder had extricated himself from Fend, and he'd crossed to the window. "I think we better get Boon in here. Firsthand really is best for this kind of thing."

"What did I miss?"

Fend strolled back to bump noses with Hisoka. *"The winds of change."*

26

CHILD OF STATELY HOUSE

Argent didn't mind being abed so long as Tsumiko nestled with him, but as soon as she left their suite, he was done with confinement. Dressing in the first clothes that came to hand, he skulked—slowly—down the hall to his receiving room. The largeish parlor was a secure space in which he played host whenever other members of the Amaranthine Council were visiting.

Make that a *formerly* secure space.

"Hello, sweetheart," he murmured, joining Bother in Lapis's favorite chair, the one closest to the hearth.

His new daughter wrapped shimmering coils around his middle and pressed her ear to his heart. Her addition to the family felt appropriate somehow. A child with Ephemeral heritage. Could she have found a more doting parent? Not that she was something to collect. This girl was theirs to protect and theirs to cherish. Hooking the footstool with his toe, Argent pulled it nearer and propped his feet. And promptly dozed off.

"Here, guv. Your tea."

Argent startled and glared at Nonny, who studiously pretended nothing was out of the ordinary.

"Sonnet sent muffins. She's in a fine mood this morning. Been baking up a storm."

This tendency to nap was Argent's least favorite part of healing. It made him feel doubly vulnerable. He peered around. Bother had gone, and the sun was high. He uncurled enough to accept the teacup Nonny proffered.

"Speaking of storms, Kyrie wants a word."

Argent took a heartening swallow of hot tea before remarking, "He hardly needs an appointment."

"That's what I thought, but he still wanted permission. On account of his hangers-on. We've been subject to sudden gusts, which is bad for bookshelves. And drizzle, but that happened in the onsen, so nothing was damaged. And the kids loved it."

Argent didn't particularly like that an Eldermost Storm had access to the children. But he trusted Ginkgo and Kyrie to have the family's interests at heart. So he only said, "I will endeavor not to trigger a blizzard."

"Anan's … different. It'll be good to get your opinion. And Jacques'."

"Send for him. I want him." He grumbled, "A return to normalcy would be welcome."

"Not sure that's possible. Going back to normal, I mean. Too many big changes."

"Forward, then. Toward a new normal. I have never been one to cling to the past."

"Right. Yeah. Adjustments all around."

Argent knew that tone, and his eyes narrowed. "Well?"

Nonny pointed at the footstool. "Okay if I sit?"

He moved his feet, and the goat-crosser settled there, close enough for confidences.

As a child, Nonny had been afraid of him. Not because of anything Argent had ever done, but because of what he was. A fox. Like many of the children who'd found shelter at Stately House, Nonny had bad memories—and bad dreams—involving vulpine tormentors.

Nonny took a shaky breath, then surprised Argent by announcing, "I love it here."

"As do I." Argent affected unconcern. "It is a fine thing to love one's home."

Nonny stared fixedly at the hands clenched in his lap. "I … aww, hell. I love it so much. You don't even understand."

"Then help me understand."

"There's so much happening. I'm not one to gossip, but I do like to keep up with what's up, so to speak. And there's so many changes. Big ones. But it's not bad, it's … I dunno. It's like one of them bardic tales Opal swains on about. All the happenstances and coincidences are fitting together, like things are getting to the way they were always meant to be. Only how the hell could anyone have guessed? It's one bloody miracle after another."

Nonny's gaze was the pleading sort, but Argent wasn't sure what this boy—one of their original orphans—was trying to say.

"And things'll keep changing, because that's how it always is. And I don't want to miss any of it." Nonny waved a hand, and his voice took on a strained note. "The future is gonna be amazing, and I want to see it."

Ah. This. Argent raised a hand, wanting to spare Nonny.

But the crosser had it out anyhow. "I don't want to *die*, guv. Can't you fix it so I can stay? Maybe one of them tattoos? Or y'know, something like what Akira found? I know I'm not important for the future of the world or whatever, but ... let me stay? *Please*?"

Already pulling Nonny close, Argent grumbled, "Take a breath and give me space to answer."

Heedless, he blathered on. "Why'm I the only one? I know it's just shitty luck, but why me?"

Nonny had always been small for his age. He'd stopped gaining height around the same time he'd achieved Argent's, so he was an awkward lapful. Even so, Argent made it work and brought out his full flourish. Wreathing his fosterling in silver fur, Argent quietly ordered, "Stop panicking."

His boy bit his lip and fell silent.

For years, Nonny had claimed to be glad that he hadn't inherited an Amaranthine's years. Unlike the rest of Stately House's orphans, he'd leapt through his adolescence, aging like a human. Though nobody could say for certain, it was safe to suppose this meant Nonny's lifespan would match a human's as well. So brief. Too short.

But up until now, Nonny had claimed that this was perfect for him. He'd wanted to grow up as fast as possible. To catch up. To close the distance between him and the one—the *ones*—he loved. But those big changes Nonny had mentioned included Jacques.

Chances were good that Dayith's and Solace's blessings had altered the man's years. But even before this unforeseen inheritance, Argent had been searching for a way to keep Jacques. To that end, he'd already been in communication with Kikusawa Shrine in hopes of securing the two golden seeds resting in their reliquarium.

Argent said, "I had already given the matter some thought."

"You ... did?"

"I would not lie, Nonny. Not about something so important." With a gusty sigh, he whispered, "I am trying to be wise."

"I'm willing to be the exception. Just so you know."

Argent was equally willing, so he lifted his face and quietly called, "Hajime?"

The soft *ting* of a bell. The gentle drift of red petals. "I am here."

"Is Naoki similarly available?"

"A moment." And in less than a minute, the tree returned. "We are here."

"Has there been a relapse, Argent? Or ... oh, my. Is something else amiss?"

Argent said, "You remember Nonny? One of my more reckless sons."

Nonny's face registered surprise.

Did he really not realize the place he held?

Letting his tails drop so Naoki could see that Nonny was in one piece, Argent said, "About that matter we discussed earlier. I am recommending Nonny as a candidate for pairing. Or parenthood, if he and his are so inclined."

"What?" Nonny squeaked. "What are you on about, guv?"

Argent sternly said, "This requires the utmost secrecy."

Nonny immediately made a handsign to swear it.

"When Dr. Naoki came to us, he carried precious cargo. A single case, filled to bursting. Dozens of tiny bottles and jars, holding the results of Kodoku's experiments."

"*Seeds*," whispered Nonny. "You smuggled golden seeds?"

"As many as I could carry," Naoki confirmed. "I managed Kodoku's collection, kept records, preserved samples. They *are* golden seeds, but they're experimental hybrids. I honestly have no idea if they'll behave as golden seeds should. We had no luck simply planting them. And many were born without a twin. Variations cropped up at every turn, but I wouldn't call them failures. For example, Kusunoki didn't conform to what's usual, yet he thrived."

"I know him," said Nonny. "He's nice."

"Yes." Naoki smiled at Hajime. "A true son of trees."

"I carried him," the imp revealed.

"It was the only way." Naoki gestured between himself and Nonny. "It may *still* be the only way. For them. But for you ...? Hajime is fruiting. If you would prefer to wait for a seed you can simply plant, his will be ready long before the new grove reaches maturity."

Nonny flung his arms around Argent and cussed him out with a vehemence that only made sense if you understood Nonny. Smiling and petting his hair, Argent mildly translated, "He wants to. Very much."

When Sibley turned up at their door with a summons, Jacques brightened … and immediately rounded on Anjou, casting a critical eye over his attire and finding no fault. "Right, then. Shall we?"

Anjou had been quietly dreading this moment. He tried to protest. "You are the one he wants."

"And he shall have me, but with all my assorted baggage and consequences." And pulling Anjou's arm through his own, Jacques murmured, "Courage, *mon ami*. There's nothing to fear."

"What if your fine lord objects to me?"

Jacques didn't hesitate. "Then I'll rebel against him by treasuring you with unapologetic flagrance."

A little breathlessly, Anjou asked, "You would do that?"

"I would, but there won't be any particular need to rebel against Argent. He'll come around once he realizes that the things you want are simple and good. Sonnet's opinion will sway him as well." Jacques radiated so much confidence. "Keeping your lady mistress happy will go a long way toward appeasing any ruffled sensibilities."

"She has become my *raison d'être*."

"Argent is similarly smitten with his lady, so I'm sure he'll sympathize. Privately, of course. He doesn't like to let on." They reached their destination, but Jacques paused on the threshold. "Ready?"

"*Non.*"

Jacques simply nodded.

Anjou was startled to realize that the man was willing to wait. For him. Delighted by such consideration, he confessed, "I would do anything to stay by your side."

"That's the spirit." And still he waited.

"A kiss for courage?"

Jacques lifted Anjou's hand, kissed its back, and showed no sign of impatience.

"A bolder kiss would make me a braver companion."

"Remind me to test the veracity of your statement later."

Something in Jacques' smile suggested that he wouldn't need reminding, but Anjou liked to be asked for things, wanted to please, enjoyed imagining where bolder kisses might land. He bit his lip and tried to keep the volume of his purr to polite levels.

And still Jacques waited.

Anjou rather wanted to stay like this, so he prolonged the moment by asking, "How should I call you in front of your foxy lord?"

"I suppose it would get confusing if you were 'my lord'-ing me whilst I'm 'my-lord'-ing him. Are there any feline precedents for a term that applies to your bonded?"

Anjou's breath caught. "What?"

"In theory, the male equivalent of lady mistress is lord master, but I don't care for it. Too pompous, and it hardly fits Sonnet's cozy ideal."

Again, he whispered, "What?"

Jacques paused. "What?"

"*Sonnet* is your bonded."

"Certainly. We're thoroughly, enthusiastically, devotedly bonded. As are you and I. Or did you forget your part in the proceedings?"

"Consorts don't … ah. That is … the toms at a lady mistress's hearth cannot aspire to such ...." He trailed off, because Jacques had a pained expression.

"See here, Anjou. I'm aware that in the feline courts, toms can expect to be bartered and borrowed and bedded by various and sundry, but you're *ours*."

"*Oui*, I am your man."

"Well, yes. In terms of employment."

"And I am Sonnet's consort."

"Which could *also* be described as a job, since you've taken on the management of our hearth. A very traditional role, one most toms aspire to. But *Anjou*." Jacques pressed a soft kiss to his parted lips. "In terms of dearness and duration, you are just as thoroughly, enthusiastically, devotedly bonded. Rather than consort, you are he-wolf and husband, *n'est-ce pas?*"

Anjou hadn't wanted to presume.

His upbringing forbade it.

But isn't this why he'd used his wiles?

To have something denied most toms.

Without compulsion or compunction.

Without end.

"Lord, I'll speak with Sonnet. Give us another chance to impress upon you the fervor of our attachment and the permanence of ou–"

Anjou cut him off with a finger to his lips. "Husband."

Jacques glided into a receptive posture. "Hmm?"

"I am ready."

With a light kiss for Anjou's finger, Jacques whirled in order to burst through the door, moments later exclaiming, "*Mon dieu! What* are you wearing?"

Jacques carted off his lord and master, insisting on an immediate change of attire. Anjou was intrigued by the cavalier manner with which he treated the fox, as well as the tail-settling calm that overtook Lord Mettlebright as soon as he was in his man's capable hands.

Here was a great and abiding trust. One Jacques clearly expected the fox to extend to him.

All at once, Argent's gaze found Anjou's and he drawled, "Smythe. Explain yourself."

"Lord. Are you going to be difficult?"

"I do have a reputation to uphold. You so rarely introduce me to your bedmates."

"*Difficult* it is, then." And without any sign of perturbation, Jacques presented Anjou in the glowingest of terms, calling him a country gentleman, comparing his beauty to moonbeams, and framing his indispensability in flatteringly salacious terms.

Argent blandly asked, "Are you certain you should be taking so much exercise?"

Anjou blushed, but Jacques cheerfully said, "Dr. Naoki performed a thorough inspection, and Dr. Elara credits the uplift in my mood to all that healthful exercise."

"And the child?" Argent pressed.

"Clinging quite tenaciously. The tendril will spiral outward for another turn or two before we can expect the pod to make its appearance." Jacques startled Anjou by calmly adding, "He'll be Papa, and Sonnet will be Mum."

The fox didn't seem at all surprised. "And you?"

"To tell the truth, I fancy *daddy*. Unironically, of course."

Anjou had expected to care for Jacques' child, looked forward to it with a gladness that was growing by the moment. But to be assigned a parental endearment ...? No, it was more than that. "I'm going to be a *father*," he realized aloud.

"That, too." Jacques indicated his lord and master. "But I was thinking of something more along the lines of undersecretary. If you can be available during the hours when I need sleep, his lordship will no longer be inconvenienced."

"You have never been a detriment, Smythe," grumbled Argent. "Do not even imply it."

"Yes, my lord."

And then the fox faced Anjou with a peevish expression and his tails all askew. "What am I supposed to do with you?"

"I am ... open to suggestion."

Jacques stepped in with a ready answer. "Anjou is from a large rural enclave. I suggest your having me keep my focus on Council business while entrusting Anjou with more practical matters."

"The house and grounds are Ginkgo's area."

"Wouldn't he welcome assistance in one or more areas? There's the household, the school, the enclave, and the grove. And it bears mentioning that Anjou is the Bonhomie tribute."

Argent's gaze returned to Anjou, and he felt he should speak for himself. "I must see to my lady mistress's hearth, but until our baby comes ...? I am available to take on any suitable occupation."

"*Anything* I deem suitable?" the fox challenged.

It felt like a trap.

Jacques smoothly interjected, "Something Sonnet would approve."

"Agreed," Argent sighed.

Anjou appreciated the condition, which reinforced his sudden elevation. He belonged to a household, would rule over its hearth, and could expect the support—and protection—of two formidable bondmates. Thoughts wandering in the direction of all the ways he could show himself grateful, Anjou slipped into a receptive posture.

"Will you be needing a house?" asked Argent.

Jacques hummed. "Perhaps once this little one is ready to plant their seed, I'll need a bit of something with a front step. Largely to uphold tradition. But I'm content to remain in the family quarters for now. Provided we're welcome."

"I have no objections."

"And you need me."

"I need you," Argent acquiesced, sounding amused. "But that one is rather more needy."

Anjou realized they were both watching him, which was pleasantly flustering.

Jacques remarked, "I have finally gotten what I deserve. Wouldn't you say this arrangement suits a man of my inclinations."

"Shockingly well." Argent carefully levered himself up out of his chair, a sobering reminder that his injuries were only a day old. "Anjou, I have sorted out your first duty as my man's man."

"*Oui*? But of course! Happily."

Again there was that hint of amusement in his gaze. "You say that now."

Crossing to a cloth-draped table, he lifted away heavy fabric, revealing the toddler who'd been hiding beneath, a muffin clutched in each fist. Scruffing the boy, Argent tucked him into the crook of his arm. Crumbs scattered everywhere, and Jacques whispered, "Lord, there goes the silk. Why do I even bother?"

Heedless of the fresh smear of half-chewed baked goods across his shoulder, Argent said, "Anjou, meet Etienne. Mind his claws. They're poisonous."

Anjou swooped in, though it was hard to say if he was trying to rescue the child or the silk. "Oo la la laaa," he crooned. "What have we here? Are you enamored of my lady mistress's baking?"

The boy—a dragon crosser with the most atrocious haircut—perked up at the sound of his mother tongue and offered Anjou a mangled muffin.

"What a generous soul! How could I refuse?" He opened his mouth, and Etienne pushed in a morsel. Humming appreciatively, Anjou tucked the dragonling under his chin and asked, "What is my duty? His diaper? His bath? Dare I hope ... his hair? All three need attention."

Argent flicked a finger. "Etienne himself. The whole of him."

Anjou's gaze jumped to Jacques, who asked, "For how long?"

"However long he has need of you."

"You're giving us one of your sons?" Jacques asked. "To raise."

"Etienne will be registered as a child of Stately House, and I will forever consider him a son. But yes, I wish to foster him at your hearth. If Anjou is willing, I will consider the matter settled."

Anjou waited to see what Jacques would say.

But Jacques seemed to be awaiting his opinion.

Embracing his newfound freedom to choose for himself, Anjou nuzzled Etienne's cheeks, purring and whispering invitations and promises in French. The little boy lapsed into trilling giggles. But after Etienne caught his breath, he spoke the name Anjou surrendered along with his heart. *Papa.*

27

TOTAL DREAM TEAM

Sinder sat on the floor in Michaelson's room, surrounded by sheets of paper. He'd turned the bedside table into a cramped workstation where one of his backup laptops teetered on stacked packets. Heralds had begun arriving within an hour of his first text to acting Spokesperson Canarian Evernhold, and they were *still* arriving at regular intervals.

He'd caught up before visiting Hisoka, but that was different from staying caught up.

Printed reports. Scanned articles. Meeting minutes. Also detailed dictation, all handwritten on Dimityblest paper and protected by sigilcraft, all intended for Spokesperson Twineshaft's eyes only. Which was fine. Sinder had clearance. He'd been Hisoka's eyes for long enough to know what to look for.

Sinder was peripherally aware that Michaelson was nearby, moving around the room. At one point, a sandwich had been thrust into his hand. And there was always tea in his cup—hot and spicy and slightly sweet. Much better than the stuff Sinder had been repeatedly dosed with last summer.

Speaking of ...! Sinder scanned a report from Torloo-dex Elderbough, which included an update on the allotment of reavers Sinder had helped train. Naroo-soh's finest had all been matched with Kith partners.

"You're smiling."

Sinder dragged his attention from the page, only to wonder where the hell he was. "What did you *do*?"

"Just a little rearranging. To make you more comfortable." Timur was dressed for bed, pajama pants and a T-shirt. He glanced around, then shrugged. "Fend helped."

The idiot had redecorated, just like he'd done at Zisa's cottage in Wardenclave. Rugs and screens and hangings and lampshades and crystals. Everything in shades of yellow. Sinder's comfort color.

Belatedly, he grabbed his phone and checked the time. Nearly eleven, which was late enough to be rude. "I'm keeping you up."

Timur shrugged and shook his head. "Why were you smiling?"

"A pile of shiny new dossiers. Some old friends reached their attainment. Want a look?" He flapped the files invitingly.

Timur lowered himself to the floor at his side and soon sighed. "How can you be happy for them?"

"Why wouldn't I be?"

"They tormented you." Timur slipped an arm around Sinder's back, spreading one big hand over his side. "They scarred you."

"Oh, don't be so grumpy. Look at her face." A young woman was aglow, caught mid-laugh by the camera as her new Kith companion rearranged her battler braids. "She worked damned hard to win that hawk's good opinion. And this guy. He's in love, and that Nightspangle wolf's just as smitten. Total dream team. They'll do great."

Timur relented enough to reminisce. Sinder tried not to be distracted when the man's chin came to rest on top of his head.

"So ... where's Fend?"

"Out. Something about going hunting with his uncle. He's probably with Catalan."

"Pretty sure he's with Hisoka."

"That so?" Timur didn't even sound moderately surprised. Or interested. Just sort of ... distracted.

Sinder flipped through the rest of the profiles before asking, "Do you *actually* think you and Fend can take down the Rogue alone?"

"Not alone, no."

"Then why humor your cat?"

Timur mildly inquired, "Why do *you* humor my cat?"

Sinder slouched into Timur and suggested, "Self-preservation?"

The man squeezed Sinder's shoulder. "Come help me warm our wardstone."

"I'm on rock-baby duty? Hold up. Where's Gregor?"

"On loan. Papka is trying to acclimate some of our new dragonlings to the feel of a reaver's soul, so Gregor, Vanya, and Lilya are bedding down in the naproom for the foreseeable future. Normally, I'd be there with them, but ... well. I thought we could take advantage of the quiet."

"To sleep. You *need* sleep."

"I don't need to be awake for you to access my soul."

Sinder went very still. "Unsafe much?"

"I trust you."

"I'm flattered and all, but no. You shouldn't tempt dragons."

"No?" Timur folded down blankets revealing their wardstone. "I'm very good at it."

Sinder was catching whiffs of crisp linen and checked the bedsheets. The man had added an electric blanket to the bed, and the thing was cranked to toasty. "Okay, you're good. Maybe even too good to be true." He slapped his laptop shut and dove under covers.

Timur pottered around the room longer, and Sinder watched him in a state of limpening bliss. Until it occurred to him that the wrong person was basking in bed. "Are you avoiding your responsibilities? I thought you were supposed to be helping me warm the proverbial egg."

Without a word, the man doused the lights and slid into bed. A moment later, a hand found Sinder's shoulder and began to knead. Sinder had expected it. Michaelson had been just as clingy all last summer, but the wardstone was definitely a hinderance.

"Let me try something," the man murmured.

As the blankets and pillows shifted, Sinder retreated further under the covers, not wanting to lose his pocket of heat.

Eventually, Timur stopped flapping cold air into Sinder's burrow. "Safe to come back."

Sinder didn't resist when he grabbed hold and pulled him into an achingly familiar embrace. Shit, he'd missed this. Might always miss this. Timur might not be a beacon—not technically—but that wasn't going to stop him from ruining Sinder. And making him want to twine like a tree.

"Put your hand here," Timur ordered.

"Huh?"

The man guided his hand to the wardstone, which he'd used to prop their pillows. Sinder rested his palm against the chrysalis, which met his touch with a tuneful hum.

"There," Timur said with satisfaction. "Our little one doesn't feel slighted, and I can make sure you're cared for, too."

Sinder should have been airing protests and reminders that the man needed sleep, but ... dunce and double dunce, the guy was *good* with his hands. There may have been some level of cosseting underway, too. Sinder needed a distraction, so ... he got nosy. "What's Fend's deal?"

"Hmm?"

"I get why he's being friendly. Needs my cooperation. Fattening me up for the kill. Whatever. But why's he keep saying I'm meant for you?"

"Mmm. Probably because he's decided you're the ideal candidate for a bond."

"Okayyy. Maybe you should explain."

"Well, Fend is Kith-kin."

"Oh, I figured that out. And I know he's good at deciding things for other people. I'll even grant the ideal part, on account of your kids needing a dragon to pick on. But ... why bondmates?"

"You know how tending can prolong a reaver's lifespan."

"Sure. Plenty of documentation. Not that it's public information. Yet."

"Well, Fend wants that for me."

"He can do it himself. Kith-kin have the years and the means to share them with a partner. You don't need a third party."

"Fend would prefer to keep his status as Kith-kin under wraps. If I stop aging, he'll be outed."

"*Flimsy*, Michaelson. He *has* to have a better reason that that."

"I suppose ...." And he tried to change the subject. "You don't think I'm a match for the Rogue?"

"No offense, but my money's on Juuyu."

"Your partner."

"What's with that tone? You have a partner, too. Juuyu and I work well together. Complementary strengths, and all that. It's probably not much different from ... uhh ... actually, I don't know what you and the fiendish Fend get up to. Not sure I even want to know."

Timur's tone definitely went all pensive. "Fend was there for me when times were tough. He calls me his other half."

Sinder was actually kind of confused. "Sounds like you're set."

"If that was true, you wouldn't be here."

"What, like you're somehow lacking? No way. And don't you go thinking he prefers me, because that's not possible. You're his whole world. Me, he treats me like the family dog—no offense to Starmarks everywhere—but you guys, you're the family." Sinder said it again. "Fend's your partner. You're raising Gregor together. Just like all those dossiers. Total dream team."

For a little while, Timur just kneaded.

Sinder spent most of that while going to mush.

Finally, Timur asked, "Why do you think you're here?"

"Can I take the easy out and say, 'confluence of destinies'?"

"I'd rather know what you really think."

"Well, shit." Sometimes, Sinder hated being good at his job. "Fine. He changed his tune about me because he's an opportunist. He's going to take advantage of two things that are way too obvious in hindsight. You have a thing for dragons. And … I'm hooked."

"I've been careful. There's no way you've become addicted to my tending." He reminded, "I made sure Mikoto looked after you most of the time. And Tenma."

"Skies and storms, Michaelson! I'm talking about this. The way you touch me. How it affects me." Sinder fluted wearily. "Look, it's not a romantic thing, but that doesn't stop it from being attractive. Even sexy. Though some of that's probably Fend's fault. Between the licking and the tending and the purring. It's damned seductive, even if you're not trying."

"You were kissing Fend."

"Jealous?" Sinder had meant to be flippant, but Michaelson answered seriously.

"I don't think so. I still don't feel particularly gay."

"*Still* don't? What, you've had your orientation assessed?"

"Jacques was interested."

"Oh, well. Yeah, that checks out. You did something to make him wonder?"

"Then? No. But now?" Michaelson pressed his thumbs into Sinder's muscles in a way that made him squirm. "Jacques would probably read all kinds of subtext into how much I want to touch you."

"Because … I'm a dragon."

"And I apparently have a thing for them."

"You totally do."

"Shut up."

"Never happening."

"Unless I shut you up?"

Sinder snorted. "If that's a prelude to a kiss, I'm out."

Timur chuckled. "No, but ... try something for me?"

"What kind of something?"

"Partial transformation. Bring out your wings?"

"Under blankets?" he asked incredulously.

"I'll hold them out of the way."

"Sounds cold."

"I'll tuck you right back in again," Michaelson promised.

Sinder owned that he was curious. Also, this man was a big part of the reason he'd regained the sky. So he sat up, removed his shirt, pulled his hair out of the way, and focused.

"Very good," Michaelson praised. "Now come here where it's warm."

Mostly sprawled against the man's chest, Sinder soon had his folded wings pinned by blankets. And then warm hands slid up, cupping the place where each wing connected to his back. Timur's grip tightened, and Sinder hissed.

"Give it a chance," coaxed Michaelson.

Sinder did, but he spent most of the next few minutes swearing under his breath. Nothing and nobody had ever touched him there before, and it was ... well, it wasn't bad, exactly. Sensitivity made his wings jumpy, and the blankets were starting to remind him a little too much of the nets they'd thrown over him last summer. He didn't like that part, but when Michaelson stopped, Sinder warbled peevishly.

"Easy does it. Catch your breath. It shouldn't hurt."

"Doesn't."

"I can feel your distress."

"Need to lose the blankets," Sinder admitted.

"Not a problem. Shed them." And Timur's hands fell away.

Sinder wrestled free. Straddling Michaelson's thighs, he flung his wings wide. Flexing was a relief all the way up until he noticed Timur watching him in frank admiration. Which was appealing in its way. Sinder liked being noticed. Liked the attention. Liked this man.

But was that enough? Fend wanted him to bond with his partner. Timur didn't seem opposed, but Sinder had always assumed that bonds like this were about love. Could compatible goals be equally valid? Could Sinder share his years with someone and stay platonic?

Okay, sure.

Maybe.

But what if Michaelson managed to find the right girl, wanted to marry, start a family, build a life, all while keeping Sinder on the side?

No.

Bigtime no.

Dragons like him were greedy, possessive, obsessive, focused. Sinder had been sent into the heights because he wasn't as strong or generous as the fathers. Even Juuyu's recent match had smacked of betrayal, and that was just … stupid. But that was instincts.

"How is nobody treasuring you? If this was mine …." Sinder left the idea lingering there, unfinished.

Timur huskily asked, "You'd consider it?"

"What? An eternity of pampering on this level? Of course I'm considering it. But you'd be limiting your options in a big way. What if you wanted a wife? She'd have to get through me, and I don't like her odds."

"None of the women I ... ah. All they wanted was ... mmm. Let's just say that I like that you're not interested in my biological profile or in our progeny projections."

"Oh, I like your pedigree just fine. You and your dynasty-class soul have wrecked me for anyone else. Except maybe your dynasty-founding father." Sinder wryly added, "And progeny isn't out of the picture. Or did you forget our rock baby?"

Michaelson growled, "Don't go to Papka."

"Yeah, yeah. I was kidding. Uhh, Michaelson ...?"

"Call me Timur."

"Sure. Fine. Timur." And when the man didn't stop drawing sigils onto his skin, Sinder asked, "What are you doing?"

"Adapting a medical barrier."

"So ... what? You're marking me? Dibs or whatever?"

"I can be possessive, too." He shot him a stubborn look and kept right on tracing delicate patterns that sparkled with power. "It's more like armor."

"You want to keep me safe."

"I want to keep you." He winced. "But I'll settle for keeping you safe."

"From danger or from competition?"

"From all comers." Timur's smile was wry. "It's childish, but it's making me feel better. I think I got my hopes up."

"Trust for trust, okay? My hopes are up, too, but we need to look at ...." And then the import of Timur's words diverted him, and his eyes widened. "From all comers."

"Hmm?"

"Fend."

"He'll approve. This whole thing was his idea."

"This *is* his idea. Probably. There's a slim chance it's all mine, but he'll take credit. Because it's brilliant."

"Fend respects your intellect." Timur kept right on embellishing Sinder's torso with pretty patterns. "I think it's part of why he's smitten with you."

Sinder waved that off.

Didn't want to be distracted.

This was too important.

"You normally ride Fend into battle, yeah? You're a dangerous combo. A flight-capable, dragon-slaying dream team. But for all his smarts, Fend has his limits. You can't talk when he's in truest form, and he doesn't have a dragon's reach or dexterity."

"Opposable thumbs."

"Comes standard for my clan."

Timur frowned. "Fend and I have trained extensively. He knows all the attack patterns, and he excels at evasion."

"I'm not criticizing. I'm improvising. Maybe even improving." Sinder leaned down, planting his hands on Timur's shoulders. "Do dragon slayers ever fly out against a dragon ... *on* a dragon? Wouldn't you prefer a field partner who can get you and your Spomenka know-how and your ambuscade arsenal right up into another dragon's personal space? Especially one with a direct line to a kick-ass phoenix whose goals align with yours?"

For several long moments, Sinder could tell Timur was picturing it. The man's heart thudded hard. "You'd carry me? Into battle?"

"Bet you never saw that coming back when you were helping me find my wings."

Timur whispered, "Oh, *Zolottse.*"

Sinder was getting embarrassed, but he wasn't going to let that stop him. "We could consider it a bondmate's privilege."

Timur pulled Sinder down and gruffly urged, "Bond with me, Sinder Stonecairne of the Icelandic Reach. Be my dragon."

"If you're sure then ... sure." Which wasn't even close to the usual formalities, but theirs wasn't the usual kind of arrangement. Their bond was more of an intellectual thing, high-minded and forward thinking and ... damned if every thought was wiped away when Timur sealed the deal with traditional enthusiasm.

Not that the enthusiasm was traditional.

That was probably just a Timur thing.

But a kiss *was* traditional, and kissing Timur was nothing like kissing Fend. In large part because Timur's was mostly perfunctory ... and also a prelude. Because he didn't waste any time baring his soul. All of it. Which was risky and shameless and joyous and ... okay, maybe even sexy.

Timur was wooing him to his side, not with a song, but with everything he had to offer. So Sinder let himself be greedy. Voice thick with sway, he urged, "Take from me."

"Not sure how."

Which wasn't a problem. Sinder knew.

Except this was nothing like tending Tenma. Because that had been neutral and polite and restrained, and Timur was none of those things. The two of them were a good match, in their way—greedy and needy and driven and ready.

Sinder was embarrassed to find the bond already there, half-knit and feeble from neglect, but Timur was delighted. He rumbled and coaxed and praised Sinder's instincts, then managed a tending session that left Sinder dazed and maybe a little drunk.

And just a tiny bit worried.

About what Fend would think.

28

SWAY ME

Sinder tensed when the doorknob turned with a miniscule *click*, letting in a shadowy figure who slunk on four paws toward the bed.

Timur was sound asleep, and Sinder still had plenty of work to do, but he hadn't wanted to leave the bed. Some of it involved body heat, sure. But there was another part of him—probably something instinctual—that didn't want to casually set aside something Timur had sacrificed sleep to nurture.

And there was another thing, too. Something that hadn't been true for a long while. Sinder *belonged* somewhere. So he was sticking by Timur because this was his rightful place now. Only problem was, it was Fend's place, too.

Blankets shifted near the foot of the bed, and Sinder jumped when cold fingers touched his ankle, then his knee, then glided along the outside of his thigh, pausing in their unhurried ascent to twirl. Damned cat was exploring the glittering patterns Timur had made.

Tense and still, Sinder awaited Fend's verdict.

And waited. Because the cat wasn't in any kind of hurry.

The building suspense was probably Fend's goal.

But then Sinder began to feel … admired, and as soon as he relaxed, Fend purred in approval.

"Aren't you ornamental! May I explore your wings, lovely one?" he inquired, the internal words as gentle as his touch.

Answering in kind, Sinder said, *"I don't mind, but don't blame me if you get knocked. They're touchy."*

"Softly then," Fend promised.

Sinder couldn't help the jerk and jump of his wings, but the cat didn't complain once. He kept right on familiarizing himself with every knuckle and slender digit, then stroking the supple membranes until their shivering settled.

Hours passed before Fend pressed against Sinder from behind. He lifted his wings to make room, then draped them over the cat.

"You gave in," Fend whispered. "I knew you would."

Sinder simply shrugged.

"Are you giving me the cold shoulder?" Soft kisses trailed across Sinder's blaze. "I have news."

Curiosity snagged, he half-turned. "Something about Hisoka?"

"You're worried about Uncle."

"Yeah."

With a glance at Timur, Fend switched back to an inner voice. *"He said little, but he was looking past his own whiskers for once. We prowled the borders, and we stopped for a glass of star wine from an old friend."*

"*Andor.*" Sinder wished he could see Fend's face better. "*And … Eri?*"

"*The visit did him good. Uncle was in a mellow mood when I turned him over to Rhomiko. But there are more interesting things afoot.*"

"*Like what?*"

Eyes alight, Fend dropped another kiss onto his shoulder. "*A phoenix has been summoned.*"

"Juuyu!" he softly exclaimed.

"*Shush.*" Fend somehow managed to boff his nose with the tip of his tail. "*We caught and claimed you just in time. Your partner cannot take you from Timur this time.*"

"*You were glad enough to be rid of me last time.*"

"*Things change.*" Fend demanded, "*Put away your wings so you can turn my way.*"

Sinder complied, and Fend stole him out of Timur's unresisting embrace, rolling him into a clumsy tangle of limbs. Sinder came out on top, pinning the cat, though he couldn't think why he'd done it. Self-preservation again? Yeah, no. That didn't apply here. Not with Fend gazing up at him with so much approval.

The cat coyly asked, "*In the mood for dominance?*"

"*Not really, no.*" Sinder figured this was as good a time as any for plain words. "*Was this bond your aim all along?*"

"*All along? Clearly not. But as I said, things changed.*" Fend reached up with one hand and caressed Sinder's cheek. "*Thank you.*"

Sinder drooped, relieved.

Fend pulled him down and whispered, "*My turn.*"

"*For what?*"

"*I want a bond, too.*"

"*Tending only works with reavers.*"

"You know *we've been bond-building since you washed ashore.*"

"*Hey, being used to your scent and your softness and your voice ...
that's too flimsy to count as a true bond.*"

"*Is that your way of demanding something truer?*"

Sinder frowned. "*You're the one who asked for a bond.*"

"*Then we both want the same thing. How fortunate.*"

Did they want the same thing? Sinder had doubts. "*Look,
I'm not some kind of ... acquisition. You can't expect me to follow
orders or betray secrets or help you take over the world.*"

The cat solemnly promised, "*If a takeover seems imminent, I'll
make certain you think the whole thing was your idea.*"

Sinder swore softly.

Fend's kiss was softer still. "*Relent.*"

"*I'm not being stubborn. I do want peace with you. And to trust you.*"

"*Such humble ambitions, wanting what you already have.*"

Sinder drooped anew. "*Then what is this about?*"

"*Alliance. I've been saying so from the start. An unassailable
alliance—brains, brawn, and beauty.*"

Fend's purr was a soothing rumble, and Sinder pondered
alliances and allegiances and applicable instincts. "*So ... all you
want from me is cooperation?*"

"*No. I expect more from a person of your abilities.*"

Sinder was almost afraid to ask, but this was important. "*You're
expecting something? From me, I mean?*"

"*So much.*"

"*Like what?*"

"*I expect you to sway me.*"

Sinder shook his head. *"Kith are immune to dragon sway. Kith-kin, too."*

"Yet with one word, you could forge bond as intimate as the one you share with Timur."

"What ... you want me to say please*?"*

Fend nuzzled close and whispered in Sinder's ear. "Reward my attainment. Choose a new name for me, and I will be yours."

29

LONG DISTANCE RELATIONSHIP

Usually, Isla had no trouble juggling multiple conversations, but after a brief meeting in the corridor with Sylphon Basqwend, she sank gratefully into her favorite chair, kicked off her shoes, and realized her mistake.

Sorry, please disregard
wrong screen
long day

Lapis texted back.

Who was that meant for?

Uncle Jackie

My mystification redoubles
Why is Jacques applying to you
about feline consort culture?

He has a new employee or something, "his man"
Anjou was raised in the feline courts
Did you know they have Dichotomy Day
gift-giving conventions that vary widely
depending on whether your locale is experiencing
the longest day or the longest night?

                              I did not
              At least not with regards to hearthcats

This being a winter solstice at Stately House
The color of a tom's blaze has import,
As opposed to the color of their eyes
Except, of course, in those rare instances
when eyes and blaze are the same color,
in which case, a lady mistress's whim
will dictate the appropriate colored stone,
A novelty which led to a fad two millennia ago
To breed for matching blaze and eye color
Blue being the most successful
Ah. I'm rambling.

                              Nonsense.
                  I hang upon your every word

Are you being snide?

                        Do not think it, my dear
              Should I call so you can hear for yourself
                          Every nuance of my interest
                          I assure you, it's real enough

No need to call
I believe you

                              How gratifying

Isla smiled. She was aware that her enthusiasm for any given topic exceeded that of the average listener. One of the diplomatic arts was listening, so she'd learned to curb her tongue. But with some people, she never had to check herself. Lapis was one of the few people who listened attentively, no matter the topic. Perhaps it was because they were both scholars at heart. Or maybe it was because they trod similar paths, both in public and behind the scenes. Either way, Lapis never came empty-handed to their discussions.

> Dragons have similar obsessions with color
> The accumulation of a full spectrum
> of brides became popular
> once Beckonthrall's children
> began arriving in
> every conceivable hue

> Aren't four brides traditional?

> Exceedingly so, however
> some harems aspired to more
> collecting beauties in every
> color was fashionable
> thankfully, the practice has
> fallen by the wayside

> Why *thankfully*?
> Were there not enough
> brides to go around?

> Obsessions often have a dark side
> Children with unusual coloring were prized
> The purpose of harems became warped

In what way?

> Ask me on another day
> In any case, I am at Stately House
> So I can see for myself that Jacques
> is pleased with his man

Why are you back at Stately House?

> To rest

I thought ...!
Weren't *we* going to meet?

Isla checked her calendar. December tenth. According to what Lapis had told her earlier, there was another week before he'd planned for a long sleep.

What changed?

> Please, don't be hurt by my little whim
> I'd hoped Jacques would be available, but alas!
> Instead, I prevailed upon the Evernhold toms

Isla *was* disappointed in Lapis for thwarting her plans. She'd wanted to be the one pampering him and protecting him. And there was the rock imp to consider. If he'd only waited a week, they might have been able to learn something of import about their chrysalis. Weren't they uniquely suited to the task, being specialists in crystals, lore, and the like?

> But in an unforeseen twist of happenstance
> I have been welcomed into Hisoka's care

She gasped. Then slowly typed,

You're with Sensei?
Is he there?

No, my dear
I have been strolling through the house
Admiring Nonny's decorations
The greening of the foyer is underway

Lapis sent through a picture that showed most of Stately House's entryway—marble floor, double staircases curving up and away, and a tree so fresh from the forest, snow clung to its branches. Four wolves steadied the lofty pine—Adoona, Ninook, Boon, and Pim.

Nonny was looking dapper, his Dickensian top hat at a rakish angle, and Jacques supervised, a toddler braced against his shoulder. One of the new dragon crossers, that much Isla could tell. She hadn't really had the time to get to know any of them yet. Suuzu and Akira were in the thick of it, though, alongside Sonnet, doling out cups. Probably cocoa.

She searched greedily for any sign of Sensei, but both he and Rhomiko were missing from the scene. Which meant they were elsewhere. Possibly alone together.

A knock startled her. "Yes?"

Boniface Smythe entered, a sheaf of papers held in front of him like a shield. "The information you requested? I would have forwarded it, but Sylphon seems to think everything should be handwritten. Lord, why don't more Amaranthine know how to type?"

"Hello, Uncle Boniface." He was new, and she hadn't gotten to know him yet, either. Hisoka-sensei would have called her priorities into question. If he'd been here. Which he wasn't. Making more of an effort, she said, "You're looking festive."

"Am I?" He glanced down at his suit.

"Who chose your tie?"

"It was a gift. From Sylphon."

"That's really very sweet of him. In naga culture, fizmer are highly prized."

Boniface untucked his tie in order to study the wavering patterns of green lines. "What now? What's a fizmer?"

"They're a type of Ephemera that can be found in long grasses." She set aside her phone and came around the desk, which seemed to fluster Uncle Boniface. Isla indicated the knotted silk. "I'll just show you, shall I?"

He slowly, slowly shifted into a receptive posture.

She didn't budge. "I make you uncomfortable."

"Entirely possible."

"Why, please? I'm willing to adjust my behavior in order to put you more at ease."

He tucked a lock of his chin-length bob behind an ear. "It's not like you can stop being female."

That surprised her. "I wasn't aware you have gynophobia."

"I don't. Well, maybe I do. If you ever met Maman, you'd understand. I have cause to be wary."

"Do I remind you of her?"

He held up thumb and forefinger. "No offense."

"None taken. You must tell me when I do something that makes you uncomfortable."

"Right. Much appreciated. Will do. So ... I'm sporting fizmers?"

"Fizmer is both the singular and plural form. And they're just here. Among the reeds." She drew a finger along the fabric, which had a subtle pattern of wavy lines. "The teensy orange dots are their eyes."

"Lord, you're right," he whispered, as if afraid to frighten away the eensy amphibians. "Why are they prized? Not for their looks, surely."

Isla smiled. "For their songs. Fizmer have been called riverbank minstrels and Nicobar crooners. In the old literature, one bard even calls them the wolves of the wallows, since their soaring calls are reminiscent of wolfsong. For Sylphon, this pattern would be traditional and nostalgic. You honor him by wearing it."

Boniface went very still. "I haven't blundered into a courting ritual, have I?"

"A gift like this amounts to a traditional blessing, not a proposition. Sylphon likes you, and with naga, that leads to generous impulses."

"Is wearing his gift a sufficient compliment, or should I be considering a return gift."

Isla was impressed. Her newfound uncle was good at social cues. Magarr was already singing his praises, albeit behind Boniface's back. "A return gift would be entirely appropriate. Perhaps something for Christmas, since that's part of *your* heritage? I was just talking to ... oh, no! Lapis!"

She hastily retrieved her phone.

So sorry!
Didn't mean to leave you hanging.

> **Do not worry yourself over me**
> **I am willing to wait as long as necessary**
> **For your attention to bend my way**

Boniface is here

> **What a coincidence**
> **His brother just mentioned him**

Did he, now?
Do me a favor
Call Uncle Jackie over
Ask him to think of a color

> **As you wish, my dear**

Moments later, Lapis texted a selfie showing him and Jacques cheek-to-cheek. The man was fairly sparkling with happiness.

> **We are, as he says,**
> **neatly situated**

Holiday cheer looks well on him

Isla pointed to Boniface and ordered, "Think of a color!"
The man frowned, shrugged, and said, "Auburn."
Lapis texted Uncle Jackie's response.

> **He says peridot is too predictable**
> **So his official answer is auburn**
> **"for personal reasons"**

"Uncle Jackie has some personal attachment to auburn?"
"One of his middle names is Auberon. With an A and U, not

O, like the Shakespearean king of the fairies, which would have been hilariously on the nose. Anyhow, when he was little, Jackie thought Auberon was a reference to his hair color."

"*One* of his middle names."

"Maman has always been exceptionally pretentious. We are both of us *quite* encumbered."

Isla wanted to ask for more particulars, but instead she said, "Right. Pick … umm. Pick an animal." Then she typed the same order to Lapis.

Boniface's expression was baffled, but he answered, "Hedgehog."

> **Hedgehog**
> **And he wants you to**
> **blow Bon-Bon a kiss**

Lapis, they're in sync

> **I'm not so sure**
> **Jacques is aware you're**
> **with his brother**
> **He's answering with**
> **Boniface in mind**

Granted but … okay
Name ANY Christmas carol

And she turned to Boniface. "What's the first Christmas carol that comes to mind?"

He warily said, "Coventry Carol."

Isla's phone rang. It was Uncle Jackie, and she picked up. "What did you pick?" she asked. "I haven't typed anything, so even Lapis doesn't know.

"Lord, this is diverting. But also vexing. Put me on speaker, but before you do, swear."

"Anything."

"Tell me if he forgets himself and sings along." And then Uncle Jackie—in his usual flamboyant style—began to sing. "In the bleak midwinter, frosty wind made moan …!"

She hastily put him on speaker. Then did a little happy dance. Another match.

Boniface looked vaguely worried. "Yes, well. So?"

Isla was too busy typing to answer.

Lapis, they're in perfect sync

Perhaps, perhaps not
They had the same answer
They're drawing upon shared history
You may only be seeing
What you hope to find

"Don't forget the lamb cravings," she muttered as she typed her retort.

Boniface tentatively declared, "Jackie doesn't care for lamb."

"Exactly!" she exclaimed.

Is Papka around?
He needs to know!

On the other end, Jacques' impromptu concert grew in volume as more voices joined the chorus. But Lapis must have gotten her message across because someone handed Jacques' phone off to her father.

Papka said, "Isla! It's the most remarkable thing …!"

"I *knew* it!" Isla pointed between Uncle Boniface and the phone. "I was right!"

"About *what*?"

"You and Uncle Jackie," she announced. "You're *resonating*!"

"Lord. If you say so," Boniface muttered as he put his tie back to rights. And began to hum along.

30

TAKE RESPONSIBILITY

inkgo had never been so glad for backup before. Things were happening fast, but Anjou was quick on the uptake. Digging through his jean pockets, Ginkgo came up with a jumble of crystals, all tuned to the entrance gate. "We're careful with these, so pay attention to who gets one. The wolves know the routine, so they'll help."

"What beauties," Anjou murmured, holding a pale blue stone up to the light. "Your spares put to shame the stones I handled back home."

"Michael's got expensive tastes, I guess. Get these to Boon's people—phoenix, stallion, wolf, and a bat-crosser. And anybody they vouch for, since they might have tagalongs. They should be arriving soon, but not all together. Sorry if you end up having to hang around for half the day, but they're carrying priceless artifacts. Hence the added security."

"Thank you for your trust."

Ginkgo took the cat by the shoulders and said, "Once I get a little more room to breathe, I'll get you proper access. Sigils and stones. Introductions all around. Seriously, you're gonna be a big help."

Anjou sighed happily, kissed his cheeks, whispered another *merci*, and slipped away.

He seemed like a good kid.

Sibley asked, "How come you didn't give any names?"

"Whose?"

"Phoenix, stallion, wolf, bat-crosser. They have names, you know."

"Well, yeah. But I'm not sure Anjou's met them all."

"Then how's he supposed to let in the right people?"

"Good questions." Ginkgo rumpled the boy's hair, then smoothed a hand over Etienne's freshly-cropped locks. "Not many people know how to find this place. Dad hid the road. And there are illusions, barriers, wards, and wolves between us and anyone. And pretty soon, we'll be adding pollen to our list of protections. You remember Hajime, yet?"

"My tree grandpa? Yeah. He's helping me practice my words." Sibley grudgingly admitted, "Japanese is kinda hard, but he hadta learn English. So he knows how it is."

"Plenty of time to learn. Me? I'm working on French."

"Guess that'd be useful. Right, Etienne?"

The toddler babbled something neither of them could translate. But it was cute, and the kid was happy. The rest would come with time. Ginkgo said, "Gotta go. Dad's waiting on me."

Sibley helped Etienne wave goodbye.

Ginkgo left at a run. Because he was late. Had been all day.

Even before sunup, he'd had to be roused from the naproom to sit in on a meeting with a newly-arrived Juuyu, who immediately left to meet up with one of his other teammates. Because they'd all taken different routes, stayed in different safe houses, and planned to arrive at Stately House at different times.

Having secured all four of the Junzi—ancient weapons that were the bane of dragons—Dad wasn't about to risk them. Not when Kyrie had promised them to the eldermost storms he'd saved ... or who held him hostage. The way Anan grumbled and glared, it was kind of hard to tell which was truer.

Ginkgo let himself in through an out-of-the-way window in one of the spare rooms, jogged down a back stairway, and tapped the wardstones that would alert Dad to his arrival.

But in the hallway outside his receiving room, a dark stain was creeping across the carpet. Ginkgo's pulse leapt, and he hurried forward just as the door opened and Dad exited—tails puffed, hair soaked. Raindrops chased after him as if flung by a brisk wind.

From inside, Kyrie's voice called, "Sorry, Dad! Please, Anan. Help me explain!"

And then the door clicked shut.

Dad stood with head bowed for several moments, then looked at Ginkgo with a weary smile. "I *am* glad I warded the bookcases earlier."

"Who's having a hissy fit?"

"Dima. The typhoon. This token protest will end soon. In the meantime ...." Dad gestured toward another, dryer parlor. "There is a very different matter we need to discuss."

"Sure." Ginkgo wondered at his tone. Dad rarely treated him formally anymore, and he didn't fancy going back to the stiff hauteur that had convinced him that his father hated him. "Is there a problem?"

"Hard to say." Argent warded the door, cast a few desultory sigils, and crossed to the window. Pushing distractedly at his hair, he announced, "We had an early arrival last night."

"Uhh, yeah. I was here for the thing with Juuyu."

"Not him. Revic Nightbide is here. Jacques is showing him around."

"The new chronicler. For our grove." Ginkgo didn't see the problem. "We've got his place ready to go. In amongst the cranes, since they have a few guest houses."

"I sent for him because I have changed the date for the Scattering. Our young colonists will be here in time for Dichotomy Day."

Ginkgo's ears drooped. "We're *less* ready for them. The cottages are built, but they're standing empty. The plan was spring. Why aren't we waiting?"

"Nona and Senna already had reason to hate me, and they also resent Wardenclave. I want to bring Wardenclave's tree-kin here before the Hightip sisters learn of the move. For the safety of the children."

"They're safe at Wardenclave. They'll be safe here. But you're worried about the journey."

"Hannick Alpenglow approved the new timeline. Indeed, he will accompany the children in order to ease their transition. Beckonthrall will be contributing a barge for the transfer, and the entourage will include Starmarks, Highwinds, Duntuffets, Glimsleeks, and volunteers from the Queen's Path Song Circle.

Apparently, there will be reindeer.”

“Sounds appropriately festive. But I’m sensing there’s a catch.”

“Yes. Of a sort. There was also an *unexpected* arrival last night.” Dad patted at his pockets, then brought out a slightly damp letter. “This got them through the gate.”

Ginkgo caught the shine of copper on the page and guessed, “Harmonious?”

“No.” With a cautious tone, Dad began, “I did not wish to intrude upon your summer away, but I believe you omitted certain details from your accounts.”

There were traces of accusation there.

“What, you mean my apprenticeship with Salali?”

Dad beckoned him over and pointed out the window.

Down in the snow-filled yard, a dozen or so kids were playing. Ginkgo didn’t need long to pick out the newcomer. An auburn dog was tearing in big, goofy circles, tail flagging, pausing to lick the cheek of any crosser that got in range.

“Playful pup,” murmured Dad. “His mother brought him, and she is insisting you take responsibility.”

“Huh?”

Dad searched his face, tucked away the letter, and blandly announced, “That boy came looking for you. Do not disappoint him.”

Oh. Okay, maybe this did look bad. “Dad, don’t misunderstand. I’ve never actually …!”

His father opened the window.

Ginkgo took the hint and jumped out.

There was really only one pup this could be. At summer’s end, Ginkgo had needed to say goodbye to Wardenclave and everyone there. Including a chubby, fuzzy puppy whose whimpers had just about broken his heart.

The little guy had grown a lot. Leggy and flop-eared, with a glossy, wavy coat that made him look a whole lot like other Starmark Kith.

Ginkgo whistled in the old way, and the pup's ears pricked. Then he was barreling toward Ginkgo with an enthusiasm that was going to bowl him over.

Resigned to his fate, Ginkgo set his feet and called, "Hey, Pact! Look at … you …?"

He trailed off in shock.

Because halfway to reaching him, the puppy tumbled and righted himself, churning up snow under two furred feet now, his arms flung wide as he called, "Da! Da! Found you, Da!"

Ginkgo scooped him up and spun him around. "Hey, kiddo. Wow. This is a big surprise."

Happiness shone in silver eyes.

"Pact. You're Kith-kin."

Even though he'd been born this past June, Pact Starmark looked like a six-year-old boy. He had brown skin and silver eyes, the spitting image of Glint Starmark, if not for the floppy dog ears. And the furry feet. And the tail that twirled in uncontainable delight. Pact was sniffing and sighing and whining and clinging. Because this boy—even though he wasn't really Ginkgo's son— must've decided that Ginkgo was his dad.

Maybe Snow had brought her boy to Stately House to enroll him? That was probably best for the kid. Given the rate at which Kith and Kith-kin aged, he'd be a young man in just a few years.

"Does Moon know about you?"

"I love Unca Moon." The boy smiled like he was the happiest person in the world. "But Da is best."

"Thanks for that. So where's your pretty mama?"

The boy beamed and pointed toward the house.

"Have you been inside yet?"

"Nope. I was runnin'."

"All the way from Wardenclave?"

Pact pushed closer, eyes crossing, as he revealed, "We took a bus, then a barge. There was dragons!"

"Sounds exciting. Do you like dragons? I sure hope so, because Stately House has a bunch of dragon crossers. They're my little brothers and sisters."

The boy's face scrunched in confusion. "Your pack?"

"It's a little different for foxes. We do have dens. This is my dad's den." He carefully explained, "I'm a Mettlebright, same as him."

"Mama says I'm a Starmark."

"Some of my favorite people are Starmarks."

"Like who?"

"You, of course. But I think you'd like Ever Starmark. He's close kin to you since your fathers are brothers."

"You're my Da."

"I'm talking about Path. Your mama has to have talked about Path, yeah?"

"He's my dog. You're my fox. Mama's a wolf again."

"That so? Wolves are good people."

Pact said, "I think Mama's good, too. But Da is best."

"How'd I get to be so lucky?"

The boy wrapped him tight and sighed happily against his neck. "Love you, Da."

Ginkgo hoped like crazy that he wasn't going to hurt this little boy. But it was easy and honest when he answered, "Love you, too, pup."

Because how could he not?

But he needed to talk to Snow.

Following her scent was simple enough. Through the kitchen door, he veered toward the spot he'd created. His winter garden had a lot more visitors these days, since so many of their crossers liked to crowd onto the couch in order to enjoy the sunny nook with its many hanging plants.

Pact's mother was in one of the rockers, a baby at her breast.

"Well look at that," he said, too glad to be awkward. "Someone's finally getting a proper meal."

One of their newest dragon crossers, a baby whose scales were somewhere between the standard purple and a deep mulberry, had turned out to be a fussy eater. None of the kids were sure he *could* eat, but Snow had him well in hand, rumbling her approval.

Ginkgo set Pact down, and the boy trotted to Snow's side. He set one hand on her knee, and he popped the first finger of his other into his mouth. If he was weaned, it couldn't have been for long.

Taking a seat on the rug at Snow's feet, Ginkgo offered a quiet, "Hey."

Snow's tail lifted, and her copper gaze roved his face. She was Transcendence Starmark, one of Radiance Starmark's younger sisters, formerly a wolf of the Ambervelte pack. Or possibly realigned, since her bondmate—Glint Starmark's Kith son—had died.

Ginkgo ventured, "You're sporting a tail?"

"Solidarity with my son. And his Da."

Ginkgo's tail—white-tipped silver—puffed and settled. "So are you here to enroll Pact in school?"

"I'm here so that you can take responsibility."

"That's what Dad said. Maybe you should explain what you mean by that."

"Pact wanted you. Wants you."

He reached over to tweak one floppy ear. "Pact's a smart pup."

The boy grinned, showing tiny fangs.

Ginkgo could tell Snow wasn't going to make this easy. Wolves liked to see courage, and he had plenty. "So how'd the world's best nanny end up with a pup calling him father."

"You were there."

"I get why he became attached, but ... why are you encouraging this?"

"Because I want you, too."

"As a nanny? That's not gonna work out. Dad needs me here. You have to have noticed how many new little ones we have, and Sansa's gonna give birth any day now. So I'm spoken for."

"If you require courting, I'll do whatever I must to achieve my purpose."

Ginkgo's ears flattened. "But I'm a fox crosser. And I have responsibilities. Here. At Stately House. Even if ... even if I *wanted* ...." He trailed off, hardly daring to believe what Snow was saying. "I can't go with you. I belong here."

"That's why *I* am *here*. You may consider this proof that my intentions are fixed."

"You're thinking of moving here?"

"Oh, I *am* here," she countered, challenge flashing in copper eyes. "And I've secured a position. I'm the new head of security for Stately House."

31

CLAN SMYTHE

Anjou spent most of the day at the gate since the members of Boon's team each chose to linger there, waiting for the others to arrive. He wasn't bored, precisely, since the group was lively and interesting to watch. Anjou was especially intrigued that all the incoming guests were armed. Were they tributes like himself? Curious though he might be, he remained where he was, quiet on the fringes. Await, await, await.

Patience had its reward when Boon said, "You remember Anjou? After all the upheaval, he landed on his feet. Double bond and a fosterling. Huh. You sorted out clan names and whatnot yet?"

"We have." With shy pride, Anjou said, "We all wanted Jacques' name. I'm a Smythe now—clan, crest, and colors."

"There you have it," said Boon agreeably. "All right. Bar the doors. Nobody else is expected today, so let's get this lot to the house. Seems to me, we've got an antsy imp on our hands."

Anjou considered the little girl in Juuyu's arms. She was clingy and quiet, and yes ... he knew what it looked like to await, await, await. So he showed his palms and asked, "May I hasten you to your heart's desire, little mistress."

"Twosies?" she whispered.

"It would be my pleasure to reunite you with the young sir."

She peeked up at Juuyu, whose expression gentled. "Anjou is a well-spoken and swift cat, a good friend to have."

"Go all in, sweetheart," advised Boon. "He's your Uncle Anjou."

She leaned away from Juuyu, both arms stretching, and the phoenix yielded her with a smile.

Cradling her close, Anjou complimented the flowers on her crown of branches, the dress, which was pink to match, and her bravery for making such a long journey. All while lengthening his stride.

"Your name?"

"Seventh Try. Or just Try. Until I have a new name. I want Twosies to choose." She shyly added, "I remember you. You were there."

"I *was* there. And now I am here and happy." Anjou thought it was important to add, "Now that you are here, Twosies can be happy."

She smiled a beautiful smile, and he hurried even more for their sake.

Such devotion should be rewarded.

It made him miss his bondmates.

He fairly flew toward home.

Boon and some of his people kept up. In fact, Juuyu opened the door for them, and Colt sauntered through first. The horse clansman had made many young friends during the rescue mission, and he was soon carrying and cuddling as many crossers as could find purchase. Juuyu was quieter about it, but he also began checking in with each child. For his part, Anjou had a star-child to find and … ah. Twosies huddled next to Eiji on a bottom step, away from the rest.

The other cat spoke in soothing tones, declaring that Argent's promises were not cruel tricks, even if he was a fox. It was safe to trust. It was safe to believe. It was safe to make plans. Wouldn't his best friend need to learn her way around Stately House? Which parts would Twosies show her first?

Anjou carried Try closer.

Eiji looked up and dimpled.

And all activity seized up when Twosies spotted Try and shrieked a note that was probably more suited to skies than foyers. Before its echo had faded, the reunion was accomplished, accompanied by an excess of scolding and weeping and the peaceful drift of pink petals.

Feeling unaccountably shy given all they'd shared, Anjou sat on the step beside Eiji, who took his hand, kissed his cheek, and murmured, "You are radiant."

"This is a good place."

They searched each other's faces, and Anjou was still trying to think what to say when Jacques came to sit on Eiji's other side. Taking Eiji's other hand, Jacques kissed its back and lightly inquired, "Have you settled in with Deece and his boys?"

"Quite comfortably," Eiji assured.

"Anjou is mine now."

Eiji shyly sought Anjou's gaze. "He is the most fortunate of toms."

"He founded our hearth and graces it." Jacques' gaze was steady, his posture commanding. "Sonnet cherishes her tom and will not want to share him with any but me."

"I understand." Eiji brushed a kiss to Jacques' cheek and glanced across the foyer. "I think we are each suited to our place."

They followed Eiji's gaze to where Deece stood, fingers gently tugging Rake's ear while he listened to something Ninook Elderbough was saying. As if sensing his audience, Deece glanced over. And immediately went pink.

"Lord," Jacques breathed. "Deece is always saying Minx spoils him. You're proof."

Eiji said, "If a lady mistress is pleased, all at her hearth have reason to purr."

"Which is why I'm jealously guarding my man. But that doesn't mean you should shy away from the courtesies of friends."

"Friendship is the strength of a community." With a grateful gesture, Eiji added, "I will respect your clan's wishes."

Jacques beamed, bussed Eiji's cheek, then announced, "I must steal Anjou. Come along, my good man. We've an appointment to keep."

Bidding Eiji an affectionate farewell, Anjou leapt to follow the man who would jealously guard him. Jacques angled his head, encouraging him closer, and so they proceeded along Stately House's halls arm-in-arm. A necessity, as it turned out, for the section to which Jacques led him was as exquisitely guarded as the passage that had first brought him to Jacques.

Which is why Anjou was caught up in thoughts of stars and sendings and the sorts of places where a tom might steal away to tryst with his bonded.

Jacques stopped walking.

Anjou glanced around, glanced up.

"When we're like this—the closer the better, especially touching—I catch impressions. Not thoughts, exactly, but a mélange of moods and cravings and hopes and intentions. It's hard to explain. I just know things."

"*Oui?*"

"Lord, I've said it before. You're an ego boost. It's lovely to be wanted, and I'd love to be wanton, but needs must." He warned, "Our appointment is with Hisoka Twineshaft."

Anjou thought it was only natural to be nervous about finally meeting the spokesperson for his clan. Hisoka Twineshaft had shaken up Anjou's ideals. While most of the young toms in his acquaintance whispered and wondered why their leader was both unattached and abstaining, Anjou sat in awe. Their spokesperson was cordial, articulate, and comely. A powerful male.

But today, Hisoka only looked wan and weary, and Jacques' soft sound of concern was as good as a command. It was only natural for Anjou to rush forward, but then he remembered himself and wavered there, feeling young and foolish and every kind of clumsy.

In a voice known the world over, Hisoka said, "Good evening, Kinsman."

"May I ... offer something?" Anjou shot a pleading look at Jacques, hoping for guidance. "What though? What do I even do? I am too moved to be of use to anyone, least of all the best of toms."

Jacques, who had his arms around the half-star who sometimes drifted through the house, said, "We were invited to make certain Hisoka sleeps."

"Invited by whom?" Hisoka asked warily.

"Lord, who *didn't* weigh in? Harmonious was certainly the loudest voice, and Lapis did his share of hinting. But Sinder's the one who all but ordered me here. Apparently on Fend's behalf. So you've a nephew to thank for today's intervention." Jacques petted Rhomiko's loose hair. "Let us teach your Romeo what you need in order to go deep."

"Romeo ...?"

"They're a star crosser, so why not? Rhomiko can be your star-crossed lover."

Hisoka looked increasingly unsettled. "That is not the nature of our connection."

"Nor will I allow your story to descend into tragedy," vowed Jacques. "Can you trust me?"

Gaze downcast, Hisoka said, "Jacques, I owe you so many apologies."

"You don't, though. Not one. But you may require some from me. I ... well, I presumed a bit. Anjou, the door?"

Grateful for something to do, he withdrew in order to swing it wide. And immediately began to purr.

Jacques said, "And here is Sonnet."

The wolf hesitated on the threshold, clad in loose pants, hair falling around his shoulders, and feet bare. "Sensei?" he ventured. "Can you endure another? I'll go if you need me to, but Jacques thought ... perhaps?"

Hisoka seemed confused. "Good day to you, Sonnet. You may enter. But why ...?"

Jacques released Rhomiko in order to kneel before Hisoka. "I will always want what you want. That hasn't changed. But other things *have*. How much can you tell?"

The cat's gaze darted from face to face, and he finally whispered, "What have you done?"

"Chosen once. And then again." Jacques' happiness seemed to suffuse the room. "Are you shocked by my selfishness?"

"Shocked? No. Threes and trees go deeper than roots, and trinities are as strong as braided cords. But ... what is this radiance? You *have* become something more than you once were."

"A Smythe. *First* of Smythes, and if it's not too *outré*, a founder. Do you think I'd be allowed a clan? Officially, I mean." Placing a hand over his belly, he confessed, "I'm in a state of expectancy. Impish influences. I'm carrying a beautiful legacy. Nobody said?"

"Michael."

"Good of him. Did you have any questions?" Jacques gently added, "Concerns?"

Anjou slipped his hand into Sonnet's and drew him closer, wanting to lend Jacques their support. They knelt on either side and awaited Hisoka's verdict.

Finally, the cat asked, "May I see?"

"Certainly."

While Jacques slipped vest buttons, Hisoka's attention veered. "Anjou Bonhomie ...?"

"Anjou *Smythe*. I am Jacques' man."

"So you *are* bonded?"

Sonnet raised his palm, and Anjou gratefully set his fingertips upon it. "Twice. Sonnet is my lady mistress. I wanted—begged—to be chosen, but I also aspired to be like you."

Hisoka's brows rose. "In what sense?"

"I am *free*."

The spokesperson's eyes widened, but then his whole expression softened. "Your bonded cannot rule over you."

"My lady mistress, she is perfect."

Sonnet made a soft noise of protest. "I'm male at the moment."

"Oh, I know." Anjou let his gaze rove appreciatively. "Must I say it again? You are perfect."

Suddenly, Rhomiko dropped to their knees beside Anjou, hands on offer. "Is that important?"

"Which part? Male or female?" He took their hands, turned them, and kissed their knuckles. "*Non*. A cat can find pleasure no matter their partner's form."

Rhomiko's lips parted, but they slowly shook their head. Withdrawing their hands, they sat back on their heels while Jacques passed along his vest, then his necktie.

"Did I misunderstand?" Anjou prompted as he folded fine cloth.

Rhomiko's fingers rested fleetingly on his arm. "Why was Hisoka pleased that your bonded cannot rule over you?"

"That? How to explain. It is like an instinct. A tom lives to please their lady. He can refuse her nothing." Anjou shrugged. "That is the way of things for cats. Very traditional. Customary."

Sonnet shyly contributed, "Anjou treats me like a lady, and

I like that. More than I expected. It was ... surprising? Like the fulfillment of a wish I didn't think to make, didn't know I *could* make. But because I'm also often ... err ... *this* way, Anjou is not so gentlemanly because he *has* to be. He *wants* to be."

Rhomiko said, "You are both. Sometimes male, sometimes female."

"I wanted to be a mother. So yes, I'm both."

"But I am neither."

"What of it? You have your own perfection." Anjou nuzzled the half-star's cheek. "And I do not think you are lacking in admirers."

Romiko whispered their thanks, but Anjou understood why they might not be convinced. Words were nice, but vows ... ah. A vow could bind you and free you and change you.

Just then, Hisoka murmured, "Oh, my," and all attention swung his way.

"Lord," Jacques whispered. Then raising his voice, "Hajime, come look! There's a *leaf*."

Hisoka had always been able to relax in Jacques' keeping. For years, the man had seen to his comfort, providing chocolate biscuits and paperback romances. Now, Jacques guided Rhomiko into his former place, and most of the comforting was coming from an unapologetically motherly male. Sonnet smelled faintly of lavender, but there was something else in the air. Not a scent, perhaps but definitely something. Finally, he murmured, "What *is* that?"

The young tom quietly answered, "You are sensing our Jacques, no?"

"Impish allure," Jacques said, apology in his gaze. He'd traded places with Catalan, who'd been on dragon duty when the rest arrived. Jacques reclined amidst pillows, fingers gently sifting through blue hair, while a sleeping Lapis clung like a long-lost friend, his head now pillowed upon Jacques' thigh.

Jacques inspired this kind of affection.

Or perhaps *trust* was a truer word.

He certainly inspired intimacies.

And he knew how to coax for passion.

Hisoka got a little lost in memories, and Jacques sought his gaze. As if guessing the direction his thoughts had taken, he offered a sultry sort of smile. Then with a subtle lift of his chin, Jacques indicated the person in Hisoka's arms. As if to say, there is your Romeo, waiting more patiently than you deserve. Reward their devotion.

There was sympathy in the man's gaze.

Hisoka wasn't sure if it was for him ... or for Rhomiko.

Jacques' expression grew pensive, and he said, "Even warded, even across the room, I have an effect. Probably on any Amaranthine. Am I keeping you awake? I could go. Leave you to the tender mercies of my very capable bondmates."

"Stay." Hisoka shook his head and absently pulled Rhomiko closer. "You are affecting, but ... what are the effects?"

"Not sure," Jacques admitted. "Not much to go on. These are early days. Argent will sort it all out eventually."

Hisoka was nearly as baffled by Jacques' new soul sense as he was by the baby rock imps. New things had always been so rare, yet he was surrounded by them. And he didn't think he minded. Indeed, he was feeling younger ... adventurous ... daring ... ready for anything.

Jacques asked, "Do you sleep, Romeo?"

"No."

"I suppose that makes you an ideal guardian."

Hisoka could feel Rhomiko's gaze and cautiously met it. That shimmer of living light, gentle green sparks, still captivated him. He was held by Rhomiko's gaze just as effectively as he was by Sonnet's arms. And he couldn't look away.

They said, "I do not sleep, but I can dream."

"Is that where you learn the truth of things?" There was a whiffling mumble from Lapis, and then Jacques confessed, "My dreams have been a mess of hopes and fears and memories and ... well, they can be perfectly lovely, too."

"Dreams raise questions," said Anjou. "Which are said to summon answers."

Rhomiko said, "I have never questioned a dream. Does that make me naïve?"

"*Non.* But a shared dream may be the safest place for questions. And confessions. And new beginnings, come to think." Jacques warmly confided, "Argent is at his most honest in dreams."

Hisoka grew increasingly aware of Rhomiko's gaze. "Hmm?"

"I cannot rule over you?"

"Not in the manner of lady mistresses. No."

"But I am the wish you did not know you could make. I am

the answer to everything."

Hisoka wasn't often cornered. He could have rebuffed the imp in his arms. But with Jacques, Anjou, and Sonnet for witnesses, he ruefully acknowledged Rhomiko's claim on him. "So it would seem."

32

TREASURED GIFTS

Argent laced the walls of the meetinghouse belonging to Stately House's sedge of cranes. After the drenching of his receiving room by the eldermost storms, Randolla had volunteered the hut, which stood upon stilts above the marsh his family had created by damming a creek.

It was a picturesque spot, near enough the forest to be partially in its shadow, far enough from the other cranes' homes to give a sense of seclusion. But more importantly, the highly-polished wood floors, hinged storm shutters, and thatched roof had been built with monsoons in mind. The high-ceilinged room was a traditional design, according to Randolla. A welcome port for three storms. And for the son who knelt before Argent, head bowed, as if awaiting judgment.

Juuyu asked, "May I see?"

Kyrie's gaze swung to Anan, who slouched moodily at his side.

"Why should we listen to this person? Who is he?"

Even though they'd gone through all the formalities already, Kyrie answered patiently. "Juuyu is a tribute of the Farroost clan. A skilled phoenix who is part of an elite taskforce. He has an imp's blessing because his bondmate's sister is a tree. Juuyu watches over one of the hidden groves." In a subtly sterner tone, Kyrie added, "You should be more grateful. He brought the Junzi."

"That's what he says, but where are they?"

"Close," Argent smoothly assured. "Now ... if you would be so good?"

Anan grumbled like distant thunder, and Kyrie flashed him a radiant smile before presenting his palms. Juuyu warbled a soothing cadence before approaching. Movements slow, he knelt before Kyrie and took his hands, carefully smoothing his thumbs over marks that Argent had confirmed earlier.

Argent did not fully trust this eldermost storm. Even less did he like that two more had holed up inside his son, sapping his strength to add to their own. Like parasites.

But Juuyu had closely observed Mikoto Reaver, whose bond with another of these storms had spun itself into a love story. The phoenix thought symbiosis a better term. A relationship of give-and-take, not unlike the bond Argent shared with Tsumiko. Or that of a tree and their twin.

Argent thought Kyrie much too young for such a bond.

Tsumiko had gently pointed out that Mikoto had been even younger when Tzefira had first favored him. And that she'd gone on to save his life. And later helped to emancipate every crosser they'd carried from Kodoku's clinic.

Nobility had probably been Tsumiko's point, but Argent erred on the side of power. If Anan, Dima, and Haizea were a safeguard on Kyrie's life, Argent *might* permit them to linger. But he was still wary. The good behavior of one wind imp didn't guarantee the cooperation of another any more than the treachery of one dragon should damn the rest.

"Your marks shine," Juuyu murmured, his gaze lifting to Anan's.

"I noticed." The imp testily admitted, "They are brighter than when bestowed."

Juuyu blinked. Blinked again. "Kyrie, are you doing something?"

"I do not want them to fade. So I have been … encouraging them." He folded his hands over his heart. "Gifts should be treasured. Is that not so?"

Argent blandly opined, "I do not think your imp expected to be loved."

Kyrie cast a sidelong look in Anan's direction. "I do not think he minds."

"Who would know better than one's bonded?" asked Juuyu. It wasn't a question.

The air crackled with the promise of a squall, but Kyrie went to set his small hand on Anan's arm and calmly inquired, "Is he wrong?"

"He presumes too far."

"Should he call you my friend instead?"

"Now *you* presume too far, little terror."

Argent thought the imp protested overmuch for one who'd given Kyrie a startlingly perceptive endearment.

Juuyu tutted at the both of them and carried on. "I know stories of Dima and Haizea and Tzefira. Anan as well. There is little doubt that these winds are Bethiel's former companions."

"*Little* doubt?" echoed Anan in mocking tones.

"*No* doubt." Juuyu's hands formed a plea for peace. "I consider our meeting an honor, and I make myself available to help the four of you find your balance."

"I thought you were meant to be arming us. Against dragons."

Kyrie slipped then, using touches of sway. "Not until you make peace with Opal."

Anan snorted. "Why should I?"

"He is an ally. We cannot do without him." The boy tipped his head to one side. "Have you forgotten that he will ask Bethiel to come and mediate between us?"

"Maybe I do not need anyone else meddling."

"Maybe you miss your friend."

"Would a friend abandon us for so long?"

"Can anyone go against songs or stars or sovereigns?" Kyrie boldly said, "*I* was meant to find you. If your friend had meddled sooner, we might never have met. Is this not a good outcome?"

"Is it?" Anan grabbed Kyrie by the scruff of his tunic and dragged him out of Juuyu's reach. "I have yet to see any of the promised outcomes."

Argent caught Juuyu's eye and asked, "Well?"

"These good imps cannot use the Junzi unless they descend, and they will not descend except to claim one of the Junzi." With a graceful flutter of fingers, Juuyu said, "Invite them here. Reveal their prize. Await their decision."

Having amassed a great deal of respect for Juuyu Farroost,

Argent inclined his head and waved a hand, banishing sigils and revealing a long leather case propped like a broom in the corner. Also a squat case like those musicians used, its hard sides plastered with stickers. And a lacquered box with golden latches, its glossy length bound by crisscrossing red ribbons. And finally, a relatively small circular case that looked very much like an antique hatbox covered in lavender brocade.

Argent said, "Thanks to Juuyu's preparations, the Junzi made the journey safely. You may assure yourself, Anan Eldermost. I would not want there to be any doubts to *their* authenticity either."

"Ohhh. Oh, my. This is my first time meeting them!" exclaimed Kyrie, who crawled across the floor. He caressed the cylindrical carrier, then lightly tapped the ribbon-bound box, as if unsure which gift to open first.

But then he hurried to the long leather case, laid it on the floor, and unzipped it. The Bamboo Stave, a flute shaped from green crystal, glittered against thick black padding. Lightly touching its silver fittings, Kyrie warbled softly to the thing, then lifted it with both hands. Eyes alight, he carried it to Anan and presented it.

"I needed help to do so, but I have kept my promise, Anan."

"You'll just give it to me?"

"I think it was always meant for you. The resonance is right. Can you tell?" Kyrie pushed the instrument against Anan's chest, forcing the imp into contact. "I think the stone remembers you."

Anan claimed the ancient weapon, but he muttered, "I don't even know how to play."

"We can ask Opal for lessons."

"I would sooner clout the blaggard with the Chrysanthemum Blaze."

Juuyu warbled a soothing cadence. "I would like to hear more about this meeting he is arranging. Do you truly expect a visitation from Bethiel?"

Kyrie hesitated. "I do not think it would be so formal. An old friend will be dropping by. Unofficially."

Argent was entirely proud. Or perhaps a more accurate term was ... impressed.

But every vestige of maturity vanished when the boy hurried to open the stickered case, then fluted over the Orchid Saddle like it was a kitten. Kyrie was—quite predictably—in love with the pale lavender stone, and his storm looked vexed to have lost his attention.

"All four Junzi, three storms, and an angelic ... ahh. An old friend dropping by," said Juuyu. "It is as the children have been saying for weeks. The song is still culminating."

"Yes. I do not think it is over." And with bland amusement, Argent inquired, "Would you agree, Sibley?"

The boy was uncommonly good at hiding in plain sight, no doubt an upshot of his clandestine forays through Dr. Kodoku's lab. Yet again, Argent was impressed.

Sibley stepped into notice.

Kyrie tensed. "What is it?"

"Nothing bad. Nonny sent me over." From the back pocket of his jeans, Sibley produced a phone, poked at its screen, then proffered it. "It's for you."

33

GENESIS

Tsumiko rocked slowly, calm despite the shocking truths Opal was spinning out. "None of the books in my current collection mention Dima by name. I had no idea that the Changing Winds had such a large role to play in human history. Or ... should I say shared history?"

"Dima predates the Amaranthine people. Impressions mostly do. Not always, mind you. We do see bright new lives adding spark and spice to the world at intervals. Baby stars are especially sweet." With a teasing glance at the child huddled against his chest, he added, "Usually."

Twosies made a face.

Opal smiled benignly.

From Tsumiko's lap, Try contributed a soft giggle.

Tsumiko was touched that Twosies had decided that his official tour of Stately House should start with the naproom. Or more specifically, with her. Try had taken one look and loved her. Not because she was a beacon, but because she somehow knew that Tsumiko was also a tree's daughter.

Twosies was the surprising one, boldly taking comfort from the same sort of Amaranthine who'd made his young life a misery. But Opal had starry acquaintances and starry stories and knew more than a few starry songs, which added up to one little boy's fascination.

Opal asked, "What resources have you gathered?"

"The Tellridge Scriptures, the Chronicles of Fynwen, and the Petalwaft Papers. As well as some anecdotal stories that Josheb Dare confided once he realized that my interests included the genesis of the Amaranthine people."

"While the Amaranthine do mingle with imps, we do not have the same nature. Rather, we have a part in the balance. It is said that the Maker wanted to be able to converse with his creation, and so the Impressions came to be. Which was good, for the Maker's friendship with the world inspired the addition of humanity."

Tsumiko had read as much. "That was humanity's genesis, but why were Amaranthine added to the world? The only references I could find were so oblique, they barely qualify as accounts."

"The mystery *isn't* one. All of the eldermost remember where they came from. And why."

Something in Opal's tone invited more, so Tsumiko asked, "Are you one of the eldermost?"

"As it happens … I am."

"Would you be willing to unravel this non-mystery for me?"

"I am a bard, Lady Mettlebright. Telling stories is what I do." And with a rueful smile, he lowered his gaze and began. "In the aftermath of Dima's destruction, all were told, 'be fruitful and multiply,' man and animal alike. And so the Widelands flourished anew. One season to the next, one generation to the next, new lives sparked and spread. Territories were reclaimed. Cities were founded. People were scattered."

"Babel," Tsumiko murmured.

Opal inclined his head. "As you may recall, authority was given to humans over the animals. There were those who took this to mean stewardship. Flocks flourished. Boundaries were established and protected. But there were those who took the Maker's intention and twisted it. Dominion became an excuse for hunts, nay for slaughter. Many sought to be named among the mightiest of hunters."

Tsumiko blinked. "There's one oblique reference. Nimrod?"

"Just so." Opal shook his head. "In a few decades, many species of the animals that Noah had preserved upon his ark were in danger of extinction. Hunted out of existence by men and women whose only goal was acclaim. Saddened by this state of affairs, the Maker stepped in once more. Or so the stories say."

"Do you know if the stories are true?"

"My dear woman, I penned those stories. I would hardly contradict them."

"Oh. Oh my goodness. I hadn't considered that." Tsumiko searched Opulence Windlore's eyes with a growing sense of certainty. "You penned your people's scriptures."

"Our songs, certainly," he murmured. "Which are just as

revealing, though vastly less prophetic. More anecdote than authority. But … yes. I threw in my lot with chroniclers and story-keepers through the ages. There are things that should not be forgotten."

"Like the first Emergence of the clans." She couldn't help plying for more. "Do all of you remember where you came from?"

"Certainly. Though none of us liked the Maker's mercy. At first." Opal's eyes took on a shine. "You might be interested to know that our genesis explains—at least in part—one of your lesser mysteries. Why crossers are even possible."

Tsumiko's mind leapt to a simple explanation, and she stopped rocking. She bluntly asked, "Why are humans and Amaranthine genetically compatible?"

"Because the Amaranthine were once humans." With a twist of his wrist, he indicated himself. "For our sins, we were changed."

Before Tsumiko could think what to ask next, Kyrie burst in.

"Mother!" He held up a phone, his face alight with happiness. "He has arrived!"

Anan skulked in after Kyrie, and he glowered silently at Opal.

The dragon beamed. "Ah, reunions. So fraught with meaning … emotion … potential."

Tsumiko thought perhaps Opal was referring to the leather case now slung across Anan's back. Argent had shown her the Junzi before they could be scattered to the winds. Lovely as the crystal masterpieces were, none had resonated with her, which was just as well. If one had, Argent might have decided to keep it.

"Mother," Kyrie tried again. He'd composed himself, but excitement still sparkled in his eyes. "Will you come to the kitchen, please? That is where I asked Grandfather to bring him."

If her father and her son were conspiring, the results could only be good.

With murmured excuses, she left Try with Opal, who changed the course of his tale-telling to a story about a tree, a star, and the foundling they raised together.

In the kitchen hall, they met Nonny, and Kyrie asked, "Bring Jacques?"

"Headed there now," he assured.

"Keep it a surprise?" Kyrie begged.

"Think that's wise?"

"Yes. They'll both have their guard down, and that is better for honesty."

"Right, then! Mum's the word." Nonny spared her a wink before trotting off to find his mentor.

They arrived in the kitchen just as a gust of cold air scattered red flower petals across the floor. Haji-oji had a wolf on each arm, acting as porters for all of their guest's baggage. Said guest was currently being smothered by Sonnet, but he turned toward the gate guards to say, "Terribly sorry about the excess. Is that all of them? Thank you Ninook, Boon. I couldn't have managed without–"

"Uncle Boniface!"

The man left off, twisting around at Kyrie's glad cry.

Sonnet turned him loose just in time for Boniface Smythe to enfold his oncoming nephew within his snow-dusted cloak. "Good lord, are you actually glad to see me?" And catching Tsumiko's gaze, he doffed a holly-sprigged hat and murmured, "Lady Mettlebright."

Then a voice came carrying along the hall at her back, and everyone took a breath. And held it.

"Lord, are you sure? I can't be imagining it." And Jacques preceded Nonny into the kitchen, already saying, "Sonnet, love, your ears are better than mine. There's a ... sort of ... ringing ...? Oh, damn."

Sonnet tutted.

"Beg pardon. Terrible manners." Jacques took in the general air of festivity surrounding his brother's arrival and settled on a neutral posture. "Boniface?"

Tsumiko could only wonder at the silent messages passing between the estranged brothers, but then Boniface reset his feet, taking a similarly receptive posture, albeit feline in origin. And when his hands cautiously formed a plea for peace, Jacques looked stunned.

"I was sent for," Boniface said, snippily defensive. "Argent issued the invitation himself. Well, it was really more of an order. So ... here I am."

All eyes turned to Jacques, who'd taken to frowning.

"I say," Boniface tried again. "Is that note quite natural? It's two notes, I think. And getting louder. An alarm? Lord, have I set off an alarm?"

And then Michael burst into the room, his arms wrapped around one of the wardstones. "Boniface! Good to see you again. Welcome back, and all that. Would you just ... here, now." And he thrust the green crystal into Boniface's arms. "Bear up, there's a good fellow. Yes, that's done it. You're the one they want. Or ... one of the ones."

Jacques covered his mouth with his hand. Probably to keep from swearing in front of the children again.

Michael looked his way. "This *is* interesting. Did anyone ever mention these to you? The team brought back four."

Finding his voice, Jacques said, "Hisoka has one."

"That simplifies matters!" Michael crossed to Jacques, then herded him toward his brother. "I may need to rethink my theories as to the source of a pair's appeal, but you're clearly a set."

Jacques rested his hand on the curve of the chrysalis in his brother's arms and murmured, "Hello, you. This is a rather pleasant surprise. More of Dayith's lineage. But, Michael. Isn't there meant to be a deep-seated, unrequited *tendre* that sets off the resonance?"

Boniface was looking worried.

Jacques stole his brother's hat and passed it to Nonny.

Tsumiko moved closer, not wanting to miss any part of this reunion ... and not wanting any misunderstandings to mar it. Up close, it was possible to tell that both brothers weren't sure how to proceed. Boniface was all cautious peeks and colored cheeks, and Jacques grew unusually solemn. That was good. He was taking his brother seriously.

But a shared past could be as much a hurdle as a bridge. And Jacques had confided enough for Tsumiko to know that his family had disapproved of his choices. She dearly wished Argent wasn't halfway across the property. Should she ask Hajime to fetch him back?

But then Boniface changed his posture again.

Jacques' eyebrows shot up. "*Mon dieu*, do you even know what you're asking?"

"Did I get it wrong?"

"*Non*, but I doubt you'll like the answer."

"Whyyy?" Boniface asked warily.

With that, Jacques seemed to make up his mind. He smiled in his haziest, laziest, flirtiest way, and with an exaggerated sigh, he said, "Lord, if I must. It's only good manners. If his lordship sent for you, who am I to say you nay? Especially since it would seem that you're harboring feelings for me."

"Harboring? Don't be overly dramatic. Err … Jackie? Bloody hell, Jackie!" exclaimed Boniface. "What are you doing?"

"Nothing I haven't done before. Take notes. This may come in useful."

"For *what*?" he all but squeaked. "I'm not gay!"

"You say that now." And with a low laugh, Jacques nuzzled his brother in an entirely polite feline welcome.

"Oh. Err … right. I know that one." And rolling his eyes, Boniface delivered a basic nonverbal rebuff.

Jacques' smile widened, and he broadly announced, "The hearths of Stately House are many and wide. And Nonny's currently bent on their greening. Good of you to cast in your lot with us. We shall merry-make and festive-be. But first … where's Suuzu? He'll want to know his man has arrived."

34

SPOKESPERSON FARROOST'S MAN

Suuzu pored over a letter from his staff members, patiently unraveling the cypher that was Sylphon's spiky handwriting. Having finally recalled hiring Boniface, Suuzu had inquired after the man. He especially trusted Magarr Oathbide and wanted the magpie's opinion. All three staff members spoke in glowing terms of Boniface's current capabilities and untapped capacities.

Sylphon's early reservations had been summarily banished. He praised Boniface's manners and the healthy respect he yielded, even for "Argent bloody Lord Mettlebright."

Lyra found him endlessly amusing—noisy when ruffled, wise in the way of jaded souls, and a sly wit.

Magarr, whose blindness made him perceptive in other areas, conceded that while *any* human had the potential to flourish under their tutelage, nobody *wanted* this place more than Boniface did. Some of it may have been sibling rivalry, for "Jackie" was often mentioned and muttered over, but it was the magpie's considered opinion that Fandriel's good fortune had brought Suuzu and Boniface together. All would be well.

"What did the guys have to say?" asked Akira.

Suuzu tossed aside the letter and crossed to the small sofa, crowding in next to his nestmate. "They are pleased with Boniface's appointment. And amused that I took so long to remember him. They made wagers. Magarr won."

"Jacques' own brother. It's hard to picture. Are they much alike?"

"No. And yes."

Akira laughed a little. "I can't wait to meet him."

"I will speak to Argent about inviting him back. Although ... Magarr hinted that I would soon see for myself that my man is thriving."

"Good. But I'm not sure I like you calling him your man. *I'm* yours."

Suuzu blinked in surprise. "Boniface is my man in the same sense that Jacques is Argent's. A gentleman's gentleman. That is how he ...!"

Akira halted him by pressing a light kiss to his lips. "I know. I'm teasing. Mostly."

"I will find another term if it would ...."

The next kiss lingered longer, and Akira's smile was genuine. "It's fine."

Suuzu touched the tip of his tongue to his lower lip and tried to calm himself.

Gaze steady, Akira asked, "Why are you holding back?"

"I do not wish to trespass in any ...."

Another kiss, and this time, Suuzu gave in. They were alone in their room, so it was safe to indulge and ... well, it wasn't imposing if Akira initiated, was it?

Drawing back, Akira quietly asked, "Are you afraid of this change?"

Suuzu took his time weighing his thoughts. "Perhaps? I do not like to think of losing anything. Your friendship is precious to me. It has sustained me."

"I seriously doubt that becoming bondmates cancelled out our friendship." Hands on Suuzu's shoulders, Akira said, "I can prove it."

"Prove what ...?"

Again, the kiss was light. Eyes sparkling, Akira said, "See? Still friends."

Suuzu managed a warble of protest. This was silly. Or ... was Suuzu being silly?

Akira straddled his lap and sat, relaxed and right there. It was the easiest thing in the world for Suuzu to wrap his arms around his waist.

"Just because one thing changes doesn't mean everything changes." Akira promised, "I won't change. You won't change. We're still ourselves."

"We are," Suuzu conceded.

"So, hey. I know there's no hurry. We have all the time in the world, but really. Stop holding back." Seated like this, they were nearly eye to eye. Actually, Akira was a little higher. "You're mine, right?"

"I am."

"And I'm yours."

"Mmm." Suuzu gently bumped noses with him.

"Are you glad?"

"More than I can express."

Akira cracked a smile. "I'm trying to tell you that you *can* express it. You know, you could stand to be a little less polite, a little more demanding."

"I do not wish to make you uncomfortable."

"I appreciate that." All seriousness, Akira said, "Try me."

Suuzu hesitated. And then he was glad he had, because Akira began pressing little kisses to his face. Fingers worked their way into his hair, tugging through curls. Suuzu's heart began to thud, and he lifted his face in a silent plea for more. "I thought ... you did not wish to ...."

"I'm pretty sure I asked you to take the lead, but maybe that was unfair. You're even more nervous than I am. And I kind of get it. At least, I think I do." Akira smiled crookedly. "You don't have to hold back."

Suuzu shook his head. He really didn't know if they were ready for all the things he wanted. And he was keenly aware of the leafling pressed between them. He should probably be careful.

Akira's hands framed his face. "Hey."

"Mmm?"

"You can hold me. You can touch me. I like it when you do. And this." The kiss was soft and simple. "I like it when you kiss me. I like kissing you, too. You get sorta flustered. And I like that, too."

Suuzu let a little more of his restraint slip, and oh ... it was good. But it only made him want more.

Akira laughed a little breathlessly and asked, "We can do this, yeah?"

Closing his eyes, Suuzu managed a tiny nod.

"Just to be clear, I still have no idea what I'm doing. Well … mostly. But I want you to be honest, to be yourself, to … to be sure of your welcome. You can have this, Suuzu. You can have everything."

Suuzu focused on Akira. There wasn't a trace of fear. No sense of worry or doubt. Only a strong, steady heartbeat. So calm. Suuzu wasn't calm. Maybe that's why he'd waited? But was he waiting for something Akira couldn't give?

"I've been thinking. While we were away, I learned a lot from Jacques. We did some things."

Hurt lanced through Suuzu.

"Hey, look at me." Akira waited for him to lift his gaze. "This is important. I want you to understand that in order to protect me, Jacques let himself fall in love. And I could tell. It was *easy* to tell. He made sure I knew I was special to him, so for a little while, I got to see what it was like being the person Jacques cared about most. And I think he did it on purpose."

"I know why he needed to … to become close," Suuzu said bitterly. He was jealous that Jacques had been able to flaunt his affections. Suuzu had needed to be so careful, not wanting to frighten Akira with the strength of his attachment.

"Yes, Jacques was keeping me safe. But I think he also wanted to *show* me."

Suuzu warbled quizzically.

"It's hard to explain, because it was all little things. Simple, nonverbal stuff. Romantic gestures. We talked through a bunch, so it was all upfront and intentional. But Jacques has always been sort of *extra*, and I think a lot of it just came naturally. He joked about seducing me, but really ... honestly? He was cherishing me. And it kind of broke my heart." Akira softly admitted, "He made it easy to love him back."

"You do."

"Yes, I do. But Jacques is Jacques, and you are my bondmate. It's different, okay?"

Suuzu tightened his hold. "And he has his own bondmates now."

Akira's expression softened. "It all worked out. But ... I was trying to explain."

"Go on."

"All the things he did—the things *we* did—they were simple and gentle and thoughtful and most of all, they were *easy* for me. But I was so busy getting flustered by all the attention that it took me this long to realize that while Jacques was being *so good* to me, he was showing me how to be good to you."

Suuzu finally whispered, "Truly?"

"So I'm going to cherish you. And enjoy it when you get flustered." Akira radiated satisfaction.

"Please do."

Much to Suuzu's delight, Akira kissed him again. And in many ways, it was the same as always—friendly curiosity, refreshing honesty.

"I like this," Akira murmured. "It feels right."

Suuzu needed to correct some of his assumptions. Akira wasn't shying away from intimacies. Neither was he passive or simply putting up with Suuzu's hopes where the delights of the nest were concerned. If anything ....

"Are you trying to seduce me?" Suuzu whispered.

Akira chuckled. "Is it working?"

"Yes."

Then Akira did something that made Suuzu gasp and stammer, "W-wait."

His bondmate eased back, still relaxed and right there. So calm. In control.

Suuzu grumbled, "I might be furious with Jacques."

"You can blame Eiji and Anjou for that one." Akira offered a little shrug. "They thought I should learn how to please a gentleman lover, so they were always giving advice. Which usually involved ... well, let's just say they'd get caught up in each other. Their demonstrations were embarrassing, but also instructive. They were trying to help."

Suuzu hid his face against Akira's shoulder.

Akira began stroking Suuzu's ear, which unraveled the last threads of Suuzu's self-control. He felt cherished and wanted and increasingly wanton. Akira met his urgency with murmurs of encouragement, gazing up at him with mingled pride and peace.

Suuzu couldn't remember moving to the bed. He blushed over his own behavior and yet ... Akira had said he should be honest. That he would be welcome. But he'd barely begun to sort out how to cherish Akira in return when Jacques walked in.

"Hey, Jacques," Akira said wryly. "Great timing."

"Oh, I agree." The man laughed. "Come now, Suuzu, you mustn't be embarrassed. Lord, do you know how long I've been trying to catch you two in an intimate moment? I feel richly rewarded for years of patience."

Suuzu hissed.

Akira petted his hair.

Jacques didn't leave. Instead, he perched on the bed's edge. "I do apologize for the necessity. You see, I've left my brother standing in the hall. May I invite him in? He should see you this happy. It's a good look."

Suuzu eased away from Akira. "Boniface is here?"

"Arrived three-quarters of an hour ago, more or less. Bit of a shock for me. Seems Bon-Bon and I are resonating. Michael's chuffed, but I'm ... lord, I don't know. Catching up would probably be the done thing, but I'm not sure how he'll take it. Or if he'll even believe me. Help a fellow break his news ...?"

Akira whispered, "Oh. The baby."

Suuzu crawled closer to Jacques, touched his shoulder, and called, "Boniface? You may enter."

From the hall, a worried voice carried, "Are you sure? Jacques said you were *in flagrante*. Are you and your chap decent?"

"I've checked their zips. Your sensibilities are safe. Though they're both looking thoroughly kissed." And in a pleased aside, Jacques added, "I approve. About time."

"Yet you interrupted," muttered Suuzu, even as Akira slipped away, aiming for the uncle he'd so wanted to meet.

"Just as well," Jacques said, softer still. "I'll send Anjou around with accoutrement. He's a tribute, and he has the necessary experience. Let him guide you. Or go to Naoki, if you want a doctor's insight. Or ... well. A nestmate is here, and I'm the farthest thing from shy."

"I do not want ...!"

"First go-around, I recommend a safe word and someone you trust in earshot. Speak with Ginkgo if you want corroboration. He looked after things for me, once upon a time." Jacques' posture was neutral, his gaze soft. "Pack custom. For a human partner's protection."

Suuzu realized all at once that Jacques was trying to be wise. Wilting into a receptive posture, he took a very different tone. "I do not want ...."

"Your beautiful boy knows what he is about. Rely on my man, and you'll soon find your balance." And raising his voice a trifle, Jacques declared, "And here is *your* man. Sure you want him?"

Keeping his hold on Jacques, Suuzu straightened as much as his kneeling position allowed. "Boniface is a friend."

"Avian approval," Jacques drawled. "Impressive."

Akira backed into the room, leading the uncle who was just blurting, "Lord. Has anyone ever mentioned you look just like Tsumiko?"

"We get that a lot. I wouldn't have guessed you were Jacques' brother, though. Should I call you Uncle Boniface?"

"If you *must* tack on honorifics, that's the most suitable." And turning keen eyes on Suuzu, Boniface complained, "Jackie, you're a beast. We're intruding."

"Don't worry about us," Akira quickly interjected. "When Suuzu remembered about you, it was a huge surprise! But I could tell you make him happy, so I've been so curious to meet his man. We'll probably see a lot of each other. Say, will you be moving to Stately House?"

Suuzu watched Akira dismantle Boniface's worries and almost cooed, he was so proud.

Jacques, whose senses were too keen these days, bumped shoulders with him.

Meanwhile, Boniface was dissembling. "Me? I really couldn't say. Isn't that up to Argent and … well …." His gaze flicked briefly to Jacques before he awkwardly repeated, "I really couldn't say."

"Relax, Bon-Bon. You're here at his lordship's invitation, aren't you?" Jacques quietly added, "And Suuzu clearly wants you."

Boniface stood there, uncertainty still lurking in his gaze.

And so Suuzu hurried forward, took Boniface's hand in both of his, and drew him to the sofa. They sat together, and the man relaxed enough to ask, "Are you eating enough?"

"Ah. Perhaps not. My appetite is still lacking."

"There are no trays lying about. Did Nonny give up on feeding you?"

"Akira coaxes him along. He cannot refuse his beautiful boy." Jacques dropped to a seat on Suuzu's other side, crowding them together.

"If you're done being forlorn, then I shan't worry." His head tipped to one side as he considered Suuzu. "And bravo to the ascendance of coral nippets. Friends to lovers. That's the ticket."

Suuzu's fingers sought the pin, which had indeed been rotated so the orange nippet egg was uppermost. "We are newly bonded."

"Many felicitations." And with a blink, Boniface ventured, "Does that make us family, I wonder?"

Akira perched on the arm of the sofa closest to Jacques. "Definitely family. Doubly so since Jacques is a nestmate."

Boniface seemed put out.

Jacques reached behind Suuzu's back in order to flip up Boniface's collar.

"Jackie," he chided. "Don't be childish."

"Don't sulk. You got to Suuzu first. Mine's a more recent concession, and I've already changed hands."

"What does that even mean?"

Jacques twirled a strand of Boniface's hair around his finger and tugged. "It means I'm happy."

"See here, you," his brother grumbled.

Akira piped up. "Preening is one of the ways nestmates show belonging and affection."

Boniface missed a beat. "Look, I know that much. But Jackie and I aren't avian."

"If Argent approves residency, we're essentially denmates, too," said Jacques. "Your hair's in magnificent condition, by the way."

To Suuzu's amusement, Boniface resorted to a standard feline rebuff, and Jacques lapsed into an appropriately apologetic posture. This seemed to confuse Boniface, but Jacques radiated a cautious sort of happiness. A good start.

"We should begin," Suuzu decided.

Boniface's gaze was expectant.

"Right. Well," Jacques began, sounding uncharacteristically awkward. "I've asked Suuzu to help me explain something out-of-the-way. I doubt you'd believe me, but with Suuzu vouching ... and if needs must, I could slip a few buttons."

"Is something the matter?" asked Boniface.

"As matters go, it's on the momentous side."

Suuzu stepped in. "There will be a child."

Boniface rolled his eyes. "Yes, yes. That's already been explained. Rock imps and whatnot."

"That is a separate matter." Taking Boniface's hand, Suuzu quietly said, "My memories are hazy, but I do believe ... did I not explain to you that I have been sprigged?"

"Yes. The whole seed business."

Jacques lifted a hand.

Boniface blinked. "*Non.*"

"*Oui.*"

"Bloody hell."

Suuzu slouched back into the sofa cushions and watched the brothers sending silent messages for several moments.

"Right then," Boniface finally managed. "Lord, I hope you don't expect me to pitch in. I'm pants at kids."

"I'd settle for your not telling Maman."

"I blocked her."

"Brave man."

"I think most of the bravery is on your side. Blazing trails and whatnot. But ... lord, Jackie. What possessed you?"

"We're not entirely sure. But I'm rife with impish consequences. Nobody can say what I've become."

"Oh, don't be daft. You're just Jackie."

Jacques cracked a smile. "I hope you stay."

Boniface just sort of scowled and reached over to tweak one of his brother's curls. Not in any gentle way, but Suuzu thought it was a peaceable gesture. Because Jacques relaxed.

But then Akira cleared his throat and asked, "Did you guys cover bondmates yet?"

35

CHICK IN HIS NEST

All of Suuzu's hopes for privacy dwindled away to nothing because Akira wanted to accompany the Smythe brothers to the kitchen in order for Boniface to meet Anjou. And to welcome Sonnet to the clan. Or something along those lines. Meanwhile, Juuyu summoned Suuzu to one of the first-floor parlors.

He was every kind of glad to see his brother again. Juuyu pulled him close, kissed the top of his head, and fussed a few of Suuzu's curls into better positions.

"Your leafling?"

"Thrives."

"Your nestmate?"

"My bondmate."

Juuyu sharply studied his face, lapsed into a softer expression, and angled his head to signal his need. "I have made promises, and they bind me. And so I need help, brother mine. Will you keep my daughter? If she is a chick in your nest, I will not worry."

Suuzu had always assumed that if he was to raise a child, it would be a younger sibling ... or perhaps another clan's tribute. That Juuyu would entrust a child into his care was staggeringly generous. But what daughter could he mean? Fumiko had only been his bonded for a matter of months, too soon for a child.

Taking a receptive stance, Suuzu asked, "A chick?"

"Perhaps leafling would be more accurate." His brother raised his voice somewhat. "Try? I am ready to introduce you."

The air changed, and the scent of flowers made Suuzu breath more deeply. He slipped from his brother's embrace in order to face a tree-child. A daughter. Of course Juuyu would have given shelter to a youngling tree. Sinking to his knees before the little girl that *everyone* knew was Twosies' best friend, he showed his palms. "My name is Suuzu."

She studied him closely, then looked up at Juuyu.

He said, "I took responsibility for you, and I am not releasing you lightly. Here is my own brother, whom I cherish, for I helped to raise him. More importantly, he understands the needs of trees. All the trust you place in him will be safe."

"Your own brother," she said softly.

"Try has been added to the family registry. Father and Letik are ecstatic. Fumiko and Zuzu will miss her dearly." Letting his fingertips rest lightly atop the little girl's head, he made his hopes clear. "Foster this child of mine. Love her as your own."

"I will. If she will have me."

"I think she will. Suuzu, will you tell this new daughter your secret?"

Suuzu warbled a willing note.

Try asked, "You have a secret?"

"A precious one. I have been sprigged."

Her eyes rounded. So she knew what that meant? But of course she would. Suuzu knew that experimental sprigging had been responsible for many of the unusual children who now counted Stately House as home. This probably included Try herself.

So Suuzu went on. "I found a golden seed and wanted to protect it. So I willingly took it in. That means that in the course of things, a chick—a baby—will be added to our family. You will be a big sister."

"I will be a sister?" she whispered.

He inclined his head. "And I have a nestmate, a man I dearly love. Akira is tree-kin. The golden seed he carries will be planted beside the front step of the home we will build together."

"Is there room for me?"

"There is." And looking up into his brother's face, Suuzu asked, "May I tell Akira?"

"Of course. Should I go find him?"

With a small headshake, Suuzu called, "Hajime, could you bring Akira? Ah, and Naoki would be welcome as well. We have a new family member to greet."

Juuyu chirped a startled note when three people arrived in a swirl of red flower petals. But then Akira crashed into Juuyu with his usual enthusiasm and began introducing—and reintroducing—his parents.

Dr. Naoki quickly noticed Try, and exclamations and

explanations were made.

Akira accepted the news of a fosterling with a frown that only worried Suuzu for a few heartbeats. Until Akira asked, "What will Twosies do?"

Try clasped her hands together and appealed to Suuzu. "Is there room for him, too?"

"A daughter can ask anything of her parents." Suuzu urged, "Let Akira and I see to your every happiness."

"Where *is* Twosies?" Akira asked.

Hajime spoke up. "Sitting on the floor outside the door, rather like a lost puppy."

Dr. Naoki smiled crookedly. "Twosies is not a dog crosser."

"He's part star," Akira murmured, though his attention was still patiently fixed on Try. "Are you part tree?"

"All tree. But ... culled."

Juuyu said, "Argent has hidden Try's pot among the other trees in his bonsai collection. Alongside Hajime's."

That caught Try's attention. "You, too?"

"I was the first."

"First Try?" she asked.

He solemnly corrected, "First success."

Akira said, "He's my father. He'll be part of your family, too. All the crossers are learning to call him ... well, everyone kind of has their own version of *grandfather*. And I'm your Uncle Akira."

Suuzu called, "Twosies? Please join us. Try wants you closer."

The boy poked his head around the corner, his gaze full of sulk.

Akira held out a hand. "Want to be with us from now on?"

Twosies warily demanded, "You're going with them? I thought you came to be with me."

"Suuzu and Akira will take care of me." Try offered her arms, and Twosies wove through the rest of them, then wrapped himself around his friend. "Not like gardeners. They'll be *parents*."

"What's so great about that?"

"I will be a big sister. I never got to be someone's sister before."

"What about me?"

"I don't want you for a brother. You're my star. It's … different."

"How come?"

Akira wisely chose that moment to interrupt. "Hey, if you let me and Suuzu take care of you, you'll be nestmates."

Twosies looked at him and in lilting words said, "Classmates. Roommates. Nestmates. Bondmates."

"That's right," Akira replied easily. "Suuzu and I were best friends almost from the moment we met, and now we're together for good. Say, Try? Can I see your pot? Argent gave Hajime a new one, and it's really elegant. Did Juuyu set you up?"

And the conversation flowed onward.

But Twosies was staring at Suuzu with wide eyes and pink cheeks and an expression of star-wise clarity.

Suuzu twitched his fingers, beckoning anew. "Do the stars sing of us?"

This time, the boy let go of Try and came to stand over Suuzu, who still knelt. Twosies' gaze slipped out of focus. "A house in a tree. A brother and two others. Phoenix song and dragon song and star song and storm song. Flower petals in every hue. Heart of a grove."

"And do you see yourself in my nest, little oracle?"

Twosies looked at him, startled this time. "Is that my name?"

"Hmm?" Suuzu coaxed him nearer. "Names are a good beginning. Many bonds are begun with the giving of a name. Have you been waiting for someone to speak yours?"

"I did not know it until I heard it." Tugging at Suuzu's sleeve, the boy asked, "Can I really stay with Try?"

"I would insist."

"And you'll guard us and guide us?"

"Those would be the more practical aspects of our role—Akira's and mine. But growing attachment and displays of affection will be unavoidable."

"Really?"

Suuzu carefully tousled the boy's shining curls, then began to preen them. "Would you like me to call you Oracle from now on?"

Eyes shut, expression serene, he mumbled, "Twosies for now. Oracle when I grow up."

"And what will be my daughter's name?"

"Do you mean Try or your baby?"

Suuzu blinked.

Twosies wrapped his arms around Suuzu's neck in an unspoken demand for closeness and raised his voice to carry. "Seventh Try will carry forward her mother's name. That is how it must be."

Several moments of startled silence followed. Then the girl asked, "I have a mother?"

Dr. Naoki spoke up. "You did, my dear. A brave and beautiful tree."

"She's gone?"

Hajime said, "Yes. But you are here. And there will be another."

With a small smile, Dr. Naoki explained, "There was a seed. Either Dr. Elara or Pim took it in. They are carrying a child whose twin will share your lineage. Your mother's name … *your* name is Trinity."

36

BEGUILING DRAGONS

Timur needed to run. Sure, it was training, but running would give him time to think. And time with his son. So he bundled up Gregor, slung him wolf-style to his chest, and took off cross-country. Route didn't matter, so he picked a path at random and pounded along it, hoping the steady rhythm would push his thoughts into formation.

Because he'd taken a male bondmate. Willingly. Eagerly. And it wasn't hard to fathom why.

Back when he was eighteen, doing his part for the In-between had seemed like a great idea. Sex for a good cause. And there had been a lot of sex. Much of it overseen by a healer. Always while blindfolded, to spare his partner any embarrassment. Because the women were usually already married, already mothers, and also just doing their part.

Timur had managed to fulfill his contract, but the whole

business had put a damper on his libido. Maybe he was just burned out. Tired of the mechanics. Uninterested in something casual. Waiting for the right woman to come along. But Timur thought that deep down, he was probably broken.

And yet he'd found an unexpected refuge.

Someone who didn't want him for paternity.

Yet clung and sighed and melted under his hands.

A friend who accepted his attentions in the spirit they were offered.

"You should be the first to know, Gregor," Timur said gruffly. "Your papka has beguiled a dragon, and I belong to him now. Is good, yes?"

His boy was utterly relaxed, so trusting.

"When I was first tapped by the Order of Spomenka, I lived and breathed dragons. Learned all I could. Heights and harems both. Then last summer, when Damsel needed me so much, I ended up needing him. Honestly, I didn't realize we were bond-building. But it explains why I missed him so much."

Timur increased his pace, which made it harder to talk. But he forced out the words, wanting to be honest. With himself. With his son.

"Always wanted a dragon. Never thought to try. A wife was more ... expected, I guess. But it wasn't as easy to find one as I thought." He was breathing hard, close to tears. "But I have a dragon now, and he is magnificent."

He slowed his pace but kept slogging on. "I think I've been enormously selfish. I probably should have tried harder to give you a mother, but ... I gave up. I'm sorry, Gregor. I couldn't even bring myself to try again. But I'll share Mum. And you'll have aunties aplenty, honorary and otherwise."

Gregor blinked up at him, solemn in his sleepiness.

"I did think of a way to make it up to you. Maybe. I'll have to ask Fend. He'll know what's best. Always does." Timur rounded a bend and stumbled to a stop at the sight of Juuyu.

The phoenix glanced his way, then strode over, plainly concerned. "Are you in distress?"

"Me? No. Just … needed a run."

Juuyu reached out slowly and righted Gregor's hat. Then with the same deliberation, he dragged a knuckle up Timur's stubbled cheek, erasing a tear track. His posture invited confidences, and his hands formed a silent promise for secrecy.

"Thank you. Truly. But … I don't … ah."

Just then, Stately House's two wind dragons reeled through the trees in a rippling, twisting race. They shied away from Juuyu, all scolding cries, then circled back. The female draped herself around Timur's shoulders with a smug *tootle-peep*, while the little male cautiously nosed Juuyu's fingertips.

"Sorry, little girl. Did I take away your boy?" Timur asked gruffly.

And then there was a crash in the undergrowth, a spate of grumbled oaths, and Sinder tumbled into the open. He was clad in jeans and a T-shirt with a band logo on it, and he was barefoot. He looked frightened and frazzled. No, Timur could *feel* that he was frightened and frazzled. But then Sinder spotted his partner.

"Oh, shit. I mean … umm. Well … heyyy, Juuyu. Long time no see."

The phoenix angled his head to one side, then the other. "Are you in distress? Ah. I see. This is *mutual* distress? Sinder, what have you done?"

"Why's it my fault?"

"You are sometimes thoughtless. You are repeatedly reckless." With a sidelong look at Timur, he added, "You are *never* barefoot in the snow. What drove you into the outdoors for which you have so little fondness?"

Sinder stood there, shifting from foot to foot, then muttered something about dunces before hurrying to Timur. "You okay? You didn't feel okay, and I don't have any safety protocols in place, but all I could think was ... get to you. *Are* you okay?"

"I'm ... fine."

"Okay, now you're lying to me. Do you regret me? Was it a terrible idea after all?" With a skittish glance Juuyu's way, he muttered, "I think we're pretty good together, y'know?"

Timur felt like an idiot, but it was vastly more important that his dragon was shivering. "Juuyu, will you take Gregor so I can sort out Sinder?"

"Gladly." Moments later, the phoenix was warbling over the little boy while casting sidelong glances their way.

"Calm down, *Zolottse*. You are good and right and best for me. I swear it." Timur shed his coat and peeled out of the hoodie underneath, shoving it down over Sinder's head before hauling his dragon off the ground. "My only regrets where you are concerned involve your suffering and scars from last summer. And your current distress. I was thoughtless, and now you're cold."

"It was so weird. One minute, I was going through Canarian's notes, and the next ... *wham*! You were sad or stressed or ... something. You weren't happy anymore, and that felt wrong, and I asked the twerps to help me find you. Jumped out a window. I was … I guess it was stupid.”

“The bond is fresh, and that can lead to erratic impressions. The impulse to reach for and protect is entirely natural.” Timur should have been more careful, more considerate. “I apologize.”

Fend stalked into the open then, ears laid back, tail lashing. He hissed at Juuyu, whose brows lifted.

The phoenix firmed his stance and calmly asked, “Do you have something of import to share, Sinder?”

“Guess I do. You remember Timur?”

“Quite well,” Juuyu assured.

“He’s my … or … I’m his …? Guess it’s the same either way.”

“We’re bondmates,” supplied Timur, keeping it simple.

Juuyu hesitated. “*Not* a love match?”

“It’s more of an alliance. But it’s messing with my head. And impulse control is apparently shot.” Sinder fidgeted. “I like it best when we’re touching.”

“Are not all dragons greedy?”

“So you think it’s normal?”

The phoenix considered them for several moments. Finally, he said, “Your responses to your bondmate are entirely natural. And if memory serves–”

“Your memory *always* serves,” Sinder interjected.

“Even before this new development, your attachment was evident, as was your appreciation for Timur’s touch.”

“I blame the Order of Spomenka. Dragon slayers are so good, it’s scary. Which reminds me. It’ll be in my next report, but … him and me. Work with us, and Timur can ride out against the Rogue.”

“Hmm.”

"He has access to ambuscade weapons."

"That's true, and I look forward to a lengthy discussion on battle tactics and training schedules, but …!" Timur lowered Sinder onto Fend's back and retrieved both his jacket and Gregor. "It will have to keep until later. I have a dragon to warm."

"I can only applaud your priorities." And more softly, "Yours is a dangerous combination."

Timur frowned. "You don't approve?"

"Indeed no. I am astonished. And grateful. Surely as a member of the Order of Spomenka, you realize how rare it is for a dragon to accept a rider. The possibilities have me giddy." The phoenix waved a hand between them. "We will train in the manner of comrades. And if you like, we will talk in the manner of friends."

Timur glanced toward Sinder, but Fend had already moved out of earshot. "I just … things didn't turn out how I expected."

"And you are disappointed?"

"No! No." Timur tucked his son under his chin and sighed. "*I'm* astonished. And relieved. But also … I don't know. I claimed something exceedingly precious for myself, and … what gives me the right to be this happy?"

Juuyu warbled a cascade of notes, light and joyous. "I can only applaud your perspicacity."

Timur felt a little teased and a little approved of and embarrassed enough to try to change the subject. "So … what are you doing out here?"

"Ah. I was tracking a small dragon, but I keep encountering hinderances. Tiny sparks of resonance, they overlap and interfere." The phoenix peered around. "What has Kyrie done to the trees?"

"He copied something Salali Fullstash did at Warden-clave. Or ... adapted it, I suppose. Ever since last summer, for weeks and weeks, Kyrie would go to Papka for chippings and shards from any remnants he'd shaped. In the end, he sent to Glintrubble, begging for a shovelful of scrap from their workshops."

Juuyu peered at the surrounding forest, expression thoughtful. "He gave every tree a voice."

"And when Kyrie's conducting, these woods sing."

"To what end?"

"Papka has partially replicated the effect on a much smaller scale. It's an array, but it's much more than that." Timur walked to the nearest tree, circling until he stood under its shard. "Kyrie names them and befriends them. He teaches them to get along with their neighbors, and he sings to them of Stately House. And when each little spark resonates, they tune their voice to his. His will is their will."

"It must be lovely."

"And terrifying." Timur began backing toward home, toward the dragon who was missing him. "Didn't Sinder mention ...? Or Moon? He was there, too. So was Ginkgo. Ask them, though I'm not sure anyone can explain how it's done. Even Papka had to admit defeat."

Juuyu trailed after him, hands framing a plea. "What has Kyrie done?"

"You *could* say he's added to Stately House's defenses. If anyone ever got past Papka's barriers and Argent's illusions, they'd find themselves in among the trees."

"An intruder would be tracked."

"Oh, they're a bunch of tiny tattle-tales," Timur agreed easily. "But any wolf in these woods can track. Don't forget. Kyrie is an ambuscade."

"I was aware." Juuyu beckoned with a quick flick of his fingers. "What is the crux?"

"An ambuscade uses remnant stones to focus their will." Timur saw understanding kindle in the phoenix's widening eyes and nodded. "Before any of us fully realized what he was about, Kyrie had turned the whole forest into a weapon."

37

GUARDIAN AND GARDENER

Ginkgo wasn't sure if it was Sansa or Dad who'd made the decision that Snow should take over security, but the arrangement was made, accepted, and summarily vowed. No takebacks. She was staying, and Stately House's defenses couldn't have been stronger. Really, it was great. She was perfect for the job.

As usual, Dad came off looking masterful, even though he couldn't have actually planned for some of the shifts.

Snow's addition freed up Sansa, who would look more to their houseful.

Anjou would manage enclave affairs, serving as a community liaison.

Jacques was back to work, which meant Dad was calmer. And tidier.

Nonny was tenaciously pulling off Christmas for the kids.

And loving it.

Elara was heading up plans to add a maternity ward to the campus. Because they were apparently a campus these days.

Revic Nightbide was all set up to act as chronicler, and with a team of preservationists due to arrive with the Alpenglow contingent in time for Dichotomy Day, Ginkgo was going to officially have more help than he knew what to do with. For the first time in a long time, he could slow down a little, look to his garden, and play with the kids.

But the prospect of puttering in the potting shed wasn't why his heart was doing flips.

Snow's gaze was steady and fierce and ... danged if it wasn't possessive.

Ginkgo wanted nothing more than to go along with her plans, but there was also a part of him that needed to make sure he wasn't dreaming. So he'd asked the people he trusted most to bear witness to Snow's proposal.

On the couch in his winter garden, three people sat in a row, gazing at Snow with polite attentiveness, probably because she'd taken a dominant posture. After some thought, Ginkgo settled on something more neutral, but he put a little sway in his tail.

Jacques was searching his face with concern. Then he mouthed something. In French. But Ginkgo caught on and nodded gratefully, then flicked his ears a few times. This wasn't the time to be broadcasting bewilderment. Not when it could be interpreted as reluctance.

Sonnet bustled over with a tray of tea things, and Jacques moved to pour. Because they were having this meeting in the kitchen.

Ginkgo hadn't wanted to hide what he was doing. And this was where he was most at home. Heart of his territory, and all that.

Then Sonnet slipped to Snow's side and tentatively offered, "Auntie ...?"

Snow hesitated a little too long, but her tail did lift. "Sonnet."

"Yes. It's been quite some time."

Ginkgo guessed she'd sorted out enough by scents to bypass a twenty-minute explanation, because her coppery gaze snapped to Jacques, who blew a tiny kiss. Then Snow enfolded Sonnet and rumbled, "Our years are not so different. May I call you sister?"

It was the exact right thing to say, because Sonnet nuzzled her cheek and murmured, "*Sister* when I'm wearing shoes, *brother* when I'm barefoot."

Snow promised, "I will remember."

"Stay, Sonnet," urged Ginkgo. "Please?"

The wolf smiled softly and settled onto one of the rockers.

"We're all here, so let's have it out. Okay if I keep the introductions simple?" Ginkgo waited for Snow, who signaled for him to run ahead. "Tsumiko is my best friend. Jacques is Dad's best friend. Boon is my big brother, and he's representing the pack I've been running with since I was just a runt. They're my people, and I trust their opinions."

Snow sized them up anew. "You want me to convince them? Or are *you* not convinced?"

Jacques spoke up. "He's not playing hard-to-get, Transcendence. We're here to pinch him and assure him that this isn't just a lovely dream."

Which was so true, Ginkgo lapsed into a smile. Jacques understood what this meant for him. Better than anyone.

Tsumiko was asking questions with her eyes, but she was too polite to say anything, so Ginkgo filled her in. "I met Transcendence last summer. At Wardenclave. She and Pact are here because they want me to be their family. Guess you'd say she's proposing. Or … making a formal offer for me."

Understanding dawned, because Ginkgo had shared plenty of puppy stories with Tsumiko. "Snow," she breathed.

"That *is* my pack nickname," Transcendence confirmed. "And it is as Ginkgo says. My son and I have chosen."

Tsumiko looked to Ginkgo and asked, "You're in love?"

This was far too sudden to go *that* far. He hadn't entertained those kinds of thoughts about Snow. Not once. "If you're asking if I want this, then yeah." He sought Jacques' gaze and added, "I mean … *wolves*."

The man agreed with a wordless joy that hit them all like a physical force. Even Tsumiko seemed to notice, which was new. Not many reavers could get a sense for each other, but an imp? Oh, yes. Jacques' impish legacy was making itself felt.

"Wolves in general? Or wolves in particular?" Tsumiko radiated confusion. "Surely you're not accepting Transcendence simply because of her clan?"

Ginkgo hurried over and knelt before her. "You're right. I wouldn't take up with just anyone simply because they're a wolf. But running with wolves means I understand that Snow's serious. And that I'm really very lucky."

She touched his cheek. "You're a fox."

"Half, yeah. And like Dad, I'll choose once and well."

That earned him a smile. "Look at you. You're *pleased* about all of this."

"Snow *knows* me." Ginkgo didn't bother lowering his voice. He wanted all of them—most especially Snow—to hear his side of this. "She wants me because I'm me. It's a first."

Jacques spoke up again, addressing Transcendence. "He's in high demand. Packets from the reavers. Propositions from the public sector. A recent bidding war between a couple of the feline courts. All unprovoked. All rebuffed. All from complete strangers who want access to Argent, Stately House, or lord, let's face it ... it could just be the ears."

Boon, Sonnet, and Snow all started growling at the same time.

Wolves. They really were the best.

"They don't matter. This matters." Ginkgo gratefully accepted Tsumiko's nod.

Jacques asked, "Will there be a ceremony of sorts? *Do* let Anjou and I fancy you up."

"You know me. Always up for a party."

Boon drawled, "Hey, little bro. You really need my say-so for this?"

"Sure. You just established a den that's ... well, it's a little different. How's it working out for you?"

"None of your business."

"I'm not after *details* ...!" Ginkgo protested.

Jacques fussed with his cufflinks. "If compatibility across clans is your concern, I'm confident that everything will—as you say—*work out.*"

Boon rolled his eyes and bluntly addressed Snow. "May as

well be clear. I have two bondmates."

"Ginkgo will be my second."

"Mine are a little more … concurrent. A she-wolf and a beacon. It's complicated. Anyhow … you okay with a fox-crosser for a bondmate?"

She flatly retorted, "You would not be the first to question my tastes."

Waving that aside, Boon said, "Nothing wrong with your senses. Every den has a heart. He'll be yours."

Yeah, that sounded about right. Wow, it sounded nice.

Boon went right on, the lilt of teasing in his tone. "Might seem like he's dragging his feet, but he's really just showing you off."

"That's not it," Ginkgo protested. "It's more like … connecting last summer with the rest of my life."

"Totally get that." Then Boon promised, "The pack will see you off with songs."

Tsumiko addressed Snow. "I'll ask our bard to honor your choice and bless your future."

"Dragon song," Ginkgo remarked. "That's high end."

Sonnet murmured, "The stars are already singing."

"I know. Nothing but portents and puppy pleas since summer's end." Snow's gaze sought Ginkgo's. "As if I didn't already know my own mind."

Jacques advised, "Make haste and state your claim, good lady. Gingko is rarer than moonbeams."

Without batting an eye, the she-wolf declared, "He is mine."

Ginkgo pivoted slightly to look up at her and answered, "My choice is made. All good?"

"Witnessed!" Jacques sang out, looking pleased. "Can I get a second?"

"Right here," said Boon.

Sonnet drummed her fingers over her heart and exclaimed, "There should be cake. Oh, do you think Cherish would come? His cakes are unrivaled."

Jacques hummed doubtfully. "We can ask, but I don't know what his lordship will say. There's a lot going on just now."

Tsumiko said, "You should pick a day."

So it was going to be a wedding after all. Not really a surprise. Tsumiko was traditional like that. Ginkgo said, "Hey, Jacques. What's Dad's calendar look like?"

"Full moon's next week," Boon supplied. "That'd be the right kind of auspicious."

"Ohhh!" Sonnet breathed, fresh sparkle in her eyes. "It will be the Den Moon."

"Does that work for you?" Ginkgo asked, trying for calm even though his heart was betraying him.

Snow shifted into a receptive posture, a reserved response, if not for the glad twirl of her tail. He'd made her happy, and that meant the world.

Ginkgo firmed his stance and promised, "My den will be ready."

She spoke with supreme confidence, "All I need, you will be."

38

FOSTERLINGS

Sibley woke from a doze, shocked with himself. Maybe all these peaceful days were making him lazy? He didn't need sleep like Etienne did, but curled around the toddler, surrounded by Anjou's soft fur and purring, he'd drifted off.

A gentle hand was making slow circles against his back, which was nice. He knew it was Anjou, and Etienne still clung to Sibley even in sleep. He pressed his nose into wispy-soft hair that smelled fancy from all the pampering the little guy had received from his new papa. Lucky boy. Good for him.

Finally, Sibley lifted his face to find Uncle Jackie's cat quietly gazing at him.

"*Bonjour.*"

"Hi." Sibley wasn't sure if he was intruding. Argent had handed Etienne over for fostering, and maybe that meant he was in the way. "Didja want to hold him?"

"I can hold you both."

"Not sure you should. Etienne's the one you got from … from Mr. Mettlebright." Sibley had a hard time thinking of Argent as dad, even if that's what the fox had invited all of them to call him.

"What is this?" Anjou asked, gently ruffling Sibley's hair. "Tell me what has you worried, and I will banish it."

Sibley searched the cat's face and wondered how someone could look so much like this place's lord fox … but feel so different. Silver hair. Blue eyes. Pale and pretty. But where Kyrie's dad was sharp and quick and cool, Anjou was all softness and smiles.

"I'm not yours."

"*Non*? Jacques is your uncle, and Etienne is your brother. These are strong connections."

"But … you and me. It's not like I'll call you p-papa or anything. That's for Etienne."

Anjou asked, "Would you like to? I can speak to Argent on your behalf. Such a thing … yes, I know it would please my bondmates."

Sibley's heart was skittering, but he had to warn this guy. So he repeated, "Not sure you should. On account of these." He held up a hand, curling the fingers. "They're poison. Same as Etienne's."

"*Oui.*" Anjou didn't look nearly as worried as he should be.

"Doncha care?"

"For cats, caring happens with startling swiftness. A few hours in my arms, and I find myself unwilling to let you go to another."

Sibley shook his head, afraid he was misunderstanding things. "You care about me?"

"*Oui.*" Anjou went back to rubbing slow circles on Sibley's back. "This is not the first time I held you. Do you remember?"

"On the barge? Kinda." With a shrug, Sibley admitted, "I had a hard time telling you and the other guy apart."

"And I did not know then that Jacques would come to see me as his own. Or that you would honor me by wishing to become mine." Anjou gently added, "Let me ask for you. Join our hearth, and you will have your uncle, a mother, and me. And Etienne will be surrounded and protected and loved."

"But ... I want Kyrie to be my brother."

"He will always be your brother."

"Well, yeah. I guess. But ... but ...." Except Sibley couldn't come up with any other protests. Because Anjou was all softness and smiles, and he made Sibley feel safe. "You feel honored?"

"Two bondmates, and now two sons? And our joy will be redoubled when Jacques delivers his child and their twin."

"But ... my claws ...." Nobody would want his claws near their precious baby.

"I shall beautify them with all my skill." Anjou took Sibley's hand and gave his fingers a gentle squeeze. "How fortunate for you that your papa knows all about sigils for sealing away that which is precious ... or precarious."

"What?" Sibley quickly checked his claws, then shook his head in confusion.

"I tamed Etienne's while you were sleeping. Can you tell?"

Sibley carefully took one of the baby's thin hands, which curled trustingly around his bigger fingers. He studied the neat point of each small claw, shining softly from the previous night's manicure. And yes, there. A faint shimmer betrayed Anjou's sigilcraft.

"You did this?"

"I did."

"Is it safe?" asked Sibley. "He can't hurt anyone now?"

"He can break my heart with a whimper, for his nightmares wound me. But *non*. So long as I refresh the wards, he cannot harm anyone with poison. It is contained—fingers and toes."

Sibley gruffly asked, "Do mine?"

"*Naturellement*. I was only waiting for permission to proceed."

It was too good to be true. Or ... just good. Really, really good. Sibley's mind was more than made when he asked, "How do I say *yes*?"

Anjou hummed. "I think you just did."

"But what's your way? How do cats say it?"

"A little at a time, so that good things last as long as possible."

Sibley thought that sounded kind of nice, but he was mostly stumped. "How's that work, though? Or do you mean I gotta wait for permission?"

"*Non*. I will see to everything," Anjou promised. "Trust your papa, *n'est pas*?"

"Okay, sure. I can do that." And because it probably counted as a little, and it might take a lot of times before he got used to it, Sibley cautiously added, "Papa ...?"

Anjou began to purr.

Sibley had no idea what Etienne was chattering about, but his little brother sounded happy, so that was all right. He toted the boy to the kitchen, straight to Sonnet. She scooped up her *darling boy*, promising him a lovely breakfast, and Sibley held very still, half-hoping Uncle Jackie's wolf would forget about him. Then he could slip away. But her gaze fixed on him in a way that made Sibley wonder what Anjou had done.

"Pardon me, love." Sonnet dropped into a crouch, her skirts puffing out, her nostrils quivering as she took deep breaths. Finally, she whispered, "Sibley?"

"Yeah?"

"Oh, I do think …. Yes, it must be true. Sibley, love, are you one of mine now?"

"Kinda. If that's okay." And because he was curious, he asked, "You can tell?"

"Anjou is quite serious when it comes to matters of the hearth, and for felines, that includes the care and protection of children. You and Etienne are sparkling with proof that Anjou is a good and wise tom."

"Did he mark me?"

"Beautifully." She confided, "Jacques and I have been encouraging him to be more possessive, and it's a fine thing he's done, claiming another son."

"He said I should call him … papa."

"Oh, love, I do hope you will." Very solemnly, she asked, "Will you let me mother you?"

Sibley couldn't remember his mother. It hadn't taken long at the lab to figure out that she'd probably either died or disowned him. "Is that okay? I mean, aren't you practically everyone's mother?"

"That's true." Sonnet nodded absently, then leaned closer.

"Isn't that just right for us, though? You look after your brothers and sisters more than anyone. And I do my part. Then there's Jacques, who is everyone's favorite uncle. We're all taking care of Stately House, but ... well, Anjou is most insistent that someone should be taking care of us."

Sibley studied his claws. With sigils, they were almost as beautiful as Kyrie's adornments.

And Sonnet was beautiful, too, smelling like cinnamon and happiness and Jacques.

He confessed, "I wanted to belong to Uncle Jackie. He was brave and stupid and fancy and ... and I knew right away that if he was my family, that'd be good."

"It was the same for me," Sonnet confided. "I loved him from the beginning, even though I didn't realize how much. I think that a heart knows what it needs."

"Yeah." Sibley edged nearer to Sonnet. "If you wanted to mother me, I think it'd be okay. How do wolves say *yes*?"

"Ohhh, usually with closeness and songs and the wagging of tails."

"I've got a tail," Sibley reminded, lifting his to slip around Sonnet's wrist.

Her lashes fluttered, and her eyes went all shiny. And then he and Etienne were squished together in a strong embrace that rumbled with wolvish approval. Sibley grinned at his little brother, whose surprise melted into a pleased giggle.

"What should I call you?" asked Sibley.

"I'm Sonnet," she said. "It's simplest. But if you decide to give me a different name, I'll answer to that."

He'd never named anyone before. Even Bother was still Bother. Deciding on a name for someone felt too important for someone like him. Maybe Uncle Jackie would have a good idea. Or ... *oh*. He suddenly wanted very much to talk to ... well, to someone like him. So he asked, "Can I tell Kyrie?"

39

NEW VENTURES

Even a strategist like Argent couldn't see any alternative. There was a gap in the Dichotomy Day schedule that had been left too long. Was Isla being overly optimistic when she'd left Hisoka Twineshaft's appearance on the calendar? Did she think that would conjure him up? Or was she hoping that Argent would force him out of seclusion?

Much as he appreciated everything Isla had done for the In-between, he wished she'd made alternate arrangements sooner. Because the only person who could step in was Argent himself. And that meant he was going to miss Ginkgo's bonding ceremony.

So be it. He would do his part. But the necessity put him in a mood.

Escaping out the nearest window, Argent considered his options and soon spied a suitable diversion. Veering toward

Bon-Bon, Argent stepped across his path and announced, "You will do."

He flinched away, then exploded, "You utter beast! Don't *do* that. I know you're lord of the bloody manor and all that, but there are basic courtesies that must be observed. Always."

Argent allowed himself a moment of smug satisfaction. Boniface might startle easily, but he refused to quail. Indeed, there were definite signs of an underlying trust. Suuzu had secured a capable counterpart. One who was currently burdened by a chrysalis. Bon-Bon hugged the swaddled and swagged bundle to his midriff.

"I apologize."

"You ... err ... really?" And with honest bewilderment, he offered a wary, "Right."

With a roll of one wrist, Argent indicated that Boniface should continue along the path. Then he fell in step beside the man. It didn't take long for him to speak again.

"To what do I owe the pleasure?"

"You need not pretend to enjoy my company."

"And you don't normally seek mine," Boniface crisply countered. "*You will do.* That's what you said. Do for what?"

"How are things with Suuzu?"

The man frowned, but he accepted the change of subject. "If you mean me, it's too soon to tell. But Suuzu is surrounded by good people. Magarr has taken charge of the day-to-day running of the office. Honestly, I think he already dealt with most things. To be clear, Suuzu isn't a figurehead for the avian and fabled races. Rather, Magarr is an exceptional mentor with a vested interest in Suuzu's happiness."

"You have also found Magarr's guidance helpful?"

"Invaluable."

"You may rely upon the greater experience of my staff, as well."

"Your staff? Oh. You mean Jackie."

"If it would make things easier, I could formalize an apprenticeship."

"Hardly necessary." Boniface stopped in his tracks and muttered, "Lord, don't you start, too."

A harmonic keening had started up.

Argent pressed his palm to the rock imp snugged against Boniface's belly.

"*Resonance*, they're all saying," Boniface grumbled. "But you can't expect two people who've never gotten on to simply … get over it and get on with it."

"Do I need to take Jackie to task?"

"As if. He's … he's a tribute to your den, and you bloody well know it." Boniface admitted, "He's been decent enough, but we're as good as strangers."

"Except you're not."

"Very not."

"Mmm. So what's set this little one to singing?"

"What else? He adores his daddy."

"*He?*" Argent pivoted, lifting his nose, covering his consternation. He still wasn't used to Jacques' missing sigils, which he'd clearly relied upon to alert him to his man's proximity.

"I don't really care if he turns out to be a she. Or one of the indeterminates. Just avoiding *it*, since he's clearly a person. A small, noisy, needy person. With a Jackie complex."

Argent slanted a look at Boniface. "Are you exaggerating?"

"About what? Him?" The man stood there, awkwardly patting the rock imp. "Understating, more like."

"None of the others have mentioned anything about personality."

"I should think it difficult to avoid. Comes with personhood." And with a resigned glance at the man catching them up, he fell silent.

Jacques slowed to a stroll before exclaiming, "Lord, here you are. Here you both are. Ah, you want acknowledgment as well? You'll have more luck with that if you're no longer a lump."

Argent was startled when the chrysalis essentially whimpered.

"All right," Jacques soothed, putting a hand against the crystal. "Uncle Jackie's here."

"He calls you *daddy*," muttered Boniface.

Jacques' gaze softened. "Clever boy, aligning yourself with Clan Smythe. Wait a tick. What's he call you?"

"Not sure. It's not a word, exactly. More of a trill. Maybe it doesn't translate from impish?" He addressed the chrysalis again, "If you came out and found your feet, you could simply follow your daddy around like a proper toddler."

"Assuming rock imps have precocious young."

Argent was several varieties of stunned by this exchange. Between two men who generally referred to each other in snide tones. Yet here, in a shining lump of crystalline potential, they'd found common ground. And quite possibly a united front. He found himself asking, "What did you two *do* with this one?"

Jacques glanced between Argent and Boniface. "Nothing special …?"

"Definitely just bearing up under the responsibility," confirmed Boniface.

"The others have been comparatively quiescent," said Argent. "Even Michael's."

"Ours is clearly the pick of the litter," Boniface said smugly.

"*Speaking* of Michael." Jacques eyed Argent. "I take it you already know?"

"Mmm."

Boniface shifted into a quizzical stance. Avian, of course.

Jacques responded as if it was the most natural thing in the world. "Sansa's gone into labor, and birthings trigger his lordship's flight instinct."

"Why? Are you squeamish? *I'd* be squeamish."

Argent opted for honesty. "I am sensitive to the mother's stress and the accompanying strain on the child. Especially when potent souls are involved."

Boniface pointed in the direction they'd been walking. "More distance?"

"Please."

"Is it worse because there are twins? When I was here last, Nonny mentioned twins."

Argent said, "So it would seem." It was as good an excuse as any.

But then Jacques suddenly asked, "Will this small distance really make a difference? I can tell you're … ah. Shall we say *invested*?"

Argent favored his man with a warning look. Really, it was unnerving how much Jacques could see. His man made a subtle sign for secrecy, and Argent could *feel* Jacques' approval, which somewhat diminished Argent's pique over being found out.

When Tsumiko had first arrived at Stately House, he'd been near death from depletion and ready for the respite. But presented with a beacon's resources, he'd taken full advantage of her ignorance and her generosity, only to realize that the more strength he pulled into his reserves, the more he found. At first, he could only be relieved. Then greedy. Then alert enough to shore up his defenses, lest his new mistress break him.

And still he took.

Adding to his flourish.

Building his reserves.

And still there was more.

Perhaps he'd done it to please her. Maybe he'd wanted to see if it could be done. Softly. Slyly. Because Tsumiko's first wish—her first command—had been for Michael and Sansa to become family, and Argent was inclined to protect that wish.

So he took and took.

Stealing in abundance.

Bestowing by increments.

And them none the wiser.

He'd known someone would notice eventually. That the couple Tsumiko considered kin were sharing her years. At least, that was Argent's perspective. Because it would be unseemly for a fox to bind three lives to his own. His role was ... conduit.

For her sake. And for his own. But also for Stately House.

Its future would spring from her faith and his foresight.

He doubted any would quibble over the consequences, which were largely good. The only upshot thus far had come to light during Vanya's birth.

Invested? That was understatement.

Privy. That was closer to the truth.

Argent occasionally worried what Sansa might do once she realized their connection existed. She might take exception. *He* certainly would have.

Jacques redirected by asking, "Are the babies beacons?"

"Probably not this time."

Boniface's eyes widened. "Lord, there's a beacon in the enclave. Isn't that meant to be incredibly rare?"

"Has nobody mentioned?" Jacques asked. "His lordship is too subtle by far. Tsumiko is a beacon, as is Michael's and Sansa's daughter Lilya."

"We've met. Kyrie made sure to introduce me to both his best friends."

"Boon brought home another beacon. Dr. Elara Perrine is still operating with a seal. Much like Tsumiko, she's had no formal training. And ... I would rank Naoki at beacon-class. Not that we'll be publicizing either doctor's presence in our enclave."

"Come to think ... Kyrie did mention that the chauffeur was a dynasty founder. He left out the particulars, though. I suppose he was trying to make certain I was showing proper respect."

He sounded exasperated. With himself.

"While not beacons, I am putting stock in Nonny's prediction that these twins will wreak havoc. Already there are signs of ... synergy."

Boniface asked, "Is anyone surprised? Resonance is clearly the done thing at Stately House."

With a short laugh, Jacques said, "Synergy or no, Sansa will have her progeny well in hand."

True words and truer.

Argent dragged his attention to the fore and brightened at the prospect of further distraction. Quickening his pace, he accosted Suuzu and Akira and genially lied, "I do not wish to intrude …?"

Suuzu tutted dismissively, and Akira's smile was as artless and endearing as ever. Keeping hold of Suuzu's hand, he spoke for both of them. "We don't mind. We were actually waiting here for Boniface."

This was news to Argent. They were on the path that led in the general direction of Randolla's shop, so he'd assumed Boniface intended to consult with the tailor. It was a very Smythe thing to do.

"We've been walking all morning," Akira went on. "I wanted to see where the grove would be. And places with room for another tree. For my tree.

"I would be happy to show you the sites I had in mind." Argent considered the Smythe brothers' shoes and warned, "It would involve a great deal of walking."

"My bit won't take long. Wait here while I rally the powers that be." And Boniface sauntered off.

"What's he on about?" Jacques asked curiously.

"He asked us to meet him here," said Akira.

Jacques peered doubtfully at the frozen marsh. "Here?"

Argent didn't know what Bon-Bon was up to, which was mildly vexing.

The man was already returning, bustling along despite his

burden, beaming as he placed an antique-looking key in Suuzu's hand. "There you are. Best I could come up with on short notice. It's a bit early, but Happy Christmas and all that."

Jacques broke the sudden silence. "What does that key unlock?"

Boniface spun in place and pointed to one of the sedge's several huts. "That one at the very edge. With the ladder. I had it added for Akira. Rustic, I know, but there's a little stove and basic plumbing. Cabinets and shelving. A window seat. Otherwise unfurnished, but Randolla assured me that Suuzu would want to feather his own nest."

Akira glanced up at Suuzu, who looked utterly stunned.

More tentatively now, Boniface said, "He's laid in several bolts for you to choose from. We could go along now ...? Have a look ...? *Non* ...?"

Argent decided to intervene. "You bought Suuzu a nest."

"Arranged for," Boniface corrected. "It's a rental. Ready for immediate occupancy. I thought ... well. Even if they keep their suite in the main house, don't all newlyweds like a bit of privacy?"

Jacques warmly declared, "Bravo."

Boniface flushed and cast another worried glance Suuzu's way, only to have the young avian step closer and pull him into an embrace that Akira quickly joined. Not much was said, but Boniface grumbled about getting soppy and only doing his part.

Jacques tucked his arm through Argent's. "Good man," he murmured.

Argent confessed, "I hated you both. Or perhaps ... I resented the hold you had over me. I was at your mercy."

"You still are."

"By choice," Argent countered. "Having a choice makes all the difference."

"*About* that."

Concern jittered through the connection that contact fostered, and several tails flashed into the open before Argent could get himself in hand. He coolly asked, "What has you worried."

"It's ... well, I came to a realization." Jacques sighed. "Lord, don't go snarly. It's nothing to do with enemies at the door or portents of doom. It's more personal. But it's affecting the people I care about."

Argent brought out more tails, wreathing his man in a show of support. "Tell me."

"As you may recall, I have considerable experience when it comes to pursuits of a pleasurable nature."

"Is that pertinent?"

Jacques nodded. "I have—shall we say—basis for comparison."

Argent couldn't imagine why he was mincing words. "You hardly need my advice when it comes to the needs of one's bonded."

"*Non.*" The man glanced toward Suuzu's celebratory cluster. "I apologize for bringing up a delicate subject."

"You've never minded before."

"I'm not teasing, Argent. I wouldn't. Not when I know how important this is. And for how many." He lowered his voice. "Not when I know what it will mean for you. What I've already gone and done."

"You have effectively established your feelings on the matter. The facts, less so."

Jacques took a deep breath, then quietly announced, "I know what I am."

Argent straightened. "You have realized something about Dayith's legacy?"

"Mmm. Rather." But instead of stating it plainly, he asked, "You know how Tenma is the answer to the Broken? It has to be due to impish meddling, either directly or somewhere in his bloodline."

"That *is* the going theory."

"My legacy is similar-ish. And devilishly *apropos*."

"In what sense?"

"Look, I didn't know. And I apologize. But … it'll be fine."

Argent stared blankly, trying to sift through the sudden shift of emotions. "Jackie, what is it you think you've done?"

"I'll just say it."

"I think you had better."

"The thing of it is, Tenma is the answer to the Broken." With an apologetic sort of smile, Jacques revealed, "And I'm the answer to the Waning."

40
CHANGING WINDS

After introducing Anan to Randolla so that the tailor could fit him for a festival coat and some regular attire, Kyrie determinedly guided the eldermost storm to the theater, where Catalan Evernhold was leading a rehearsal. This year's Christmas play would be a reprise of the previous year's *A Christmas Carol*, which was going to be very interesting. Because Cat had decided that Uncle Boniface should be Uncle Jackie's understudy for the role of Bob Cratchit.

He was really very good. Not scared at all about being on stage. Even with Dad standing in for Ambrose Scatterlight, who would arrive on Christmas Eve, just in time to take the lead.

"Found you!" came a hushed exclamation.

A hand slipped into his, and Kyrie smiled. Sibley had a knack for finding him, no matter where he might be, and it was nice. Kyrie was glad that Sibley liked the idea of being brothers as much as he did. Blood ties might not be the *only* way of belonging to someone, but he couldn't deny the many new bonds that had been forged because of a shared sire.

"I am here." And noticing the dusting of flower petals in Sibley's hair, Kyrie began plucking like a preening avian. "Did you ask for Grandfather's help?"

"Had to. When there's a lot of ground to cover, a tree's a good friend to have."

Kyrie hummed happily and pulled Sibley firmly to his side, ignoring Anan's moody glance. Thankfully, the wind imp was interested in the play, so his attention returned to the stage.

But then Kyrie noticed something new and gasped, putting Sibley at arm's length. Where …? There! "Show me your claws!" he whispered excitedly.

Sibley surrendered his hands, which had been neatly warded.

"These are wonderful. Did Papka do this? But no … the sigilcraft does not feel like his."

"Anjou." Up on tiptoe, Sibley quietly shared, "He wants to be my … my papa. Mine and Etienne's."

Kyrie was dumbstruck.

As silence lengthened between them, Sibley grew increasingly worried. "Are you mad?"

"No! I am *pleased* for you and Etienne. I was only wondering if there will be others within the enclave who might want to foster our brothers and sisters. We are a big family. Perhaps we are too big?"

"Me and Sonnet and Uncle Jackie are going to take care of everyone at Stately House. And … and then Papa will take care of us."

"That is a good plan."

"We're still brothers, though. You and me."

Anan loomed over them, interrupting Kyrie's answer. Without a word, he scooped them up and began walking.

"Where are you taking us?" Kyrie asked.

"I want to be outside."

Sibley asked, "Where outside?"

"The woods."

"Oh, yeah?" Gazing around curiously, Sibley pressed, "How come?"

"I prefer open skies. And I need a place away from prying ears."

"Are you gonna thunder again?"

Anan grumbled, "I do not answer to you, little brother."

Sibley blinked. And smiled.

Kyrie rested his cheek against Anan's chest and relaxed. Being in the arms of a thundercloud was a little like flying. Something about the scents and the smoothness of his wind's stride. He reached for Sibley's hand and curled their fingers together, glad to share this moment.

Sibley matched him, leaning into Anan and murmuring, "In stories, only the best dragons tame winds."

Kyrie shook his head. "What if Anan has tamed us?"

"Hey, Anan? *Are* you our brother? Like … Ginkgo is our big brother, and you're our eldermost brother?"

A soft trill escaped Kyrie, who peeped up through his lashes to see what Anan would say.

"You aspire to much, little brother."

"What's that mean? Aspire."

Kyrie said, "To want something very much. To do your best to reach it."

"That's a good word. But I dunno if there's anything left for me to aspire about. I've got a home. And a hearth. And bigger brothers." He nuzzled Anan's chest. "Even an eldermost brother."

"You aspire to take care of your family," Anan reminded. "But the gathering isn't complete."

Kyrie immediately realized what he meant. "There are more of us."

"That's the way the stars sing it."

"Can you help me collect them?"

"No small feat, little terror." But eventually, Anan added, "Perhaps. If Dima was willing. Perhaps."

Kyrie waited to see if Dima would have anything to say on the matter.

And waited.

He'd adjusted to her presence, and perhaps she was adjusting to him. But he wasn't sure what kind of person she was, and that bothered him. Sure, these three were part of a group known as the Changing Winds, and historians agreed that they were the companions of Bethiel. But Kyrie was interested in the wind imps as individuals. How could he not be?

He was a crosser, but not all crossers were the same. He was a crystal adept, but his talent took a different shape from others with the same classification. He was a child of the Rogue, but he and his siblings were many and varied. In the end—or from the beginning—Kyrie was Kyrie. So it would be almost *rude* to lump together these three.

Yes, they were wind imps.

Yes, they were eldermost storms.

Yes, they were historic, even legendary.

But before all of that, they were Anan, Dima, and Haizea.

So Kyrie said, "Anan is taking us in among the trees, Dima. I wonder if you would like my woods? To rattle through bare branches and to tip snow from pine boughs."

Anan blandly asked, "*Your* woods? Are you claiming swaths of land as well as sky?"

"In a way." Kyrie tried to think how to explain. "Every tree in these woods shares a bond with me. They have names and voices and a part in my plans."

Sibley said, "It's true. He showed me. Listen for it. They know he's close."

Anan stopped right there in the snow and cocked his head to one side. Raising his voice, he announced, "Dima, I believe him."

It reminded Kyrie of that first night on the shore, when he'd been soaked through and too cold and at a loss. Anan had said, *he believed me*. That time, Kyrie was embarrassed to admit that—for a moment—he'd thought Anan was triumphing over him. That Kyrie had trusted amiss. Believed a lie.

But Kyrie understood the thunderstorm better now. Anan had been telling the truth when he said he didn't really understand lies. The newly descended wind imp had been telling Dima something about Kyrie. That Kyrie had believed Anan.

According to lore, not many people believed in winds. Too fickle, too flighty. They could be a passing fancy, but winds—supposedly—never stayed. Kyrie thought that perhaps, long ago, another person had believed Anan. And that's why his wind still treasured his friend Bethiel.

Anan added, "He's right. You'd like these woods. They're sturdy. And full of wolves. And the trees whisper small songs. It would be impolite to flatten them."

Kyrie wondered if Anan was trying to give Dima reasons to descend. So he offered, "I walk among these trees, and I tell them their names. They welcome me into their midst, and they sing for me."

Sibley asked, "Is it the trees that love you or the crystals you put in them?"

"Both, I think. A ring becomes a ring once the stone is in its setting. This forest is the setting for remnants and their songs."

"You took two things and made something new?"

"He changed them," said Anan. "Reshaped them like the winds that dance among the dunes, sculpting as they go. Right, Haizea?"

The whirlwind didn't answer. But Dima did, blunt and bold.

"Shepherd of woodlands, lowlier than skies, what are they for?"

"The trees?" checked Kyrie.

"Why take them? Why remake them?"

Something in her tone made him ask, "Do you think I should not have done it?"

"Answer me. Explain yourself."

"Yes, all right. It is an interesting question." Kyrie peered around as Anan began to walk again. "Normally, I would say that trees are for shelter and shade and food and climbing. Trees have their own beauty."

"But you intruded upon their simplicity," challenged Dima. *"You complicated their existence. Why?"*

Anan added his own accusation. "You found a use for them,

and so you became generous. You gave them voices so they could serve you."

Kyrie weighed their words carefully. Did these winds think he'd enslaved the trees? Their perspective was unique, being embodiments of nature. Finally, he shook his head. "I do not think I am looking down on them."

"Would you know if you were?" countered the thunderstorm.

"With a friend like you to call my motives into question? Yes."

"Friends, are we?"

Kyrie silently offered up his free hand, where Anan's mark shone so brightly, nobody would consider it subtle. Or even hidden.

"Strange boy," muttered Anan.

"*Suits you,*" accused Dima.

"And you? What will you do, Dima?"

The typhoon fell silent, and Kyrie thought it was a brooding, building sort of silence, like the gathering of a storm. It would break eventually. Probably directly overhead.

41
NAMESAKE

Juuyu remained at Stately House in order to help prepare the way for a Scattering. Nothing new for a tribute of his years, but neither was it usual. To make safe a group of tree-kin colonists, most of whom were children. To mingle with refugees who remembered him and trusted him and took to calling him *uncle*. To arrive in time to see his brother's delight in his bondmate … and to celebrate the nest they'd establish in this good place.

Reasons to sing were multiplying, and he didn't hold back.

And it was a heady thing, dueting with a dragon bard.

Nearly as exhilarating as catching the songs of stars, who drew near to this place, full of portents and promises. Tuning their lullabies to the baby talk of the four wardstones, one of whom had found a thread of longing Juuyu had missed. Or at least mistook.

Sinder.

Juuyu was pleased to note that the dragon was humming again.

It was a sound that had faded over the months, and its absence was a clue that Juuyu had overlooked. Why had he not noticed? It had begun last summer, after Juuyu extracted the young dragon from Wardenclave. At the time, Sinder had been glad enough to return to his side. But perhaps there *had* been a certain amount of … pining.

Waaseyaa and Zisa were often mentioned, but had Timur been the true source of the wistfulness in Sinder's shifting moods? Mmm. Perhaps. Even if they had not formed a love match, dragons held tightly to the things that mattered to them. Juuyu should have guessed there was a bond in place the moment he saw Sinder go limp at a touch from Timur. Had that relaxation been—at least in part—relief?

But the feline. Timur's Kith partner. That one … mmm.

Maybe it was boredom that had caused Juuyu to bend his focus Fend's way. And maybe it was none of his business. And yet he had a scant handful of days before the Scattering would arrive. Juuyu checked his pocket watch and nodded to himself. Four more days. He would decide whether or not to confront Fend in four days.

In the meantime, he had three eldermost storms to consider.

He rapped on the door to the Rosewood Parlor precisely at eleven.

Nonny shot him a look that might have been exasperated. "It's open. You don't have to knock if it's open. And as you can see, we're the farthest thing from warded." He rolled his eyes toward the passel of crossers crowding Anan. "This is what they don't tell you about gathering storms. They gather stuff. Mostly crossers. How do you take your tea?"

Juuyu needed several moments to take in the unexpected glut of information, and once he had, he found Anjou at his elbow, a dainty cup on offer. He took the tea with murmured thanks, tasted it with appreciation, and held the gaze of Jacques Smythe's older brother long enough to earn comment.

"How do you do? I'm Boniface, recently attached to your brother's cortege." His posture was pointedly polite, and the angle of his head suggested avian instruction. "Still in training. Still pants at kids. Not that this one seems to mind."

Boniface Smythe perched primly on a tuffet, and he was thoroughly entwined in the coils of the girl-child who was part midivar.

"Do you need assistance?"

"What? No. We're getting on well enough. I've had to get used to coils and scales and things, haven't I? Once I arrived in Keishi, they put me in with Sylphon Basqwend. Been flatmates for weeks. Most mornings, I wake to coils. It's less nightmarish once you get over the shock. He's a good sort."

"Sylphon. Younger brother to Spokesperson Krail Basqwend." Juuyu had looked into all the members of Suuzu's staff as a matter of course.

"That's the chap. Fabled races and all that." Peering into faceted eyes of iridescent yellow, Boniface murmured, "You're enough to make a bloke believe in pixies."

"Bother is half-star," said Kyrie. "And half midivar."

"Half ... what now? Wait a tick. Did you just call her Bother?"

Sibley spoke up, calling Juuyu's attention to his presence.

"Lady asked me to think of a better name for her, but ... names are hard."

"Lord, they *can* be a trial. I've more than my fair share."

Kyrie trilled amusement and said, "Tell him, Uncle Boniface. Share your whole name."

With the hint of a self-deprecating smile, he announced, "My full name is Boniface Percival Christobel Yves Smythe."

Nonny said, "There you go, Sibley. We can call her Bon-Bon."

"That may be the *least* appealing namesake you could propose. Aside from Yvette. I couldn't bear it if you called her after Maman. And besides, it might get confusing if there were two Bon-Bons. It's the only thing my brother ever calls me."

"Your offer is very generous." Kyrie looked to Sibley. "Do you like any of Uncle Boniface's spares? If they share a name, that will be another bond. They will be family."

Juuyu thought Boniface might like to protest, but the little girl lay her head upon his shoulder, and he eased into a receptive posture. Feline nuances this time.

Anjou began to purr.

Sibley brightened. "Hear that, Bother? You and me, we'll be cousins."

Boniface seemed wary, but he held his peace, letting the children make their plans. Juuyu decided that at heart, Boniface Smythe was a kind person. When he next spoke, it was only to murmur, "I wish Sylphon could get a look at you. I think he'd be charmed."

"Careful what you wish for, Bon-Bon." Nonny had just warmed up Anan's tea. "She's a barrier dodger and a professional stowaway. You might get back home and find her in your baggage."

"I thought Uncle Boniface belonged here," said Kyrie. "With Uncle Suuzu."

"I have work," the man countered. "At the embassy."

"You could work from home."

Boniface hesitated, but he shook his head. "Hardly feasible. I've mentors and tutors and meetings and … lord, there's so much I need to learn before I can be useful."

Nonny said, "Going away to school's not so bad. Bon-Bon will be back after he's had enough lessons."

"Perhaps. If that's what Suuzu needs from me." Refocusing on Sibley, Boniface asked, "Did you need me to run through my names again. Or we could dip into Jackie's many monikers, since he seems to be an especial favorite of yours."

"He saved me."

"Good of him," Boniface mildly returned.

"Guess I already forgot your names. They're different."

So Boniface reeled them off again, this time spinning out family lore, grumping even as he reminisced.

Finally, Sibley asked, "Christobel?"

"If you're sure."

"I mean … it's kinda girly."

"I've always thought so, too." And arching his brows at the clinging girl, he asked, "What's your opinion, mademoiselle?"

She flicked the trailing end of her tail in Sibley's direction. It must have been something unique to them, because he immediately twined his tail around hers. "Yeah. Okay. We both like Christobel."

While Boniface lapsed into a discourse on feminine endings in French, Kyrie slipped to Juuyu's side and said, "Thank you for coming."

"Of course. You mentioned a predicament. And mediation ...?" He inclined his head toward Anan. "Between you and these imps?"

"Between these imps and Opulence Windlore." With a small shrug, Kyrie said, "I have tried to reason with them, but we are at an impasse."

"Mmm. Perhaps a quieter setting?"

"Yes. Thank you." The boy turned toward Anan and announced, "We are going with Juuyu."

With unhurried care, Anan extracted himself from his many admirers, returned his teacup to Nonny, and pulled the case holding the Bamboo Stave from atop a sizeable armoire.

Only when the eldermost storm was ready did Kyrie nod and say, "Lead on."

Juuyu strode into the hall, but he drew up short. "What shape do you want peace to take between your new friends and that old dragon?"

Kyrie smiled. "Music lessons. But Anan does not want to make peace with Opal before making peace with the Bamboo Stave."

"Mmm. My bondmate once played this instrument."

Anan stepped forward, stance aggressive. "Bring them. At once!"

"An impossibility. Fumiko is tree-kin. She is as rooted to her place as her sister. They are the heart of a grove."

"She could still give lessons," posed Kyrie. "Michael has an apprentice in America, and all of their lessons are accomplished over great distances."

Juuyu could see the sense, but technology wasn't his forte. "Sinder. Let us go where Sinder is."

Thanks to the tuned crystal in his necklace, Juuyu had a bearing, but he noticed that Kyrie turned in the correct direction a beat before he did. As if he knew where every soul at Stately House could be found. Perhaps he did.

Juuyu asked, "Do you have him marked?"

Kyrie simply nodded.

Amused, he asked, "Does he realize?"

The boy softly asked, "Have you realized?"

It took some time. Indeed, they were crossing the railroad tracks before Juuyu was sure that the three small sigils he'd found were all there were to find. He was impressed. "You are the most subtle person in my acquaintance."

Ears gone pink, Kyrie asked, "Should I remove them?"

"I could have done so, but I will not. I choose to remain as I am." He thought he understood, and so he added, "They are the gifts of a friend."

Anan snapped, "You will *not* mark him."

"No. I would not dare to impose upon your claim," Juuyu assured. "But perhaps a tuned crystal? I have a small bead that would suit you, I think. Deep within the amethyst range, with a subtle sort of authority. You could forge the connection yourself."

Anan glowered, but Kyrie warmly replied, "I would welcome such a gift from a friend."

They turned from the road, following tracks in the snow toward one of the sturdy fences along the boundary of a pasture.

Randolla Demoiselle and Fairlee Longbrawn perched there, along with a dozen dragon crossers. And Opal the Sage.

Something in the air changed. Charged.

Kyrie took Anan's hand.

The stormcloud sighed and stood down. Calmed.

A shadow swooped overhead, and laughter rolled, rich and full. Timur had begun training and was clearly enjoying his dragon's looping flight path. Juuyu thought Sinder looked happy, too. It was a shame to interrupt.

"Sinder."

The dragon spun his way and slipped gracefully from the sky, only shifting after Timur slid from his back. Hurrying over, Sinder briskly asked, "Need something?"

"A phone."

"You really should carry your own. I'm going to let you in on a little secret. Most people do."

Randolla and Fairlee brought out theirs, waving them demonstratively.

Timur, who'd been checking his messages, was quickly mobbed by youngsters begging for rides.

"I am aware that there are others whose phones I might have borrowed. However, yours is the most secure."

"You need me to call someone?"

"Anan wishes to confer with Fumiko."

"Oh, yeah?" Sinder gave the eldermost storm a considering look, but he brought out his phone, tapped a few times, and held it out. Tones indicated that a call had been initiated.

When Anan made no move to take the phone, Sinder rolled his

eyes and offered it to Kyrie instead. "Show him how it's done?"

"I will. Thank you."

"Not a problem." And once the two of them drifted apart, Sinder beckoned to Juuyu. "Want in on this? I've mostly figured out how not to drop him, but some kind of saddle or harness would be better than bareback. That's why Randolla and Fairlee are here. But if Timur wants to start swinging ropes or nets or whatever, it'll be a pain keeping my wings clear. I'm open to suggestion."

"Mmm." Juuyu slipped off his suit coat and began rolling up his sleeves.

Sinder looked relieved. Which was probably optimistic. But gratifying nonetheless.

42
AFTER HOURS

Timur's everything ached. But it was the good kind of heaviness that came from an intense day of maneuvers. How long had it been since he'd put in this much effort? Mum had needed a break from the usual rigors while carrying the twins. Honestly, Timur hadn't trained this hard since Gregor. Having a baby changed things. Would having a bondmate change things again?

But that reminded him. He needed to see if Fend liked his idea.

Giving his damp hair a final roughing up, he pulled on a clean hoodie and trekked upstairs. Easing past Sinder's new wards—the dragon had felt better once they were in place—Timur walked into his room. Or tried to. Coils of pearlescent dragon scales barred the way, stranding him on the threshold. "Budge over?"

Sinder scrunched, and Timur wedged himself far enough into the room to close the door.

He worked his way around until he could meet Sinder's gaze. The dragon looked vaguely sheepish, probably because he was cradling a purring Fend to his chest. The panther sprawled on his back, paws kneading the air while Sinder petted him.

"I'm not sure who's spoiling whom," Timur remarked. "Is Gregor somewhere in this tangle?"

Sinder produced the boy by lifting his tail, which was looped under Gregor's arms. The toddler dangled cheerfully and waved with both hands.

"There's Papka's little battler!"

With casual dexterity, Sinder ferried the boy to Fend, who captured him with all four paws and dabbed his tongue against one round cheek. Gregor chortled and clung, then peered around. He gabbled a string of syllables, and with an answering *tootle-peep*, his wind dragon unspooled from the nest Sinder must have made, given the abundance of yellow cloth.

She draped herself around Timur's shoulders. Then Fend reached out, and a velveted paw hooked around Timur's thigh, pulling.

"Am I wanted, then?"

The end of Sinder's tail wrapped Timur's ankle, twining up his calf. Thanks to their nascent bond, his hopes were easy enough to guess at.

"Did you want tending?"

Sinder's hand formed a swift negative, then gestured gracefully between them.

Catching on, Timur smiled crookedly. "Right. You want to tend me …? I'd like that. Will you remain in truest form? I must confess, I love the feel of dragon scales."

His bondmate blinked.

Fend shifted in order to relay, "You've flustered him. We should flatter him more."

"Is it really flattery if everything we say is true?"

Settling Gregor on one arm, Fend pressed his free hand to Timur's chest. "He likes your hands on him. You like the feel of dragon scales. And I am *so* easy to please, if only you would try."

"You're hardly neglected. I saw the state Sinder had you in."

"Hardly neglected … but hardly satisfied." And going up on tiptoe to steal a kiss, Fend whispered, "More, *ma moitié*. Be lavish with us both."

Fend did kiss him sometimes. Not often, and not at any great length. Timur had always written it off as feline impulse, proof of an affection he didn't always want to put into words. Was he worried about his part in their little family's new balance?

Timur hauled Fend to his side in a one-armed hug. "Did *you* want tending, then?"

"Always. And only from you."

"I'm at low ebb or I'd offer to brush you." Meeting Sinder's gaze, he said, "You have to be as bone-weary as I am. I should be warming oil and looking after any aches caused by carrying me aloft."

Sinder shifted, protesting, "Dunce and double dunce, there's such a thing as being too generous. Fend, help me get him into bed."

Timur wasn't that bad off, but he humored them. Sinder unseated the little wind dragon, and Fend rearranged pillows. It really did feel good to stretch out and go limp.

"You tend, I'll knead," said Fend.

"What about Gregor?" asked Sinder.

"Wants his papka. We'll see them both to sleep." Fend plunked their boy onto the mattress.

Timur rolled onto his side to pull his son close. Right away, he noticed something new. Really, it was a wonder he'd needed this long. He was a ward, for pity's sake. "Someone has a new bracelet."

Gregor lifted his arm, proudly announcing, "Lellow."

"Did Papka's dragon share a stone?" He arched his brows at Sinder. "It's a fine one."

"Lellow," Gregor repeated, poking at the line of seashells that further decorated the strand.

"Yes. Yellow. A sign of favor, since it's our dragon's favorite color."

Sinder fidgeted. "I thought I should get around to those safety protocols. I know Kyrie already has him decorated with stealth sigils, but I wanted a share. You … don't mind?"

"Your plans for our boy are good." Which reminded him. But before he could frame his idea, a plaintive humming came from under the pillows.

"You'll have yours, but only after you figure out how to *share* a pillow instead of prop one."

Their rock imp.

Sinder rattled on. "Gregor will probably love being a big brother. Assuming we get to keep you. Which I hope is an option. Because I'm going to want to keep you. I swear, instincts are scary as hell."

Fend lightly inquired, "Pretending to be greedy again?"

"I'm a dragon. It's part of my birthright."

Timur thought Sinder's greed could be easily mistaken for generosity.

"And your rock-child already believes that your lullabies are *their* birthright." Fend leaned into Timur and took on a tattling tone. "He's making certain that little one knows the sound of his voice."

Timur could remember wanting that for Gregor.

Sinder eyed him worriedly. "So? I mean … singing to a rock makes more sense than hugging a rock. Doesn't it?" And in a bid for support, he added, "Fend cuddles the impling when you're not looking."

He yawned and smiled and closed his eyes. "I'm in favor of both lullabies and cuddling."

"Speaking of birthrights," said Fend. "Where's mine, hmm? Stingy dragon."

"I'm working on it, okay? It's harder than I expected."

Timur asked, "Now, Fend. Are you making things difficult for my bondmate?"

"How was I to know he'd wallow in indecision."

"Hey, I tried. I keep trying. You've rejected everything I proposed."

"Dare I ask … what's the nature of these propositions?"

"Don't make it sound weird," begged Sinder. "He wants a name. It's traditional for Kith who show themselves to be Kith-kin to earn a new name. Usually something with more than four letters."

"What have you suggested so far?"

Fend immediately jumped in. "*Nothing* worth repeating, I assure you."

Timur was pleasantly surprised that Fend wanted a bond. "A new name is a big deal. A big responsibility."

"Yeah, yeah. It's an honor. I get that." Sinder stole into bed, trapping Gregor between them, borrowing a corner of Timur's pillow in the process. "But how am I supposed to find something that fits? You may not have noticed, but he's kind of a lot."

"Well said, lovely one." Fend, who'd crowded in behind Timur, leaned past in order to press a kiss on Sinder.

Stuck in the middle, Timur felt Sinder go still, then stretch up to kiss Fend back. The dragon suddenly pulled back, flashing Timur a guilty look.

"All right there?" And Timur played at cosset, letting loose a bit of shine.

Fend sighed endearments and licked Timur's ear, lapsing into encouraging purrs.

Sinder's shoulders hunched. "*I'm* supposed to be tending *you*."

"Is good, yes?" Timur let his mother's accent slip in, trying to lighten the mood. "I know how to look after the ones I love."

"But we agreed. We've made an alliance. This isn't a love match." In a smaller voice, he added, "Juuyu said so."

Timur hadn't realized that the phoenix's assessment had been bothering him. "Juuyu wasn't slighting you. Or us. I'll say it again, Sinder. You're good and right and best for me."

But was that the same as being *enough*?

"Right. We need this sorted." Timur tried to catch the dragon's eye. "Our bond's a big deal, too. And a big responsibility. And an honor."

"I want you for myself." Sinder grimaced and admitted, "But I want Fend, too."

"Dragons *do* accumulate brides."

Sinder snorted, then sighed. "I'm more comfortable with *unassailable alliance*, thanks. But here's the thing. I think I want … yeah, I'm sure I do. Look, maybe it's just me being a greedy dragon, but I want you to love me. You don't have to fall in love, but I want to … to matter. What can I do about that? What can I do to … to matter more? Because Fend's suggestions *aren't* very helpful."

When he rambled to an awkward stop, Timur had to laugh. "I can imagine the sorts of things our cat might propose."

"Mmm," offered Fend, sneaking in another lick at Timur's ear. "He wants *more*. Let's be generous."

"Stop teasing him."

"Never," Fend vowed. "Now answer his silly question. Ideally with a kiss."

Sinder grumbled, "That's not what Timur wants. That's you. I can tell that much."

"But you're overcomplicating things. Here. I'll go first," Fend said with exaggerated patience. "I want my ears petted. By either of you. By both of you. But *only* the two of you, since it is an entirely personal matter. Intimate, even. But I would welcome such a thing in private moments."

"Your ears, huh?" Sinder beckoned.

Fend hooked his chin over Timur's shoulder so the dragon could reach. Much purring ensued.

Timur guessed he should do as he was told and answer Sinder's question, which wasn't silly at all. "You matter, Sinder.

You don't have to do anything to matter more."

"But do you think you'll ever love me?" Sinder pressed. "Eventually?"

He couldn't understand his dragon's doubt. Timur loved this, and he loved being with both of them. This closeness. The only thing lacking was … well. You couldn't have everything.

Sinder propped himself up on an elbow, gaze suddenly keen. "What was that? That thing just now? The awful pang."

"I know, right?" sighed Fend. "Doesn't it make you want to kiss it away? I wasn't enough to mend that rift. Help me make it better?"

"But what *is* it?"

Timur couldn't answer. Didn't need to.

Fend slipped into a deadly dangerous tone. "They broke him, and then they stole what matters most. You will help me give it all back."

Sinder glanced down at Gregor, who'd fallen asleep. "Is this about the kids?"

"You *see* the necessity," Fend challenged.

"Yeah, of course. There are strings I can pull. Names I can drop. Forms to fill out. But … sure. I can make it happen."

"Invitations by Dichotomy Day?"

"I can probably manage. Hardest part will be getting together enough heralds. They're booked solid this time of year. Christmas at the latest?"

Timur was glad Fend had found someone whose mind made similarly agile leaps, but he was feeling especially dull-witted. "What are you on about?"

"The kids. Your children." Sinder quietly stated, "You want to know them. You want to matter to them. So we'll use the system that used you, and we'll bring them here. What reaver parent would refuse an offer from an exclusive school run by the very dynasty they wanted a piece of?"

"We invite them. We enroll them here." Fend nuzzled Timur's ear and whispered, "They will know their papka."

"I thought maybe someday ... summer courses at Wardenclave ...?"

"Why settle for summers when you can oversee *all* their training?" posed Fend.

"Guess I can let them paw at me if they need practice. And we're flush with dragon crossers at the moment."

Which reminded Timur. "Firstly, yes. If you can figure out how to bring them here, even some of them ...? I want that. But also. Fend, listen. I had an idea. Tell me if it's good?"

"As good as mine? Doubtful. But I'll hear you out."

"I want something for Gregor." He tried to pull his reasoning into some semblance of order. "I was, hmm, twelve I think ...? That's when Argent and Tsumiko came home with Kyrie. He was tiny and beautiful, and he helped me decide about becoming a Spomenka. Kyrie's a big part of the reason I learned to love dragons, and I'm still learning from him."

Sinder and Fend traded a look, but they held their peace, giving Timur time to explain.

"You probably already know. About how Mum took him and nursed him, since he and Lilya were born the same day. Lilya's always had Kyrie, and Kyrie's always had Lilya. Do you think we could give that to Gregor?"

Fend inhaled sharply.

Sinder was tapping his fingers. "Twenty-five baby Spomenka ... and if relative age is important ... we might just squeak by. A partnering program adds gloss to the invitation. Good thinking."

"I wasn't thinking of it as a school thing." Timur frowned. "I want Gregor to have someone he can't imagine living without. A best friend. A training partner, sure. But more than that. Kin. Family."

"Sure. There's that, too. But with a little spin, we can get that kind of bond for *all* of Kyrie's siblings." Sinder hesitated, then asked, "Did you have one in mind? First dibs?"

"No. I usually leave the big decisions to Fend. And now you."

"Okay. First off, Gregor *does* technically have someone. That little wind dragon is going to loom large in his future. She's sentient and plenty opinionated. She's part Impression, but in essence, he's already got a lock on a Kith partner."

Sinder paused long enough that Timur suspected he was conferring with Fend. With a nod, he went on.

"As far as the crossers go, I think you should talk to Jacques. Etienne's close enough in age, and Anjou will go for it. Pairing off kits and cubs is common practice in feline households. Also Sonnet will totally step in and cover the mothering angle. Added bonus, your kid will probably end up fluent in French."

"That would be *brilliant*. I'll talk to Jacques first thing."

Sinder raised a hand. "You have another option, too. If you want to keep your boy. It's one of those big deal, big responsibility, big honor things. Both limiting and unlimited.

Good for the dynasty, bad for travel."

"You have the means?" demanded Fend.

"Naoki's packing golden seeds, not that you heard it from me. If you applied to him, Gregor could become tree-kin. He'd share a tree sibling's years."

"While you share your dragon's," Fend added, sounding supremely smug.

Sinder nodded. "The best part is … you don't have to pick and choose. All of these things stack. Gregor would be able to keep everyone that matters to him—best friend, tree twin, wind dragon, rock imp, and us."

Timur let himself imagine such a future—schemed by his wily cat, arranged by his generous dragon, shared by his littlest battler— and dragged them all just a little bit closer before whispering, "Is good, yes?"

"Yeah, yeah," mumbled Sinder, looking pleased.

"Is good?" countered Fend, sounding amused. "Don't be shy, *ma moitié*. You love it and you love us and this lovely one wants to hear it said. Greedy thing."

Sinder looked ready to retaliate, but Timur soothed, "I should have spoken sooner, Sinder. I think I was trying to spare your feelings, since … well, it sounds romantic, doesn't it? But you are good and right and best. And loved."

He didn't mind saying so. It had been true for longer than he'd realized.

As true as the note that rang through their rock imp.

As real as the rumble of approval at his back.

As shy as the kiss Sinder stole. Or gave. But definitely meant.

So Timur accepted it in the spirit it was offered. And felt unassailable.

43
SAVE THE DATE

Cyril Sunfletch's holiday gala to celebrate his election to the White House had been tentatively scheduled two years ago so that prominent Betweeners could save the date. His landslide victory at the polls had locked in tonight's extravaganza, which would be attended by everyone who was anyone—and then some. The guest list and media attention Cyril had drawn easily rivaled the hoopla made over Kimi's courtship.

Ages ago, Isla had secured adjoining suites at the venue. For Hisoka-sensei's convenience, of course. She'd plotted even longer over her wardrobe.

Technically, she was arrayed in diplomatic green, which was fitting for her role with the Amaranthine Council. But once the cloth had been embroidered with a floral motif, all in a rich, creamy hue, her gown became a nod to Hisoka Twineshaft's clan colors. Few realized they were, of course, since he always wore pewter and gray. But he would have known. And Isla had hoped he would see the compliment. And maybe realize how well his colors suited her.

Lapis Mossberne swept through the adjoining door, draped in shushing velvet.

His gaze swept appreciatively over her chosen attire, then he startled her by bowing over her hand ... and slipping a small box into it. "A token. A trifle, really. But who has dimmed your usual sparkle?"

"You have to know I was hoping to attend with Sensei."

"You talked of little else for weeks."

"It was going to be my chance."

"Sleep still has a claim on him, and so you are mine. Do try to bear up."

"Don't be silly. I'm disappointed, of course, but spending time with you is hardly a dirge. We'll have to be careful, though, not to seem too close."

"We can hardly avoid that. I'm your date, am I not?"

She smiled crookedly. "You don't date. And everyone knows it since you're always pointing out that you're from a chaste class."

"My chastity is well-established."

"You know, they've started making lists of the world's most unattainable bachelors. You're on all of them."

"The world at large can't hope to lay hold of me. Not when my interests lie elsewhere."

"In books."

"Ah, my heart *does* thrill over the romances we read and write, but I am not referring to fiction."

"That's entirely too misleading. You made it sound like you have your heart set on someone."

His gaze did not waver. "I suppose I did."

"But that's not possible." She would have noticed, would have known. "You'd have said something."

"Perhaps I wasn't free to speak." And before she could pursue her point, he swung the velvet cloak from his shoulders, revealing an extravagance of silk.

Isla gasped. The matching embroidery on his vest, the touches of diplomatic green. Their ensembles clearly belonged together. "But how ...? Did you go to the Scatterlights, too?"

With a smile that definitely fit into the knowing category, Lapis urged, "Open the box, my dear."

Inside, she found a set of hairpins capped by crystal flowers that were the same deep blue as Lapis's hair.

"If I may?" He turned her toward the mirror and busied himself with finding places for the midnight blossoms in her hair.

She opened her mouth to warn him about the crystal array already in place, but Lapis was a master when it came to remnants. He hummed to them and murmured soft encouragement. Her teensy green ornaments were pleased by his attention, and they realigned themselves to suit his purposes. Isla was almost miffed that they were so willing to do another's bidding. But ... the additions sparkled fetchingly among her curls.

"You're going rather far to cheer me up."

Lapis apparently wasn't finished, for he began plucking a dainty sigil from the air between them. "Humor me."

She watched closely. "I don't know that pattern. What does the sigil do?"

"For the most part, this variety is decorative. Your palms, please."

Isla offered them, attention fixed on the emerging sigil. Granted, it was a pretty bit of artistry, but what was the point if it didn't *do* anything?

"You know your lore," he prompted. "This is a pale imitation, I fear, but such marks are inspired by tales of imps and their favor."

This was familiar territory. "In lore, an Impression tested someone's regard with a kiss. They're said to leave a shining mark upon the person they favor. And if their feelings are returned, the mark remains. That's how they know their feelings are returned." She smiled when Lapis nudged the first one against her skin and began another. "There's ample evidence that they're not fiction. Mikoto Reaver is a recent recipient. And Persiflage Beckonthrall is *quite* decorative."

Lapis settled a second sigil on her other palm. "By such marks, an admirer knows that their feelings are returned. For tonight, let these assure you that you are dear to my heart. And do try to enjoy the evening. The Sunfletches are sure to have outdone themselves."

Isla tore her gaze from her new adornments, thinking of nothing more than thanking him, but she froze at finding Lapis so close. But ... it was just Lapis, so she forced herself to relax.

But he wasn't done. Taking and turning one of her hands, he began fitting rings onto her fingers.

As the weight of shining stones increased, Isla protested,

"But Lapis, these are yours."

"They are old friends to keep you company when I cannot be at your side. Let them shine for you and adorn you. Let them capture the attention of others; let them win for you the admiration of all. And when the evening is over and you return to my side, let me draw them from your fingers and reclaim them with kisses."

"That's not from one of our books."

"No."

"Is the wording traditional?"

"Paraphrased. It would be more potent in the original."

Isla was further intrigued. "May I hear it?"

"Unwise, my dear. The words are accompanied by gestures, like punctuation, for emphasis."

"I want to know."

He lightly said, "You have always been greedy for facts, but this is more about feelings."

She huffed. "I have feelings."

"And they are focused elsewhere."

Two more rings slid into place before she bartered for more. "Let's say it's for a book …?"

He gathered her hands into his. "We could say that."

"We haven't ever included dragon courtship. Couldn't we explore the possibility?"

Lapis didn't even hesitate. "Yes, my dear. Let's explore the possibility."

As if that had been his plan all along.

"Right then. Do it again. In the original. Tell me *properly*."

He began.

Isla was impervious to sway, but she was cognizant of the fact that Lapis Mossberne had a compelling voice. She had enough of the old languages to get the gist of what he was saying, and she let herself be swayed, just to see what it was like. This was almost as if she were the leading lady in one of their romances. Only ... well. Was she being too passive, simply waiting to see what Lapis would say and do?

But he took the lead and kept it with a confidence that was probably the product of centuries.

Her reasoned observation kept faltering, and her heart took to fluttering. Lapis hadn't lied about movement being part of the recitation. He circled her as he spoke, pausing sometimes to adjust the position of her arms, her feet. It was a little like one of those regency dances that she and Kimi had learned together back in high school. The press of palms, the graceful turns. But Lapis was taking this so ... so seriously. Like a romantic hero should.

This was fascinating and ancient and inspiring. She was smiling, and he was pleased.

When it was over, she pouted. "That was all?"

"All you might want."

"So there's more."

"There is more."

"Don't leave anything out!" she demanded.

He lowered his gaze, which showed off the shimmering color on their lids. "Do not blame me."

She was enjoying this. It was new and exciting, better than anything in books.

Lapis slid a ring of crystal from his little finger and placed it in his mouth.

"What did you do that–?"

A gem-tipped claw pressed against her lips, commanding silence. Then he hooked that finger under her chin, tilting her head, and his lips lightly brushed across hers. He quietly ordered, "Open."

Isla let herself be swayed.

When he passed the crystal ring to her, a familiar note sang across her senses. This was a little like the crystal rods Betweeners routinely used to keep anyone from overhearing private conversations. What an interesting application! But why would anyone …?

"Isla," Lapis murmured against her lips. "Stop thinking."

She wanted to protest, but there was a ring of crystal on her tongue. So all she managed was a vague, "Mmm?"

"Dragonish courting game," he offered.

Then he was dipping in, stealing the ring with the tip of his tongue, then returning it.

Isla wasn't sure what the rules of this game were, but … well, there was a lot to catalog, really. Flavors and scents and textures and responses. Also, she was catching hints of Lapis. She'd never tended him, of course. He was an abstainer, even after Tenma had set him to rights.

"Isla," Lapis sighed, easing back.

She blinked, focusing. "I'm sorry, what?"

"You're still thinking."

"Well, yes. I'm not sure it's possible to stop."

Lapis inclined his head. Or ... well, it was more like he hung his head.

She urged, "Do go on. I'm *interested*."

"In the dragon clans, courting games usually involve dares. With a ring such as this, we could be kissing in front of every camera in the press box, and nobody would notice."

"Where did the ring go?"

"It is in my cheek."

"And if I wanted it back ...?"

"Another kiss." Lapis explained, "Dragons can hide in plain sight, and seductions can be secret even when they take place in public. Such games have great appeal, especially for dragon lords who must woo multiple brides, often away from other potential suitors. Or from some fine and famous lord to whom they've been betrothed since birth. Seduction became an artform."

Isla may have been a cultural liaison, but she had a few strongly-held personal ideals. "What do the dragonesses think of being squabbled over and accumulated by males?"

Lapis tutted at her. "We say 'the fathers are strong,' but do you understand why?"

She hesitated. "I know the saying. I've always taken it at face value. The dragon lords hold power. They're the rulers of your clans. Their strength is passed on to future generations ... like selective breeding."

"Not so, dear heart. Will you listen to one who is lesser, a lord in name only?"

Isla immediately shifted into a receptive posture. "Help me understand."

"We are terribly selfish, dragons."

"Well, yes. No offense."

Lapis's eyes sparkled with amusement. "One in four males is elevated. By whom, do you think?"

"Is there a selection committee for dragon lords?"

"Yes, and it is entirely peopled by females. The ladies of our clans are exacting in their standards. Only one in four males shows promise. The fathers are strong … and rare. Because we are terribly selfish, dragons."

The reasoning was frustratingly circular, but Isla caught a glimmer of his meaning. Perhaps because her own father was exceptional. "Dragons make terrible fathers."

"The fathers are strong because they are generous. They willingly pour their lives into others. Fond of children. Wise and patient and loving."

"But you're all those things!"

"According to my father, I loved books too well, and my charms were better spent on the crystals that loved me much and love me still."

"You can be both! Look at Papka."

"I have often considered the idyllic life of Michael Ward and envied him his place." And pivoting, Lapis asked, "Would you like to claim my little ring? It's an especially fine remnant. Unrivaled. Exquisite. Winnable."

"You'd let me keep it?"

"Courting games often involve prizes." Lapis bent closer. "There will be distractions and dares. I'll test your courage, expand your creativity, sharpen your wits. I'll behave foolishly, wax romantic, and make you wonder why you didn't make me part of your plans in the first place."

She wanted to prove herself, to impress him, to win. "It *is* a pretty ring."

"You could take it from me. But I wonder if you can keep it from me."

He was challenging her to a game. Wasn't that all right? A game to pass the time. A game to keep things interesting.

"Do you require persuading?" He held her gaze while he kissed her palms. "I like challenges, too."

He knew her so well. If this had been anyone but Lapis, she would have rebuffed him soundly, then deployed her defensive array. But Lapis knew her secret hopes. Lapis shared her love for romantic gestures. Lapis could be entirely dashing. And for tonight, he was inviting her to shed restraint and join in on a dragon's revel.

Isla's imagination swirled with all the things she might learn. And ... perhaps more importantly ... he was trying to distract her with something fun. A distraction she probably needed. So when he angled his head just so, she took up the challenge.

Her kiss was tentative, but he hummed approval and angled his head.

She tried again, and the way he sighed against her lips ... oh, that felt like winning.

With a touch of sway that was both rude and riveting, Lapis murmured, "Deeper."

44

SAVING HERSELF

Isla knew her duty to the In-between, and not only because of the fee she paid at regular intervals because she'd been putting that duty off. She fielded a fair amount of criticism for refusing so many offers. Reaver families would have loved to elevate their status by bringing her in and riding Papka's dynasty-class coattails.

Honestly, it was exhausting. When she'd been little, both Mum and her older sister had explained just why she was so popular at school. Everything had become awkward, both for her and for the boys who were under pressure to make a good impression. During summer courses and at academy, she'd quickly earned a reputation for snobbery.

Which was just sour grapes, really. And stupid. It wasn't as if choosing a partner would have made all the rest any happier. But because she abstained, she was somehow the problem.

Her lineage, her ambitions, her connections—they kept most men at a comfortable distance. She was universally disinterested in the many packets that arrived with bids for her cooperation. Early on, Mum shredded and burned them to ash. Later, they piled up in Isla's inbox—unopened, unwanted. These days, she was a little more polite about refusals. Her staff issued a standard letter, all very grateful, all very diplomatic.

But her years of single-minded devotion—to her books, to her craft, to her mentor—added up to a lack of firsthand experience. She'd been saving herself since *always*. For Hisoka-sensei. Who was either blind to her charms or pretending he was. And forays into fictional romances weren't the same as having one.

She wasn't entirely sure she was having one now.

Maybe she should check.

"I've never done this before."

Lapis hummed. "Won't matter."

"Have you?"

"Doesn't matter."

Which was vexingly evasive. She hated answers that didn't. So she pulled back, even though she hadn't secured her prize. "What does *that* mean?"

He nibbled gently at her earlobe, which was definitely interesting, in a we-will-readdress-this-topic-at-a-later-time way. Then he sighed. "Isla, my dear, could we possibly deal with one variety of curiosity at a time?"

She redirected her focus, because they really should stay on-topic.

Lapis was beautiful. It was the unattainable sort of beauty for which dragons were famous. They were often compared to elves or ascribed eldritch qualities, especially in the sorts of romances Isla reviewed.

Again, she had to rein in wandering thoughts. Was she avoiding the facts? That wasn't like her. Wait. Was she missing something? But surely ... not? All those times when they'd discussed the romantic bits of their books. Or written love scenes together. Even going so far as to stage them, hiding in armoires and whatnot. In all those times, never once had Lapis kissed her lips.

"Why have we never done this before?" she asked.

"Why have we stopped doing this now?" he countered, a trifle sulky.

And she let him draw her in, even though she'd never really considered Lapis before. When they'd met, she'd been eight years old and quite seriously in love with Ginkgo. And not long after, her affections had locked onto Hisoka-sensei. Lapis was around as a friend of the family, in much the same way as Harmonious Starmark or Adoona-soh Elderbough.

Yet here he was, jewel-like eyes half-lidded and ... and he was kissing her.

Which meant she was being kissed. For the first time. And, oh. She wanted something more. "Would you mind ...? Will you hold me?"

"May I?" He sounded pleased to be asked.

"Err ... well, yes." And as she was carefully crushed into silk and surrounded by familiar scents, she murmured, "Where's the ring gone? I've lost track. Do you have it?"

"Mmm. Do you want it?" One of his hands supported her as he bent her back. His other tugged at her hip until they were flush.

He kept her off-balance, effortlessly in control.

And it occurred to her again that he was beautiful ... but more importantly, that he was not the sort of person to toy with a woman. Papka had tried to tell her, to warn her. She'd been imposing on Lapis. Thoughtlessly using him. Never truly seeing him. And yet he murmured her name.

"Err ... what?"

Lapis managed to look patient. "I am declaring myself."

"Well, yes. But should you? We're friends. We've always been friends."

"Friends to lovers has always been one of my favorite storylines."

Isla was floored. Again. "Oh, for ...! You're *so* soft for unrequited love!"

"As are you."

"But ... I have Sensei."

"I am aware. As for myself, it has to be you." His gaze didn't waver. "You could have me back. I'm not sure the same can be said for Hisoka, but you must choose for yourself."

Isla shook her head. "Am I breaking your heart?"

"That remains to be seen."

"I ... Lapis, I don't want to be the kind of woman who loves one person but kisses another."

"Does that mean you want to kiss me again?"

She was so used to being frank with him. "I might. Is that terrible?"

"No, my dear. It's promising."

His next kisses were gentle, coaxing, and they made it difficult for Isla to form thoughts. She murmured, "Are my knees actually weak? It's a real thing?"

"Isla." He was smiling, and there was the ring, trapped between his fangs. "Come, my dear. Take what is yours."

"You can't be mine."

"I can be. In some respects, I already am." Was that his tail wrapping around her ankle? "If you will allow it, I'll use all my wiles to woo you to my side. And then I'll grant you the constancy you deserve."

"Just to be clear … do you mean to say that you love me?"

Lapis fluted sweetly.

"But you never said!"

"I would hardly intrude upon a friend's good fortune." He patiently explained, "Your heart was set on Hisoka, and there is none finer. I admire him myself. You hardly needed me and my burgeoning admiration making things awkward."

"What changed?"

"With all due respect, my dear, very little has changed. Except your notice. Ah, and the kissing." His lips touched hers, and his tone went all husky. "While I was willing to place your happiness before my own, this is more to my liking. May I court you, Isla Ward?"

She shook her head. "I'm not in love with you."

"Leave that to me." He touched her hair, where his crystals sang. "A dragon can be persuasive."

When Isla sailed into the ballroom upon Lord Mossberne's arm, she had a smile on her face and a new ring on her first finger. The press was there in force, and she heard the snap of shutters on every side. But Lapis ignored the paparazzi. All his attention was directed her way.

"I should tell you that my intentions have been made clear, at least to any dragons in the vicinity."

"How is that possible?" she whispered. "Did you say something to them?"

"Your lip color." After all the kisses they'd shared, Lapis had needed to retouch her lips. And at that time, he'd added the same shade to his own. "It's an old trick that allows for stolen kisses. You can always tell when two dragons are entangled, because they paint from the same pot."

Isla tried to smile for the cameras. But under her breath, she asked, "You're going to kiss me in public?"

"Perhaps." He tucked her arm through his, then tweaked the crystal ring she'd won. "We both have duties this evening, but I will fit in occasional romantic gestures. As long as we both touch the ring, none the wiser."

"Gestures?" she wondered aloud. "Things dragons do?"

"Things I like. Things you like." Lapis blandly pointed out, "I have the advantage of knowing exactly what makes your heart race. Your taste in reading is quite telling."

Isla felt suddenly vulnerable. And somewhat defensive. "Don't even pretend we don't have similar tastes. How else could we ...!"

Lapis bent to bestow a careful kiss that wouldn't disturb her makeup.

She was so stunned, she lost her train of thought. But there were no shutter sounds, no gasps, no whispers. Glancing around, Isla asked, "Did nobody see us?"

"When a dragon does not want to be seen, he rarely is." His open expression and crooked smile were almost boyish. "Ah, the things we could dare!"

"You're ... you're having fun."

He lifted her hand, kissed each of the rings he'd placed there, and urged, "See to your duties, and I'll see to mine. But I will find you every so often, to make certain you are also enjoying the evening."

"What will you do?"

"I wonder," he countered, tone light. "There are traditions to uphold, customs that might surprise you, and little tokens that may find their way into your hand. I could teach you the steps to a dance, tempt you with drinks and delicacies, or smuggle you into any available armoires."

She had a thousand questions, but before she could frame the first, he lightly tapped a finger against her lips.

"Tonight is mine. Enjoy it with me." Lapis quietly vowed, "I will not leave you wanting."

And without a backward glance, he strolled toward a knot of ambassadors, beginning his evening's rounds. Leaving Isla in a state of unaccustomed disarray. Was she really going to let Lapis Mossberne seduce her? Some shred of feminist pride rebelled, but her romantic inclinations put up a good fight.

In the end, she decided that yes, courting games appealed. She wanted to be adventurous for once. But she didn't want to be a first draft heroine this time around, sitting back and waiting to be swept off her feet. Lapis may have bragged about knowing her favorite tropes, but she knew his, too. And intimate understanding gave her certain advantages.

With a flash of fingers that sparkled prettily thanks to the addition of a dragon's treasures, Isla began to weave sigils.

Why should she leave everything to Lapis? Games were meant for two to play, and seducing a dragon? Oh, that felt like winning.

45
SCATTERING

Sibley had come to Stately House with only the vaguest recollection of Christmas, but Nonny wanted everyone to love it as much as he did. So the house was filled with good smells and snatches of songs and fun plans. But for the Amaranthine—and reavers, too—Dichotomy Day came first. Sibley was having a harder time figuring out why it was such a big deal. Something about the shortest day ... or was it the longest night that was important? Either way, he was up before the sun, waiting for the festivities to begin.

There was going to be a wedding in the Song Circle, since Ginkgo and Snow were going to be a family with Pact. And there would be a bonfire on the beach. And they'd fix up the festival booths, some of which had toppled with the waves Dima had pushed ashore. Sibley had overheard Lady talking to Sansa, so he knew that the Christmas festival was also a birthday party for Lilya and Kyrie.

But before all that, they were going to welcome a Scattering.

The grownups kept talking about today being the best, most auspicious—a good word Opal had taught him—day for a bunch of new children to arrive. They weren't dragon-crossers, and they weren't escaping from anything bad. But they were meant to be a secret, which is probably why they were supposed to get here before sunrise. Sneaking was easier during this longest, darkest night.

"Will they tease me?" asked Trinity, who liked her new name.

"I won't let them," promised Twosies.

"But I have a pot."

Kyrie quietly pointed out, "Grandfather has a pot."

Sibley knew for sure that this was a comfort to Trinity. She'd confessed that hers now rested in a safe, secret place that belonged to Argent. She wasn't allowed to talk about it, but knowing it was there was enough of a clue. Sibley figured that with a little poking around, he'd find it.

Last-minute stuff had kept most of the house up all night. Uncle Jackie had dozed off after midnight, but Papa Anjou had woken him again with coffee and kisses. And Sonnet was relying on Sibley to help make sure all the new kids felt welcome. Because he was in a new position.

Nudging Kyrie, Sibley said, "I'm like you this time."

"How do you mean?" Kyrie asked, his gaze letting Sibley know that he was really listening.

"When we were new, you welcomed us to your home. Now, I belong here, so I get to welcome new kids to *our* home. And then it will be theirs, too, and they'll help us welcome whoever comes next. Like that."

Kyrie said, "I would be pleased if we can bring all our siblings to live here. Well, all who want to come. There might be some who also found a good place."

"Good for them."

"But maybe they could visit with their own families. So we can know each other. Like a reunion."

Sibley had overheard some things, so he knew what that meant. "It's a good word. Reunion."

Just then, Kyrie tilted his head to one side and smiled. "They are here."

"Did the trees tell you?"

"Yes."

"Can we go see?"

Kyrie's smile widened. "Yes. I will tell Lilya. Do you want to bring Etienne?"

That was a great idea, since this was his little brother's first chance to welcome someone new. He hurried to Papa Anjou, who had Etienne snuggled against his shoulder. Sibley didn't want to interrupt, since he was talking to Ginkgo, but the half-fox's ears angled his way.

"What's up, little bro? Need your papa for something?"

Hearing that said must have pleased Anjou, because he began to purr.

Sibley asked, "Can I bring Etienne to meet the new kids?"

Ginkgo's ears pricked. "That time already? Let's all go. Something this momentous deserves a big welcome."

Anjou snagged a blanket off the back of a rocker and swathed it around Etienne. "I'll be along. Keep each other warm, hmm?"

"Yes, Papa."

"I will bring your uncle. *Non*, both uncles." He nodded to where Uncle Jackie and Uncle Boniface were helping Sonnet set up long tables. They'd be having something called brunch, which was another good word. Sibley liked that it came from mixing two other words into something new. A breakfast-lunch crosser.

Back outside, he found that Kyrie had waited.

Lilya waved from where she stood hand-in-hand with Dr. Elara. They were together a lot lately, on account of the doctor needing beacon lessons.

Some people were already headed along the road to the gate. Ginkgo walked with Lady. They were in charge since Argent was away, doing Dichotomy Day things on television. He was standing in for someone Sibley had only heard about. People mostly called him Sensei, except for Rhomiko. They called Sensei theirs.

Anan squatted in order to scoop them up and stride after the rest.

Sibley said, "This is Etienne. He only knows French."

To his utter amazement, Anan rumbled a string of foreign words to the little boy, who wriggled up in order to kiss the thunderstorm's cheek.

While Etienne snuggled back down into his blanket, Sibley asked, "What did you say?"

Anan only grunted.

Kyrie, who knew lots of French words, probably thanks to Uncle Jackie, answered instead. "Anan said that Etienne is as gentle as a summer breeze and just as welcome."

"Good for you." Sibley ruffled his little brother's hair, then searched Anan's face. "Guess that means you figured it out?"

His eldermost brother frowned.

Kyrie asked, "What do you mean, Sibley?"

"Nuh-uh. I'm not saying anything else. It'd spoil Ginkgo's surprise."

All at once, Anan took to running, and Kyrie's laughter trilled. Then came a sound almost like thunder. Sibley couldn't place it, but then he saw the horses. They were louder than a hundred Nonnys, their big hooves thudding the ground as they came. One of the horses carried two riders, and Kyrie sounded real glad when he called, "Mikoto!"

But that was nothing to Anan's shout. "Tzefira!"

Kyrie guessed this was the first time that Anan had left his side since his descent. After weeks of constant looming, the storm's sudden absence was jarring. Anan might not speak much, but his presence was commanding enough that Kyrie was always being buffeted.

He shyly admitted, "This is a lonesome sort of feeling."

Dima was in high dudgeon. *"Do not call him back! That's Tzefira he's holding!"*

Anan had all but dropped his passengers in a snowbank in order to reach the fourth member of the Changing Winds. Mikoto had helped her slide from their horse's back, straight into Anan's waiting arms. He hadn't exactly run away with her, but they were far enough away—on the edge of the woods—that Kyrie couldn't overhear anything. In fact, he was quite sure that the little winds who usually carried whispers to him were keeping things from him instead. Tzefira may have descended in order to become Mikoto Reaver's bride, but she hadn't forgotten how to shepherd winds.

"*Anan dotes on her,*" Dima said. "*It was cruel to part them.*"

"He loves her?" Kyrie asked, worried that Anan might unleash a storm on Tzefira's husband.

"*Like a daughter,*" boasted Dima. "*She's the newest of us. And the sweetest.*"

"*Tzefira descended?*"

That was Haizea's voice, and Kyrie's heart leapt. He said, "Yes. Tzefira found someone with a noble heart. He called out to her, and she descended. I was there. It was a happy day."

"*She chose a human?*" Dima was incredulous.

"Yes, she did. He is a good man. A distant cousin of mine." With a small smile, he added, "We are related because we have the same tree somewhere in our lineage—Hajime."

Haizea murmured, "*Trees and dragons. An unusual combination.*"

"For me, it is a tree, a dragon, and a star." Kyrie glanced at his palms. "And I am favored by winds."

"*Kept by a storm,*" Dima countered. "*Anan dotes on you now.*"

"Is that what this is?" Kyrie asked doubtfully.

"*Mmm. Perhaps not,*" admitted Dima.

"*Not,*" echoed Haizea.

"*I wish Bethiel was here. He would see the truth and say it.*"

Haizea softly said, *"I … I also wish Bethiel was here."*

Dima laughed darkly. *"Maker mark and maker move."*

It sounded like a challenge.

Kyrie was disappointed when Haizea lapsed again into silence. But maybe he should be grateful that she'd decided to speak at all. Surely that was a good sign.

Across the way, Sibley was proving to be much more outgoing than Kyrie had ever been. He was right in the middle of a group of newcomers, introducing Etienne and promising everyone that they'd found a good place. As far as Kyrie could tell, the tree-kin were all humans. And even though they'd brought friends—a small herd of Alpenglows—they were looking rather nervous.

But then Ginkgo waded in, wrapping his arms around Sibley from behind and adding his own greeting. Then Snow was there, and everyone from Wardenclave knew her, which seemed to chase away any lingering worries. Which was when Gilen announced that there was a basket of kittens in the kitchen, and Sonnet was calling everyone to come in out of the cold.

Things were going well, but something niggled for Kyrie's attention, so he stayed where he was, letting people's notice of him fade. What was this feeling? Why was it so worrisome? He pivoted, senses straining, hoping for a helpful gust. But … no. Stepping lightly through the snow, he pressed his hand to the trunk of one of his trees.

An instant later, something snapped, warped, and slipped off-key.

Heart racing, Kyrie looked to see who was closest. Boon stood a little way off with some of his team members—Moon, Hallow,

Colt, and Juuyu. Before Kyrie could take a single step in their direction, Sibley was at his side. Somehow, in the middle of everything, his brother had noticed.

"You feel it, too?" Kyrie asked.

"I feel *you*. Something wrong?"

"You noticed me?"

"Well, yeah. We're brothers, aren't we?"

Maybe so, but Kyrie doubted that many brothers were as attuned to one another as Sibley was to him. It was almost like resonance, and Kyrie wanted to both explore it ... and tune it. So they could use it. But not just now. "Yes, something is wrong. Take Etienne inside where he will be safe. And ... do me a favor? Quietly."

Sibley's gaze darted, and he turned his body slightly, shielding Etienne. "Anything."

"Tell Fend."

"Timur's panther?"

"Yes." Kyrie decided it would be best if his brother knew this much. "When things happen, especially when Dad is away, always tell Fend. Quietly."

Sibley lowered his voice. "Why him? What's a cat gonna be able to do?"

"I could not say. But I made a promise. Help me keep it?"

"I can do that." And Sibley sprinted away.

Only after the kitchen door shut behind them did Kyrie turn back toward the elite taskforce. Raising his hand in a tracker's signal that begged for help, Kyrie crisply called, "Boon!"

The wolf moved fast.

Almost as fast as Anan.

"Easy there," Boon drawled, hands upraised. "Your boy wanted a word."

"He is alarmed."

"I picked up on that, too. Well, kid?"

Kyrie had to step around the eldermost storm. "Boon, somebody is testing the boundaries. A wardstone is missing."

"Bearing?"

Kyrie pointed.

"On it."

46

INTERLUDE

Hisoka stirred, but only to stretch. Waking could be taken slow when there wasn't a schedule to keep. His agenda—if he even had one anymore—held no obligations, and he wasn't in a hurry to leave Rhomiko's arms. Because that's where he found himself. Draped and petted and on the verge of purring.

There was a scent unique to stars. He'd been catching whiffs all his life, but this close, where it was thick and warm and nuanced ...? Hisoka nuzzled and breathed deep and deeper. Memorizing. Making himself at home.

Rhomiko began humming, and Hisoka knew the song.

Old enough to be ancient, a song once sung by a tree.

His tree. His twin.

Taken and taken again.

Yet here was Rhomiko, giving back something so long gone,

Hisoka hadn't realized he'd forgotten it. A small thing. So simple. And precious.

Slowly, deliberately, he wound his arms around Rhomiko. Holding onto the starry remnant who was holding him in turn. And humming along.

Hisoka had eaten every bit of the food that Anjou and Sonnet brought from the kitchen, then allowed his nephews to smuggle him into Jacques' *en suite* for a much-needed grooming session. Jacques laid out festive attire, because somehow Hisoka had slept straight through to Dichotomy Day.

When he returned to his room, which Sonnet had freshened, he was feeling more like himself than he had in … well, he supposed if he was honest, it had been a few years. A communique sat on the table, and he pulled it closer, turning his head to read the headlines.

The world, it would seem, had been carrying on without him.

How freeing.

When Rhomiko slipped into the room, they set a thick journal and a pen on the table before taking over the bed in order to cuddle the rock imp. Hisoka got the impression that Rhomiko had chosen their spot in order to keep him from returning to his former cocoon. But Hisoka's sense of freedom had his mind racing, and it pleased him to commit plans to paper.

Lesson plans and practicums.

Field trips and mentorships.

He was so caught up in possibilities that he barely heard the bump that came low on the door. Only belatedly did he realize that Michael was there ... and that he must be using his foot to knock. Hisoka glanced Rhomiko's way.

"It is for you," they said, a secretive smile on their face.

Unsure what to expect, Hisoka hurried to open, then quickly stepped back, pulling the door wide so that Michael could enter. The man's arms were filled with a doubly precious burden.

Michael smiled crookedly. "Did we actually manage to surprise you?"

"I *am* surprised. Nobody mentioned your news." Hisoka had always liked this part of Michael. Fatherhood suited him.

From the bed, Rhomiko called, "Bring them. I want to see! Oh. Oh, they are so new."

Michael angled his head, and Hisoka accepted the direction. Closing the door, he followed the man, who asked, "Room for another, Rhomiko?"

The star-crosser swiftly set aside the wardstone and extended both arms.

"This little man is fresh from a bath, during which he squalled with hearty disapproval. But he's as ready as we could make him for an introduction. He is Pavel."

Rhomiko kissed his down of blond curls. "Perfect."

"When did they arrive?" Hisoka asked.

"Sansa would tell you they've been here all along. But they were born a week ago, more or less. While you were sleeping."

"A week and a day," said Rhomiko, whose face was radiant.

"Pavel is easily differentiated from his twin," Michael began.

"By their wards …?" guessed Rhomiko. "Such strong ones."

"Well, yes. I did a bit of sigilcraft when they arrived. The precaution seemed wise with so many Impressions joining the household. I'll be curious if they can build up a resistance to impish allure, having been exposed since birth. But if need be, Argent and I can maintain our assortment of wards against starshine and pollen and whatever else the winds may bring." Michael turned toward Hisoka and offered the other baby. "He is Nikolay."

Hisoka caressed a tuft of dark hair. "Fraternal."

"Yes."

This wasn't the first time Hisoka had been in this position. He'd dared to renew his acquaintance with Michael and Sansa in order to settle Deece in their household. And since then, Michael had been presenting Hisoka with babies. It was flattering of course. The enormity of trust involved. In this way, Michael had given his former mentor the most precious thing he could, since he couldn't give himself.

"Two sons. Congratulations."

Michael's fingertips came to rest on Hisoka's shoulder, and his gaze took on a hopeful quality. "Sansa and I have a tradition. It began with Ginkgo. We placed our children into his hands, and they flourished in his care. Every one of them, right through Lilya. He fostered them. Then with Sonnet's arrival, Sansa asked to let the honor pass to the wolf she counts as a sister. Vanya considers Sonnet his second mother."

He was leading up to something.

It wasn't difficult to see what.

But … *why?*

Michael went on. "I would have spoken sooner, Sensei, but I wanted to be certain. I've never really hoped before—for a girl or for a boy. But this time, I did hope—for your sake—that there would be a son. Here are two. And there are two of you. Would you and Rhomiko do us the honor of taking these boys to your hearts? I know they'd benefit from your guidance and affection. Much as I did."

"I … I never expected …."

"Then I shall bask in the rare triumph of surprising you twice. Very appropriate, don't you think. Twin surprises."

Rhomiko spoke then, and their voice held the lilt of command. "Come here, Hisoka. These boys want to be together."

So he left Michael's side in order to take his own place.

He didn't think that the softness in Michael's gaze was entirely for his sons.

Chances were excellent that he knew what this honor meant. A fostering bond now linked him and Rhomiko, overlapping their connections, deepening their closeness. They would share Michael's gift. And eventually, they would share everything.

Tsumiko decided not to remark on Hisoka-sensei's sudden appearance in the kitchen. One of Michael's twins snugged in the crook of his arm, he greeted Hannick Alpenglow, chatted amiably with Revic Nightbide, and apologized to Transcendence for taking so long to wish her and Ginkgo well.

Calm, poised, and present.

Argent would be so pleased.

Children were everywhere, trading names and touching palms. Lilya wove among them, facilitating introductions, and Dr. Elara was sweetness itself, making sure that everyone had a nametag. Tsumiko should have been right there with them, but she was doing her best to take her friend Kimiko's advice and savor the moment. This was a new beginning for so many people, and watching over it felt right.

While Jacques and Anjou guided the newest members of their community toward the spread in the dining room, Rhomiko arrived, moving straight to Hisoka's side. They also had a babe in arms, and they nudged Hisoka toward the two rockers over by the battered sofa.

"Pull your chair nearer," Rhomiko urged. "Pavel is vexed that we parted them."

"Is that so?" Hisoka asked. "Why don't you hold them both?"

"I do not wish to be greedy."

"Ah, but you could take Nikolay for Pavel's sake. And I will go steal our rock imp back from Michael."

"And return here," Rhomiko said, their gaze steady.

"And return here," Hisoka promised, mild in his obedience.

He met Tsumiko's gaze, and he inclined his head in that same regal way that Argent adopted whenever he was feeling awkward. She was glad for him, and she thought he could tell. And that was enough. Sensei was such a private person.

She crossed to Rhomiko, who had also watched Hisoka leave.

Reading the imp's expression could be difficult, and she found herself asking, "What are you thinking?"

So much for allowing Sensei his privacy.

Without a trace of embarrassment, Rhomiko answered, "That he is mine."

"Is he?"

"Is that strange?"

Tsumiko sat in the neighboring rocker and began to sway in gentle tandem. "I suppose, like anything else, it depends on how you mean it."

"We belong together," Rhomiko stated. "And we belong to each other."

She hummed to show her interest, but she didn't pry further.

But Rhomiko continued anyhow. "For a very long time, my world was safe and small. Barely large enough for two. Hisoka is my other, now, and that is good. But we are not alone. You are part of my world, Lady Mettlebright. And so are Pavel and Nikolay. My world grows every time the enclave grows."

"Yes." She pondered all the things that had happened since their last Dichotomy Day celebrations, when the house had felt so empty with Kyrie and Lilya away at camp. "This has been a growing season for Stately House. So many answers to prayer. So much happiness."

"This is a good place." Rhomiko's gaze turned inscrutable

again. "I do not want it to be imperiled."

Tsumiko's chair stilled. "Is that a thing we can avoid?"

Rhomiko sadly shook their head.

"I see." Having stars and half-stars in their community meant the odd brush with prophecies. But they weren't always practical insights. "Can you guide my next steps? Is there anything we can pass along to Argent? Or to the wolves?"

"Can a message be sent with haste?"

Dipping into her cardigan pocket, Tsumiko held up her phone. "If I know their contact information, yes."

"Begin with a message to Isla Ward, please. She did not listen. She needs to be reminded."

47
TEXT BUBBLES

Isla woke to a series of dainty pings from her phone and fumbled under her pillow, which was her usual place for it. When one roved through innumerable hotel suites, living out of a suitcase even during brief stops at home, one never knew which side to reach for the bedside table. So ... pillow. But no phone.

She propped up on elbows and pushed rampant curls out of her eyes. Another departure from her normal routine. Ever since Uncle Jackie had coaxed her into accepting the most miraculous of oils and a soft cap for sleeping, her hair was better behaved. But she could tell at a touch that it was a fright. And all at once she recalled why.

Because there were rings on her fingers.

And a dragon lord on the chaise lounge.

Lapis had spent half the night running his fingers through her hair—hence its current disarray—his slow kisses curling her toes. She'd liked that almost as much as the breathy sighs and low hums she'd wrested from him. Yet he sat there, arrayed in fresh silks, clan colors ascendant, calmly reading.

He spared her an assessing look, then lifted a packet. "Do you want to read these yourself? Or do you trust my ability to abridge down to the most pertinent points?"

Council business. He'd moved on to work.

"Umm. Just a mo, and I'll take a look."

With a nod, he went back to reading, and she caught up a few items of clothing and tried to scamper in a dignified way into the bathroom. Staring at herself in the mirror, she resigned herself to the *full* hair-washing routine.

Her thoughts spun and tangled. What had she done?

She'd flirted with Lapis. Encouraged his attentions. Played at courting games, then tried to seduce him. They'd been in bed together, and yet ... well, things had gone far enough that there was no going back. She'd never be able to look Lapis in the eye without remembering. She'd been curious, and he'd been accommodating. And intent. And so intense. Of course Isla would be swept away. And of course dragons *would* be sexy. They probably couldn't help themselves.

Oh. How long had she been standing under the spray, staring at the ceiling?

Had Lapis noticed? He'd be able to hear from the next room. He could also probably get a read on her mood. He knew her so well, knew she needed time to think. He was giving her space. Time to process. Time to come to terms with her own stupidity.

Or stubbornness. Or willful blindness.

His declarations were staggering.

And she'd put up no resistance.

And yet her wards were intact. She couldn't detect any of the bonds that were described in lore or textbooks or even in recent journal articles covering the phenomenon of interspecies mating bonds. Which was the next logical step.

And yet ... he hadn't tried. So this was a tryst?

What were his exact words, back at the beginning?

She couldn't seem to recall. Was dragon sway in play? Isla knew she wasn't susceptible, but clearly she could be distracted by beautiful males who used courting gifts and games in convincing ways.

Finishing up, she wrung and toweled and started to dress. Partway through, she cracked the bathroom door and called, "Lapis?"

"Yes, my dear?"

"What are we?"

"Somewhat behind schedule."

She cast about for her phone, but it wasn't close to hand. "I can't miss my flight!"

"We are only somewhat behind. Not entirely late." Lapis calmly invited, "Come and have some breakfast."

"Is there time?"

She pulled on standard-issue breeches and a tunic in diplomatic green, then skimped with her hair and skin care in ways that Uncle Jackie would have tutted over. "Don't *you* have a flight?"

"Not until evening. I've that congressional luncheon, followed by an interview and photoshoot for the *Emergent*."

It took mere minutes to repack her things and zip her case. Draping the garment bag with her gown over it, she patted distractedly at her pockets and asked, "Phone?"

"Here. Beside your teacup." He filled it, then summarized the information from Canarian's staff. Which somehow led to questions about the manuscript she'd traded back to him. And a completely unnecessary reminder that Argent would be filling in for Hisoka for her next appearance. "He'll already be there when you arrive. In Iceland."

She didn't like it.

How could Lapis be treating her so normally?

Plucking up her phone, she quickly scanned her emails and checked the most urgent messages. There was something from Papka and a message from Tsumiko. Probably Dichotomy Day greetings. She'd answer them once she was through airport security.

"Isla?"

She pushed away the plate he fixed for her and stood, though there wasn't really anything left to do. Except ... leave. But she didn't want that, either. So she collected her share of the mail and spent too long straightening the pile. Why was she disappointed? After an evening filled with romance and foolish games and thrilling caresses, did everything have to go back to how it always was?

"*Isla.*"

His hand caught hers, bringing her attention to the rings that still sparkled on her fingers, then to sapphire eyes that were suddenly very close. "In my efforts to make you more comfortable, have I managed to make you uncomfortable? How clumsy of me. I do apologize."

"Right. Well. I mean ... it all seems so far away. Those things. That happened."

"Those things are neither far nor in the past." Lapis gently inquired, "Am I not right here? Is that not yet enough? I am quite willing to recapitulate."

His kiss lingered light upon her lips, giving her room to escape, but when she let the right moment for a rebuff pass, his hold shifted, and then there was silk and hot skin under her hands, and ... right then. So Lapis *was* willing to kiss her silly while breakfast went cold.

When he eased back enough for her to see how pleased his smile was, she asked, "I didn't imagine it?"

"Can you be more specific?"

"This."

"Charmingly vague." His hand pressed to the small of her back, and it was the easiest thing in the world to arch against him. Like a dance. Like lovers might do. He hummed approvingly.

She wanted more. "May I tend you?" she blurted.

Lapis immediately turned pensive.

Isla saw how inappropriate her question might be, asking for intimacies that skipped past the physical, opening the path to permanence. It was probably her right to ask for proof that this wasn't dalliance, but she also knew that he'd been Broken once. And that he abstained.

Worse, what if he thought she wanted him for his years. He had to know she wasn't that kind of woman.

"Not today, my dear. I will want to. I will. But there are things I should tell you first. So that you understand why I was ... the way I was."

She'd tried not to speculate about Lapis's status as one of the Broken. It was impolite to ask in the first place, and all of his answers would probably expose something he'd rather forget. She knew stories. Amaranthine could become addicted, which led to excesses. Or they were mishandled, misguided, misappropriated. It always came down to greed and sadness and tragedy, with bitter consequences. If not for Tenma, Lapis would still be stricken.

"Isla." Lapis touched her hair, finding his pins tucked amidst her curls. "You may have my every secret, even the woeful ones. But there is no time to satisfy your formidable curiosity at this juncture. Indeed, I doubt you would thank me for making you late. Or for taking advantage of last night's reckless abandon."

"Why didn't you?"

"Neither of us likes that trope. Though my disdain is now tempered by sympathy. I *barely* resisted. And I doubt my restraint will last must longer." Brushing his lips across her parted ones, he warned, "Keep your wits about you, dear heart. I am in pursuit."

Isla fretted. How could she not? Even though the Office of Ingress had sent a car, they were stranded in traffic. She couldn't tell if they were in the middle of the morning rush or if this was holiday traffic. Dichotomy Day was finally gaining in popularity in America, and official celebrations involved a skywatching extravaganza. Brake lights flashed, and people leaned out of car windows as a herd of enormous horses—Thunderhoofs by their coloring—galivanted overhead.

While en route to the airport, they were similarly delayed by a flight of heralds trailing streamers and the languid flight of a lone dragon that she would have sworn was Lord Shywind, simply out for a stroll.

As they were now in public, Lapis kept to his side of the car, radiating contentment despite the risks they were taking. There was no good reason for him to accompany her to the airport, and yet he insisted on seeing her off.

Would there be paparazzi?

Deciding to err on the side of caution, Isla quietly slipped Lapis's ring into her mouth. Just in case he wanted another private-in-public kiss.

Belatedly, she realized she could have been responding to messages, and she checked her phone. As soon as she did, a new message popped up. From Uncle Boniface.

Since that was out of the ordinary, she tapped it first.

Miss Ward, may I beg
a moment of your time?

I'm here.

I am but a humble messenger
With something to pass along
Are you familiar with a young chap
Two hundred twenty-two, as was
Goes by Oracle now
For official matters
Of which this is apparently one

**I'm sorry, who is with you, please?
222?**

Twosies

Isla did seem to recall there being a lot of numerical labeling among the children Sensei had helped to rescue from that awful island.

One of the children. A crosser?

**Indeed, yes
Bright boy
Very articulate
Very insistent**

**And he has something
to say to me?**

**Here's the first bit
Word for word
"Do not forget again.
These words are true."**

She frowned, and her gaze flicked up to where Boniface had given the boy's name. Oracle? Was this meant to be some kind of prophecy?

Uncle Boniface's next message arrived with all the subtlety of a slap.

"Hisoka will never call you to his side."

48

WHIRLWINDS AND ROMANCE

Nothing was happening. Kyrie couldn't detect any further tampering with the barriers, and though he strained his ears, no wolf raised an alarm. He didn't want to, either. Not with Ginkgo's and Snow's bonding ceremony set to take place in the Song Circle. It would be soon. Almost next.

Anan gruffly announced, "Tzefira went inside."

"Should we go inside, too?" asked Kyrie. Because that was obviously what the thunderstorm wanted.

The imp stalked ahead, and Kyrie drifted after, most of his attention still on the peaceful hum of the forest. Michael's barriers were exceptional. And Dad's sigils added wily failsafes to their boundaries. Nothing should be able to get past. And yet ... there were exceptions. Like trees who could pick and choose where to manifest. And like him. A boy who could coax remnant stones.

It bothered Kyrie that the missing wardstone was purple.

He'd always gotten along best with stones in the amethyst range.

What if his knack for slipping past barriers was inherited?

Had the Rogue come to reclaim his many children? Or was he more the type to want revenge? Greed and grudges were at the heart of many stories about dragons.

Kyrie could not allow his sire to threaten any of the people that were under his protection. So while he allowed Anan to lead him inside, Kyrie wasn't paying any heed to his surroundings. His mind was caught up with possibilities and plans.

Tzefira wanted to be close to her old friends, so Kyrie was soon crushed between her and Anan on the kitchen sofa. Mikoto had gone off somewhere, and Jacques murmured something about an impromptu bachelor party for Ginkgo. Hosted by Andor and Doran.

Boniface seemed puzzled until star wine was brought up. "To toast the groom, as it were?"

Uncle Jackie said, "They're probably trying to distract him from Argent's absence. Last-minute scheduling snafu, but he couldn't very well leave Isla in the lurch. I offered to go myself, but … *non*."

"Timur and Sinder also went with Ginkgo," said Tsumiko. "They were all friends together last summer."

Uncle Jackie said, "So long as they return Ginkgo to me in a fit state to stand, Anjou and I will see him beautifully arrayed and gilded in silver. As per tradition."

"Silver?" asked Kyrie.

"Have you never seen your father decked out in the Mettlebright tradition?"

"No."

"Full makeup, with the most dramatic silver eyeliner. Gorgeous."

Kyrie asked, "May I have silver eyeliner? I am a Mettlebright."

"Do you want it?"

"Opal's star had red eyeliner, and I liked it."

Uncle Jackie considered the matter. "Many dragons do go in for that sort of thing. And you're thirteen in a few days' time. Seems the right sort of thing to mark your embarkation into adolescence."

Mother's small smile was permission.

Tzefira murmured something about clouds and silver linings.

Anan referenced the silvering of the sky whenever lightning deigned to strike.

Uncle Jackie suggested that Anan join them and be adorned, and Anjou exclaimed that he hoped it would be so. But while he went into rhapsodies over how honored he'd be, Kyrie's attention turned inward.

Dima said, *"Wasn't Bethiel ever-arrayed in blue and bells?"*

"Was he?" he asked. He couldn't recall any description of what Bethiel looked like. Only things about his responsibilities and the many friends he made while carrying them out. Kyrie asked, "What else?"

"Quick to smile. Ready to laugh. Kind to a fault. Always gentle."

Somewhere deep down, Haizea made a sound. It took him a minute to understand, but once he did, he slipped away. No small feat when one is seated between two imps. But Kyrie ran lightly along a hall, then whispered to the wardstone guarding a locked door. Once through, he was out-of-doors and running. Only when he was well away and tucked between a thicket and the thickest tree did he ask, "Why are you crying, Haizea?"

"My fault," sighed Dima. *"Or his. Where* is *Bethiel? He has*

much to answer for! Poor, sweet Haizea."

"What can I do?" Kyrie asked.

"*You? You can do nothing. Least of all elude a sworn storm.*"

Thunder cracked overhead, loud enough that Kyrie felt it in his bones, followed by a deep roll that held notes of displeasure. Oh. He'd gone without a word to Anan. Stricken, he huddled on his knees in the snow, face in his hands, a dragonish display of contrition.

Slow stomps crunched in the snow, and the air popped and sizzled. For the first time, it occurred to Kyrie that Anan had more destructive potential than most of the people in his acquaintance. And having been nested in Kyrie's very soul, he probably knew all the things that would hurt most, should he wish to make a point.

Then large hands closed around his shoulders, and he was looking into Anan's worried face.

"This is a thing you must not do," the storm ordered. "Never do this."

"Does it hurt?" Kyrie whispered, suddenly sure he'd inflicted pain. "Why must you be near? Did I enslave you after all? Are you bound to my side?"

"Near is my choice." Anan took one of Kyrie's clenched hands and pressed it open. "I descended for you, little terror. Have you already wearied of the responsibility?"

To his amazement, Anan grimly checked his other hand. Or more accurately, he checked to make certain his marks were still there. As if they could ever fade. Kyrie treasured them too much to neglect them.

"You were worried?"

"You hid from me."

"Haizea has been too quiet. I do not think it is natural for a whirlwind to be so still." Kyrie quietly added, "She was crying. I only wanted privacy to ask why."

Anan frowned. "And how did she answer?"

Kyrie could only shake his head. "I have not done anything that I know of, but ... could there be something I left undone? I do not wish to be guilty of neglect. Will you mediate for me?"

"I can do it!"

"Dima?" Kyrie asked.

"Anan may be your favorite, but that doesn't mean he's always best. Not for this."

Kyrie wanted to protest. Anan may have reached him first, spoken first, descended first. But did that mean he was Kyrie's favorite? Had he slighted the other two winds? Was that the problem here? He ventured, "I would be glad if you can help, Dima. Please?"

"You're a safe harbor, but can you be home? I think not."

"If my help is no longer needed, you are free to go. If you *can* go ...?" Kyrie admitted, "I have heard that bonds can form accidentally."

"If I wished to stay, I could. But I'm not the sort to share."

Kyrie thought he agreed, which meant Dima knew it, too. Because he couldn't hide anything from her. Or from Haizea. But it seemed he could hide from Anan now that they weren't sharing space. That's why he'd been able to get away from the eldermost storm. It also meant that he needed to speak his mind if he wanted Anan to understand him.

But he was curious about something else. "Would you *want* to stay, Dima? With someone else?"

"*I might. If I found someone suited. But more to the point, Haizea is waiting. And I can be plainer. She's waiting for Bethiel.*"

"*I want my friend,*" came Haizea's small voice. "*If he is a friend. He abandoned us.*"

Kyrie asked, "Should we talk to him? Find out why?"

"*No. I do not want to know that I was not missed. That I was not worth finding. That I was never loved.*" And in the barest of whispers, a confession. "*I love him. More than anyone.*"

"*True words,*" praised Dima. "*I don't like that they pain you.*"

All at once, Kyrie wished that Tzefira had followed Anan. Because Haizea might be heartbroken. And if anyone could understand this longing for love, it would be her.

"*The boy sees now. Look how his heart has broken for you.*"

Haizea sighed. "*He is not the one I wish to move.*"

"Haizea." Anan looked away as if embarrassed by what he had to say. "Do you want Bethiel to hold you?"

Little tendrils of wind whirled around Kyrie.

The thunderstorm grumpily declared, "An impossible hope."

Such heartless words. Kyrie trembled along with Haizea. But then Anan caught and held his gaze, speaking to the old friend harboring close to Kyrie's heart. "Can he hold you in the way you want to be held if you do not first descend?"

Kyrie saw the difficulty, felt the sudden spark of hope. "Oh, that would make a good story. Do you think–?"

But before he could finish the thought, there was a dainty

woman kneeling before him in the snow. She had a round face, wideset blue eyes, and an abundance of loose brown curls.

"Ohhh," he breathed. "Oh, that was very brave, Haizea."

"*Now* look what you've done," grumbled Anan, who actually sounded impressed. Slipping off the fur vest he'd taken to wearing—a gift from the wolves, who liked his wildness—he settled it around Haizea's slim shoulders and pulled it shut.

Wanting to balance out Anan's scolding tone and recalling Tzefira's qualms when she'd come to the point of descending, he said, "Hello, Haizea. You are very pretty."

Anan scowled. "What do you mean by that?"

"Umm. Haizea has an open countenance, and I have always liked curly hair."

Brows furrowing, Anan said, "You never said such things to me."

"Do you feel slighted? I apologize." Contemplating Anan, he declared, "You strike awe. And sometimes fear. But I find I like how my heart trembles in your presence."

"Is that even a compliment?"

"I think so. And ... since I really *do* like curly hair, may I touch yours?"

Anan's expression grew wary. "What for?"

"Curiosity." Kyrie felt he should be as honest as possible. "And I do not want you to feel neglected. Should I go on?"

"Can you?"

He nodded. "I like the lines of your face and the color of your skin and the deep of your voice and th–"

Anan wrapped one big hand over the lower half of Kyrie's face. "Enough." But he seemed happy.

Instead of drawing his hand back, Anan ran his thumb over the freckled scales at Kyrie's temple. Like he'd been curious, too. He prodded at one of his horns, then let his hand fall away.

Kyrie lifted both hands. "Do you think I am pretty?"

Crouching and bowing his head, Anan answered, "You are a dragon."

"Only half." He confined himself to a short exploration of Anan's wild hair, then stepped back. "And I am not proud of my lineage. If I am a little terror, it may be because my sire is truly terrible."

Haizea caught the hem of his tunic and whispered, "You are a *noble* half-dragon."

Kyrie sometimes wondered if he needed to be good in order to offset the deeds of his father. But no, he'd only learned about the Rogue this past summer. All his life, Dad had encouraged Kyrie to try to live up to Mother's ideals and to stay in his good graces. Mum was all about courage and tenacity; Papka was more about generosity and creativity. And there was Uncle Jackie, who listened and loved them all ... and showed them what it meant to be a gentleman.

But somehow, earning the good opinion of an imp was uncommonly nice, and he flushed with the pleasure of it.

Dima demanded, *"Tell him the truth, Anan. He wants your opinion as much as you want his."*

Anan snorted. But then he re-took one of Kyrie's hands, pressing his thumb into his palm, where his mark spoke for him. Probably spoke for both of them. Still, the eldermost storm handed down a compliment of his own. "Beauty only adds to this one's ability to sway his foes."

Haizea wryly asked, "Is that even a compliment?"

Which was funny. Until Kyrie realized Anan was taking her question seriously.

After an appraising look, Anan asked, "If the little terror is pleased, who are you to criticize?"

Dima piped up again. *"His foes? Don't you dare blow past those words so swiftly. This is the first I've heard of foes."*

"Then you haven't been listening," drawled Anan. "There are whispers on all sides."

Kyrie tensed when all three storms lapsed into a listening sort of silence. Winds stirred and scattered, then swirled back.

Dima spoke first. *"He's in danger."*

Anan grimly agreed. "He's in danger, but with us, he can prevail. So, Dima? Will you take up a weapon?"

"I might. If I found someone willing."

Anan caught Kyrie's eye and warned, "She will. A typhoon always gets her way."

Kyrie believed it. "I would be happy if you did, but ... will you at least ask nicely?"

"I might," Dima repeated. Her tone had gone all teasing. Like she was having fun. Which was probably a very good thing, since she must be feeling better. But it might be more than a little dangerous for the one she chose.

Anan helped Haizea to her feet, then grumbled under his breath before simply picking her up.

"I must learn to stand," protested Haizea. "To walk."

"You may totter in the snow another day. There are more

important matters. Or did you forget the promise we were made?"

"I remember. I know." She pouted at Anan, but the look she turned on Kyrie was as haughty as a queen's. "I shall wear a crown. Yield to me the Plum Cascade."

49
KEEP YOUR WITS

Being one of the world's foremost diplomats came with its share of prestige, and Isla liked being acknowledged for her efforts. But there was a teensy downside—hardly worth mentioning—where her personal life was concerned. Because people naturally expected her to be flawlessly, endlessly above it all.

Criticism? Blame? Misrepresentation? Speculation? She had to pretend they couldn't touch her. And even when people were beastly and made personal jibes, she had to be the better person. Because her behavior reflected upon everything she cared about—her parents, other reavers, the In-between, the clans, and most especially, upon Hisoka-sensei.

But she'd benefited from Amaranthine guidance. Members of the clans held to a necessarily long view, and they'd helped Isla to cultivate a similar perspective. Oh, but there were times.

Moments when she was sorely tempted to lash out or make a point or set the record straight. Or to tell off meddling star-crossers who shouldn't even have her contact information ... yet somehow managed to get in a triumphant little *I told you so.*

"Since when is Twosies an oracle?" she muttered.

Lapis hummed in a distracted way. But he also produced a crystal, a subtle reminder that they couldn't very well discuss one of Stately House's new—and unregistered—crossers in front of their driver.

She let her palm rest lightly over the stone, ensuring her next words were private. "It's nothing. One of the children at Stately House has a new name. Boniface mentioned it in passing."

Lapis slid his fingers between hers, though he kept a disinterested gaze on the view out the car window. "I met young Twosies. Part star. It would explain a penchant for prophecy."

"Yes, well. Just because he has impish ancestry doesn't mean he knows anything about anything."

That earned her a puzzled glance.

"It's nothing. Really. Sorry." She tried to pull herself together. According to the sign they'd just inched past, the airport was at the next exit.

"Heritage holds sway over all of us. For instance, are you a battler or a ward?"

"Neither," she snapped. But that wasn't the whole truth. "Both."

Lapis rolled his wrist in a casual gesture the clans liked to use when someone else made their point for them.

Fine. Whatever. In any event, she couldn't take out her frustration on Boniface, whose text was kindly meant. While she was trying to phrase an answer that didn't have claws to it, an earlier message caught her eye, and she withdrew her hand from Lapis's. Because Rhomiko's name was in the preview. With a sense of trepidation, she opened the text from Tsumiko.

Isla, please listen. Rhomiko is with me, and they asked me to reach out to you. Here is their message: "Hisoka will never call you to his side." Does this mean anything to you?

She stared at this fresh series of texts in disbelief. Was the whole world against her? Yes, fine. Maybe she'd been wrong about Sensei. Maybe she'd wasted years yearning for someone who was destined for another. But did they have to rub her nose in it?

As the car glided to a stop beside the terminal, Isla switched her phone to airplane mode and powered off. She was in no mood for this nonsense. Not after having spent a perfectly lovely night with Lapis. Not when she was so ready to look forward. Not back.

Then car doors popped open, and her luggage landed on the curb.

Lapis left the vehicle and turned back to offer a gentlemanly hand. She managed a wan smile.

His gaze lingered on her lips, and his quirked. Oh. Of course. His ring was there, an oblique invitation. Or perhaps a dare. Because it was nice—for once—to be the one pursued.

Lapis angled his head, and she fell in step beside him, lengthening her stride, only to check it when he swerved to circle a display of books for sale. Chastity Landis's most recent release was among the offerings.

"Do we really have time for this?" she whispered, glancing around. "Anyone might see."

"Nobody will notice. They never do if I don't want them to."

It was one of their little traditions. Well, *she'd* come up with the scheme. Lapis was the one who mostly carried it out. Essentially, if he found one of their books in any kind of shop, he'd add a signature of sorts. Isla could, too, but it was harder for her to be sneaky about it. They each carried an inked seal for the purpose— slim, capped rods, like the seals used for official signatures in many Asian countries. Only theirs didn't involve red ink or kanji. Whenever Chastity Landis left her mark, it was a tiny blue castle, twin banners flying, floating up among the clouds.

Because without Lapis, Isla's authorial hopes would have never been more than castles in the air. And Lapis had once remarked that their books let his imagination soar, so that he felt as though he'd regained some small part of the sky.

Isla had always been enormously pleased that Lapis wasn't just humoring her, that he was proud of the stories they'd written together. Enough to want to further adorn them. To give the readers who discovered them an additional reason to treasure them.

So far, nobody had connected Lapis's ports of call to the appearance of tiny castles in the vicinity. And so far, nobody had successfully duplicated the metallic shimmer of the ink he used, which made authentication possible. Fans referred to it as Chastity Blue.

While Lapis stealth-stamped, Isla's mind raced through practical matters—customs and security and gate assignments. Would Lapis escort her all the way to her flight?

And then she caught sight of someone who shouldn't be there.

He spotted her and strolled her way, and she fumbled for her phone, turning it back on, waiting for wifi to reconnect.

Tsumiko's next texts popped up.

> **I do think this is important.**
> **Stars, you know.**
> **They're good at portent.**

Isla quickly tapped in a question.

> **Is Sensei awake?**

> **He is. Yes.**

> **He's no longer locked away?**

> **No. He's back.**
> **I know you were worried.**
> **We all have been.**

So her eyes weren't deceiving her. Sensei really was back. And he'd come for her. Her fickle heart soared. Well, why *wouldn't* she be happy to see him. Here was proof that he did care. Pocketing her phone, she glanced back, wanting to share her good news with Lapis.

But she couldn't see him.

Employing camouflage, no doubt.

Hisoka had stopped across the way, looking especially fine in his gray cloak. Tsumiko was right. He was truly back—calm and smiling and *here*. Lifting a hand, he tapped a finger to his lips, which curved in a secretive smile, asking for silence. Because of course he wouldn't want to draw attention to himself. Then he beckoned with a subtle twitch of his fingers.

"Back in a mo," she murmured in Lapis's direction.

Her heels clicked terrazzo as she wove between other people, making her way to Hisoka's side.

"And here you are," he said warmly. "I knew we'd connect if I made my way here."

As if he hadn't been essentially missing for months.

As if she hadn't been abandoned without a word and warded out.

As if he could step into his usual place without so much as an apology.

But how could she scold when he was here for her? And weren't there more important matters than her complicated feelings? She loved him, yes. That would never change. Neither had the fact that she was one of the few people who could take him to task.

"*Really*, Sensei! Your schedule! Didn't you check with Canarian? We were meant to be ...." She caught herself and checked her pockets for a warding crystal. Not all of their itinerary had been made public, and there were too many people who might overhear. "Argent stepped in, despite everything. Didn't you know?"

"Are you disappointed that I came to collect you?"

"No! Never that, but ...!" She shook her head and weakly protested, "This isn't like you. I suggested Ginkgo postpone, but Tsumiko said .... wait. Tsumiko was just saying ...?"

Isla retrieved her phone, but Hisoka plucked it from her hand.

What a childish thing to do.

She responded in kind, practically pouting. "I've been waiting for you."

"Then your patience has been rewarded." He indicated the length of the sprawling airport lobby. "Shall we?"

"Of course. I'm so sorry. Your suddenly being here has completely thrown me off. I was … wait a moment, Sensei. My bag!"

"You won't need it."

"But my notes!"

"As if you didn't already have every little thing memorized backward and forward."

Was that meant to be a compliment? It hadn't felt like one. "I have personal notes. For a project I've been working on."

"Where are your priorities, Miss Ward?"

In books, it was always so lovely when the hero swept in and took care of everything, but Isla was beginning to be annoyed. "I have flight reservations. I can't be late."

"You won't be late. And you must admit, my way is faster."

"That would break five treaties!" she hissed in shock.

He steered her toward a set of escalators. His grip was quite firm.

"Give me my phone. I need to tell Lapis …!"

"I'd like all of your attention just now, that's a girl." He leaned close with a gleam in his eye that promised mischief.

She didn't like his tone. His calling her *girl* …? So Isla demanded, "What is this?"

"What do you want it to be?" he countered, evasive as ever.

Somewhere behind her, a long way off, a shout rose. It was a compelling voice, urgent and familiar and thundering with sway.

"Wait. Did you hear …?" But when she tried to turn, Hisoka pulled her into his arms, twirling her like a dance partner. She was clamped to his side with so much force, she was certain there would be bruises. "Sensei, that *hurts*."

"Look at me," he urged. "Isn't this want you wanted?"

Maybe it was. But something was very wrong, and she was having trouble focusing. So she did the only sensible thing. She closed her eyes. Because illusions relied heavily on sight. And because she could tell now that her personal wards were jangling almost as urgently as the array of remnant-studded pins in her hair.

Wind suddenly sliced across her skin, icy cold.

She was chilled through, as if she'd been outside for a while now.

Then her stomach dropped, and they were airborne.

"You can stop trying to trigger your personal wards." It was a feminine voice. Hisoka's smile twisted into something mean, then the illusion dropped. "We disarmed them at the beginning, since *we* are not fools."

"Nona Hightip," Isla greeted coolly.

"Always so eager to have the right answer."

Her sister appeared, as did the tangle of sigilcraft they'd woven while Isla had been lost in a fox dream. Senna Hightip placed a finger against Isla's forehead and ordered, "Sleep."

The world immediately dimmed.

Though her mouth had gone very dry, Isla did the only two things she could. She swallowed the ring that had been tucked in her cheek. And she wished that stars didn't make so much more sense in hindsight.

50

LEFT WANTING

Lapis might be flightless, but he could run at speeds that rivaled the wind. At least, he could when he wasn't trying to hasten through populated areas. The kidnapper's course forced him to cut through an urban district where shoppers strolled along to the tunes of Christmas music past. Putting a fire escape to good use, he resorted to rooftops for a while, pausing to scoop up an unhappy hairpin. Suburbs were somewhat easier, though a contrary course correction forced him to zigzag from one block to the next.

This was hopeless.

He needed help. But whose?

Hisoka was cloistered.

Argent didn't carry a phone.

Harmonious required direction.

Adoona-soh was in India.

But there were other Elderboughs. Choice made, Lapis kept running while he waited for his call to connect.

"*Hey,*" came the welcome answer.

"Boon, they took Isla."

"*Keep talking.*"

"Fox magic," he managed, breaths becoming ragged. "At least one. Possibly two. They have her, and they're flying east. Once they reach the ocean ...!"

"*Gotcha. You need wings.*"

"I beg of you."

"*On it.*"

And that was all.

Lapis ran on, following a trail of breadcrumbs that rained down like taunts. Isla's protections were many and subtle, but her captors were stripping them away one by one. When they'd discarded the last of her hairpin array, his rings began to fall.

This wasn't at all what he'd had in mind when he'd told Isla he'd be in pursuit.

He entered an industrial district, all shipping containers and security fencing. And then he was out of places to run. Standing at the end of a breakwater, surrounded by the lap of waves and the lonesome ding of buoys, he wavered on the brink.

Should he swim?

Much as he disliked seawater, he was willing, but his speed would be no match for a fox in flight.

He placed another call. To his staff. Because he was going to miss several appointments. And then he notified Canarian. To his surprise, the acting leader of the Amaranthine Council already knew about his predicament.

"Help is on the way," he promised. "Focus on reaching Isla. I'll handle the fallout."

So Lapis put away his phone and focused. He began to hum, seeking willing winds. And to weave sigils. And to send them flying where he could not go.

Panic was setting in. And despair. But then a sharp whistle turned his head, and someone dropped to his side.

"You?" he ventured.

"I was nearest. And more than willing." Cyril Sunfletch held out his hands. "Will your dignity permit …?"

Lapis didn't care about anything but Isla. "They took her."

"I heard. Isla Ward." Cyril hefted him and took to the skies.

"I love her."

"Dear boy!" And more softly, "You looked radiant together last night."

"I told her." Lapis pointed urgently. "I *must* reach her."

"And so you shall. We are your support." Voice brimming with pride, he added, "All you need, we will be."

Half a dozen black wolves tore past, taking their bearing from Lapis.

"My security detail," Cyril explained. "Nightspangle wolves. And the others are making their way to you."

Lapis knew he should be singing. It was almost the only thing he *could* do. Yet all he managed was a weak trill.

"Here, now. Bear with us. Canarian Evernhold is a resourceful fellow. Did you know he used to be a playwright? These days, he scripts on a grander scale, but he's a genius when it comes to directing his players toward the best possible outcome."

Cyril was reaching heights and speeds that caused Lapis to huddle against the avian's spare frame. He dearly wished for his fur-lined cloak. And for the one who'd had it specially made. All at once, he dared to hope. "*The others*, you said. Who is coming?"

"The old guard, as it were. Canarian wants you to know that you'll have the full support of the Five."

An impossibility, surely. It was Dichotomy Day. All of them had been booked for years. And would be booked for years to come. He knew for a fact that Harmonious was in South America.

"Canarian speculated that the Hightip sisters might be planning to corner Lord Mettlebright. I understand Miss Ward has strong ties to Stately House."

"Born and raised there. And fostered by Ginkgo Mettlebright." Lapis felt the first faint glimmers of hope. Argent wouldn't let anything happen to Isla. She was as dear as a daughter. She was part of his den.

"What of Hisoka?" Cyril asked.

"I don't know," Lapis admitted. But he didn't like to think how Hisoka would take the news of Isla's capture. Could one so heartbroken bear up under another blow? They must reach Isla in time.

Jacques crooked a finger to lift Ginkgo's face. "Lord, you're stunning."

"You think? I feel ridiculous."

"The pressed powder Anjou used has a hint of shimmer. Very moonbeam. Perfect for snaring the regard of a wolf."

"Pretty sure that happened months ago. And without any of this frou-frou stuff." Ginkgo grumbled, "I want my denim back."

Jacques whispered, "Shall I add glitter to your hair?"

"Save it for your own wolf."

"There's an idea." And holding Ginkgo's gaze for several beats, he asked, "*Do* you need me to pinch you?"

"If this is a dream, leave me to it."

"Wolves," Jacques solemnly intoned. "And—at least in my case—cats."

"Anjou's great. When I left, he was starting on Kyrie's makeup. Pretty sure little bro is going to steal the show." The half-fox hesitated, then quirked a smile. "You're totally picturing Anjou with glitter in his hair."

"I am caught out." Jacques dipped into gossipy tones while he fussed with the drape of Ginkgo's silks. "We enjoyed a minor stir yesterday when some lost property arrived on our doorstep. All the things Anjou and Eiji had packed along to that dreadful island."

"I'm almost afraid to ask. What kind of stuff does a young tom pack when answering a consort call?"

"Powder with a hint of shimmer, for one. But there were a few precious things: mementos of home, his favorite hearth slippers, some weaponry. But as you might imagine, it's mostly mantraps, and I look forward to falling into them."

Ginkgo laughed.

"I'm sure Anjou would loan you some harem pants, if you want to up your shimmer game."

"Thanks, but no thanks. This get-up's too glamorous, but at least you can't see through it."

"That's the spirit." Jacques was enormously glad that Transcendence had been bold enough to make an uncommon choice. And that Ginkgo would be rightly cherished.

The half-fox's expression slowly shifted. "Are you doing that on purpose?"

"What have I done?"

"When you're happy, it's sort of … catching."

"I'm a good influence, hmm? Boniface is quite sure I'm a bad one."

Ginkgo breathed deeply. "This is it, isn't it? Impish allure."

"That does seem to be the consensus."

"I don't get this same feeling from the trees. They're nice. Pleasant. But this?" He went up on tiptoe. "What *is* this?"

"I'm substantially warded, but you're inside my sphere of influence." Jacques took Ginkgo by the chin, this time to prevent him getting any closer. "Hold that thought. Actually, I'd like to hear that thought. How do you feel?"

Ginkgo eased back, his ears at odd angles. "Curious, I guess. Hate to admit it, but I really wanted a taste."

"That would be unwise at this juncture." And chucking him under the chin before stepping back, he wryly added, "Me, the voice of reason. Who could have guessed?"

"And just like that, the pull's gone. Say, does it affect the kids?"

"*Non.*"

"The wardstones?"

"Bon-Bon and I do seem to have established a swift rapport with ours, but who can say why? Our rock baby may simply find him charming. Many do. Quite the mystery."

"Oh, come on. He's cute."

"*Mon dieu*. You've taken leave of your senses."

"You're both … I dunno. Let's just say you're both something else. In a good way. It works for you."

That's when Boon strode into the room, his phone to his ear, his expression fierce. He said, "On it." And ending the call, he closed distance, gave his customary ponytail a restless tug, heaved a sigh and said, "Sorry, little bro. We've got a situation."

Hisoka hadn't been outdoors since that one night when Fend had cornered him into a prowl through the woods. Now he strolled beside Rhomiko, taking an admittedly circuitous route toward the Song Circle. It was their ultimate destination since Tsumiko had asked if he'd officiate Ginkgo's bonding ceremony. Hisoka was honored. But also uneasy with the fact that Argent wasn't here because he'd taken Hisoka's place elsewhere.

"He's missing his son's bonding ceremony because of me."

Rhomiko hummed. "Does the absence of one's parent affect the ceremony's outcome?"

"I suppose not."

"If Mother does not witness the declaration of a bond between us, will that bond fade?"

Hisoka's step faltered. "Have you become interested in such things?"

"I have learned about Amaranthine bonds and about human weddings. About reaver contracts and about the customs of several clans." Rhomiko asked, "Which do you prefer?"

"Goodness. Who have you been speaking with?"

"Several people. All of whom were completely candid with their answers."

"I'm not trying to avoid the question."

Rhomiko sighed. Actually sighed.

Hisoka felt bad. "I was only trying to understand what your reasons for asking might be."

"What do my motives matter? There is no need to align your answer to mine." And they calmly repeated, "What sort of bonding ceremony would you prefer?"

His first impulse was to remark upon the presumption of the question.

His next was to make some remark about the fickleness of cats.

But Rhomiko's stance was perfectly, pointedly neutral. And their gaze—while not unkind—did not waver while they waited.

"Something quiet," he tentatively offered. "Not a Song Circle gathering. No television crews."

"You do not want anyone to know about my claim?"

"No!" Hisoka frowned. "Wherever I go, you will be by my side. Word will swiftly spread, but for a bonding ceremony, I would greatly prefer something quiet."

Rhomiko inclined their head and gestured for more.

Even though Hisoka had never given the matter any prior

consideration, he immediately knew what would please him most. "For my witnesses, I would want there to be a tree and a star. And Jacques."

Rhomiko's expression gentled. "Will Eri do?"

Hisoka blinked. "You have met Eri?"

That earned him a flat look.

"Yes," Hisoka meekly answered. "Eri will do."

And with no further discussion, Rhomiko took him by the hand and led him onto the narrow, snow-tromped path that took them to Andor's cabin.

He bowed his head to hide his smile. After countless centuries of sidestepping propositions and proposals, Hisoka would pledge himself to the one person who didn't bother to ask.

Andor didn't look especially surprised to find them standing side-by-side upon his doorstep.

Eri drew them inside, presenting ribbon-wrapped posies, as if their impromptu plans had been anticipated. And after Andor had heard them out, he grunted and called, "Hajime."

All at once, there was a tree with them, patient with an introduction that had apparently been made several times already, and quite prepared to grant Hisoka's wish. He was gone and back with a vaguely frazzled Jacques. But the instant the man's gaze fell to the bouquets in his and Rhomiko's hands, he drew himself up.

"Am I here to witness a happy event? Or ... lord, am I giving you away?"

Rhomiko smiled softly. "You will give him back."

"Too right, I will. To you and no other." And turning to Andor, he beamed. "*Do* say there will be star wine for afters."

The bear huffed and ambled out.

Jacques wasted no time. First pulling Rhomiko into his arms, he urged, "Be good to him. He needs minding."

"He will want for nothing."

Hisoka had the sense that this was the beginning of vows.

But then Jacques' hands were framing his face, and the man solemnly said, "Thank you for your trust. I release you from our vow. So when I say *be happy*, it's not an order. Just the usual sort of felicitations."

"Thank you." A meager offering, considering how many difficulties this man had spared him. "Truly."

"Are we all here, then?" Jacques checked.

Hisoka said, "A tree, a star, and you."

"Lord. Still flattered, but a trifle confused. Which star, exactly?" Jacques pointed up. "I can't be the only one who's noticed."

"I thought Eri …?" began Hisoka.

That star shook their head.

"I thought so, too," admitted Rhomiko. "But another has come and wishes to stand with us."

Hisoka's heart leapt, for his first thought was for Novi, his oldest friend.

A knock on the door, and everyone traded glances.

"I'll just get that, shall I?" offered Jacques.

The door swung wide.

Showing perfect poise, Jacques inquired, "May I ask who's calling?"

There was a brief pause, during which Eri and Rhomiko edged closer to the door. Hisoka remained where he was, hoping against hope that Novi hadn't descended. He'd never wanted that, and Hisoka wouldn't wish for it.

But an entirely new voice genially declared, "Most know me as Bethiel."

"Lord. We're honored, I'm sure. Do come in." And turning to catch Hisoka's eye, Jacques widened his eyes and announced, "*Bethiel* is here."

Rhomiko was first to present their palms. "Hisoka wanted a star. Thank you for coming, but … did you descend? You have, haven't you?"

One of the foremost angels from Amaranthine lore, Bethiel of the Changing Winds, matched palms with Rhomiko. "I am newly descended, yes. A strange sensation. I'm sure I'll adjust."

"Just for us?"

"No, not entirely." And directing a warm smile Hisoka's way, he said, "I'm rarely sent anyplace for only one reason."

51

IN THE PRESENCE OF THESE WITNESSES

Andor lumbered in, a cask of star wine on his shoulder. Seeing Bethiel in their midst, he didn't register even a flicker of surprise. Simply tossed off a casual wave. The angel responded in glad tones, like he and the bear clansman were old friends.

Moving to stand beside Hajime, who caught and held his hand, Bethiel urged, "Carry on."

Hisoka's mind was utterly blank.

What was he even supposed to say.

"Yes. Right. Dearly beloved, and all that," agreed Jacques, who had moderated his fair share of press conferences and knew how to steer a room. "Rhomiko, love, I believe you should lead off."

The half-star made a graceful, grateful gesture that included the gathering of witnesses. "Stars. Tree. Bear. Smythe. I will say what I think, and you will tell me if it is enough."

Hisoka rocked back into a receptive posture, and in some far corner of his mind, he could hear his sister's teasing voice, ordering him to *await, await, await*. He'd never been good at it. Never wanted to lean too heavily into trust.

Jacques was his exception.

And Rhomiko was simply *his*.

Rhomiko said, "I have been watching, and I have seen. The way a gaze can follow and rest and plead. How the eyes reveal secrets and confirm them. What a glance can tell.

"Argent watches Tsumiko.

"Suuzu watches Akira.

"Ginkgo watches Snow."

The half-star hesitated. "I could make a longer list, but I think there are secrets that are not mine to speak. Rather, I will confess to kinship with all those whose gaze lingers on their beloved. Because my eyes are also drawn, and my thoughts are always dwelling on the one I love to see.

"I am bound to Hisoka Twineshaft by my mother's will and by a father's twins. But I want an even closer tie. The closest of ties. I want a vow worthy of Song Circles and dragon song. But it can be spoken quietly. And here."

And so with a star and a tree and a Smythe for witness, Hisoka Twineshaft said, "Yes."

One small word.

A scant syllable.

You'd think an old diplomat like him was capable of something more eloquent. And yet Rhomiko's expression grew more lovely, and a teary-eyed tree clapped his hands.

Bethiel spoke first. "It is good."

Andor glanced up and gruffly announced, "The stars are singing."

And Jacques quietly urged, "Uphold tradition, Hisoka. Kiss your bondmate."

This time, it was Rhomiko whose posture shifted into one of willingness. "You like kisses."

"I suppose I do."

"Show me why."

Many cats were comfortable with public displays, but Hisoka had always been—would always be—private in his attachments, reserved in showing his affection. So he confined himself to a kiss that was small and quiet, but no less profound than his *yes*.

"There is more," Rhomiko said.

Hisoka expected there would be more. Eventually. "There is wine."

"Not that. There is something yet unfinished."

He awkwardly muttered, "Not here."

"No. Not here." Rhomiko's hand found his. "You are needed. You need to go."

"Where am I meant to be, if not with you?"

"Lord," Jacques breathed. "You're adorable, but your Romeo is right. Not to hurry matters along, but things were in a bit of a muddle when Hajime pulled me aside."

"Isla did not listen." Rhomiko repeated, "You need to go. Join her rescuers."

Hisoka looked to Jacques. "Isla ...?"

But it was his bondmate who answered. "The foxes who stole Mother. They have your apprentice."

As the taskforce's information guy, Sinder got ahold of everyone who was anyone to Isla, then tracked down the closest assets so Lapis would have support. Canarian Evernhold was a big help there, calmly suggesting the most *ridiculous* option.

"Sure, why not," he muttered to himself. "I'm sure President-elect Sunfletch had nothing better to do on his *one* free day before his inauguration."

But it had worked out. In spades. Because Doon-wen Nightspangle was in charge of Cyril's security detail. *Personally* in charge. And Jiminy's pack would have Jiminy's protections. Which meant they'd be sigiled backward and forward against every possible threat. Including the kinds of foxy illusions the Hightip sisters must have used to net Isla.

Which was quite the power move. But … so, *so* stupid. And not just because that young woman had friends in high places.

Sinder smiled grimly at the string of messages coming across his screen. He was feeling on top of things all the way up until he walked through the door to Timur's room … and found Kyrie and Fend—in speaking form—sitting in the middle of the floor, heads bent over a small sphere of potent stone.

"He *knew*?"

Fend was wrapped around him an instant later. "Jealous?"

"Maybe a little. Talk about glam." Shimmying out of the cat's clutches, Sinder dropped to a seat next to Anan, whose usual glower was now limned in silver. "Who fancied you two up?"

"Anjou." Kyrie's eyes were lined with purple, and the scales on his face had been carefully edged in glitter. "For Ginkgo's bonding ceremony."

"Yeahhh, too bad about having to postpone."

"Snow understands. If he goes after Isla, she will carry him."

"Is that wise?" Sinder asked. "Your brother's not ... wait. Actually, he spent a lot of time with Salali last summer. Not for nothing. And if there's one thing last summer taught me, it's to never underestimate a crosser."

"Those vixens were unwise for taking Isla. Ginkgo is—"

"Incensed," filled in Sibley.

Sinder hadn't even realized the kid was in the room. Given Fend's soft hiss, he hadn't either. Damned if these crossers weren't impossible to predict.

Kyrie smiled in that secretive way of his. In the know as always. He asked, "You followed me?"

"I was looking for you." Sibley's gaze was fixed on the Kith-kin in their midst. "And you said that when things are happening, you gotta tell Fend. Now I get why."

"I am found out." Fend beckoned. "Come here, Sibley."

The boy shuffled forward, though his attention was fixed on Kyrie. "You're extra adorned."

"Yes." Kyrie cast a shy look at Sinder, including him in the question. "Does it suit me?"

Fend reeled in an inattentive Sibley and petted his hair. "Tell your big brother he's pretty. Dragons like compliments."

"Do we? I never noticed."

Fend said, "You are the bravest of the batch. Visit anytime."

Sibley frowned at him for a moment, then sighed. "Okay, yeah. I liked that. You give good compliments."

Noticing that Kyrie was still waiting for an answer, Sinder twirled a finger at his own face. "The glitter might be a little too over-the-top for every day, but sure. Your eyes. It's a good look."

Anan growled, "We were in the middle of something important."

"Dragons—and their needs—*are* important," countered Fend. "But yes. We have decisions to make." Including Sinder and Sibley with significant looks, he smoothly added, "Welcome to the cabal."

Sibley had already been pretty good at tracking down Kyrie, but Anan made it extra easy. Storms had a certain feel to them, and if Sibley closed his eyes, he could tell where his eldermost brother was. At least, he *thought* it was all Anan. Might be he was sensing that typhoon Kyrie was keeping safe.

One thing was sure. Sibley *really* liked guys like Anan and Boon. All that swagger and rumble and that little bit of danger. Sibley planned to be just as big and bold as them once he grew up.

He could already tell it would be right for him.

Much better than trying to be like Kyrie.

Because *alike* wasn't *same*. Sure, Kyrie was a little older and a little taller, and his nice manners made him all elegant, sorta like Uncle Jackie and Uncle Boniface. But that was stuff Sibley could learn if he tried. Those were things around the edges of Kyrie, like the liner that adorned his eyes. *Anyone* could have lines like that. But could they see what Kyrie saw?

The easiest way to put it was … there was a bigness to Kyrie. Big ideas. Big plans. He was big enough to carry eldermost storms inside him. And while everyone else was wasting time, Kyrie knew just what to do and what to say. And what to ask for.

And Kyrie had asked Sibley to do something. As part of a cabal. That was a good word. Cabal. It meant a group who did things secretly. Cabals were also perfect for Sibley. He'd had a lot of practice.

Poking his nose into one of the downstairs parlors, Sibley froze when Mum's dark eyes met his. Just like that, he was caught. She was harder to hide from than the rest, like she had a second sense when it came to sneaks.

"Hey, little bro." Ginkgo greeted him with the lift of his chin. He was sitting on a footstool, still all dressed up for the wedding-thingie they'd called off. Since they were having an emergency instead.

Sibley checked Mum again, unsure of his welcome. Some days, the lady was as stormy as Anan, and maybe that should have scared him. Except he had fuzzy memories of another dark-eyed lady. Someone who'd liked to watch battle games and that show with Aloora Longstride in it. Not his real mother, but someone who'd shared her blanket and her bowl of popcorn.

Sansa held out a big hand and said, "Here is an elusive one. Come and let Transcendence sort your scent."

Ginkgo said, "Sibley's American. English, please."

"It would have been English anywise," countered Ginkgo's lady. She had white hair, copper eyes, and all kinds of swagger in her soul.

"Is good, yes? A wolf is always welcome."

Sibley hadn't exactly been avoiding this she-wolf. She was the best kind of big and bold, too, but he'd been busy with Anjou and Etienne. "What's transcendence?" Sibley hastily adjusted his posture to make the question more polite.

"Something that goes above and beyond. And a real mouthful." Ginkgo asked, "Okay if the kids call you Snow?"

She inclined her head. "You may call me Snow."

"That's settled. Auntie Snow it is."

"Why *aunt*?" she challenged.

"Respect, mostly."

"Nobody has ever called you Uncle Ginkgo in my hearing."

"Well, nooo. I'm just Ginkgo."

"Then I am just Snow." And the lady sought Sibley's gaze to order, "Call me Snow."

Sibley watched closely. Gingko was really good at hiding things, but not his tail. It was puffed and twitchy, and even though it'd lifted when Sibley came in, it'd gone right back to being tucked between his ankles.

But Ginkgo sounded like himself when he patted the side of his leg and said, "And this is Pact. You two met yet?"

A dog burst out from under a table, fairly prancing up to Sibley and licking his chin before running to Ginkgo and trying to clamber onto his lap.

"Come on, pup. Say hello to Sibley."

And the dog shifted into a little boy with floppy puppy ears and silver eyes, who snuggled into Ginkgo and said, "Da." Then stuck a finger in his mouth.

He was cute.

Sibley thought of something. "If you and me are brothers, and you're Pact's da, am I his uncle?"

"Well, sure. I guess that'd be right. But it might be simpler if you're just Sibley. Kith-kin like Pact grow up fast. He'll be bigger than both of us put together in another few years. But don't be shy about chipping in. Big brothers are the best."

Sibley tended to agree, but Ginkgo's inflection made him curious. "Do you have any?"

"Big brothers? Sure I do. If you're paying attention, you'll notice that Boon sometimes calls me *little bro*. Same goes for *his* big brother, Roo-nii."

"You have wolf brothers." Sibley was kind of impressed.

With a knowing look, Ginkgo pointed out, "And you have a wolf mother, just like Pact. Go ahead, pup. Sibley will understand."

Glad that his claws had been rendered safe, Sibley wiggled his fingers coaxingly. "Friends?"

With an achingly sweet smile, Pact lunged for him, and Sibley swung the little guy onto his hip.

"Sibby?"

"Sibley," he corrected, rubbing their noses together. "Good for you. This place is nice. You and your mom and your da can help me and Kyrie keep it safe." He stole a peek Sansa's way and hopefully added, "Mum, too."

Pact was friendly, but he was too busy to cuddle for long. When he squirmed to be let down, Sibley let him go. Moments later, the pup was back on four paws and chasing his own tail. Ginkgo and Snow barely noticed the ruckus, they were so deep in conversation. Making plans. Ones Kyrie needed Sibley to change.

Sansa crooked a finger. "I know this look. Is important, yes? This thing you want to say."

Ginkgo's ears pricked, and his nose took to twitching. "Sibley?"

He was ready for this. Fend had coached him. And Kyrie was depending on him. So he lifted his chin and said, "I'm here, and you're looking at me."

"Yeah, little bro." Ginkgo beckoned, inviting him closer.

Sibley stayed where he was. "And while you're looking at me, you're not looking at Kyrie."

The half-fox's ears flattened. "He's not here. He's ... off that way." And to Snow, he added, "All the kids are tagged one way or another, just to be safe."

"Yes," Sibley said, calling his attention back. "He explained it real good. How I could keep you busy here while he walked out."

"Out," echoed Mum. "What is this *out*?"

Ginkgo's eyes widened. "Tell me he didn't go after Isla."

Sibley shook his head. "Kyrie thinks your dad can handle another fox. But there's this question I gotta ask you. While all of them rescuers are looking for vixens, maybe it's to keep everyone from noticing something else."

"Kyrie's worried about decoys?" Ginkgo traded a look with Snow. "There *are* two vixens."

"And the Rogue, yes?" Mum's eyes held a dangerous glitter.

"Are you the kind of people who'll listen to kids, even though we're kids."

Ginkgo promised, "I'm listening."

But Snow huffed. "He's stalling."

Wolves. They were really good at sniffing out the truth. "Yeah. I am. I'm the decoy. And I need you to promise that you won't leave, even though you love Isla. She's yours, right? You fostered her."

Ginkgo's cheerful mask slipped some. "From the day she was born."

"And you're her mum," he said to Sansa.

"Yes. Isla is my girl."

Snow warned, "He's still stalling."

Sibley smiled. "Yeah. I am."

"Why?" asked Ginkgo.

"Because there's a problem with the new head of security for Stately House." Sibley looked her in the eye and hoped she wouldn't be too mad. "Pick me up."

Without hesitation, she crossed to him and lifted him, giving him a really good look at shining copper eyes.

"Pet my hair," he said.

Ginkgo was there, and his eyes flashed warnings. "Hey, now, little bro ...!"

Because he was using sway. "Touch my nose," he ordered next.

She did. Gently. And without any sign of resistance. Fend had been right. Snow wasn't going to be any kind of help if they were facing a dragon.

"Da! Up!"

Ginkgo's expression was hard to read when he lifted Pact so the little boy could pet Sibley's hair and touch his nose. But Sibley thought Ginkgo's drooping ears meant he got it. And that was good.

Sansa asked, "How many went? How many who hurried away were the ones who know better than to listen to dragons?"

"Most." Ginkgo shook his head. "Most of the *adults*. Dragon crossers are immune. And Kith."

"Beg pardon," came a voice from the doorway. Opal the Sage offered a wave. "You left out dragons. And imps."

"And Timur," said Sansa, brimming with pride. "But these things, they are not why our boy is stalling, yes?"

Ginkgo looked worried then. "Where's Kyrie going?"

"He's got this friend. Seems like Kyrie cares just as much about rocks as he does winds. And one's missing. He went looking for it."

"The missing anchor crystal? But we checked. It's not ... oh, hell. It's not *inside* the barrier." Ginkgo shoved Pact into Snow's other arm and ran out.

Sansa said, "Michael and I, we will secure the house. Opal, bring our people here. All of them. Empty the enclave."

The dragon sketched a bow and slipped away.

"Let me down." And once Sibley dropped to the floor, he quietly said, "Pact needs his mum."

It wasn't *really* an order, but it was true. And it might keep Ginkgo's new family safe.

Because if Kyrie was right, their sire was looking for a way in.

And if Fend was right, their cabal was perfectly equipped to stop him.

52
OLD GUARD

e wants to talk to you."

Argent glanced between Hallow and his proffered phone. "Is that absolutely necessary?"

"Jacques thinks so." With a small shake of his head, the bat-crosser from Boon's team softly added, "I think it would be wise."

"Why?"

Hallow bluntly said, "You need to calm down. He can do that."

Argent huffed and put out his hand.

A moment later, Jacques' voice was chiding him from half a world away. *"Are you being difficult? This is no time to be peevish. There's too much at stake."*

"I am aware of the stakes." And in a more moderate tone, "How was Ginkgo's bonding?"

"Ah. I really wish you wouldn't travel without me. The information lag alone ...!"

Argent frowned. "To the point, please."

"The bonding ceremony had to be postponed."

And then silence.

Argent's stomach plunged. "Whoever thought you would be a calming influence was badly mistaken."

"Lord, sorry. That wasn't meant for a dramatic buildup. I was just handed a baby. Nickolay is now privy to our conversation." There was a lilt to his tone. Argent could hear the smile he was giving the baby. *"There is nothing specifically amiss, but Sansa has put the whole enclave on high alert. And I must ask. Are you certain there are two vixens in your vicinity?"*

"Senna and Nona always work in tandem."

"What if tandem means one sister is playing decoy while the other is diminishing our defenses? Hypothetically speaking."

"Stately House is one of the safest places in the world. I made sure. I *make* sure." His den was virtually unfindable, nearly impenetrable. But no sooner had these thoughts formed, than the existence of exceptions presented themselves. Like the manifestation of trees. And his son's unique ability to slip past barriers. A trait he may have inherited from his diabolical sire. "Why did Sansa delay the bonding?"

"And empty the enclave. Everyone's been moved to the main house, and the surrounding yard has become an encampment of wolves. We're striving for a festive air, for the sake of the children, but ... well. As the old adage goes, better safe than sorry."

"Why?"

"Kyrie."

"Again, why?"

"My information is secondhand, but according to Sibley, one of the remnant stones that serves as an anchor for the outermost barrier went missing. All very suspicious. But the wolves didn't have anything to report."

"Which is *also* suspicious."

"In hindsight, quite."

"When was this?"

"This morning. Before dawn. Amidst the excitement of the Scattering's arrival. Which is why Sansa wanted me to ask if you're facing one vixen or two."

Argent didn't like to sound boastful. "I cannot see either of them giving up the chance to see my face when they do their worst."

"Are you up to confirming that?"

He could see where this was headed and didn't like it one bit.

Jacques forged on. *"You're a fox. Can't you ask them?"*

"No."

"Give audience then? They may wish to gloat."

The very idea repulsed Argent, but he would do anything for Isla. Even this. After a lengthy silence, he reported, "No response. They are not yet in range."

"Right. Anjou will relay that to the powers that be. Any orders?"

"Ask Michael and Sansa to trust us. And Ginkgo should kn– "

"Ah," Jacques interrupted. *"About that. Ginkgo isn't here. Well, he's still here, but not here-here. He went after Kyrie."*

Argent's jaw clenched. "Could you expand on that as-yet-unmentioned detail?"

"Right. Sorry. Again, my information is secondhand, but that anchor stone from the outer barrier? Kyrie went after it. And

Ginkgo went after him."

"Change of plans," Argent drawled. "Tell Sansa that Fend will take the lead."

"*Beg pardon?*"

"Fend is in charge. Trust the defense of Stately House to him."

Jacques' incredulity was plain. "*Timur's Kith partner?*"

"Timur's Kith-kin partner, the sly boots." With a grim smile, Argent added, "Let him know that I will consider his success proof of his attainment."

Argent kept catching flares of light in his periphery and suspected stars. He wasn't used to accounting for impish assistance, but he liked the potential. "Could I beg a favor?"

Nothing.

"If you are witnesses only, so be it. But if you have time on your hands, could you fetch two far-flung friends?"

Still nothing.

"Harmonious Starmark. Adoona-soh Elderbough. They are making their way here, but from considerable distances. You could hasten their journeys."

"True."

Argent blinked, then narrowed his eyes against the sudden swelling of brilliance before him. A skybound star put out considerably more light than a descended one.

"Your prayer shall be answered."

Had that been a prayer, then? Perhaps begging for miracles amounted to the same thing. He inclined his head. "Thank you." And because he was curious, "Who might you be?"

"Soriel."

"Of the Dawning?"

An awkward smile. A small shrug. "Don't look so impressed. Bearing witness to beginnings is nothing compared to undertaking them. Continue what you have started, Argent Mettlebright. And ... thank you for asking. I don't often get to step in. It's a nice change of pace."

And the star streaked away.

As did two others, each in a different direction.

Juuyu skimmed to his side, his eyes wider than Argent had ever seen them. "What did you do?"

"I ... asked for help."

The phoenix blinked. "Has that always been an option?"

Argent gestured helplessly. "That was *Soriel*."

"Of the Dawning?"

"Imagine my surprise."

Juuyu peered in the direction he'd disappeared. "Where did he go?"

"To bring reinforcements. I wanted Harmonious and Adoona-soh."

"There was a third." Juuyu used his whole arm to show the final star's heading. He held Argent's gaze and asked, "Hisoka?"

It *was* the direction of home.

Argent dared to hope that the Five would face this trouble together.

Boon drifted closer, speaking into his phone. "Nothing here. But if Doon-wen's right, we'll converge soon. Hang on. Argent, what did I just see?"

"Stars."

"Huh. Okay, sure." And then his expression changed, and he glanced around. "Uhh. More importantly, what did I just *hear*?"

Juuyu's brows arched, but he shook his head.

Argent also signaled to the negative.

Boon tugged at his ponytail and uttered a bewildered, "Mom?"

Then one of the dexes whistled, short and shrill. She pointed to an arc of light streaking from the South. Argent had seen the same phenomenon mere weeks before, during their time in the tropics, when a veritable shooting star had delivered Paltry into their midst.

Adoona-soh arrived in a rush, haloed in a brilliance that simply dispersed, twirling up into the blue to join the lights that were still dancing just out of focus.

"Did you see that?" Adoona-soh looked windblown, even rattled. "Did you see him?"

Argent asked, "Did you meet Soriel as well?"

She goggled at him, then lifted a hand as if to call back her helper. "That was *Cadmiel*."

Senses sharpening, Argent demanded, "What do you have there?"

In her other hand, Adoona-soh gripped crystals. And they weren't just any stones. She held out her hand so they could all see. "Cadmiel said they were too fine to be lost to the sea. So Jashiel coaxed the tides to retrieve them." With a pleading look at her son, she asked, "Have I stepped into a bard's tale?"

Boon's smile was sympathetic. "I take it you recognize these, Argent?"

"The hairpins are Isla's. I helped Michael tune them as part of her personal wards. And while I don't keep track of *all* his jewelry, I do know that this stone … and this one … belong to Lapis. Fair to assume these are all his."

"How did Lapis's rings end up in the drink?"

"Isla may have been carrying them." Argent slowly added, "Or wearing them."

Adoona-soh said, "It would be just like Lapis to try to add to her protections."

"True." Argent tensed when Boon did.

But Adoona-soh flashed a stand-down signal, and another of the dexes whistled. A second point of light was streaking their way. The she-wolf rolled her eyes and snapped, "Stop *shouting* Harmonious. You are deafening my pack."

Moments later, Harmonious Starmark joined them. Brimming with enthusiasm, he exclaimed, "Soriel of the Dawning! Can you believe it? He guided Da, back at the beginning of everything for our pack. I've heard the story a thousand times and more, but to meet him for myself? Amazing!"

"Ah," said Juuyu, his gaze fixed in another direction. "This bodes well."

They turned to face another oncoming star. Argent's heart lifted when Hisoka arrived in their midst, as poised as if he'd always traveled this way.

Harmonious was the first to move. Enfolding their leader in a gentle embrace, he gruffly said, "You're here. Thank goodness. It's good to see you."

Argent gazed after the retreating star. "Friend of yours?"

"A new acquaintance, though his name is familiar enough. Auriel. He … well. Once upon a time, he saved my mother's life." Hisoka disentangled himself from Harmonious, giving the dog's broad shoulder a grateful pat. "I was already on my way, but his was a welcome visitation."

"We'll see Isla safe," promised Harmonious. "The Five. Together."

"That is certainly *one* of our goals," Hisoka acknowledged.

"Nona," Adoona-soh said darkly. "She goes too far."

"The Hightip sisters are an affront to peace, and the Rogue will go the way of his sire." Juuyu's fingers lightly touched the hilt of the blade at his hip, and his demeanor promised a swift end to his prey. "Maker mark, and Maker move."

"We *have* been moved." Hisoka considered the view. "Are we in a position to intercept?"

"That's the gist of it." Boon leveled his arm along the correct bearing. "Any minute now, we should be able to … hold up. Huh. There we go. I'm catching Nightspangle chatter." He missed a beat. "Hell and hellions. Why did nobody mention that these were Doon-wen's people?"

"You hadn't heard?" asked Harmonious. "Good of Cyril to step in."

Juuyu fidgeted. "Cyril Sunfletch is a public figure. Vital to the peace process."

Boon barked a laugh. "And the Five aren't?"

Harmonious was more diplomatic about it. "I understand what you're saying. But who can argue with Soriel of the Dawning? Or Auriel of the Golden Seed."

"Or Cadmiel of the Echoing Song," interjected Adoona-soh.

"There. See?" soothed Harmonious. "Maker bless, you have to

agree we're where we're meant to be."

And then the next president of the United States arrived with Lapis, ringed by large black wolves. Hardly subtle. Argent immediately began pulling sigils into order while greetings were exchanged. Hisoka was offering belated personal congratulations with regards to Sunfletch's appointment when Lapis caught Argent's eye.

Of course the dragon would recognize the remnant stones Adoona-soh had surrendered to him. The rings and hairpins rested in the breast pocket of the suit that Jacques had promised would make the right sort of impression on the world. But Lapis was too diplomatic to interrupt Hisoka. So Argent whisked the anxious dragon from Cyril's arms and dropped away from the rest for a private word.

"The angels who brought us together also salvaged several precious trinkets."

Lapis found his voice. "There is a ring. I gave her a ring. She has it still."

"Show me where," Argent urged.

The dragon looked.

Argent pivoted in order to follow his gaze. Further south than expected. Not that there was anything to see. With foxes, there wouldn't be.

Lapis's hands were trembling. "My sigils worked for a while, but they noticed. I can only be sure of the ring. Argent, it is *close*. They may be watching."

"If so, then they are seeing things."

"Illusions?"

"There has been ample time to prepare. You and I are already lost to everyone's view. All the better to stage a rescue, hmm?"

"This is all my fault, and now I'm a hinderance." Head bowed, Lapis whispered, "I *can* swim. Set me down in the sea. Free your hands. Reach her for me?"

"When the time comes, I will be relying on *your* hands. But first, tell me of this ring." Argent narrowed his eyes as he concentrated. "Teach me its song."

Lapis took a steadying breath, then began to hum. The notes were simple, but the winds were willing. Argent was soon catching resonance.

"Enough. I have her." And she *was* closer than he'd expected.

A moment later, a sly chuckle teased at the edges of his mind. *"I told you he would come."*

Senna.

A beat later, Nona's sweet inquiry. *"So eager. Should we be flattered?"*

"He can only be pursuing us, for there is nobody else." Senna radiated smugness. *"I told you the right enticements would draw him into our sky."*

This again.

He refused to answer. They were only trying to flush him out. It was a good thing Lapis couldn't hear them. Yet.

With his lips nearly touching Lapis's ear, Argent warned, "They are here, and they are cruel. They will send visions of terrible things to draw you out. They will make outrageous claims. Or make it seem that Isla is begging for you. Ignore them, no matter what you think you see."

"But Argent," he answered miserably. "I love her."

So Tsumiko had been right.

"All the better," said Argent. "You and I are closest to her—both in nearness and in knowing. Leave the vixens to the rest of the Five. Focus on the ring. It will be a faithful guide. We will take Isla back."

"I am willing."

"Good." Argent searched Lapis's face and said, "My plan is simple. They will drop her. You will catch her. And I will carry you both to safety."

"If Isla falls from this height ...!"

Argent sternly interrupted, "My pocket. Your stones. Choose the one she knows best. Use it to signal to her. If she knows we are here, that we are below, she will know it is safe to act."

Lapis fumbled through his options, placed one ring upon his finger, and whispered to its remnant stone. It whispered back.

"Good," Argent repeated. "Now. My senses are sharpest in truest form. You will ride, and we shall hunt."

53

TRIBUNAL

Hisoka supposed they weren't the likeliest of rescuers. Diplomats all, and most wearing their Dichotomy Day finery, rushed from the world stage to one vastly more isolated. Matters simplified as each of them shifted into truest form. On four paws, what needed to be done would come more easily.

Red foxes sprang into view as if surprised from a nearby den. Two. Six. Ten. Twenty. They bounced along different planes, above and below, scattering and circling with a confusion of yipping laughter. Distractions, yes. But also mockery.

Prowling along the edges of the mass illusion, Hisoka's whiskers quivered as he sifted through the scene. Cats relied on their eyes for the hunt, which left them at an inherent disadvantage when it came to foxes and their tricks. But there wasn't anything subtle about the vixens' display. And Hisoka was wily in his own way.

He was certainly savvy enough to realize that the silver fox at Boon's side wasn't Argent. Lord Mettlebright had slipped away. Readying his own plans, no doubt. Hisoka wished he knew what those plans were.

Rhomiko had urged him to go after Isla, utterly confident that he was needed. And Hisoka had bowed to their wishes. Barely away from Stately House's protections, he'd encountered his starry guide and been carried off. Mere minutes had passed, and most of those had been spent in grateful awe, not strategy.

For better—or worse—most of their group were canines. They could coordinate their efforts. But as the lone feline in this mess, Hisoka was out of the loop. And reduced to bystander.

Adoona-soh blew through an illusory vixen.

Harmonious growled and pounced, dissipating another.

Doon-wen snapped a faux fox out of existence.

Ah. So the head of the Nightspangle pack had stayed back? The rest of the cortege had gone, no doubt bundling Cyril to safety. This wasn't his battle, but Doon-wen wasn't without connection. Isla's father was his foster son's mentor. And the Nightspangles had supported the Elderboughs wherever they could during hunts for the Rogue. That made this personal.

Speaking of connections, his own was close as Kindred.

Isla.

Was she even here?

Hisoka wasn't attuned to her. Indeed, he'd gone out of his way to avoid the kind of closeness an Amaranthine usually enjoyed with their apprentices, so their bond was largely a matter of record. Would she suffer for his reticence?

A white wolf dropped back to his side, shifting into speaking form. Moon said, "I'm with you, Sensei. Boon's orders. Please don't be offended. We know you can handle yourself."

Hisoka could only be grateful. He nuzzled Moon's shoulder, then settled into an inviting crouch.

"That *would* make my job as earpiece easier. Thank you."

Polite to a fault. It was one of the reasons Hisoka had singled out Moon-kin Ambervelte, who'd served as Boon's mentor back when the whelp had first begun announcing to anyone who'd listen that he wanted to be a lone wolf. The two had distinguished themselves as the best of the best among dexes ... even though neither technically held the designation.

On paper, Boon and his people were part of Hisoka's cortege.

Off the record, they were sanctioned by the Amaranthine Council to administer justice in the ancient way. It was a solemn duty, and they took the responsibility seriously. Being sympathetic souls, their prey never suffered. Something that currently gave Hisoka mixed feelings. He wanted Senna and Nona to pay dearly for their crimes. An unbecoming attitude, surely. But it was how he felt.

"I don't know if you've seen Lord Mettlebright's declaration of intent to the powers that be." Moon quietly relayed, "As spokesperson for the fox clans, he's within his rights to call for blood. We will answer that call. Today will see the finish of a long and frustrating hunt."

A welcome finish.

But at what cost?

He still hadn't caught any sign of Isla. Had one of the vixens slipped her past them while the other bedeviled them?

Harmonious bowled through insubstantial fur and changed tack, choosing a new target.

Boon worked from the edges, circling inward, snatching at ankles and tails.

Doon-wen wasn't messing around. He scuttled each illusion by going for its throat.

And in so doing, they systematically narrowed the field until Adoona-soh's jaws closed on a fox's scruff. Suspended as they were between sea and sky, she couldn't bear her quarry to the ground. The red fox jerked and writhed, trying to scrabble free. Adoona wasn't being gentle, and the scent of blood soon tinged the air.

After a string of outraged yips, the vixen went limp.

Moon murmured, "It's Nona. Senna must have Isla."

The remaining vixens all shimmered away, and the canines converged. However, Boon made room for Juuyu.

"What is your name, Kindred?"

It was the beginning of judgment, and they were all witnesses. Hisoka shuddered, for the rote called up memories of Juuyu's questioning of Kodoku, the self-proclaimed doctor who'd dabbled with countless lives. He, too, had been Nemi's child. Parent to the Rogue, who was Rhomiko's half-brother.

Growls sprang up on all sides, demanding compliance.

The vixen shifted into speaking form. Hand clapped to the damage at the nape of her neck, she chose bravado. "You know me. You *all* know me." Nona haughtily demanded, "Didn't I earn a place with you in humanity's history books? Wasn't I part of your precious peace process?"

Harmonious was too easily baited. Shifting, he raised his voice.

"You betrayed our trust."

He sounded as much hurt as angry.

She rolled her eyes. "You *misplaced* your trust. Is that my fault?"

Juuyu's voice carried calmly. "What is your name, Kindred?"

"Nona Hightip."

"Where is Shisoku?"

"Is he the one you should be worrying about right now?"

Juuyu waved a hand. "We are not immediately concerned with your sister. She will speak for herself in due course."

Nona's gaze cut to Argent—or the facsimile he'd left as a placeholder—and she sweetly asked, "What of Isla Ward? Have you given her up for dead?"

Juuyu simply repeated, "Where is Shisoku?"

She made a rude gesture. "I have nothing to say to you."

Boon took speaking form, and a blade hissed from the sheath at his hip. The faint *shing* of steel came again, for Hallow had drawn his sword. It was only posturing, but the vixen quailed.

Hisoka stepped into the opening they'd created.

His shift unseated Moon, who touched his back in a silent promise that he had it. Hisoka raised his voice to ask, "What about me, Nona? Do you have anything to say to me?"

Lip curling, she said, "Toms should keep to their mistress's bedchambers, where their skills are appreciated."

Harmonious's growl reverberated.

Hisoka lifted his hand in a call to be wary, a straightforward reminder that Nona's jibe might be another diversion. The taskforce members turned outward, weapons drawn, and Doonwen began to prowl.

"What do you know about the devastation of an eldermost grove, during which a star was stolen from a sheltering tree?"

Nona's expression blanked. "The eldermost groves are long gone."

"My question is a long time in coming." He smiled faintly. "Surely you recall it. A grove beset. A tree aflame. A star plucked."

Her gaze drifted out of focus, then snapped back. "Are you talking about Nemi?"

Was the devastation of his first home *that* unremarkable? Or had she needed to confer with her sister? "Yes. Tell us about Nemi."

"Why do you care about one fallen star?"

Hisoka didn't know what to do with her bafflement. Was it possible that she didn't know about his connection to that tragic star? That hurting him had been coincidental?

Perhaps that was for the best. It wasn't about him. Never had been. Far better to seek justice for less ancient wrongs. For the Hightip sisters' complicity in Kodoku's crimes. For the hundreds of lives stunted and shattered and sparked by the Rogue's predation.

He looked to Juuyu, who smoothly picked up where he'd left off. "Where is Shisoku?"

This time, Nona flashed a malicious smile. "Not. Here."

54

THREAT POTENTIAL

Now that his message was delivered, Sibley kinda figured that while he wasn't *invited*-invited to catch back up to his brothers, Ginkgo and Kyrie and Anan hadn't told him not to follow. So he asked Hajime to get him close, and then he ran for it. Keeping up after that wasn't easy, since Ginkgo had ditched his fancy slippers and was making these low, long leaps on the straightaways.

Actually, that was a really good way to move.

Sibley needed most of the run to the boundary to get used to the springing gait, but he loved the feeling. Almost like flying. He'd keep practicing, if only because it was so much fun. Well, it was fun if you didn't mess up and jump into a tree.

Yeah. He was figuring it out.

Ginkgo didn't go straight to the gate where wolves were always on guard. Maybe because it was supposed to be locked up tight.

Barriers and stuff. Sibley had been sneaking past them for ages, so he knew. The ones Papka set up were much gentler than the ones he'd faced at the lab.

The sweet-natured stones were more worried about keeping bad people out than in trying to cage kids. Ginkgo walked right up to one and pressed his palm to the invisible wall. But before he stole through, he half-turned and asked, "Coming, little bro?"

"Yep." And hurrying to Ginkgo's side, Sibley muttered, "How come you always know where I am?"

"I'd love to say it's brotherly intuition ... with a side of experience. I mean, I've had Kyrie following me since he could scootch. But honestly? Dad gets the credit. He marked you. All of us are tagged. It's just one of the little ways he shows he cares."

"Wouldn't it be simpler to just say so?"

"Maybe for someone like me. But Dad? He's not the kind of person who comes out and says he loves you. He's sneaky about it. Y'know?"

"Guess so." Sibley was feeling generous. "He's allowed to be shy."

Ginkgo looked him up and down. "You've got quite the collection going. Kyrie. Anjou. Deece. Timur. Boon. Catalan. Opal. And if I'm not mistaken, this smudge of shine is from Anan."

"He's my eldermost brother," Sibley explained.

"Then you've got him looking out for you, too. That's good. Unless it bothers you ...?" Ginkgo held out a hand, then pulled Sibley through a slender gap he made in the barrier. "It's because we care."

"I like it." Sibley kept hold of Gingko's hand since it was safe now. "I like it even better'n compliments."

"Glad to hear it. Now stay sharp. We're past the barrier, and I don't know what we'll find, so use all your camouflage skills, and I'll toss out some simple illusions. I need to get to Kyrie before anything unexpected happens."

"That way, then." Sibley pointed. "He's not far."

Silver fox ears flicked. "I know. How'd *you* know."

"Anan. Probably. It's not Haizea, since she's not with him anymore, but could be it's that typhoon. Dima. Both her and Anan are sorta noisy. But not in a *sound* way." Sibley knew he wasn't making much sense. "I don't know a word to explain it."

"Mmm ... resonance. I think you're catching resonance."

Sibley had been hearing that word a lot lately. "Like with the rock babies?"

"Sure. Rock imps and remnant stones seem to have that in common. But some people are sensitive to winds or sigilcraft or soul-sense."

"So resonance is another word for love?"

"Usually, I think of it as affinity. But that's just a fancy way of saying you get along with something. That friendliness could be a kind of love." Ginkgo stopped walking. "Sometimes, resonance is kinship, though. Do you know if you resonate with the dragon who sired you? Not just your siblings?"

"Never met him."

Ginkgo waved at the woods around them. "He could be here. Could you tell?"

Sibley gave the idea a chance, peering around. "If I *can* tell, then he's not close."

"Good enough for me." They walked on, but much slower. "About Haizea. When did Kyrie lose her?"

"She's not lost. Anan put her in the wine cellar. On account of Andor's star."

"Most people don't know about Eri."

"I know, and I know you know. It was the best we could do. Eri makes her feel safe."

"Because they're both imps?"

"Could be. Is that resonance?"

"Shared experiences can be a kind of kinship."

"Like being in cages."

"Yeah, you kids have that in common. But in Haizea's case, it was a bottle. And then a boy."

Sibley wondered if that was why he could resonate with the eldermost storms. Because of the cages and the bottles. And because that meant they all knew how good it was, being here with Kyrie instead.

They circled a thicket and found Kyrie in a small meadow on the other side. He sat cross-legged in the snow, all his attention fixed on the two crystals in his hands. Anan loomed over him, scowl firmly in place, standing guard.

"Hey, little bro." Ginkgo crouched in front of Kyrie. "You're on the wrong side of our barrier."

"I *am* outside," Kyrie acknowledged. "But that does not make this meadow wrong."

"Don't quibble terms."

"I think I did the right thing." Gaze solemn, he lifted two crystals. "When this wardstone broke, its song changed. It split. Their lyrics are distinct, and they are lovely. But the change left them uneasy. I am making friends."

"Sounds like they've been through a lot, and I'm in favor of being friendly. But do it in a safer place."

"The Rogue is not nearby."

"How can you be sure?" asked Ginkgo.

Kyrie was calm and confident. "I knew Sibley was nearby."

"That's resonance," said Sibley. "Like Uncle Jackie and Uncle Boniface."

"Brotherhood is a strong bond." Kyrie offered him one half of the split stone.

Sibley knelt next to him. "What happened?"

"Ignorance. Impatience. Violence." Kyrie sought Ginkgo's gaze before saying, "The Rogue is not nearby now. But I think he *was* ... and that he did this."

Their big brother swore under his breath, messed up his hair, then finally announced, "If Anan wasn't with you, I wouldn't be half so calm right now. Do you understand how dangerous your sire is? That he'd hurt you without a second thought."

"Yes, but ... oh." Kyrie's gaze turned inward, and he wasn't talking to them anymore. "Yes, that is how it is. Should I have? The risk *is* greater here, but I have taken care. Yes, there is a dragon. Yes, he is a threat to all of us. Sibley, too. Oh? Oooh. I wonder if he w–"

It was a good thing that Sibley was already seated on the ground, because the sudden pressure of Dima's descent couldn't knock him far. As it was, he was having trouble catching his breath. And making sense of words. There was snow in his face and the roar of too much sound.

But then Kyrie was pressing a hand to his forehead, and

someone else tugged off Sibley's boot and sock and slapped the bottom of his foot. After that, the storm eased off. Dima wasn't gone, but she'd been muffled enough that he could hear Ginkgo's grumbling and the steady stream of Kyrie's calm.

"It is all right, Sibley. Ginkgo and I added to your protections. Do not be afraid. Dima only needs a moment to figure out how to hold a smaller shape. She is as surprised as we are that she towers. She did not mean to frighten you."

"Not scared," Sibley countered. "The air got heavy. Is it safe?"

"Wait a moment." Kyrie's head was turned to one side, and he was looking at Sibley out of the very corner of his eye. "It will be better once she is closer to Anan's size. Then he can loan her his shirt."

"Been doing a lot of that today." Sibley propped his chin on folded hands and kicked his feet. "That's all of them, then. Your winds."

"Yes. But I do not think they are all mine." Kyrie was smiling. "Dima's choice is an interesting surprise."

Sibley didn't see why. "I thought this was always the plan. Descend and pick a weapon, yeah?"

His brother turned his way, his gaze soft with happiness. "Dima did not descend so that she could take up the Chrysanthemum Blaze, although I do think it will suit her. She descended for a boy. For you."

55

EASTERN BRIDE

Isla's first waking thought was that Ginkgo would be terribly disappointed in her. She'd been *raised* by a trickster, for pity's sake. Foxy pranks were nothing new. At home, she was always on guard. But away? What a mess.

Nona's and Senna's illusion had preyed upon Isla's hopes, and by the simple act of wanting it to be true, she'd essentially surrendered herself to the people topping the Amaranthine Council's Most Wanted list. Isla had attended enough briefings to know what the Hightip sisters were capable of. And after the recent rescue mission that had taken Sensei away, their close association with the Rogue had gone from suspected to substantiated.

This meant that Isla was facing even odds of being either eaten or raped. Or both, though not necessarily in that order.

But after some cautious boundary-testing, she came to a heartening conclusion. She was being underestimated.

Either the dears had no idea what she could do. Or they thought she wouldn't try anything at their current altitude. Which, granted, *was* a factor. But not the first thing with which she needed to deal. Isla had sigils to trigger and wards to construct. All under the cover of her own repertoire of illusions, many of which had been handed down by her brilliant older sister Darya, whose aptitude for strategy had even kept Argent on his toes.

She hadn't played games like this in a long while. And certainly not with stakes this high.

But Isla had no trouble recalling the orderly deployment of tiny barriers that would mask the subtle movements of fingers. Moments later, she made certain that all the vixen carrying her would notice were slow breaths, a steady heartbeat, and dead weight. And by the simple act of wanting it to be true, the fox would trust her hopes ... and fall prey to Isla's cunning.

Lapis slowly loosened his hold on silver fur. He scanned upward as the confusion of red foxes dissipated, leaving Nona Hightip at Adoona-soh's mercy. Well enough, but not where Lapis's focus belonged.

His ring.

His lady.

Argent was too big to sit astride, so the dragon sat cross-legged in the middle of the fox's back, partly sheltered by two of Argent's many tails. While he prowled, Lapis scattered sigils—some to seek, some to snare, some to obscure.

Now that he was paying attention to more than his own fears, Lapis was able to pick out some of the preparations Argent had been able to make. Sigils slowly wheeled in overlapping layers. And by some command Lapis couldn't fathom, several silver foxes strolled onto the scene. Duplicates and decoys. These Argents carried other riders—Tsumiko, Michael, Ginkgo, even Isla herself.

Convincing.

Tempting.

Confusing.

Would Senna drop Isla in favor of a new acquisition?

Lapis hastily sought the spark of the remnant stone that had guided him thus far. "She's above us, Argent. Leftwise and lowering."

The fox's ears snapped up as Senna let her illusion drop. She crouched in midair, Isla hanging limp in her jaws.

Lapis gasped her name and yanked urgently at Argent's fur, but instead of rushing to the young woman's rescue, one silver ear gave a disdainful flick.

"But … she *is* there," Lapis pleaded.

Argent began to circle higher, and Lapis coaxed a largeish sigil in the ring's direction. If it touched Senna, she'd be marked. Exposed. But his handiwork passed ineffectually through the decoy even as Isla's ring—and presumably the vixen carrying her—backed up and away.

Suddenly, Isla was calling out. "Argent, I'm here! Please! It hurts!"

Lapis tensed.

Argent's ear flicked.

"How can you tell?" Lapis whispered, his stomach in knots.

But then from another direction, Isla whimpered. Hair wild, hand outstretched, she piteously asked, "Don't you care?"

He didn't need the ear flick to tell him that this wasn't the young woman he knew. She would never have taken that tone with Argent. Or anyone. He supposed the illusion had been calculated to cut Argent. But making her seem young and fearful, with that uncertain quaver? If Senna thought her puppet was a passable representation, she hadn't put much effort into researching her chosen bait.

Lapis quietly warned, "I doubt I can let Isla know we're here without Senna noticing."

Argent shot a look of pure disdain over his shoulder, then gently cuffed him with a white-tipped tail. As if to say *get on with it*.

That's when Harmonious Starmark—bless his tender heart—blundered in, unable to ignore the illusion's pleading.

Once Isla was certain she could move without her captor noticing, she opened her eyes and looked for whatever had caused the vixen's growled oaths. To her amazement, a silver fox sprang past with Papka riding his shoulders. Then came Uncle Jackie, astride another Argent, looking rakishly debonair with his aviator goggles. And yes, there was Mum on yet another silver fox, her favorite polearm at the ready.

Isla had to stifle a laugh. The whole scene was ridiculous, but Senna Hightip didn't know her family well enough to understand that all of these would-be rescuers couldn't possibly be here. But the common denominator was a clear enough message.

Argent was here on their behalf.

Sorting through illusions took a while. The sky was full of Amaranthine in truest form. She was prepared to dismiss them as more figments, but then Harmonious Starmark raced to the rescue of a decidedly insulting imitation of herself. He skidded uselessly through the image, looking as bewildered as a puppy as he snuffled around, searching for her scent.

She'd swear it was really him. But how?

Isla decided to set aside the means for now, because Harmonious, Adoona-soh, and Argent represented a huge opportunity. And there was Juuyu, and … oh, my. Unless she was being deceived again, that was Hisoka-sensei.

Truly? It certainly seemed so. Mind-boggling. The original Five had tracked the vixens? Or nearly so. All that was needed to complete the set was Lapis.

Her heart clenched as she searched the gathering of allies, however, none of them carried a rider. But then a fluting call heralded the arrival of a dragon on the wing. Blue scales shimmered as Lapis climbed in widening circles—powerful, graceful, glorious. A glimpse of what might have been, if only Lapis had the use of those wings.

And then faintly, gently, from amidst the eye-catching confusion all around, she caught the piercing note of a remnant song. She *knew* that stone. It belonged to one of Lapis's rings. One she'd worn the night before, when he'd adorned her fingers and coaxed for kisses and spilled his secrets in swaying tones.

Now, her fingers were bare of rings.

Yet that distinctive stone gleamed brighter, a sure sign, a signal.

Senna Hightip noticed it, too. And with silky delight, she said, "I've found you."

As if she'd managed something.

Anyone with the minutest trace of sensitivity might notice the veritable beacon Lapis was nurturing. No doubt with dragon song. And of course that remnant would do its best for him. Because he doted on his crystals, and they adored him in return. A dragon's admiration was irresistible. And his message was as clear.

Somewhere below, quite near the water, Lapis was calling, and Isla was ready with her answer.

Letting a key few illusions drop, she smilingly asked, "Senna Hightip? Wonderful news." And triggering the sigil she'd drawn on her palm, she slapped it against the vixen's shoulder. "You've moved to the top of the Council's schedule. They'll be able to deal with you now."

Senna's snarl cut short as luminous threads flickered to life, speedily spreading outward, a delicate tracery that inexorably unfurled. The vixen's whole body seized up, and with a shove, Isla achieved freefall.

Lapis stared with a mixture of wonderment and regret as a blue dragon beat wings that were whole and strong, gaining the sky with enviable grace. Until a scream of fury turned into a howl of pain, snapping his attention back where it belonged.

Isla was falling?

Isla was *falling*!

"Argent!" Lapis exclaimed, pulling himself up onto his knees.

The fox's narrow muzzle was already pointed upward. Argent was calmly rising, making small adjustments as the young woman plunged their way. Clearly, he was leaving the rest to Lapis. Already, the dragon's hands were moving, flinging sigils upward. Modified barriers to slow her descent, to call for willing winds, to assure her that he was ready.

Lapis was on his feet now, arms extended. His sigils had helped, but her arrival still drove him back to his knees. His heart was in his throat as he searched her face for any signs of pain or injury or fear.

But Isla laughed, and her arms slipped around his neck. "You're brilliant." As if everything had been his doing. Her eyes sparkled, and her smile was nothing but confident when she cheerfully added, "I've made up my mind to be very much in love."

56

CLOUD COVER

Sinder had been slinging messages nonstop, some by digital means, some as a Reach. Honestly, it felt like cheating, using Michael's superlative crystal arrays to boost his range. Not that he could reach Juuyu directly. Distance was still prohibitive. The action was so far north, Juuyu was practically in Sinder's old stomping grounds. Or above them, anyhow. But as soon as Goh Impleer got into position with Inti, they'd set up a relay. The secondhand information was mostly fresh and only a *little* muddled by monkey nonsense.

In the midst of all the mayhem, his rock baby had surprised him by doing their darndest to help. That had resulted in some eerily melodic feedback, but Inti had thought it was cute. Because ... well, it *was* cute. Which made Sinder oddly proud.

"You gonna be a Reach like your ... uhh. Let's go with dragon. Like your dragon. That's true without making any premature commitments. Bet you could if you wanted. Be a Reach, I mean. And just so you know, it's not that I'm not willing to commit. I *can*. I'm just worried they won't let me keep you. Or you might not want to be kept. I mean, Timur'll want you, too. And he'll insist on *papka*. But you and me can be more … less. Because all these bonds are hard enough to explain as it is."

The rock imp strapped to his front warbled like a hatchling.

Stinking cute.

Sinder couldn't wait to see if Timur had been catching any extra resonance.

But when he strolled through their door, Sinder was treated to a big dose of déjà vu. Only this time, he caught Fend—once again in speaking form—getting cozy with Jacques Smythe.

Neither of them looked even the least bit guilty. Still, Sinder couldn't quite hide his pique. "I would like to point out that, for once, *I'm* not the one who spilled your secret."

Fend made a face. "I never had one. Or didn't keep it long."

"Don't sulk," Jacques soothed. "Argent may have realized, but he let you keep your secret. *I* certainly never knew, and he tells me everything. But this is a pleasant surprise, and I want *all* the sordid details, but … after."

"I didn't know Fend's secret either, which means Hisoka didn't know. And seriously, it's not like you weren't going to be outed eventually, what with all these trees moving in. In fact, Hajime's probably the one who tipped Argent off."

Fend left Jacques' arms in order to drape himself all over Sinder.

"Yeah, yeah. You're damned smart, but he's doubly sly. Just chalk it up to superior years and move on." Awkwardly patting

Fend, Sinder arched his brows at Jacques.

"I was simply re-introducing myself. Fend and I are old friends, but … well! We've never really chatted. And now his lordship has put him in charge." And to Fend, "What can I do?"

"What's he mean, *in charge*?" Sinder asked softly.

Fend butted the underside of Sinder's chin, then looked up through his lashes. "I am acknowledged. Argent is trusting me with all he holds dear."

"No kidding? That's kind of amazing." He gave one velvety ear a gentle tug. "What do you want me to handle?"

A kiss grazed Sinder's throat, and then Fend drew himself up, a clawed hand resting lightly on the rock imp between them. "Where's Timur?"

"I thought he'd be here. I was looking for him."

"How about Kyrie? I want cloud cover."

Jacques said, "Lord, it's simple enough to find out." And lifting his voice, he called, "Hajime?"

Sinder hated that he'd forgotten about Hajime. Again. How on earth had Jacques made the leap to pollen immunity so fast?

The tree said, "There is a limit to my range. Kyrie is beyond it."

That's when Timur arrived, Anjou close on his heels, each with a child in arms.

"What's happened?" Timur asked. "Anjou said you need me?"

After a quick conference, Fend rattled off orders, and everyone—*nearly* everyone—hurried off to do what needed doing. For Jacques, that involved minding the boys, who were eyeing each other from opposite sides of the man's lap. Etienne trilled shyly, and Gregor's whole face lit up.

Sinder was just contemplating escape when Jacques led out in a cheerful sing-song. "Sinder, love. We should talk."

"About ...?"

"Affairs of the heart." His smile was coy. "You needn't be embarrassed about your gentleman reaver."

"I'm not embarrassed. And it's not an affair. Or about hearts, for that matter. It's not like that."

"I can tell there's a bond." Jacques shrugged. "Can't help myself. Add it to my list of impish symptoms."

"Yeah, well. Stuff happened." He gruffly begged, "Don't tease."

"I wouldn't. I'm not. I count Timur as a friend, and I like to think he confides in me. And you and I get on. It's a nice surprise, your being the one he needed."

"He's not in love with me or anything."

"*Au contraire.*" Jacques' smile was wry. "I understand lonesome. And I know happy when I see it. You mean the world to Timur."

"Well, yeah." Sinder shuffled his feet. "So?"

"So! As his friend and yours, I would like to make an addendum to your file on me. I assume there is one."

"You might have warranted a footnote or two," Sinder said warily.

"Anything recent?"

"I found out your full name, courtesy of Kyrie, who heard it from Boniface."

"Lord, my brother's a prig."

Sinder thought he said it fondly.

"With regards to my assorted legacies from Dayith and Solace, let the record show that I've become a good influence. Or a bad one. It's all a matter of perspective." And in even tones, Jacques explained why it was a risky business having him waft about in their bedchamber. "I *could* be more explicit, but discretion—and your pallor—forbids. If you require more than anecdotal evidence, I daresay the enclave will give proof. Three years from now."

"Aren't you sealed?"

"Well-warded. But Fend's whiskers were in a twitch over me. And while I don't mind in the least, you have been slowly inching my way. Definitely out of character. Steady on."

Sinder swore softly and dragged himself back a step. "I don't have time for this."

"There *are* more perilous games afoot. I suggest tossing me out. Gently. Preferably in the direction of the naproom, where I can mind these two and man a phone. Have Sonnet do a sweep through here. She knows what's needed. After things calm down, ask Timur to ward against me, same as you would for starshine or tree pollen."

"Can do. I can't believe your Jacques-ish-ness is contagious."

"You make that sound like a bad thing."

Sinder sighed. "No, it's not. If you really are the answer to the Waning, you're the best thing that's happened to the clans since … well, since Tenma."

"*Exactement.*" Jacques stood and hefted the little ones. "Come along, me boyos. We've naps and nappies to navigate. What say we collar Uncle Bon-Bon and call it revenge?"

But then his pocket pinged.

"Sinder, would you be so good? It's bound to be important."

He dipped into the man's pocket, tapped in a pin he probably wasn't supposed to know, and answered. "Hi, Boon. Okay if I put you on speaker. Uncle Jackie's juggling babies."

"Just you two?"

"Yeah, it's just us."

Speaker employed, Jacques immediately asked, "Argent?"

"Fine. We're all good. The Hightip sisters won't be causing any more problems, but we still have one. The Rogue wasn't here."

"Kyrie thinks he's here," Sinder said.

"Aww, hell. On my way."

Sinder snorted. "Even at top speeds, it would take ...."

But then a shrill whistle came through the speaker, and Boon shouted, *"Hey, buddy! Can I catch a ride?"*

Jacques and Sinder exchanged a look, and Sinder asked, "Who are you talking to?"

"Not sure." And then to someone else, *"You got a name?"* The response was too muffled to carry over, but then Boon was saying, *"Uh-huh. No kidding? Well, it's real nice to meetcha. Thanks for this. Seriously."*

"Who ...?" Jacques began, shaking his head. "Who would be faster than Boon?"

Sinder could only shrug.

Then Boon was back with them. *"Okay, we're all set here. Veliel is willing to hurry things along, and I'm not the only one getting a lift. Sit tight. Backup's on the way."*

Sibley's senses were taut as he scanned the surrounding woods, searching for a feeling he didn't want to find. Dr. Kodoku's gaze used to make him want to squirm away, to hide, to run. He'd developed a sort of second sense about him. "We should get back, yeah?"

Ginkgo asked, "You picking up on something?"

"Dunno for sure. Maybe. I don't feel safe."

Dima asked, "Is it me?"

He glanced up—way up—into his wind's face. Even though she was no longer a giantess, Dima was just as tall as Anan. They had the same skin and silver eyes, but Dima's hair wasn't a dark cloud. More like whitecaps on a churning sea, silver-tipped peaks that looked sharp enough to be dangerous.

"Nah. I'm not scared of you. It's just ... I don't like how this feels, and that means it's time to go."

Ginkgo said, "Then we go. Only let's use the gate this time. I want to check on something quick."

They filed along a narrow trail, with Ginkgo in the lead and the two storms bringing up the rear. Sibley glanced back in time to see Dima stumble and Anan steady her. She elbowed him, and he rolled his eyes. Their faces were expressive, but if they were talking, it wasn't out loud. Watching them, he realized something.

"You're like a brother and sister."

Anan snorted. "We *are* a brother and sister."

"Twins," said Dima. "*I* am older."

Kyrie stopped at that, his eyes bright with interest. "I did not know winds could have siblings. Does that mean you were born together?"

"The eldermost are not born. We were *made*, for that is the Maker's business."

Dima inclined her head. "We are judgment. We are wrath."

"We *were*," Anan countered. "We became companions. We became change."

"Because of Bethiel."

"Yes. Because of Bethiel."

Kyrie's attention drifted as little winds tugged at his loose hair. Sibley wondered what they were telling him, because his expression grew worried. But his voice didn't show it when he announced, "We *should* go to the gate."

Ginkgo, who'd paused to check his phone, said, "Looks that way. Message from Sinder to that effect. Oh, wait. Sinder's phone, but it's Fend. Since when does Fend send texts?"

Kyrie and Sibley traded smiling glances.

"Also ... Anan? Dima? He's asking for cloud cover. Can you lower visibility without actually storming?"

"Perhaps," Anan said doubtfully.

Dima grumbled, "You want me to hold to this size, walk upon two feet, and summon a cloud bank? All while keeping my temper?"

Anan grimaced. "Perhaps *I* ...."

"You? You are all crashes and claps," she countered. "Give me a moment. I will manage. See if I don't."

Ginkgo beckoned for them to keep following. He was moving faster now, so Sibley tried the leaping gait again. Soon, he and Kyrie were racing, and a road came into view. Sibley had never seen it from the outside, so he did his best to memorize the surroundings. Especially the biggest trees and stones. It was important to know your options for hiding places.

"Isn't it locked?" Sibley asked.

"Anyone with a tuned crystal can come and go," said Ginkgo. "Trusted friends."

"Like Lapis. Or Canarian. Or Ever and his da," Kyrie offered by way of explanation. But then he quietly added, "And the Dare brothers."

"Yeah, them, too." Ginkgo's ears were flat. "How much have you worked with them?"

"Not enough," Kyrie answered. "They never stay for long."

"Those TV guys are here?" Sibley asked.

"It was meant to be a Christmas surprise. Josheb wanted to play Santa. And if they could swing it, they were gonna be here for my bonding." Ginkgo offered Sibley a crystal. "Come on, little bro. Caleb and Josheb are definitely here, and they might be in trouble."

When Boon called everyone close and relayed his plan, there was a fair amount of shuffling while Argent decided who should stay and who would go. Because the serenely smiling Soriel was limiting their travel party to ten.

Nobody was surprised when the fox gave priority to Stately House's best fighters—Boon, Adoona-soh, six other Elderbough wolves, Juuyu, and Argent himself. The rest could return at a somewhat more reasonable pace, lending continued support to Lapis and Isla.

Which meant Hisoka was stranded.

And in Isla's vicinity.

With no polite way to extricate himself.

But then a familiar voice lightly brushed his mind, and four words had never been more welcome. *"I am here, Hisoka."*

"Novi." He turned, already reaching, and his oldest friend glided easily into his arms. Foreheads pressed together, they communicated without spoken words, for Novi's voice was meant for celestial choruses.

"I have missed you," Hisoka confessed.

"And I, you."

"Nemi?"

"Gaining in strength, overflowing with gratitude."

"Were you with these others all along?"

"No. They are Maker-sent, but I am sister-driven."

"Nemi drove you out?" Hisoka asked, only teasing.

"Nemi sings. For her child. And for their bondmate."

Hisoka felt teased in return. Perhaps he deserved it. *"I suppose I did relent."*

"Rhomiko's regard looks well on you."

"What?"

Novi slipped from Hisoka's arms in order to pull him against his side, ready to fly. *"When we reach your stately new home, once the danger has passed, perhaps you should find a mirror."*

Ginkgo had been running with the Elderbough pack since forever, so he knew both wolves at the gate. He'd attended their whelping feasts. Tussled with them when they were little. Led them on a merry chase when they were training. He trusted them both, but he didn't like the look of things when he passed through the barrier.

Jumpy. Wary. Confused.

They were slowly circling a heap of baggage, noses twitching. Their puffed tails tucked as Ginkgo approached, so he took a soothing tone. "What's all this?"

"I'd love to know," said Oolong Elderbough, his eyes darting nervously. "It just … showed up. And we can't figure out how."

"It's not like our backs were turned," added his cousin Doogh. His voice quavered slightly.

"This isn't right," whispered Oolong.

Doogh gave Ginkgo a pleading look. "What should we do? Report it?"

"Yeah. To me is fine. You all right?"

"No." Oolong looked ill. "I don't know why, but … no."

"Something's wrong," his cousin agreed shakily.

Kyrie marched up to Doogh, hands on offer. "You are safe. You did well."

The wolf clansman flinched away. And immediately dropped into a near grovel. "Kyrie! I'm so sorry! I don't know what …!"

Sibley piped up. "We know. It was him. You saw the Rogue."

"Did we?" Oolong asked softly. "Maker have mercy, what have we done?"

Anan stepped forward to loom, but though he looked like a thundercrash, his words were grace and mercy. "Kyrie is right.

You did well. He is pleased with you."

Sibley was nodding. "Yeah, this works out. So long as the TV guys don't get hurt."

Ginkgo had to admire the kid.

He was good in a crisis.

Just then, the sun simply ... disappeared. Everyone looked up as silvery clouds hid the sky, swirling steadily lower until the treetops were lost in thickening mist.

Dima eyed her handiwork critically. "How much lower? I assume the goal is blinding our enemy ...?"

Kyrie raised his hand to just above his eye-level. "Here, please."

A few seconds later, Ginkgo was forced to crouch in order to see anything. His phone vibrated, and he answered with a question. "Did Caleb and Josheb make it to the house?"

On the other end, Sinder swore.

Then a new voice came on. *"What did you find?"*

Ginkgo worked his way over to the pile of baggage. Kyrie and Sibley joined him, unabashedly listening in. "Their stuff's stacked inside the gate, but the guards can't remember how it got here. A very bad sign. That you, Fend?"

"Yes. Hello. You give excellent scritchies," he said briskly. *"More to the point, ask Kyrie to tune the trees. And if the winds are willing, bring the Junzi into play."*

"You should know that Boon called. Backup's on the way. Him. Probably Dad. They'll be here ... well, *soon*. They're being helped by stars."

"What?" Fend sounded outraged. *"He can't put me in charge, then give me no time to show my worth. Wretched thing. Well, fine.*

Let's hurry this along. The Rogue's an idiot, so it was barely a challenge in the first place."

Ginkgo couldn't help smiling. "You think?"

"*I* know," Fend countered haughtily. "*So we will get to the Dare brothers and retrieve them intact. You will focus on the Rogue. Locate him. Waylay him. But don't end him. Promise you'll wait for Timur and I to join you. Otherwise, Argent might withhold the attainment he promised.*"

And he was gone.

Ginkgo pocketed his phone, then met Kyrie's solemn gaze, then Sibley's pensive one. "You heard him. We're supposed to hold off. No dragon-slaying until Fend's here to supervise."

He'd meant it as a joke.

But Kyrie gravely countered, "Unless it becomes necessary."

As if he'd let his sire live a little longer, but only as a favor to Fend.

57

CONFLUENCE

rgent tried to wrap his head around the monumental events of the past quarter hour.

Once it became clear that Nona was done answering Juuyu's questions, Doon-wen lost patience. He lunged, and her life was forfeit. The swiftness of her demise left the whole group stunned. In fact, Nona's sister had been the first to react. Her outcry was part grief, part fury.

Tangled in a net of clever sigildry that would have made Michael proud, Senna was easy to reel in. Juuyu began again with the rote, and Senna babbled warnings and hissed invectives. She shifted blame to everyone and anything—reavers, Wardenclave, Kodoku, Argent, and even to the star called Nemi.

When Hisoka questioned her more closely on this point, Senna's lip curled. She bitterly regretted ever carrying off the star, for Nemi had become a favorite of the ancient dragon who'd sired Doku and Kodoku. Senna's ugly remarks hinted that she herself had been deposed as his lover … and that she'd gladly contributed to Nemi's suffering.

But there were no more surprises. They already knew of her complicity in Nona's treasonous acts. The sisters had consumed an unknown number of reavers over the centuries, but since the beginning of the New Saga, their number was recorded. Linlu Dimityblest's careful documentation matched unsolved cases of disappearances from the reaver community. And while not every clan claimed their crossers, Linlu kept careful records of all who'd landed in Kodoku's cages.

Broken faith. Broken treaties. Broken lives.

As spokesperson for the fox clans, Argent could pass judgment on these crimes.

With the stars as witness, the Hightip sisters had both reached an end of days. But at whose hand?

Hisoka had a right to vengeance, and Argent's grievances had multiplied with every child who'd come under his care. However, Hallow Brunwinger spared them from going home with blood on their hands. His blade's swiftness was more mercy than the vixen deserved, but the conflict was finally over.

Or … not.

"What *is* that?" he muttered.

"Your home," said Auriel, who'd been among the stars offering transport.

Argent knew that, of course. But the entire enclave and much of the surrounding area was buried under slowly wheeling clouds. From here, he knew his sigils, barriers, and illusions were intact. At their heart, Tsumiko shone, beacon-bright and beautiful.

As the angels left them, flashing away without even waiting for thanks, Boon called out, "Say *hey* to Hurricane Dima."

"Anyone else catching a weird ... is that resonance?" asked Adoona-soh.

"No. There are remnants embedded throughout our forest," said Argent. "Kyrie is tuning the trees."

"You make it sound like Kyrie's putting on a concert." Boon's gaze held challenge as he answered his mother's question more straightforwardly. "The kid's hunting."

"What's happened here?"

Kyrie turned from his task in honest surprise, for the little winds that were usually so helpful hadn't mentioned the arrival of another unexpected guest.

"Paltry!" exclaimed Ginkgo. "You're early. Not that I'm complaining. We have a bit of a situation here."

"So I see," the wolf said blandly. He'd had to hike up his kimono in order to crouch below the level of the clouds. "Boon put out a call, so we closed up shop early.

We?

Kyrie realized that he wasn't imagining any trick of the light. Paltry had a halo. A borrowed one. Because he hadn't come alone.

Paltry's moonbeam peeked out from behind him, silver eyes especially wide as he watched Anan and Dima.

"I did not know there was going to be a storm," said the moonbeam. "Are storms a Christmas tradition? Nobody said so. Not to me."

"Hey, Churlish," greeted Ginkgo. "Well, hey! You brought Patter?"

Sibley hurried forward then, and Patter immediately reached for him. They were old friends because of their former captivity.

Churlish let the little crosser go, and his gaze sought Kyrie's. "You," he said, almost sounding accusing. "You are storm-kissed? That sounds dangerous. But you like it, or else his marks would not take. Maybe it will be fine, since he has silver eyes."

Kyrie was struck by something Ginkgo had said. "You are *early*?"

"We were going to come in two more days. Because Sonnet asked me to make a birthday cake. *And* because I am a good uncle." Churlish explained, "This will be Pitter-Patter's first Christmas, and Nonny thought we should come, since Stately House will have a proper celebration. Is this storm quite proper?" With a sulky look for the lowering sky, he added, "This does not feel celebratory."

"A birthday cake?" asked Kyrie. "For me and Lilya?"

Ginkgo wryly said, "Surprise."

Kyrie was really very pleased. He kept such a close eye on his home that there wasn't much he didn't know. "I *am* surprised."

"Glad you're so glad, little bro, but get back to your tuning. I'll try to explain what's going on to Paltry."

He nodded, even though his work was essentially done.

Paltry held up a hand. "I can guess what kind of trouble you're having. I know this scent."

"You know the Rogue."

"Since way back. Yes."

Ginkgo straightened. "Okay, yeah. Dad said you're the one who knew his name."

"Shisoku. Yes."

"And ... you're immune to dragon sway?"

"Yes. Opulence Windlore is an old friend."

While they quietly compared notes, Kyrie crossed to where Sibley cuddled a toddler with green hair and tiny antlers. Patter was part moonbeam, so Churlish really was his uncle. But he was also part pitterhind, a mouse-like variety of Ephemera.

"You remember me, doncha?" Sibley checked.

The little guy nuzzled and peeped.

"I can't wait to introduce you to Etienne. And to Bother, though her name's Christobelle now, thanks to Uncle Bon-Bon." But Sibley's smile slowly faded, and he sought Kyrie's gaze. "We got time for this?"

Kyrie considered the tales his trees were telling and nodded. "He is not close. And he cannot get far."

Paltry swung his way and said, "*There*. See?" like he was proving a point. "Your brother agrees. Despite the doomsday trappings, this isn't a disaster. Far from it. We have him. Best thing we can do is reinforce the boundaries fencing him in."

Ginkgo blinked, then snorted. "Fend's right. The Rogue really is an idiot. Can we herd him inward—away from escape—without endangering our people? Hang on. I need to talk to Michael."

He and Paltry were soon bent over his phone, and Kyrie wove a few tiny sigils, which he flicked at Churlish, Patter, and Paltry.

The moonbeam noticed. "They are a little like kisses. Why are you blowing kisses at my wolf and my nephew? And me?"

"So I know where you are."

"I am right here." Churlish bent at the waist so they were nearly eye-to-eye. His eyes were the sort of silver that had a little lavender to it. Much softer than Anan's lightning-bright ones. But Churlish's eyes could flash. With realization. "Oh, I see. You are leaving us behind. You will not go alone, I hope."

"Not alone." Anan had stolen up behind Churlish, and he was looking insulted.

"That is what I said, silly storm. *Not* alone. Of course not. Not when your kisses took." And drawing himself up to his full height, Churlish primly added, "Your stone wants to sing, you know. You should be kinder to sad stones."

It was sort of funny, watching the dainty moonbeam scold an eldermost storm.

While Anan was distracted, Sibley stepped to Kyrie's side. "What's he mean ... you're leaving?"

"I need to get to the Rogue."

Sibley glanced at the otherwise-occupied members of their group before quietly asking, "Are you going to kill him?"

"I do not think it will come to that."

Sibley searched his face. "Yes, you do."

Kyrie chose a truer answer. "I want to speak with him before he dies."

And signaling to Anan, he slipped away.

Stately House's kitchen had to be the coziest war room Sinder had ever overseen. And the calmest. He figured most of that was due to Lady Mettlebright's influence. She might not be trained as a cosset, but she still radiated serenity. And Rhomiko's humming from the direction of the rockers only reinforced the prevailing mood.

Sinder had set up his laptop at the kitchen table, across from Michael, who wasn't even trying to look serious about the current conflict. The man's feet were propped as he leaned back in his chair, one of his newborn sons sprawled upon his chest.

With half an eye on his phone screen in case of more texts, Sinder typed updates to his files. It was busywork, really. They were in a holding pattern until Fend could get Timur to wherever the Dare Brothers were. Which might be where the Rogue was. Sinder guessed Timur would be a match for the monster, since his Spomenka skills ran as much to dragon-slaying as dragon-pampering. But what about Fend? Should Sinder have been the one to go?

But ... no. Trust for trust. If this was where Fend wanted him, it was because this was the most optimal division of the resources at his disposal. Their megalomaniac knew the stakes. His own attainment was on the line. He wouldn't take any unnecessary risks.

Forcing his thoughts back to the task at hand, Sinder made

a mental list of tasks-to-come. He'd probably be chasing down witnesses for days. Boon would paraphrase too much, and Hallow would pick and choose his words in an effort to be considerate. Colt was more straightforward, but he wasn't a big picture guy. And if Sinder wanted Argent's side of the story, he'd need to go through Jacques, who was insightful enough but prone to fashion-related remarks.

At least Juuyu would be able to offer a detailed firsthand account of the events surrounding Isla's rescue. And Hisoka would know how to slant things. Then Sinder could frame an official statement that the Amaranthine Council could issue to assorted criminal investigation divisions.

If everyone held still long enough, maybe Sinder could hope to kick back for a week or two. Did unassailable alliances get a honeymoon? Or the unromantic equivalent. It just sounded really good right now, letting all this busywork slide and letting Timur and Fend do … well, all the stuff they did.

"Here you go, love." Sonnet set a cup of fresh coffee in easy reach. Then added a plate of shortbread. "How are you holding up?"

"Good, I think. But awkward, too. Lots to get used to. I mean, I'd forgotten Timur snores."

Sonnet pressed a hand to her heart, eyes wide. "Oh. Oh, I *see*!"

Sinder tried to think. How many days had it been? Would Timur have mentioned their bond to anyone yet? Had Sinder just outed them? Well, it wasn't exactly a secret. Juuyu had known. And Sonnet could tell.

All at once he felt the weight of Michael's gaze and realized that he was facing his … well, shit. Did unassailable alliances incur in-laws? Recalling Timur's expression, the huskiness of his promises, the way his touch was both admiring and possessive, Sinder felt a burn in the tips of his ears and quickly lowered his gaze.

That's when Deece quietly took the chair beside Michael's.

Suddenly, Sinder was very conscious that he'd stopped typing around the same time he'd begun recalling Fend—the scent of him and the softness of him and the way his kisses lingered. Dunce and double-dunce, they were both watching him now. Could they tell he was shamelessly two-timing their sons?

Michael's eyebrows lifted.

Sinder's mind went blank.

Deece cleared his throat. "Sinder, can you reach them?"

"That's never been an issue. They keep me in the middle."

"Using the array," Michael patiently prompted. "Do you know how far they've gotten? Can you tell if they're all right?"

"Shit. Right. Yeah." In a stretch that was already becoming second nature, Sinder checked on the state of his bond with Timur. The man's presence was reassuringly steady, his mood calm, purposeful. "They're safe."

"Fretting?" Fend's voice lilted with amusement.

"Keeping tabs on everyone is part of my job."

"What's put you in a fluster?"

"Parental scrutiny."

"Bear up bravely. They cannot possibly find anything to criticize. You are a splendid acquisition."

"Thanks, I guess. Anything happening where you are?"

"Nothing worth mentioning. Distract me later."

"Yeah, yeah."

"I mean it. Promise it," demanded Fend. *"When I return, I want to be amply rewarded for my various attainments. Give me a name."*

"Sure. I promise. Just ... take care of each other out there."

"So you are fretting."

"Only because you're tracking a mass murderer."

"Trust me."

"Promise it."

A sudden, drawn-out silence worried Sinder, but then the feline softly asked, *"What do you want me to promise?"*

"Specifically? Shit, I dunno. Just ... everything."

There was an inarticulate growl that had Sinder tensing. But then Fend sighed and grumbled, *"Distract me later, lovely one."*

Sinder wasn't sure how he was going to keep his promise. He turned his mind to names that might please a feline. They needed something that would sound natural for Timur to laugh around or grumble over or say with his mother's teasing accent or even shout in battle. Something that could warm with affection or drip with sarcasm when their cat was being exasperating. Something Gregor could manage. Something Sinder could whisper between kisses.

A throat cleared.

Sinder flinched. "Like I said, they're safe. Nothing else to report."

"Right," said Michael, whose brows were still arched inquiringly.

Deece was in a pointedly receptive posture. Were they awaiting orders or ... oh, hell. "Did anyone say anything? About ... us?"

Michael was mildness itself. "Did you have something to say for yourself?"

Sinder teetered on the edge of confession, which wasn't really the best of terms. He didn't need to apologize to these fathers. Deece was a fine, upstanding sort. A tribute to his line. If he didn't know yet, he'd probably be delighted to learn that Fend was Kithkin. And Michael might be First of Wards, but he wanted Timur's happiness. Even if the one cherishing him wasn't the usual sort of damsel.

And inspiration struck.

For a name. For Fend.

"Well, shit. I think ... yeah. I think he might go for it." And waving between the two of them, Sinder exclaimed, "The fathers are strong!"

"But the brothers are not weak," intoned a familiar voice. "Sinder Stonecairne, I need a word."

Half-turning in his chair, Sinder cautiously nodded. "Hey, Opal. What's up?"

"You and I have a date with destiny."

Sinder snorted.

Opal eased into a less demanding posture. "We have a delivery to make. It should be safe enough for us to leave, our being dragons."

"Sway isn't the only threat to our wellbeing," Sinder pointed out.

"And yet!" With a small shrug, the bard said, "Zeri is most insistent."

"What are we meant to deliver? And where?"

"First and foremost, we must get the Plum Cascade to Haizea."

Sinder knew his lore.

The Chrysanthemum Blaze was both an executioner's blade and an irresistible lure, to prevent a dragon's escape. The

Bamboo Stave was a thief, stealing the power from a dragon's every word, nullifying sway. The Orchid Saddle was a taunt, for the one wielding it gained the very sky for which every dragon longed. And then there was the Plum Cascade, a dainty crown of glittering pink that made turnabout fair play, because its wearer gained sway over dragonkind.

Sinder had to ask. "Is that really the best plan, turning over a weapon? Or did you somehow forget that these storms are mightily pissed at you?"

With a forced laugh, Opal simply repeated, "And yet!"

Hisoka didn't question Novi's decision to plunge through the cloudbank that buried Stately House. He felt the whispery welcome of Michael's barriers, which had been tuned to accept him and which had never posed a problem for his starry companion. Interestingly, Hisoka was also getting fleeting impressions from the cloud itself. Fierce. Resolute. Protective.

"This has to be one of Kyrie's imps." The storms' attachment to him was an interesting outcome.

"Dima. She is showing considerable restraint."

"To what end?"

"For a covering."

"To cover an evacuation?" he guessed. Usually, Hisoka would catch a sense of life and movement throughout the enclave. The wolves in the wood. The cranes in the marsh. The cows in the pasture. The mice in the meadow. The bees and bumbers busy among the flowers.

"*I do not know the purpose, but Dima is calm. This is calculated.*"

"Agreed. And inconvenient. How well can you see?"

"*I know my course.*"

Hisoka's heart lifted. "And mine?"

"*I have always known where you are most needed.*"

"Usually for more than one reason."

"*Here are two.*" And Novi released him.

"You're leaving?"

"*For now.*" And with a gentle push, Novi quietly added, "*Hurry.*"

Hoping he wouldn't end up tangled in some thicket, Hisoka dropped. And obeying a sudden impulse, he shifted on the way down. In true feline fashion, he landed on his feet, and he was pleased to find that the restrictions still in place on his size meant he could pass easily under the low ceiling of clouds.

Nothing in the vicinity told him why *this* was the right place, let alone the right time. Still, he sat, curling his tail neatly over his paws, and lifted his whiskers to the wind. Novi had said to hurry, so he shouldn't have long to wait.

Within moments, he heard footfalls.

"Hang on a sec!" gasped a man. "Let me ... catch my breath."

"Remind me. Why are we running blind?"

"You don't remember?"

"Honestly? I got nothing. Are we in some kind of trouble? Or is this just the weirdest game of hide-and-seek ever?"

"This isn't a *game*, Josheb."

"You're totally spooked. Hey, should we do the thing?"

Caleb Dare shushed him, then said, "It wouldn't help. It's just lucky I'm less susceptible to sway than you are."

"Since when?" Josheb was patting his pockets and came up empty. "Hey, where's my phone?"

"*Please* keep it down. He took it. He practically melted it."

Josheb peered warily around, then crawled closer to his brother. "Why would someone melt my phone. Or should I be asking *how*?"

"You tried to interview him."

"Sounds like a thing I'd do. Seriously, bro. What gives?"

"We met the Rogue."

Josheb's jaw dropped. "That's ... probably really bad. Did we at least get a picture?"

"Oh, you snapped one. Right in between asking for an exclusive and getting your phone melted."

"And he's following us?"

"Yes. And I doubt it's because he's rethinking that interview."

Josheb rubbed at his forehead, then gazed around some more. "We were ... on the way to Stately House, yeah? We need to get through the gate, but ... how do we play this? Splitting up's a no-go. I can't lead the Rogue away. They always go for you."

"We're *in*." Clutching the remnant stone on his necklace, Caleb added, "Andor is bound to realize."

Hisoka decided he'd had enough of being overlooked. Sauntering forward, he rubbed up against Josheb, purring at volume.

"Whoa! Uhh ... hey, there, kitty-cat. You one of those little guys we signed a petition for?" Josheb scratched Hisoka gently behind an ear, then cleared his throat. "Say, Bro? Am I prone to wishful thinking?"

And then Caleb Dare was crowded close. "Hello, sir. Why are you so tiny?"

"Stealth mode?" suggested Josheb.

Just then, a faint noise began in the distance. Hisoka only needed a moment to recognize the hum of crystals, high and sweet. The pure note gained, then split into a cord that rippled outward, racing closer as more of Kyrie's trees took up the song.

"Can you hear that?" Caleb whispered. "What on earth …?"

Josheb grabbed his wrist and peered around with widening eyes. "Nice! Kinda pretty. Kinda eerie. Is it figments?"

Hisoka shifted so that he crouched before the Dare brothers. "The trees are laced with remnant song. Kyrie is directing them."

"So it *is* you!" Josheb grinned. "I'd have felt pretty silly if it turned out that you were just a kitty-cat."

Cuffing his brother's shoulder, Caleb took a respectful posture. "Spokesperson Twineshaft. Can you help?"

"Certainly. Give me a moment to get my bearings."

Orienting himself was simple enough. Even swamped by clouds in a pathless section of woods, Hisoka could detect the many remnant stones that were part of the enclave's protections. The four wardstones marked Stately House itself, and … yes, there was the gate. Which meant they were quite far from everything, beyond the pastures where Fairlee Longbrawn grazed his Kith.

If the trees were telling tales, then Kyrie knew where they were. That was good.

Inspiration struck, and Hisoka checked to see if he could borrow Kyrie's array to gain a greater sense of … well, anything. But the tiny crystals had different priorities, so Hisoka withdrew. But his meddling had been noticed, because an unanticipated voice cut across the strains of crystal song.

"Uncle! Where are you?"

"Here."

Fend blandly said, *"While heartening, that is hardly elucidating."*

Speaking aloud this time, he said, "I am with Caleb and Josheb. We're northwest of Fairlee Longbrawn's pastures."

"That far?" Fend muttered peevishly. *"I'll have to run. I'm bringing Timur, but I have little doubt that Andor will reach you first. Any sign of the Rogue?"*

"Signs, certainly. Caleb remembers enough."

"But can you tell where he is?"

"In this murk?"

"Must I corner you into every answer?"

"No. And no. I don't know where the Rogue is. And I would rather prevent him from claiming any more victims." He met each brother's gaze for a moment, then admitted, "Caleb is under the impression that they are being pursued."

"Teach those Dares the rules of dragons. And try to keep Andor from the kind of idiocy that leads to poisoning."

"I can do that."

"And use Kyrie's trick. Mark him if you can."

"Yes. Very sensible." And when Fend left off, Hisoka turned his attention back to the brothers. "Help is on the way, but in the meantime, a lesson. The first rule of dragons is … once you spot one, do not look away."

Josheb said, "The camouflage thing. I've seen it in action."

"There one moment, gone the next." Caleb's attention shifted, and he said, "Andor's coming."

Hisoka's wariness redoubled, because if Andor had been enough to assure these men's safety, then Novi wouldn't have dropped him into the scenario. "I don't think we should wait for him. If you'll grab hold, please?"

It was awkward, grappling the two men and carrying them into the cover provided by clouds. But Josheb was quick to adjust and coached his brother into a more secure position. Below, there came an all-to-familiar slither and the scent of unwashed dragon.

Hushing the brothers, Hisoka stayed still, but he flung a warning Fend's way. *"Have a care. The Rogue is here."*

"Mark him!"

"My hands are full."

With a growl underlying his tone, Fend promised, *"Nearly there. And Sinder says that Boon and Juuyu are on the hunt, but they're circling out from the House. It might take a while for them to reach your position."*

"Where is Kyrie?"

"Listen for the Bamboo Stave. That may be our first and only clue." A few beats later, Fend warned, *"Since you have the brothers, I'm asking Dima to pull back."*

As if on cue, a voice came from below. "This is so annoying. I know you're close. Did you climb a tree? Come down."

Josheb tried to push away from Hisoka, intent on dropping several meters to the forest floor. Sway. With a grim expression,

Caleb slapped his brother's cheek, which might have given away their position if the clouds hadn't begun a hasty retreat. Their cover scudded and wisped away, clearing their view … and leaving them exposed.

The Rogue made a half turn, watching the change, but then he looked up, straight at Hisoka. Recognition sparked in large, thick-lashed eyes, and the dragon haughtily demanded, "Drop them. They're *my* prey. Fair game."

"You're trespassing, Shisoku. You cannot hunt these grounds."

A sly smile brightened the dragon's beautiful face. "Who told you my name? Was it Father?" A wink later, he was leaning into Hisoka's personal space. "Tell me. Are you the one who killed him?"

"No," answered Josheb, who was susceptible enough to be compelled to reply.

Hisoka skimmed backward, desperate to keep the Dare brothers out of striking range.

"Hold still. Answer me! Who did it? Nona said it's somebody here. One of you. Were you there?" With a confident smile, the dragon drifted closer. "I can make you talk."

This time, Hisoka steadfastly held his position, but only so he wouldn't get in the way.

An instant later, a wolf blind-sided Shisoku, knocking him clear.

Then Juuyu was beside Hisoka, calmly crafting defensive sigils. "I am grateful you reached them in time. We would have been too late."

"They need to be taken to safety."

Below, there was a confusion of snarling and hissing, for Shisoku had reverted to truest form. His wings spread in a threatening display as he flexed poisonous claws.

Still serene, Juuyu called, "Boon. Priorities."

Hisoka was impressed when Boon simply abandoned his quarry, letting Juuyu swoop in.

Shifting back into speaking form, the Elderbough tracker showed his palms to the Dare brothers, asking, "Remember me?"

Josheb asked, "You the cavalry?"

"That's the gist. Mind a little more manhandling?"

"Rescue away, friend."

Caleb asked, "Can we run *toward* the oncoming bear?"

"You got it."

And they were safely away.

Hands freed, Hisoka immediately began weaving the tiny tracers that Fend had requested. He reached for his nephew with a report. *"Boon has the Dare Brothers. They'll intersect with Andor. The Rogue is marked, and Juuyu has waylaid him."*

Hisoka supposed his own role was to once more bear witness, though he'd step in with all speed if necessary. But before Juuyu could begin his rote, thunder crashed overhead, and the air filled with a pressure that drove Hisoka to the ground. Wind whipped up on all sides, rattling branches and slinging the snow it found there.

"Hush, Anan." Kyrie stepped into the open, and the wood fell ominously still.

The boy took note of everyone, then raised a hand in a standard signal to hold position. He reinforced the command with a single word. "Wait."

There was no sway involved, but Hisoka knew the sound of authority.

Kyrie took charge with a politeness that was astonishing, given the circumstances. And then he startled them all by demanding an ancient right. "Before you do what you must, I would like to speak to my kindred." And to the dragon warily eyeing the point of Juuyu's drawn blade, he calmly said, "Come with me. I can show you the way to Stately House."

58

IN THE BLEAK MIDWINTER

Sinder wasn't a huge fan of eldermost anything, but especially eldermost dragons. They were exasperatingly pompous and made terrible decisions based on stuff like prevailing winds, comfort colors, or sudden cravings. Opal the Sage was definitely an eldermost dragon.

"You're humming again."

"Was I?" The white dragon's smile was entirely unapologetic.

"Since when do dragons break out 'Coventry Carol'?"

"I *am* a bard, you know."

"You may have mentioned that a time or two." More like dozens of times. And Sinder had only known the guy a scant month. He hadn't even started a file on him yet.

"It eases people's minds."

"The humming?"

"The role. Dragons do love their camouflage. *Bard* gives the right sort of impression."

"What's the wrong sort?"

"I think we can all agree that the Rogue is the wrong sort."

"So you're not a bard?"

"I have bardic tendencies, certainly."

"And sage-ish tendencies?"

"That appellation is mostly due to Zeri. When one has a star whispering wisdom in your ear, it is entirely possible to convince the world that you are a sage."

Sinder couldn't decide if that was self-deprecation … or a dig at Hisoka. Either way, he still wasn't a fan.

"We should try to get along, you know." Opal's gaze was unsettlingly clear. "While this is neither heights nor harem, it has become a clan home. We are elder brothers, wise guides, keepers of kindred tales and lore, teachers of the sagas and the songs."

"You're staying?"

"My vow is made."

Sinder hadn't realized there'd be another dragon around, and it was … okay, yeah. It was a relief. "You're right. We should try to get along."

"Shall we make a beginning, then? In the old way."

"Seriously? Nobody goes through all those hoops anymore."

"I do."

"You're old."

"Come now, Sinder Stonecairne. Yield a truth I can trust, a secret I can shelter, a burden I can shoulder, and a touch that will bind."

"So you're a traditionalist?"

"Hardly. But you strike me as a lad who likes the idea of the old ways." And opening the door to their first destination with a little flourish, Opal added, "You cannot deny it. Or me."

"Fine. But you go first." Sinder reached for the box that held the Plum Cascade.

The other dragon crossed to the case holding the Chrysanthemum Blaze and rested his fingertips lightly upon polished wood. "My truth—I have never really tried to be good. But because I wanted to live up to the hopes of my best-loved person, the world was spared from another rogue beast. Will that do?"

Sinder only needed a moment to figure out what mattered. "Your person—you called him Zeri—he's still in the picture?"

"Very much so. Most people refer to him as Zeriel of the Beckoning Sky."

"No kidding? And you're his dragon?"

Opal brightened. "You're familiar with our story?"

"Who isn't?" Intrigued in spite of himself, Sinder said, "Okay, yeah. I'll trust your truth."

"Your turn."

Sinder tried to think. "I don't even know. Can it be anything?"

"Even the tiniest kernel of truth can take root and flourish." And with less grandeur, "I am unlikely to criticize, lad. The stars sing of peace, and I find I want my portion."

There were so many things Sinder could have told—about his former place, about his role in the taskforce. Nice, neutral, job-related facts. Safe topics, even if they were supposed to be secret. But instead, Sinder blurted something dearer. "I'm newly bonded."

"An unusual turn of events for a dragon of the heights."

"No shit. I mean … you're not wrong. But Timur says it's good and right and best, and I think I believe him. And since this is Timur's home, I'm home. I'm staying, too."

"I can only be delighted, both for you and for myself." Lifting a finger, Opal declared, "And now a secret. I wonder which I should choose?"

"Got anything that isn't woefully outdated?"

"As it happens, I do. But only in the sense that the information is currently applicable." And with a sly smile, Opal revealed, "I know what your adorable rock babies need."

Sinder stopped and turned. "How long have you known?"

"Always."

"Why didn't you say anything?"

Opal sighed. "All the little dramas involved were so *entertaining*."

Sinder snorted. "So you'll give me the recipe? Or whatever?"

"Everything I know. And soon. But not just now."

"Yeah, yeah. Priorities." And making another scan of the room, he said, "Hold up. Where's the Orchid Saddle?"

"Stolen."

"*What*?" As far as Sinder knew, the only other people who could enter this room were Argent and Jacques.

"That thunderstorm took a fancy, and his boy indulged him."

"Oh. That's probably all right, then. Let's get this to where it's going."

"And this." Opal claimed the long case with its crisscrossing ribbons.

"If you say so." Sinder picked up the pace, but he couldn't

outrun tradition.

"Your turn," the other dragon reminded in a light sing-song.

"You need a secret? I mean, they're part of my job. I'm not near as old, but I have more than my fair share."

"Something personal."

Sinder stewed over that until they were beyond the encampment of wolves and into the trees.

"I guess … I might be … sort of … in love?" Now that the worst was out, Sinder finished in a rush. "And I can't for the life of me figure out how it happened."

Opal diplomatically said, "To love one's bondmate is a fine thing."

"Okay, sure. I get that. But he's not the one I mean."

The old dragon got in front of him, eyes bright with curiosity. "Oh, I *do* love complications. Tell me more of your story."

"There's not much to tell. It's just that Timur's partner is really … distracting."

With a soft warble that was pure happiness, Opal asked, "You fell in love with a Kith?"

Startled by the other dragon's reaction, Sinder blurted, "Kithkin. Which may not be a secret for much longer, but he doesn't like to let on. Promise you won't tell."

"On him? Or on you?"

"Both. Please."

"I suppose I will have to put off writing your ballad."

"What? Is that a threat? Don't you dare!"

"A threat? Nonsense. Composition is a form of affection, and I am growing increasingly fond of you. Now then. A burden. How can I support you?"

"You first," countered Sinder, since he was drawing a blank.

"Ah, yes." Opal's expression turned pensive. "I am whole and well and that is wonderous in its way. But the fact remains that I broke."

Knowing the story as he did, Sinder winced. "Your wings. In the old stories, you found them to reach your star."

"Useless now. And yet the sky still beckons."

"Need a lift?"

"From time to time."

"I can do that." Sinder was startled by the vulnerability in the other dragon's expression. Eldermost or not, he had really ordinary hopes. Stuff Sinder could understand. Because once you found the place you belonged, all you really wanted after that was to be there.

Opal asked, "And for you ...?"

An answer lurched immediately to mind, and Sinder guessed he'd be in so much trouble that the support of an eldermost dragon might lend a little balance. Somehow. He slowed to a standstill, suddenly feeling sick.

"Oh, my. Calm yourself, or you will upset your bondmate." Opal adjusted his grip on the Chrysanthemum Blaze so he could reach for Sinder's hand. "Are we not brothers, after a fashion? Tell on, Kindred."

It was hard to say, this truth that was both a secret and a burden.

"You can tell me," Opal said, lacing his words with sway.

Sinder was kind of glad the guy was such a jerk. Because maybe he wouldn't think less of Sinder.

"I know where there are more," he confessed. "Have known. For years. And I didn't tell anyone. Or do anything. They were just ...

information gathered. On file. I cared enough to find them, but not enough to *do* anything."

Opal gently asked, "Who are *they?*"

"More of the Rogue's kids. More of Kyrie's half-siblings." Squeezing Opal's hand tightly, Sinder wished he had a better excuse. "I didn't think."

"We are famously selfish, dragons."

"I want to make up for it. I want to go get them. If Argent will let me."

"The fathers are strong, but the brothers are not weak." Opal bowed until their foreheads met, the touch to bind. "When you bring your findings to Lord Mettlebright, I will stand with you. Together, we will beseech a strong father to bring home the rest of the children who will be in our care."

"You think he'll just ignore that I've been sitting on something so important?"

"If I have Argent Mettlebright's measure—and I am exceedingly good at divining natures—he will be *glad.* Your information aligns with his own determination. That is a good balance."

"Eventually glad, sure. But does that make up for immediate indignation?"

"Use your much-vaunted wits, lad. Before we bring your findings to Lord Mettlebright, we will bring them to his lady."

"Okay, yeah. Let's go with that."

Opal pulled back, let go, and indicated the path. As they hurried along it, Sinder decided he felt just the tiniest bit better. But there might still be some heartfelt abasement in his near future. Like when he admitted all of this to Kyrie.

Kyrie considered the face of his biological father. It was a stranger's face. Naturally, there were traces of this person in all of his newfound half-siblings. The shape of his eyes. The curve of his jaw. The arch of his brows. The line of his nose.

Uncle Boniface had told Kyrie that he had his biological mother's smile. What legacies would he carry forward from his sire?

There was only one that Kyrie actually wanted.

So he would wrest it away, make it his own.

Because he was dragon enough to be greedy.

And foxy enough to pull off a diabolical scheme.

"They were right," his sire gloated. "You're all here."

Kyrie wanted that clarified. "Did the vixens tell you where to find the children you sired?"

"That fox stole them, hid them here. But now I'll steal them back."

"Is that why you came?" Kyrie was trying to understand. It wasn't easy. "You wished to meet us?"

"I'll begin my own clan. For that, I need to get all of you back. A father needs children."

"Like me?"

"You and more like you."

Kyrie didn't like how swiftly he was dismissed as a person. "None of my siblings are just like me."

"That won't matter. You're all mine."

"Are you certain you have any claim on us?"

"Blood." The dragon smiled proudly. "You are one of the seeds I planted. You're a success. A survivor. A successor. You and whatever other halfers the fox stole, you owe me your existence. You should be grateful to me!"

"Are these the things your father would tell you?"

His expression closed off. "My father is dead."

Kyrie dared to ask, "Are you glad?"

The Rogue's eyes narrowed.

"I am asking because you do not seem sad."

"What do you care?"

"I am trying to understand why you want me, even though you do not care about me."

"Because you're mine."

They walked in silence for several long moments before Kyrie spoke again. "I have a name."

A snort. Very rude.

Kyrie wondered if Dr. Kodoku had bothered to teach his children any basic courtesies. "In Amaranthine tradition, the exchange of names is how two people begin to know one another. All the clans take an interest in names. When a new name is given, it can become a claim. My mother chose my name. With it, she claimed me as her own, and it embodies her hopes for me. And my father claimed me by giving me his name, bringing me into his clan."

"Father?" retorted the Rogue. "Do you mean that fox? I *hate* him."

"Yes, I mean him. I know his voice, his scent, his warmth, and his care."

"I *made* you."

"That fox is my dad." Kyrie tried for a more even tone. "You are a stranger."

"I'm going to kill that fox."

He kept right on walking toward the house that was his home. "I do not think you could. But we will not know for certain, since I will not let you try."

Another rude snort. "I can make you do whatever I want."

"I am immune to sway."

"There are other ways." He flexed his claws. "I am the father now. You should listen and do as you're told."

Kyrie wasn't used to so many empty words. Did this dragon even understand what he was saying. "You want me to listen? To do as you say? What would you have me do?"

"Bring me the others."

"No."

"You will bring them!"

"No."

The dragon glowered at him, but Kyrie thought Anan was much better at this sort of thing. He withstood his sire's irritation with an increasing sense of detachment.

"You are a disobedient child!"

"Most of the time, I am careful to comply with my parents' wishes. Both their rules, which are reasonable, and their expectations for proper behavior." He got the sense that these ideas were totally foreign to his sire. Holding his gaze, Kyrie said, "Usually, I live in a way that will not disappoint them. But today, I am tempted to become a very disobedient child."

He walked on.

The Rogue followed.

Kyrie couldn't have said what he expected from a conversation with this person. Maybe he'd wanted to find a shred of decency inside the monster? Maybe he'd simply needed to reassure himself that this truly was the best course.

Yes. He was sure. And in that moment of decision, the Rogue's fate was sealed.

Sinder knew—in a cerebral sense—that Andor Skypact was cozy with a descended star imp. These facts were duly noted in the vintner's file.

Unofficially, Sinder was no stranger to stars. He hadn't been working for Hisoka very long before he'd pegged the one who sometimes stuck close enough to give his new boss a halo. But Novi wasn't a secret Hisoka shared with him. So while they were acquainted enough that Sinder could pick Novi's voice out of a chorus, they really only acknowledged each other's place in the Twineshaft cortege. And left it at that.

So Sinder's firsthand, up-close experience was decidedly lacking. Maybe someday, he'd feel more blasé about meeting impressions, but he was pretty excited to be doubling down. If what Opal said was true, then Andor was harboring his starry business partner *and* a wind imp. Plus, she was something of a rockstar. He'd grown up hearing stories of the Changing

Winds, so meeting *the* Haizea was going to be epic.

If Opal didn't ruin it.

"You can't just walk in!" hissed Sinder.

But the other dragon rolled his eyes, put a finger to his lips, and threw the door wide. Which was incredibly rude. And dangerous, if you believed all the stuff that was said about one of the world's oldest—and grumpiest—bears. But it was also pretty darn informative.

Because the cabin was harboring an extra imp. And they'd caught two of them mid-kiss.

Opal was not fazed. "What a *lovely* surprise! Oh, this *is* a pleasure. If I had only known, I would have brought a suitable gift to mark the occasion. Unless … why, *yes*, I do think this suits quite nicely. Sinder, are you acquainted with the happy couple?"

The infamous whirlwind of legend was a dainty lady with soft ringlets. She was obviously dressed in Eri's spare clothes, since they were doing the matchy-matchy thing. But Sinder doubted that the softly shimmering fabric was responsible for her glow of happiness. That apparently came from kissing stars.

"Nooo. I mean, by reputation, I guess? I've always favored an east wind." And with increasing fluster, he was reduced to a feeble, "Hi."

Haizea dimpled and said, "That is very sweet."

And the guy came forward, hands on offer. "I'm Bethiel."

"No way."

"Yes way."

"Bethiel of the Changing Winds … that Bethiel?"

"That is historically accurate, but I'm semi-retired. Or pivoting? You see, I'm facing a rather dramatic career change."

"Sooo you're Bethiel of the Changing Jobs." Sinder hated himself the moment the words were out of his mouth. "I'll just shut up now."

"No, no, little brother," countered Opal. "There are songs of celebration to sing. For their descent and for their union. Ah, the lyrics I shall write for you! Leaving the sky in order to walk with one another. And with the clans. And with humanity."

"That's great and all, but ...." Sinder held up the precious case he carried. "Aren't we supposed to be rushing the Junzi to the Four Storms so they can head off the Rogue ... or something?"

"No."

"No?" Sinder watched with increasing bafflement as Opal presented the Chrysanthemum Blaze to Bethiel on both palms.

"No and not so. *That* confluence of destinies belongs to others. *This* is our part in the culminating song."

59

PLACES PLEASE

Timur was torn between getting to where the Rogue was supposed to be … and backtracking to locate his bondmate, whose emotions were all over the place. Looming over his Kith partner, he growled, "Fend! Please! Does he need us?"

"It's all right. I got through. Sinder's safe. The discombobulation was largely incidental and partially understandable, since there are imps involved." With a decidedly sulky expression, Fend asked, "Should I be *worried* that he made a point of telling me that he's not getting up to anything with the east wind?"

"He favors the east wind."

"I know. And he's singing for her."

Timur thought he was missing something. "He's wooing a wind imp?"

"Wooing may be too strong a term, but I do think he wants to impress her. She's one of the set Kyrie brought back from Keishi.

And I'm no happier about it than you are."

"Sinder is trying to woo an eldermost storm?" Jealousy warred with incredulity. "Should we go get him?"

With a gusty sigh that was half-hiss, Fend said, "No. He's in awe, not in love. And she's spoken for. He's dueting over some sort of impish bonding. Opal roped him into it, or so he says. All that really matters to me is that our Damsel is safe."

"So ... we should move along."

Rolling his eyes, Fend re-shifted so Timur could mount.

"I can tell, you know," Timur said softly. "I can *feel* that he's singing."

Fend added a playful little jounce to his step.

Timur smiled. "We'll give him more reasons to sing, yeah?"

He was probably a little too focused on possibilities, because he had no idea how a man simply appeared in their path. Fend sprang sideways, skidding to a stop with claws gouging at snow, hair puffed, and spitting feline expletives. He shifted so fast, Timur was dumped on his ass in soft snow.

"Be more careful!" Fend exclaimed. "I could have hurt you!"

Picking himself up, Timur tried to understand his partner's reaction. "You know him?"

Fend looked his way, eyes still wide. "You don't? I suppose you wouldn't. This is Hajime."

"Hello, Fend. Hello, Timur."

"You know my name?"

"We *have* met. You are a difficult one to get to know. I think because you are warded against pollen."

"It protects him when we're away, but it does seem to be

slowing his acclimation at home." Fend patiently announced, "Hajime is an imp. The scent of his flowers and the taste of his pollen are protections for trees of his variety. People forget meeting him."

"Are Kith immune?"

"No, but with Kyrie's help, I've been systematically inuring myself." And turning to the tree imp, he groused, "What are you doing way out here? This is far from home."

"Almost too far." Hajime tried to take a step forward but flinched back. "I am at my limit."

Fend dragged his heel in the snow. "Where is Kyrie?"

"There." The imp took a step back before raising his arm to point.

"All right, old man. Don't strain yourself." With gentle pushes and pulls, Fend forced the tree into retreat. "Wait at a safer distance. Kyrie will do his part."

"Yes." And with a tremulous smile in Timur's direction, Hajime showed off the small blue marble resting on his palm. "I am ready."

"That's an unusual stone," remarked Timur.

"Kyrie asked me to hold it for him. Until it is needed."

Timur took his time sorting out his impressions of the sigilcraft lacing the remnant stone. It was definitely Kyrie's handiwork. The complexity didn't surprise him, but he wasn't sure what to make of the power that crackled behind its etchings. He found he didn't like looking away from it ... in the same way you didn't turn your back on an opponent.

"What's it for?" Timur asked.

Hajime clasped it between both hands, hiding it from view. With a grim nod, he said, "An anchor."

"Sibley, no."

With a guilty start, Sibley eased out of striking range. Not that it would have done any good, since his claws were warded. And he was pretty sure this guy would be immune to his poison. "I was just making sure he didn't try anything, you know?"

"Come here." Kyrie beckoned for him.

He circled around to his brother's side and slipped his hand into Kyrie's. There was a crystal waiting there. That was so smart.

"We will wait. Otherwise, Fend will be unhappy with us."

"Guess so." As soon as they were walking again, he mumbled, "Are you done with him yet?"

"No," he whispered back. "One more thing."

Sibley dared to meet the Rogue's gaze.

He eyed them with actual interest. "Getting children this way makes for more in the way of variety. With seeds it's just more of the same."

Kyrie gave Sibley's hand a squeeze, then left the crystal with him. "We each have inheritances from our mothers."

"But you're obviously mine." Shisoku asked, "How many of you are there?"

Sibley asked, "Don't *you* know?"

"Why would I?"

It was a little interesting and a lot scary that this dragon— his real dad—looked like a younger version of Dr. Kodoku. With

Futari, it'd been harder to tell that they had the same face, probably because she was a girl. But that resemblance meant that Sibley could read Shisoku's expressions real good. He was annoyed, impatient, and simmering close to the meanness that usually meant a cage, a bruise, or worse.

Trying for a friendlier tone, Sibley asked, "We were just thinkin' it'd be nice if we were all together."

Kyrie backed him up. "That *is* my hope."

He also stepped a little in front of Sibley, which made him feel a tiny bit safer. He wished he and his brother had that resonance thing, so he could pass along the kinds of warnings he might need. He thought at Kyrie real hard.

Watch his eyebrows. If the left one goes up, it's bad. See how he's rubbing his thumb and finger together? There'll be poison in his next touch. And that's not a happy smile. If he goes back to pouting—good. If that smile widens—run.

It wasn't words. It was mostly bad memories and fears.

To Sibley's surprise, Kyrie looked away from a dangerous dragon, which was against the rules, and touched their shared crystal. "I know. I do. Not long now. Try not to rile Dima."

"You heard me?"

"Sort of. I am trying not to worry Anan." And returning his attention back to their sire, Kyrie changed things up. "I am grateful to be alive, and I love my siblings. I have resolved to become our clan's tribute."

"If that means you'll be more useful to me, go ahead. I don't really care."

Sibley searched his brother's face, and for the first time, he saw a little of Kodoku and Shisoku there. Because Kyrie's left eyebrow had risen slightly. Sibley rubbed his thumb and finger together. Papa Anjou's seals meant he couldn't bring out any poison, but he did it anyhow. Maybe it was resemblance. Maybe it was resonance. Either way, it would be bad for the Rogue.

"May I know the name of my clan? Nobody will say, so I have not heard."

"I don't see why." Shisoku puffed up with pride. "It's a good name. The best of all clans. Special."

"May I know it?" Kyrie asked, all good manners on the outside.

The dragon smugly declared, "Celestoria."

"I know that name. That is a star's name."

"Yes. My breeding is exceptional. Dragon and star and tree."

Kyrie stopped walking. "I met a star. Celestoria Novi. Oh, I think ... yes. Oh, I see. That is sad." Wind ruffled through his hair, and Sibley thought it must have been whispering to him, because he asked, "Is your father's mother Celestoria Nemi?"

"That's right. Nemi. I never met her. I used to watch her, a beautiful lady trapped inside a jewel." Resentment flashed in his eyes. "Cradling a child. I *hated* that child."

"Why would you hate them?" asked Kyrie.

Shisoku's jaw worked, and Sibley didn't think he was going to answer. Bu then he spat out, "They were safe."

"And you were not?" Kyrie asked quietly.

Confusion turned to exasperation. "Are you stupid? I'm *strong*. They were safe *from me*. Even my poison couldn't scratch their chrysalis. It was annoying."

Even softer, Kyrie asked, "You hated them because you could

not hurt them?”

"Now you see. Yes. That was it exactly."

"This way." Kyrie indicated the way forward, his tone gone flat. "Only a little further."

Nobody had been near enough to tell Sibley that he shouldn't follow a fox into captivity. Maybe it made Sibley a bad person to be glad, but he wasn't going to tell the Rogue that he was just as stupid to be following Kyrie.

As they went along, Sibley spotted something and ran ahead. Tracks and a long furrow marred the snow, which was strewn with tiny red petals. That was good. It looked like Fend's plan would work.

Kyrie had kept to a slower pace, listening to their sire rant.

"A star in our lineage makes us special. It's in our blood to be truly splendid."

"That is something your father told you," Kyrie answered.

"And I am telling you. Because I am the father now."

"Legacies can be important." And turning so he walked backward, Kyrie lured the Rogue ever closer to that line in the snow. "I have taken many things from you. My hair. My eyes. My scales. My longing for the sky. I will also take your name for our clan. Celestoria, for the brave star who was lost. Celestoria for the brave star who searched."

"No, it's *my* name. Mine."

"And mine. That is how legacy works. But that is not all I will take from you."

Kyrie was using sway now. Sibley could tell, and he liked the sound of it. It was nice. Ohhh, nope. Sibley recognized that good feeling, should have realized sooner. Hadn't he seen red petals in the snow? His grandfather tree was nearby, and the scent of him was one of the best parts of home.

Grandfather's scent.

Lady's shine.

Uncle Jackie's smile.

Sonnet's gruel.

Argent's fierceness.

Papa Anjou's ... mmm. Maybe his accent? Or his purr. And the way he always smelled like ... *oh*. Sibley snapped to attention. But then the wind shifted, and the scents were gone.

Kyrie raised a hand. Sibley was still learning tracker signals, which were a whole lot easier than Japanese. He was pretty sure this one meant *wait*.

"I will also be taking your inheritance."

Shisoku laughed. "Not so fast. It is *my* turn. Your time will come. Eventually. If you are a good boy."

"You are not listening. You must listen. I want you to understand what is happening."

The sway held Sibley's attention in a way that was new and unsettling. Had Kyrie always been able to do this?

"The Celestoria clan is founded, and I will serve as their tribute."

"Yes, yes. You said so before. But I am the leader. This is my clan."

"You *are* founder, which is too generous a term, given your crimes. And so you will be removed." With a small sigh, he went on. "You did not ask, but I will tell you anyhow. My name is Kyrie Hajime-Mettlebright. And as the Celestoria tribute, I will do what I must to protect our clan. From you."

In the instant his sire looked away, dismissing him as a threat, Kyrie wanted to prove himself superior. Which alerted him to the fact that he *felt* superior. To a dragon who was too busy feeling superior to realize that his young guide was contemplating his death.

The Rogue was too proud.

He had done terrible things.

Was Kyrie similarly prideful?

Would he be terrible in his turn?

It was a little frightening that if he wanted … if he tried … Kyrie felt quite sure he could put an end to this threat. And this time, he didn't hear any stars singing. Or telling him to stop.

Instead, he heard a long, low note and knew that Anan had unleashed the Bamboo Stave. Grateful for the reminder that his part in this plan was nearly at an end, Kyrie urged the surrounding trees to tune themselves to that sustained note.

Beside him, Sibley said, "This feels like foxes."

Which was almost true. "One and a half foxes. Father has returned."

The Rogue was the only one who didn't realize that it was over. His time would end. Indeed, the only reason it hadn't was Kyrie himself. Because he'd asked Fend for this chance. To meet his father face-to-face. To learn the sound of his voice and his scent. To be able to answer any questions that his siblings might one day have about their sire.

This had been a duty. And curiosity. And disappointment.

Having nothing more to say, Kyrie let his hand drop to his side.

Immediately, arms wrapped around Kyrie's shoulders from behind, and Dad—his true father—softly said, "You did well."

Turning in his embrace, Kyrie hid his face and whispered, "I do not like him. At all."

"Why mince words? He is vile."

Ginkgo spoke then. "You did good, little bro. Satisfied?"

He shook his head, then raised it to meet his older brother's searching gaze. "No. Not until it is over."

"That is best," said Dad. "We will not have long to wait."

"Bear witness," said Anjou in solemn tones.

Kyrie pulled away enough to see that Sibley was similarly safe in the crouching feline's arms. And that there was a particularly wicked blade in one of Anjou's hands. It was easy to forget that Sibley's new Papa was a very capable tribute.

Sibley offered a shy smile, and they both turned to watch.

Timur scanned the gathering of allies. Even if forced to fight Shisoku in truest form, they were more than enough to bring down a dragon. Especially since Juuyu Farroost stood poised on the fringes. He was speaking into a phone, but his eyes never strayed from the Rogue.

Wolves ringed the area, a handful with riders. Battlers. Trackers. Some were survivors from past encounters with the Rogue. Any of them would gladly use their strength and their skills against this enemy.

Timur shook his head. "What was he thinking, strolling into Elderbough territory?"

"Why would he worry?" posed Fend. "He's eluded them often enough."

"Most of these trackers are immune to dragon sway. He can't talk his way out of this."

"All of us are immune, assuming the Bamboo Stave is working properly. I can only assume the thing isn't fussy about the lack of any kind of melody line. I suppose monotone is technically music, and he certainly has the wind to maintain it."

Timur let his loaded crossbow come to rest against his shoulder as he glanced up to the position Anan had taken. The eldermost storm had somehow procured the Orchid Saddle, and he balanced gracefully, bare feet set upon the softly-glowing crystal that held him aloft. He made an awe-inspiring picture, haloed in darkening clouds, his silver eyes flashing in time with the silent licks of lightning flirting at the storm's edge.

The Rogue was blind to all of it. Lost in the illusions that Argent and Ginkgo had concocted so that Kyrie would have his chance. With each passing minute, new protections sprang up—barriers and blinds and battlers.

"Did we even need the Junzi?" Timur asked in a low voice.

"Maybe if he was still somewhere out there, ranging free and raging unchecked." Fend waved a hand dismissively. "But as you pointed out, he strolled into our territory, and that simplifies everything to a ridiculous degree. It's a wonder nobody thought of it sooner."

"Sinder pushed for it. Last summer."

"He's a clever one, our dragon. I will shower him with compliments later." Fend shook his head pityingly. "I stand by my earlier assessment. Shisoku is an idiot. He was probably doomed the moment those vixens left him to his own devices."

"That may be, but it doesn't diminish the danger he poses." Timur returned his attention to the Rogue. "He's a dragon. Take care."

Boon ambled over, hand resting lightly on the pommel of a blade. "Any way I can make myself useful? Argent says you're in charge."

Fend shot a sour look in the fox's direction. "Yes, actually. If Kyrie tries to put down his sire, intervene. It's two centuries too early for him to take on that particular burden."

"On it."

While Boon positioned himself, Timur quietly asked, "He wouldn't *actually* kill his own father, would he?"

"You're giving him too much credit."

"I think ... I *do* think Kyrie might believe it's his responsibility."

"True. Hence Boon. But I meant that you're giving Shisoku too much credit. He isn't any kind of father."

"Ah." Timur cleared his throat. "I suppose that's true. Conceiving children and leaving them to their own devices is hardly admirable."

Fend whipped around so fast Timur jumped. "Do not *ever* think that what you did compares to what he's done!"

"Until this moment, Kyrie had no idea what his father was like. Isn't it the same for my children? They've never known me."

"You kept yourself from them to spare their mothers. But you took the time to learn their names, and you love them from afar.

For pity's sake, you talk to them in your sleep."

Timur was needled for snoring often enough. "I talk in my sleep?"

"Sometimes. I can't prove it, but I suspect Argent's to blame."

Timur frowned. "I talk to them? You think he draws them into dreams?"

"It's the sort of thing a fox can do. And definitely the sort of thing Argent would." Fend pressed their cheeks together. "I'd wager my attainment on it. Your sons and daughters know your voice, your smile, your heart, and your hopes for them. When you meet—a feat I *will* see accomplished—they'll run into your arms and feel right at home."

"Mmm." It was all Timur could manage. He doubted it could ever be that easy.

Fend drew back and grumbled, "So many distractions. Shall we attend to more pressing matters?"

Chastised, Timur fell back on his training and watched as stoically as he could while Kyrie's expression slowly closed off. It broke his heart.

From his crouch nearby, Boon casually announced, "The kid's resolved."

Timur could feel the shift, because the chorus of tiny crystals started up again, and they'd changed their tune. This could be bad.

Fend touched his arm and softly begged, "Stay with me?"

"Aren't we always together?"

"In everything." And facing forward, Fend crisply ordered, "Scuttle the illusions, my good foxes. Let the Rogue face what's left of his future with clearer eyes."

It did Timur's heart good to see Argent and Anjou so swift to their son's defense. The boys had been brave, but they were still just boys.

The Rogue peered around with a superior sort of annoyance. "Oh, go away. I have things to do." And when nobody budged, he asserted himself. "Nevermind me. Turn around. Walk away."

Fend stepped forward. Not far. Just enough to draw the dragon's gaze. Timur was proud of his partner, who might toy with their own dragon and make snide quips at home. But in this setting, he gave proper courtesy.

"Welcome to Stately House. We are its defenders."

The Rogue looked Fend up and down. "Are you one of Father's mongrels?"

"I am not."

Fend's tail puffed and switched beneath the hem of the tunic he'd borrowed for the occasion. Timur's stuff was far too big, but Fend hadn't wanted anyone else's. Belted into battler teal, he held his head high. And higher still when Deece took up a position on Fend's other side. Timur thought Fend's father still looked a bit dazed over the revelation that Fend was Kith-kin.

"Were you taught the ancient rotes?"

The Rogue eyed Fend warily. "How would I know?"

"Mmm. Thought not. Very well. We are prepared to simplify. Do your best to keep up."

Timur took charge. His role was a little different than Juuyu's would have been. As a reaver, and more importantly as a member of the Order of Spomenka, he'd been vested with the necessary authority to speak for the dragon clans. And perhaps more importantly, to speak for the victims.

"Celestoria Shisoku, you stand accused and must answer for your crimes."

"No. Stop this. I'm leaving." But the sway didn't work, and when he turned, he found his way barred by the ring of wolves. He next tried to fly and found he couldn't. "What have you done?"

Harmonious Starmark spoke up. "We're here because of what you've done."

"I don't answer to anyone. Father is dead. I can do as I please."

Timur brought out his phone. There hadn't been time to prepare anything more formal. Canarian Evernhold had sent what he could. "I have here the names of your known victims. Even though there are probably many missing, it's a heartbreakingly long list. Dead men. Ravaged women. Search parties. Innocent bystanders. Abandoned children. In a more formal setting, it would be my duty to confront you with their names, but the Council has agreed that a full reading will take place at every Song Circle."

Adoona-soh Elderbough declared, "We will sing for those lost, and the survivors will gain our support. All they need, we will be."

It was an enormously generous promise.

Timur made a grateful gesture before extending a final courtesy. "Do you wish to speak for yourself?"

"What is this?" Shisoku demanded.

Argent butted in then. "It is a kinder end than you deserve."

"You!" the dragon snarled, claws flexing. "I *hate* you."

And then thunder rumbled, the moaning flute stopped, and Kyrie's voice rang out. "Open your mouth."

Timur needed several moments to pull himself together, and

when he did, he realized that all of them—every person in the circle—had dropped their jaws. All of them were supposedly immune to sway, yet they'd been compelled to obey.

Fend recovered with a soft hiss. "And here I thought we'd need the Plum Cascade."

Again, Kyrie raised his voice. "Take it, Celestoria Shisoku. Accept my parting gift."

Timur's fingers twitched, but he governed the impulse to take something, anything. Perhaps because Kyrie had used his sire's name this time. And then Timur realized that there was another person in the center of the circle.

"Kyrie suggested this," said Fend. "It's a unique form of justice. Quite obsolete. He found it in a book and decided it was fitting."

Timur wasn't privy to this part of the plan. "Is that a tree imp?"

"Yes. That's Hajime. And trees are capable of frightening things."

The imp stood fearless before the stunned dragon, whose jaw remained slack. Shisoku didn't resist when the tree imp placed a small sphere of crystal into his mouth. The remnant was blue, no bigger than a marble, and Timur felt certain he'd seen it somewhere before.

Then Hajime set his hand over the dragon's heart, and they vanished together.

"What just happened?" Timur asked.

Fend held up a finger.

A few heartbeats later, Hajime returned and knelt before Kyrie. With a grave smile, he announced, "He sleeps like a stone."

60

MIND MADE UP

Lapis could have retreated to his usual chair in the Blue Parlor. Instead, he perched on a vastly less comfortable stool in a comparatively drafty upstairs hall. The mares put too much faith in fresh air for his tastes. They must have left a few windows cracked. And at midwinter? Suppressing a shiver, he continued his shameless eavesdropping on Dr. Perrine's gentle questioning of Isla.

"Look, I'm *fine*. Truly. No injuries. No trauma. No lasting effects. Take my side, Pim! Surely you can tell that nothing untoward happened?"

"Are you sure you want to bring my nose into this, Miss Ward?"

"If you'll confine your remarks to the impositions of foxes, certainly."

There was a husky laugh.

And probably a knowing smile.

But for once Isla didn't let it rile her. Hardly a surprise, given this and that. Isla-in-love had always been dauntingly undauntable. Except this time, there was less stubbornness about it and more in the way of ... joy. It suited her. She suited him. And so Lapis kept to the sparsely-appointed hall and waited his turn.

The checkup was a formality. One Isla had attempted—and failed—to decline. Sansa had put her foot down. Isla had retaliated with a counteroffer, conceding to consultation, but only with a healer of her own choosing. Lapis suspected that Isla didn't want the mares getting back to her mother about the very scents Pim had detected. In a sense, it was a power move. Isla was forever asserting her independence. He was still contemplating the interplay between mother and daughter when the father surmounted a nearby stairway and strolled his way.

"Good day to you, Lord Mossberne. Or ... well, it's close on toward evening now."

"Midwinter day is necessarily brief," Lapis returned.

"And exceptionally momentous." Michael placed a gleaming green chrysalis across Lapis's knees. "This one's been softly keening since your arrival. There, now, little one. Here is the dragon who stirred your heart. You're safe in his arms at last."

"Ah, yes. You have been sadly neglected."

To Lapis's surprise the baby imp grumbled in discordant agreement.

Michael laughed. "They're increasingly responsive. And becoming more distinct. They have more than each other, so they no longer sing in unison. You'll see how it is, since you'll be staying."

"Will I ...?"

"Argent asked me to tell you that you're officially on holiday. Jacques is managing the necessary shifts in schedule. You're to spend Christmas with us. We've all the usual festivities planned. You won't be needed for any public appearances until New Year's Eve at Kikusawa Shrine."

If Argent had sent Michael, then it was very likely that the fox had relayed at least some of what had occurred between him and Isla while on his back. Lapis supposed that had been rather reckless of him. But he'd been so relieved. And Isla had been so ….

Michael cleared his throat. "I'm also told that there's time enough to call for a press conference. For the thirty-first."

Lapis blinked.

Isla practically skipped out the door he'd been guarding. "Oh, but that's brilliant! I'll need to check with Canarian about auspicious dates and possible lulls in the Council schedule, but definitely yes. New Year's Eve is perfect. We can use our news to undercut any speculation over the sudden cancellations that the Five were forced to make. Canarian can script something, and then Kimiko can make the announcement."

Michael all-too-innocently asked the obvious question. "*Is there something to announce?*"

She took a dominant stance and rested a hand possessively on Lapis's shoulder. "Our engagement, of course!"

Their rock imp thrummed in contentment.

Lapis had always known that to win Isla, he'd need to appeal to both her intellect and to her heart. If she'd made up her mind to love him, then he knew himself to be chosen. And if she was prepared to be very much in love, they'd finally found their balance. Lapis was prepared to be exquisitely happy.

Except.

He feared that his bondmate-to-be was going to try to outdo Kimiko Starmark, and he wasn't ready to resign himself to a three-year courting period. So on the morning of the twenty-fourth, while the rest of the household was making final preparations for Christmas, Lapis invited Isla for a stroll.

Draped in fur-lined cloaks, he escorted her along a snow-skimmed path while fat flakes drifted lazily from pale clouds. She was talking—she usually was—and he listened contentedly to her suggestions for edits to their current manuscript. Having learned of his enforced holiday, she'd immediately proposed an accelerated schedule so they could finalize the book before their meeting with Canarian next week in Keishi with a proposed schedule for their betrothal's publicity campaign.

Normally, Lapis applauded Isla's work ethic, but he'd rather hoped to spend the week in other, more intimate pursuits.

But there was an order to such things. Before they could go forward, he would keep a promise he made in passing. So once the book talk was tabled, he made an oblique beginning.

"When I was born, I was greatly admired for my coloring."

Isla caught his mood and lost her smile. "Tell me more …?"

"Blue isn't common. My mother, who was born after the Waning, is still considered a rare beauty. Sky blue, you know. My father is nothing special. A brown. One of Beckonthrall's younger brothers, as a matter of fact. I inherited his eyes."

"Will I ever meet them?"

"Ah. I'm sorry, dear heart. They went into seclusion long ago. After ... well, I was at the center of some drama, which was embarrassing for all involved. And disastrous for me."

Isla's intuition had always been keen. "Is this about your breaking?"

"Before you succumb entirely to my charms, you should know why I am ... as I am." With a faint smile, he added, "You always did like a tragic hero. Though I've never been the brooding sort."

"You certainly don't have an air of tragedy about you. If you're sure you want to tell me. I must confess, I *am* curious."

Lapis fixed his gaze on the path ahead. "In passing, I mentioned an old ... hobby. Before the current mode, with the dragonesses seeking out our strongest males, some of the eldermost and ancients did as they pleased, including the collection of a full spectrum of brides. Though in truest form I have the same azure scales as my mother, in speaking form, I was unique. An indigo dragon.

"The bidding for future daughters—sight unseen, as yet unborn—must have seemed a windfall. When a powerful old dragon came to call with expensive gifts and generous promises and veiled threats, my parents agreed to bind their next daughter to him. But there was a catch, because the lord was as impatient as he was greedy. And so I was sent as a stand-in for my someday baby sister."

Isla tugged at his arm. "You were held hostage?"

"Worse. I was a bride. His tenth. And a child bride at that." Lapis patted her hand. "I spent most of my adolescence arrayed as a female."

"Was it terrible?"

Lapis inclined his head. "I was unhappy."

"None of the dragon lords behave this way nowadays!"

"Not officially, no."

Isla gaped at him.

"I would love to say it was a different time, lost in some long-distant past, but alas, I am not *that* old." Firmly steering her forward, Lapis said, "Many dragons see no reason to change their ways simply because the times have changed. Traditionalists, you know."

He could see the protests she wanted to make, watched her training as a cultural liaison kick in, and was grateful when her only response was a reluctant nod.

"While I was living in my non-existent sister's place, the dragon lord who'd bought me found a new novelty. Reavers. Before long, he secured a young man with a superlative soul and no resistance to sway. But this new pet had a sway all his own, and soon the lord succumbed to addiction. The balance of power shifted, and the cosset found himself a lord in his own right, with a harem of beauties eager for his touch."

With a sigh, Lapis confessed, "The hatchery grew cold, and the dragonesses whispered that the cosset's influence was to blame for a spate of stillbirths. But looking back, I think that they were quietly putting down crossers, lest any learn of their shame."

"What about you?" Isla asked.

"I broke," he said simply. "But a human's life is short. In a few decades, after every member of the household had shattered, he left us bereft. I don't know what would have happened if Lord Beckonthrall hadn't come to see why his messages were going unanswered. I believe four of the dragonesses in the harem were his granddaughters."

"So you were rescued."

"And bustled off to a secret place for rehabilitation. And eventually placed in a remote height, where books became my escape ... and then a bridge of friendship between myself and the very sort of human who ruined me. Because the brothers of my new home worked in tandem with an order of reavers who had long allied themselves with dragons.

"Five generations later, my trust in humanity was renewed, my expertise had expanded into areas of remnant songs and sigilcraft, and my book collection exceeded my living quarters. That's when a cat came to call. And I liked him and his plans. And his dog."

"You've always been close to Harmonious."

"He's been good to me."

She tugged at the folds of his cloak, exposing the reddish fur that lined it. "He and Anna treat you like one of their own."

"Harmonious, Hisoka, and humanity have been much kinder to me than members of my own clan." With a small shake of his head, Lapis redirected. "I simply wanted you to know that while I did succumb to addiction, it wasn't something I sought. My situation would be considered the mishandling of a minor."

Isla pushed up into his personal space. "You know, I never once thought you were Broken for personally nefarious reasons. And you're *not* a tragic figure. You're generous and gentlemanly and romantic and … and good."

"Thank you, my dear. I'm flattered by your regard."

"It's not flattery. It's the truth."

"It is true that I survived an ordeal. It's similarly true that I live with the consequences." He let his chin fall to his chest. "Another truth will have a bearing on the future. I sympathize a great deal with the Rogue's children. I cannot always be here, but I will often be here."

"Of course," she said warmly. "You're more at home here than anywhere."

"Mmm." He lifted his gaze, peering at her through his lashes. "Grant me a boon?"

"If you want him, you'll have to wrestle Pim and Elara for him."

Brushing snowflakes from her hair, he lapsed into swaying words. "Give me what I want, Isla. Let me have my way. Concede to my terms."

"You're waxing redundant. Very bad form."

"I will say it as many ways as the thesaurus permits. Yield. Entrust. Bestow."

That won him a laugh. She said, "You're always telling me to be more concise."

"Do not make me wait, Isla. Not one more day."

She frowned. "I gave you my answer. I'm quite sure I did."

With a small shake of his head, he firmed his hold on her arm and ushered her briskly to his intended destination. The Song Circle was still decorated for a bonding ceremony. Standing with her at its center, Lapis made his meaning plain. "If you so desire,

I will submit to a lengthy and ornamental courtship, with enough trimmings and trappings to rival Kimiko's. But that will be for show. A celebration after the fact."

He waited, worried he'd disappointed her.

Pageantry was expected for someone in his position.

And their bonding really would benefit the Council.

But to wait longer after waiting for so long?

He repeated in pleading tones, "Not one more day."

Isla couldn't help wanting to use their engagement to titillate the masses. Not only was it a prime opportunity, it was a much-needed one. Because once the hype surrounding Cyril Sunfletch's inauguration died down, he would pass into the realm of politics. A new, high-profile romance would be just the thing. Tried and true. Dream-come-true. Canarian was sure to give their match some flare. Unattainable Bachelor Takes a Bride. Or something.

"You mean … elope?" she asked doubtfully.

"Since neither of us is where we're scheduled to be, I think it's fair to say we've already run away together."

"Don't be daft. We came home."

"A good place to begin. As is this." He indicated the Song Circle.

"Can we do that? Just … become bondmates. Oh, but of course we can. For nearly every Amaranthine clan, the establishment of a bond comes down to consent and copulation. Any other trappings are either cultural or instinctual gestures, usually attached to the courtship phase. In fact, for most clans, the introduction of any form of bonding ceremony hearkens back to the addition of reavers to their community. The additional formalities are largely considered adoption or adaptation as a nod to human expectations or sensibilities. For example …!"

She trailed off when she realized that Lapis had been slowly encroaching.

He smiled and pressed his lips to hers. "Are you willing?"

"I … well, yes." Her mind was still racing. "We can still have all the press conferences and photoshoots and interviews and whatnot?"

"Are we not ambassadors for the very peace our union represents." Another soft kiss. "We might even reveal ourselves as the *tour de force* behind the novels of Chastity Landis, since my years of patience and pining for you will appeal to romantics."

"Ohhh. Oh, that's *brilliant*!" She hesitated. "Unless people will think the whole thing's a publicity stunt?"

"I will not hide the fact that I am ardently in love." Another kiss, this one more lingering. "We are highly demonstrative, dragons."

"But … our books sales."

Lapis shrugged. "Give them away. Perhaps a new cause. Something for children of interspecies unions …?"

"Kimiko would definitely support us! And Harmonious and Anna, of course. Argent and Tsumiko. Actually, I'm quite sure we could get the Sunfletches involved. And Ash is a crosser."

"And our own children."

She blinked. She cautioned, "My current schedule won't allow for a three-year maternity leave."

Lapis mildly pointed out, "My years are yours. I'm merely

thinking ahead. For now, we can concentrate on securing the rights and respect due to all people, no matter their provenance."

Isla was pleased with this course. "Should I place a call to Canarian? He'll want to know ...."

"He'll be here within the half-day. To spend Christmas with his family. Let's not interrupt his holiday. Or forget our purposes here." He indicated the Song Circle.

"Right. Sorry." She eased into a receptive posture. "I'm no more familiar with the forms of a dragon's bonding ceremony than I was with courting games. How should we proceed?"

Lapis took her hands, rubbing his thumbs over her fingers. "You need warming and adorning, which I am prepared to do in the privacy of my suite. But according to the traditions of my clan, lasting vows are made where the winds can bear witness."

His expression was peaceful. His gaze gentle. But anticipation was building beneath the surface. He wanted more. He wanted *her*. And it was wonderful, being wanted. Somewhere, deep down, Isla had begun to doubt her desirability. Too career-oriented. Too outspoken. Too strong-willed. Too famous.

Lapis was perfect for her.

And he was waiting for her.

Because her thoughts had strayed.

A faint smile welcomed her back.

He really was perfect.

The slowly falling snow had been catching in his midnight hair, giving him a pure white crown. A rare beauty. Was he the only dragon with this coloring? With a sudden jolt of inspiration, she said, "Wouldn't your child also be an indigo dragon?"

"It's certainly possible. Who can say which characteristics a crosser will inherit?"

"But if *you* carried the child. Like Uncle Jackie and Suuzu?"

His eyes slowly widened. "A fair and equitable proposition. How forward-thinking of you, my dear. I am willing to do my share. Perhaps after Suuzu's seclusion ends?"

"Right. Well. I can add that to the agenda for our meeting with Canarian."

"Please, do."

And he drew her into a stirring kiss that could have meant anything, but probably meant everything. At least, she was confident that's where this was leading. Wanting to be equally as fair and equitable, Isla retreated enough for whispered words. "May I tend you?"

Lapis looked a trifle fraught, but his trust was hers. "Please, do."

Of course, it wasn't simple. He was sigiled from tip to toe, and her personal wards were nearly as formidable. But they worked together, puzzling out a pathway that would leave them with sufficient protections.

It was an unexpected intimacy, teasing past barriers.

Her awareness of him took on fresh nuance, and she supposed she was similarly exposed. It was throwing her off more than she liked to admit. Her love for him was brand new, though it had its foundations in a longstanding friendship. But his soul reached for her with a wistful, hopeful, needful sort of yearning.

"You've abstained ever since then," she murmured.

He pulled her against him and nodded into her hair.

Isla felt a tremor pass through him. "It's all right, you know.

Papka might get all of Sensei's compliments, but I'm really very good."

Another nod.

She fed a gleaming thread through the way they'd made. That's how she pictured it. Fine as silk, shining like starlight, ready to meet him and bind him, so that Lapis would be hers.

He sighed.

And then he made a flattering little trill.

And then he began to speak.

> "First and foremost, eastern bride,
> Let your rising fill these eyes.
> Wise and windmost, northern bride,
> Let your tumult quell my storm.
> Right and highmost, western bride,
> Let your singing guide our course.
> Kind and softmost, southern bride,
> Let your warmth undo your drake."

Isla was delighted. And enormously curious. "Did you just propose to me four times?"

"Four times," he echoed, a trifle dreamily. "You are my every direction."

That was really a very romantic thing for a dragon to say. And also telling. "Are you telling me that all four bride's chambers are mine?"

"Yours entirely. Rule over them long and well."

"When I convinced you not to take Tenma as your eastern

bride, I didn't realize I was protecting my own place. I'm rather glad I succeeded in putting you off."

"A few years ago, I succumbed to a bout of optimism and prepared for future eventualities. Both the north and south brides' chambers have been done over."

"You renovated? You never mentioned."

"I was embarrassed. I had no right to presume."

Isla pushed him enough that he straightened and met her eyes. "What did you do?"

"Bookshelves."

She was stunned. "You made room for my books?"

"I almost offered the rooms to you a dozen times, once they were ready. I never did like that your library was under Hisoka's roof. Perhaps there is some form of instinct at play? A dragon's home is where he keeps his trove."

Isla shook her head and breathed, "You made room for my books."

Lapis looked entirely pleased by her pleasure. Actually, Isla could *feel* his satisfaction.

Happiness and hopefulness added lilt to this answer. "Yes, my dear. Room enough for yours and mine. And should we begin to overwhelm the available space, there's always the western bride's chambers."

Moving her collection would be an undertaking, and then there were her offices at the embassy. But should she move those as well? Being in Keishi was certainly convenient, but if Lapis didn't want her books under Hisoka-sensei's roof … but, wait. Her responsibilities could mean uprooting her entire staff, and that would be enormously impractical.

"Isla. My dear. Do stop drafting agendas. For a bit?"

She wasn't sure she could. "Sorry. There's just so much."

"Most of which can keep. However, one thing cannot. It's a formality, really. You haven't given your answer. May I hear it?"

"About the rising and quelling and guiding?" She lowered her voice. "And that last bit. *Highly* euphemistic!"

"And—one dares hope—not overly optimistic."

"Certainly not." She paused, "Which is to say ... properly optimistic. Is there a traditional answer that the brides usually give to their pursuing dragon?"

"Yes."

She waited.

His smile warmed. "All you need to say is *yes*."

"Oh! Right, then." And easing into a more confident posture, she said, "Yes, Lapis. Very much yes."

With a gracious inclination of his head, Lapis took up a new rote:

> "Twain songs now twine;
> Words before the wind
> Make this drake a lord,
> For he has won a lady."

And then he pressed a quelling finger to her lips, which *had* parted, since Isla wanted to know if he was now a lord in more than name, which was certainly implied. And if she was truly a lady. And if she should take his name or perhaps hyphenate. But instead, she smiled into laughing eyes and allowed Lord Mossberne to finish.

"Enter my harem and complete it."

61

LORDING OVER

rgent was back. And so, to his softly thrumming satisfaction, was Jacques.

"*Really*, my lord. You have no right to look so pleased. I've had to order three new suits for you. With the worst over, do you think you take a step back from wanton destruction and resume kinder, gentler forms of dishevelment?"

"I really couldn't say. Oh. Bother." And lowering himself to the floor, he crooked his fingers toward the shadows under the chaise lounge. "What have you there, sweetheart?"

The little girl peeked out at them, then glanced back over her shoulder. With a peep, Patter appeared beside her.

"How in all the Widelands do you keep getting past my barriers?" Argent coaxed Patter into his arms and quietly remarked, "I *am* glad Churlish brought him. I have been curious ever since I heard about him from Hisoka."

"His claws are snagging your silk," Jacques chided mildly.

"Mmm." He let the little one snuggle in, too charmed to care.

"Up you come, little miss." And having secured their other interloper, Jacques said, "They've chosen her name, by the by. Bother has become Christobelle. They borrowed from Bon-Bon, who may not fully realize that the giving of a name is a solemn bond."

Argent hadn't had the chance to sound out Jacques on the matter of his elder brother. "Should we be asking him to stay?"

"I don't really want him. But I also can't begrudge him." With a careful tone, Jacques admitted, "He'll be good. Actually, he'll probably be grand."

"In the end, it's Suuzu's decision."

Jacques acceded with a nod. Then lightly inquired, "What have we here? Oh, you *are* wonderful! I was looking for this just yesterday. Thank you, Christobelle. You're a treasure."

"What has she found?"

"A lost cufflink. One of mine. Since this set is the right hue, I thought ... well, nevermind. It's rather shabby now that I can appreciate that little extra something of living crystal. Though I suppose with gifts, it's the thought that counts."

"Last-minute Christmas shopping?"

"Yes and no. There's this midwinter custom amongst the feline clans. A gift to match the color of a consort's blaze. Sonnet wants to surprise Anjou, so I've been pawing through my assorted haberdashery and gee-gaws, trying to find something appropriately gorgeous."

Argent eyed the cufflink. "What color is his blaze? Or ... too personal?"

"*Non.*" He tilted it, showing off the inset glitter of peridot. "As it happens, Anjou was born with a blaze in a sprightly green. Which is perfect, since I am—as Nonny loves to say—going to do the *outré* thing and claim it for my clan's color."

"An appropriate choice."

Jacques brightened, and the radiance of his mood suffused the entire room.

Patter peered around and chittered softly.

Christobelle lay her head against Jacques' vest and petted his tie.

Argent supposed he should speak up. "I may be able to help. I have a few things set aside for … well, I imagined they would be for birthdays or anniversaries or milestones. They are rather fine, and they are the correct color. And they have always been meant for you. In a way, I already gave them."

"I'm intrigued. Tell on!"

Pointing to a paneled section of the wall, Argent asked, "Can you see the sigil just there?"

Jacques followed his gaze and narrowed his eyes. "Lord, I don't know. The whole room is reeling with foxy excesses."

Argent stood, plopped Patter on the chaise lounge, and framed the pertinent sigil with his hands. "There's another cupboard behind here."

"Why would you hide a cupboard from me?" Jacques asked suspiciously. "I thought you gave over the whole of your closet."

"Ah." He supposed he was in for a scolding. There were several 'missing' garments stashed inside—spoiled or itchy or sequined. But mercifully, Jacques only had eyes for the items displayed on two shelves at eye level.

A fussy atomizer for scents and a hand mirror set with crystals. A shapely vase and a stoppered decanter. An exquisite bottle of expensive oil and a softly-whirring clock that was keeping perfect time despite being locked away since last summer.

"These are from the array!" Jacques exclaimed. "The crystals I smuggled into the tropics."

"These pieces were models for the illusions I used on the array."

His man picked up the vase, trailing light fingertips over its decorations. "Every one of these is a work of art."

"Mmm. Take them. Do with them as you like."

"What to do …." Jacques touched each item, and his happiness became a giddying force. "May I take one for Sonnet, too?"

Argent gruffly reminded, "They are yours. I can give you access to the cupboard, should you wish to bring them out or bestow them at intervals."

"*Merci.*"

But before Jacques could make his selections—or remark upon a particularly loathsome pair of shoes that both pinched and creaked—there was a rap.

Argent frowned. "That cannot be Nonny. He will be at the playhouse already."

Jacques muttered, "Lord, *this* should be interesting." And he went to swing the door wide.

Fend—in speaking form—stood in the hall, Gregor propped on his hip, the little female wind dragon draped around his shoulders. His gaze was almost a glare, full of challenge.

Recognizing the import of the combined sigilcraft the threesome represented, Argent cracked a smile. "So *that* is how you manage it."

"Yes. There's a gap in your defenses, and I thought you should know."

"I cannot imagine that anyone else would be equipped to exploit it as you have."

"No, but there may come another time when *I* am exploited."

"Another?" echoed Jacques.

Fend adjusted his hold on Gregor, boosting the squirming boy higher. "Who do you think brought you your beloved Anjou?"

"*Mon dieu*, but of course! He shouldn't have been able to reach my door. But with one thing and another ... I suppose I was so glad to see him, I didn't question his arrival."

Argent snorted lightly.

Jacques offered an unapologetic shrug, then moved to steal Gregor. "He's only trying to get to Patter."

Indeed, the green-haired boy beckoned from the nest he'd built from a cashmere throw and two castoff tunics.

Fend nuzzled Gregor's curls. "You *are* your daddy's boy, hmm? Go on, then. Make a new friend while I claim my due."

Argent pretended not to hear and immediately changed the subject. "Where did Bother get to?"

"Christobelle," Jacques corrected distractedly. "Come, me boyo. Uncle Jackie shall be your ally. You must help me introduce young Master Patter to Etienne. He will be similarly charmed."

Fend propped his hands on his hips, looking unamused.

"She's in my new cupboard, exploring the castoffs *somebody* ferreted away." Jacques blandly added, "*She* understands the appeal of sequins."

Argent was vastly more interested in another point that had been glossed over. "You implied exploitation. Who told you to bring Anjou past barriers?"

"A star," said Fend.

"Which star?" Argent pressed.

"Bethiel."

That gave him pause.

Jacques startled him all over again by remarking, "Nice chap."

Argent pivoted. "When did *you* meet Bethiel?"

"Mmm. Dichotomy Day, so three days ago."

"And you failed to mention this ... why?"

Jacques replied evenly. "Because not all news is mine to tell."

It was a mild rebuff, but Argent let the matter go. For now.

Fend pushed forward. "Argent! You made me a promise."

"So I did." Rising to his full height, he added, "I am prepared to offer an apprenticeship."

"Don't change terms. Recognize my attainment!"

"I do. Jacques can bear witness. Or if you prefer, we can stand before your father and brothers and uncles ...?"

"No need. If *you* say it, I'll be satisfied."

"Because you respect Argent," interjected Jacques. "More than any other person at Stately House, his opinion holds value."

Argent blinked.

Fend sniffed. "I have so few peers. Intellectually."

Jacques said, "I agree with Fend. Apprenticeship implies a step down, not a step up. Far better to expand your cortege. You're past due."

Argent didn't like to be cornered, but this was Jacques. So

he didn't refuse outright. "Past due?" he countered instead. "I only just added Anjou."

"We are fortunate, indeed, to have so many capable felines at Stately House." Jacques gazed at Fend, his expression thoughtful. Finally, he said, "Bring him on in an advisory capacity. Include him in all Council business. Make him your sounding board."

Fend eyed them critically. "It's the only sensible thing to do. Provided he trusts my judgment. And accepts criticism."

"Trust for trust." And in a warning tone, Jacques added, "Respect for respect."

"I would appreciate that, yes." And brazenly meeting Argent's gaze, Fend announced, "I'll lend you my full support. On one condition."

More amused than anything, Argent said, "I am listening."

In a posture that made it clear that Fend considered himself equal to anything, especially Argent, Fend said, "I'll join if Sinder does."

"You *are* a brazen one," Argent drawled.

Jacques helpfully interpreted, "He likes you. You're hired."

The children were nestled, all snug in their beds. Or would be soon. Argent was waiting for Tsumiko to finish her evening rounds. No small feat, given all the excitement for tomorrow, which would be Christmas. He didn't expect her for another hour, and then they'd join Michael, Sansa, and the rest in staging several surprises. Nonny and Sonnet had most everything else well in hand.

So Argent's feet were propped before the fire. Indeed, he was in real danger of dozing off when a light rap sounded. He banished a sigil, and the door opened to reveal Anjou, who escorted Hisoka Twineshaft.

"I found him in the hallway," explained Anjou. "He needs a word. We are not intruding?"

"Not at all." Easing out of his slouch, Argent extended a hand. "Join me?"

With quiet efficiency, Anjou pushed Twineshaft inside, and retreated. When the door shut behind him, there was a gentle wash of wards to supplement Argent's own. Really, Jacques' new man was quite good. A welcome addition.

Argent waved to the seat opposite his, but Hisoka crossed to him instead. A pointedly deferential posture banished any sense that he was looming. However, he seemed at a loss how to begin. Argent's gaze dropped to the cream-colored envelope in Hisoka's hands, and he prompted, "Something for me?"

Hisoka looked vaguely embarrassed, but he proffered the thing. "I … yes. For you."

Argent accepted it with a good deal of curiosity. The envelope bore no name, and it wasn't sealed. Inside was a single sheet of paper. Superior quality. And Hisoka had stamped the bottom corner with his seal. So … something official.

He read.

He read it all again.

Hisoka tentatively said, "Dichotomy Day may have passed, but this is still the season for new ventures …?"

Argent raised his hand, forestalling further explanation. He read the lines a third time, thoughts racing. Finally, he said, "There is much to discuss, but before any of that … *yes*."

The cat practically crumpled, dropping gracelessly to his knees and bowing his head until it touched Argent's knee.

He gently rested a hand on Hisoka's shoulder. "Did you think I would try to dissuade you?"

"I did. A little."

"Then you do not know me as well as you ought. I suppose I am not the easiest person to know." He mildly added, "To be fair, you are similarly enigmatic. But with *this*, perhaps we can do away with polite distances …?"

Hisoka lifted his face. "I am in your hands."

"Oh, I doubt *that* is the case." Argent contemplated the intricacy of the mark that now graced the cat's brow and lightly asked, "What of Rhomiko?"

"My bondmate?" Hisoka ran a hand over his hair. "They intend to keep me."

"Then you shall be well kept."

"I realize this may cause trouble for the Amaranthine Council. But I cannot return."

"Set your boundaries, and I will reinforce them." Argent dared to caress pewter hair. "You can shape the future from here. Guide our children."

"There will be those who'll criticize …."

"That is like saying there will be those who sneeze." Argent firmly countered, "There will also be those whose trust cannot be shaken. Those who respect your priorities. Those who support your choices. And there will be *me*."

Hisoka bowed his head again, so Argent brought out his full flourish. Draping his friend in silver fur, he said, "Welcome home, Hisoka-sensei."

Tsumiko had been just the tiniest bit worried that Churlish's arrival would cause problems in the kitchen, but Sonnet had welcomed the prickly moonbeam with the fondness of familiarity. Churlish was soon perched on the countertop, consuming a bowl of Sonnet's gruel, humming over each bite.

"I grew up underfoot in the Moonglade Tea Room." Sonnet's tail did a happy shimmy. "Churlish taught me everything I know."

Churlish tapped a silver spoon against his bottom lip. "After birthday cake, we should make more gingerbread. Paltry likes gingerbread. *Everybody* should like gingerbread."

Tsumiko left them to their plans, strolling past the parlor where Catalan and Canarian had commandeered the piano. Most of the cast from the evening's play were there, singing carols. She was pleased to see Uncle Boniface in their midst, pulled snug against Cat's side as they harmonized.

In the front foyer, Jacques and Nonny had organized a stealthy brigade. Gifts that had been stashed who-knew-where were arriving under the tree. Josheb stood with Michael, their heads bent together over each tag as the young man made certain of his pronunciation. He'd be presiding over the morning's distribution.

Andor had broached an enormous cask of star wine, and Anjou and Eiji roved through the room, topping off drinks. Harmonious Starmark's laugh rumbled to the ceiling over something Rhomiko said, then he cuffed Hisoka's shoulder. The dog clansman's mood had brightened considerably with Sensei's return from seclusion.

The front door swung wide, letting in a breath of fresh air and two latecomers to the festivities. Boon had apparently volunteered to cross international borders on their behalf, and before he had his companion fully unbundled, Uncle Jackie had Harrison Peck in a bear hug.

Usually, they only had the pleasure of Harrison's company during summers. Tsumiko wondered who'd organized to have him brought. She wouldn't be surprised if it was Argent.

As if summoned by her thought of him, he came striding her way. His tails were out and puffed, and his intent was clear, and people stepped out of his way. Nobody seemed overly concerned, and once he was close enough, Tsumiko could read his expression. Something unusually fine must have happened, because her bondmate was nearly aglow with a pleasure he rarely let others see.

Behind fanning tails he dipped down to press his lips to her answering smile. "Here you are."

"Here I am," she acknowledged.

"I could not have contrived it on my own," he began. "Though I would have loved for you to see. We are most fortunate. I am honestly staggered. Jacques never let on, and how was I to guess? But I am glad for your sake."

He'd pulled her arm through his and was guiding her out. She wondered what had excited him to such an extent, he was almost rambling. But then they were at the door to the Blue Parlor, and Opal was within, chatting with someone new. Tsumiko was certainly familiar by now with the characteristics of a star clansman. So Argent had wanted to introduce her to an imp?

The dragon bard was complimenting the star, who'd apparently used the Chrysanthemum Blaze to mollify Dima. Did that mean ...?

Argent nuzzled her and murmured, "If anyone deserves an angelic encounter, it's you."

Opal stepped back without another word, a coy smile on his face.

"Oh," she managed. "How do you do ...?"

"Lady Mettlebright. Tsumiko. Please meet Bethiel," Argent said with all the formality he'd once used as her butler. "He will be joining the Amaranthine Council."

62

GIFTS THAT KEEP ON GIVING

Jacques woke to a soft warble and lisping French. Gilen or Arnaud must have tattled on him, for he was back to being Papa Zha-Zha, which was fine. Better than fine. Indeed, it was splendid. He didn't even have to open his eyes to know who'd led Etienne to his naproom nesting place. "Hey, Nonny nonny. Is that coffee for me?"

"Might be. Might even be enough for your friend there."

"That's welcome news," Harrison said in a sleepy mumble. "Merry Christmas, Nonny."

"You, too. Glad you could make it. Now get some of this in you, and get downstairs," he ordered, sounding supremely happy. "Sonnet wants the two of you fed before the festivities begin."

"We will be there anon."

"Faster than anon, or I'll send Anan to drizzle on you." A hoof gently prodded his hip, and Nonny wheedled, "C'mon, Jacques.

594

It's *Christmas*."

Jacques propped up on elbows and peered around the hushed naproom. "Dressing gowns and hearth slippers okay?"

"Yeah, of course. Same as always."

When Jacques sat up fully, Etienne clambered onto his lap. Nonny passed along one steaming mug, and Harrison wrestled free of his blankets in order to accept the other. The man looked rather dapper in his candy cane print pajamas.

Pausing with his coffee cup halfway to his lips, Harrison lowered his voice to ask, "*How* are the children still asleep?"

"A masterful combination of barriers, illusions, and visions of sugarplums," said Jacques. "Argent will turn them loose once the rest of us are in place."

"Want me to take Etienne back to Sonnet?"

"*Non*. My bonny wee boy and I will face the festal morning together." He took a sip of excellent coffee and thought to check. "Is Sibley with Anjou?"

"Nah. Bon-Bon collared him." And with a saucy salute, the goat-crosser hurried to his next task.

Jacques took in the bare minimum of coffee, angled his chin at Harrison, and pushed to his feet. They wove through the room, Harrison pausing here and there, tweaking blankets into place. Jacques noticed that Vanya and Perse had Gregor tucked between them. And Sonnet's granddaughter Linnea had stolen in at some point, probably to get close to Ever. In his turn, Ever had his arms around Pact, who'd been understandably smitten with his Starmark cousin. But Kyrie's usual place beside Lilya was empty.

Out in the hallway, he grumbled, "The sun's not even up."

Harrison patted his shoulder and reminded, "It's Christmas."

Reason enough to soldier on.

By the time they reached the kitchen, Harrison had donned a long-tailed Santa hat, and Jacques wore one in the same style, only green.

Anjou swooped in for a kiss and twirled away with Etienne in his arms, crooning promises of breakfast. Sonnet came over, touched Jacques' freshly-shaved cheek, trailed fingertips along his shoulder, and then moved back to the stove.

Harrison watched the interplay with a little half-smile on his face.

"Something to say?" Jacques inquired.

Harrison, who was probably the kindest, most generous friend Jacques would ever have, said, "No wonder."

"Let's see if you'll say the same once you meet dear Bon-Bon."

"Oh, my, yes. Where is your brother?"

He pointed the way, but before they'd fully left the kitchen, the back door swung wide as Ginkgo entered. Heads turned, and he received a flurry of greetings that implied that the half-fox hadn't simply been out shoveling paths. He'd been out all night. Jacques took a longer look. And perhaps due to his impish legacy, he saw through the trick.

Relying on the trickster's sharp ears, Jacques softly said, "You can't fool me."

Ginkgo touched a finger to his lips and winked.

Harrison, who was waiting on Jacques, took an inquisitive posture.

"Oh, you know how it is," Jacques said breezily. "Christmas is filled with secrets and surprises."

Not the least of which was Ginkgo, who was now swinging *two* tails.

They found Boniface in the Rosewood Parlor, the entrance to which was being guarded by Anan and Dima. They let them pass without comment. Bon-Bon had accumulated an interesting cortege, considering how often he complained about children. Sibley and Kyrie. Twosies and Trinity. The five of them were assembling gifts, pushing small boxes into festive paper bags, then affixing tags with ribbons.

"What new mischief is this?" Jacques asked.

"Do you need help?" offered Harrison.

Boniface glanced up, took in every detail of their attire, and refrained from comment. Instead, he asked, "Can you help with ribbons? Kyrie's trying to teach the others, but it's slow going."

Harrison grinned. "Tying bows is something of a specialty of mine!"

"That's true," said Kyrie. "Give us a lesson, Harrison-sensei?"

Soon the man was kneeling with the rest, and Kyrie had handled all the necessary introductions. So Jacques set aside his coffee cup and lowered himself to the floor beside his brother. He missed a beat when he realized that under his plush dressing gown, Bon-Bon was wearing pajamas with a pattern of tiny hedgehogs.

"Good lord. You kept them?"

"What? Oh. Well ... why wouldn't I?"

"Because I was twitting you ...?"

"Well aware." Boniface passed him one of the little bags and a red satin ribbon.

Jacques recognized the swooping calligraphy on the tag as his brother's. "Wait a tick. Who's Twila?"

"One of your new colonists. A filly, or so I'm told." Boniface cut another length of the wide ribbon. "With this lot, I needed my selections approved, and then I needed help matching them to recipients. This lad was more than up to the task. He's a bloody oracle."

"Language," Jacques said mildly.

"Right. Frightfully sorry."

"You brought gifts for everyone?"

Boniface rolled his eyes. "For the children anyhow. I mean, it's Christmas."

"So who approved your gifts?" Jacques had always enjoyed asking roundabout questions, since Boniface was easily frustrated by non-linear explanations.

"Argent brought in Juuyu and then Naoki. And I asked Hajime, of course."

With that, another person joined them at the table.

"Gosh!" exclaimed Harrison. "Well, hello!"

Kyrie introduced his grandfather, and the children talked over one another as they gave Harrison a largely anecdotal explanation of family trees and the nature of pollen. It was slapdash at best, but Jacques guessed it wouldn't really matter, since Harrison would soon forget it all. Maybe when he returned for his usual round of summer courses, he'd have enough time to acclimate to Hajime's presence.

Jacques snugged a cheery bow onto the bag and reached for another. "What did you find for them? May I see?"

"If you must."

Jacques carefully slid the small box out of the next bag and lifted the lid. He frowned in confusion. "A pocket watch?"

"More of a locket," said Boniface. "There's no inner workings."

"It is neither," countered Kyrie. "These are like the reliquaries at Kikusawa shrine."

Jacques was familiar enough. Akira had one. "What possessed you?"

Boniface shrugged. "Sylphon suggested it, and Ginkgo liked the idea. He said some of your tree-kin are keeping their golden seeds in pouches. These will be more secure, since Argent and Juuyu added sigils. And they can hold onto them as a keepsake, even after they plant their seeds.

It was surreal, hearing Bon-Bon talking calmly about long-held Betweener secrets. Jacques asked, "How do you even know ...?"

"Suuzu's a tribute. So's Sylphon. And ... well, I suppose it's poor form to rattle on. Does your bowtie savant know about you?"

"Harrison? Yes. We were up half the night spilling the tea. Bondmates and rock imps and babies, oh my."

"All very fascinating," Harrison assured.

"Would *you* like to be sprigged?" Hajime suddenly asked.

Harrison startled and exclaimed, "Gosh! Well, hello!"

Which required a whole new round of introductions, which Kyrie patiently made before moving on to Boniface's gifts. "Different styles are designed to fit a seed, acorn, or cone, depending on the variety of Amaranthine tree that will sprout when planted."

Boniface pushed another package his way.

The attendant label stunned Jacques. "Lilya?" he whispered.

Twosies finished adding a lopsided bow to another gift and pointedly passed it along.

"Lord. And Tenma, too. Is he here?"

"Yes. Da brought him when he brought Ever." Kyrie's smile was wistful. "Their reliquaries are empty for now, but Dad is letting them know the shape he wants their future to take."

Any further explanation was forestalled when Harrison exclaimed, "Gosh! Well, hello!"

While Sibley made the introductions this time, Boniface rummaged in a case at his side. "Here. Have a look. I've a few spares. They're rather prettyish. Sylphon's people make them."

The ornamental seed cases were each unique. One like an oval locket. One a perfect sphere. Another boxy and hinged, with a faceted remnant on its face. Each was tastefully embellished. And skillfully warded.

While he was fiddling with catches and sliding panels, Nonny came in with a tray. "With Sonnet's compliments," he said.

Twosies and Trinity moved finished gifts into a waiting basket to make room, and Nonny set out pastries, cocoa, and—bless her—a fresh pot of coffee.

"All right there, Kyrie?" Nonny asked. "You're looking a mite peaky."

The boy murmured something vague, but then Boniface was saying, "Here, Nonny. Since you're here. Seems your name's on this one."

Jacques gasped.

Nonny shot him a puzzled look, then reached for the bowtie-bedecked bag. "I'm sure that's very generous, Bon-Bon."

"Open it." Indicating Hajime, Boniface added, "Twosies says this sort is best for your sort."

Nonny held an egg-shaped pendant on a long chain. He teased open the catch, peered inside, and snapped it shut. "Thanks ...?"

"It's for a seed," Twosies said helpfully.

"Yes, yes." Boniface took a beleaguered tone. "I was getting to that. Argent wanted me to say that he'll see to any missing pieces and parts if you'll pop by and ... ah. He's gone."

Indeed, Nonny had fled so fast, even his hoofbeats were lost in the distance.

"That went well enough, I suppose," Boniface said. "I don't see why Argent has to be so sly about everything. Or put *me* up to it. You do these? More your thing."

He set two boxes in front of Jacques. And wouldn't meet his gaze.

"What have you done?" Jacques whispered.

"Don't blame me." Boniface pursed his lips and softly added, "And don't thank me, either. We both know that Argent bloody Lord Mettlebright likes to spoil his man."

There were tags. "What do they say?"

Boniface sighed. "I know you can read, Jackie. I taught you myself."

So he pulled the boxes closer and flipped the first tag. Then the second.

Josheb

Harrison

Jacques just stared at his brother.

Boniface gazed back without expression. "Empty, of course. But on reserve and theirs for the asking, or so I'm told."

From under the table, a resonating note broke into a tuneful cascade. Tattling on Jacques, but also breaking the sudden tension. "You brought our rock imp."

"Couldn't be helped," muttered Boniface. "He doesn't like to be left out."

"Oh, blast and dash! Give me one of those tags. A blank one."

Boniface located one and passed it along.

"A pen, love. Do try to keep up."

He uncapped a fountain pen and extended it. "I'm not your love."

"*Non*. You're my brother." And with as much flourish as he could manage in the space allowed, began to write. "My pompous ... priggish ... persevering ... bird-bound ... brassy ... bloody well brilliant brother."

"Language," Boniface chided. "And don't be unctuous. It's unbefitting a Smythe."

"Then when you're giving reading lessons to your *next* little brother, teach him better manners." He presented the tag with both hands.

On it he'd printed Bon-Bon's full name—**Boniface Percival Christobel Yves Smythe**.

"Tiresome brat," was all the thanks he gave. But he tucked the tag into his vest pocket. Then pulled their rock imp onto his lap, absently shushing and tutting as he patted the tuneful stone.

Sibley asked, "What if your tree's a sister?"

Jacques suggested, "Sonnet?"

"That's a good idea. I mean, she'll probably want ... umm ... oh. Uh-oh." Sibley leapt to his feet, spun around, and called, "Anan?"

The storm imp stepped through the doorway. A moment later, thunder rumbled ominously. "Where's Kyrie?"

63

LITTLE TERROR

Before Kyrie could think it through completely, he was coaxing his way past the barriers surrounding his dad's conservatory. Visits to this inner sanctum were rare. And always chaperoned. Which meant he was out-of-bounds and probably breaking trust, yet he kept going.

A minute. That was all he needed.

Wending through the hidden garden that flourished behind beveled glass, ironwork, and illusions, he spared a glance for the sky beyond. Pink and gold were gaining. The sun would soon rise. Christmas morning had arrived.

His birthday.

His and Lilya's.

They were thirteen.

This year, Kyrie's present from his parents had come as a surprise, probably because his father had settled on something at the last minute. He was to be given a room of his own, outside his parents' suite. Because he wasn't a little boy anymore.

Dad had probably expected gratitude, not the opening of negotiations.

But there was Anan to consider. While Kyrie didn't like to imply that the eldermost storm wasn't housebroken, there had been enough inclement incidents to give weight to his argument. Yes, a room would be nice, but a house would be better. For everyone.

In the end, the decision had required a whole committee's input and agreement. Kyrie's four parents worried over precedents, and Ginkgo and Uncle Jackie brought up attainment. Fend and Anjou were called upon to give their opinions, and even Boon and Sinder weighed in. Kyrie would get his house. Building it would be a summer project.

He had swayed them.

He had surprised them.

People were often surprised by his actions, but he rarely surprised himself. Kyrie was careful and cautious. He made plans and then he implemented them. But stealing into the conservatory felt … different. Reckless. Maybe even a little dangerous.

Part of him—probably half of him—obeyed instincts that pulled more strongly than ever before. Was it because he was entering adolescence? Or maybe something had changed because he'd taken in three storms? He was storm-touched and storm-kissed and storm-kept.

Could Sinder help him sort through these sudden, strange impulses? Like now, as he plucked several clusters of forget-me-nots, which Dad managed so there were always some in bloom.

Taking them felt right, even necessary. But were they important enough to risk Dad's disappointment in him? And why was he making so many excuses?

He wouldn't be gone long.

He wouldn't be going far.

But as he fled with his posy, he could hear the sounds of a storm building in the house at his back. He was being foolish. He could not outrun the wind. Yet he kept going. Leading the storm away? Or just following another instinct? Was he being selfish? Was it allowed, this once? As a birthday treat?

Kyrie ran faster, adding long leaps that blew back his hair, cooling his face.

Maybe ... maybe he wasn't thinking too clearly. Why was that? Was he starstruck or imp-addled? Something was definitely strange.

And then Anan was upon him like a crash, except that he didn't thunder. His grip was gentle, and his eyes held concern. "Where do you think you are going? And why are you scattering flower petals?"

He looked at his stolen bouquet. Why hadn't he protected it better? More than half the petals were missing, leaving it limp and ragged.

"I told you not to go without me."

"But the danger has passed."

Anan dropped into a low crouch and peered up into his face. "Am I only needed for emergencies, then? You're done with me?"

Kyrie shook his head.

Reaching out, Anan pried one of his hands away from the

bouquet he now cradled to his chest. The storm silently inspected his mark, rubbing his thumb into Kyrie's palm, perhaps checking to see if it had come loose. A fanciful notion. That's not how sigils worked. If it was going, it would fade, not fall off.

"Are you in pain?" Anan asked softly.

Kyrie blinked and peered around, disoriented. "No ...?"

"Mmm. Restless?"

"A little ...? I was going."

Anan slowly straightened. "Where are we going?"

"That way. Not far."

"Show me." And Anan took his hand.

Kyrie grabbed hold, suddenly grateful that he wasn't alone.

"Tell me what this is, little terror."

But he didn't know what this was. Only that they were going the right way. "Can you hear it?"

"What am I listening for?"

"My anchor stone."

"Is that what draws you?" Anan seemed doubtful.

Ginkgo caught up with them then. He barged right in, and Anan let him. "Hey, little bro. What's up?"

He showed his ruined bouquet. "I thought ... flowers."

"Okay, sure. Can I come, too?"

Kyrie simply walked on, sodden slippers crunching through snow. Warm cloth settled over his shoulders. Ginkgo's usual blue shirt was comforting. It was cold. He should have noticed.

When he could feel the stone below, he stopped. "It is here. The place. He is here."

"Who's here?" prompted Anan.

When the silence stretched, Ginkgo answered. "This is where Hajime buried Shisoku."

One by one, Kyrie plucked tiny blue petals and let them fall upon the snow.

The flowers were mangled and scattered, but each petal was tiny and perfect.

Like the mothers.

Like their children.

As the last fell, Ginkgo turned Kyrie toward him. Concern showed on his face, but his ears were pricked forward, like he was on the scent of something. "Trust me?"

"I do."

"Let's bring Damsel in on this, okay? Timur, too."

That sounded good. A keening sort of noise slipped free before Kyrie could stop it. He twisted the flower stems between his hands, wringing them.

Anan acted first. "Hajime," he called, confining himself to a half-roar. "You heard him."

Several beats passed, and Anan had begun to grumble, but then there were familiar scents and soft sounds and red petals mingling with the blue.

Sinder took Ginkgo's place. "Hey, little cousin. Okay, wow. Fraught much?"

"I do not feel well."

"Too much birthday cake for breakfast?"

Kyrie just stared at him.

"Sorry. Lame joke. I'm taking you seriously, I swear." Sinder asked, "How *do* you feel? Besides not well. Can you describe what's going on?"

"I am ... not myself?"

"Okay, sure. I don't think there's any great mystery here. Well, I'd love to know *why* ... but I think we can cover other important stuff, like who and what and when and where. Actually, I'd be interested to know *why here*?"

Kyrie offered the twist of stems to Sinder. "I brought flowers. For the stone. Forget-me-nots are the emblem of dragon-slayers. We became dragon slayers, that stone and I. We felled a giant."

"Yeah, you did good. Actually, Fend said you were perfect, and he doesn't give compliments lightly." Sinder ventured, "So you wanted to thank this remnant stone."

"And to keep my promise. This stone is my tribute. My oath is made."

"You know about that, do you? I'm impressed. Tributes are pretty tightlipped about membership to their little club."

"I hear things." Kyrie didn't apologize. He wasn't sorry.

"Understatement. And it might explain some of this. I mean, big-time vows can trigger some pretty interesting consequences. Especially when imps are involved. Lucky for you, I have just the thing for an occasion like this. Big fella. Total pro. Authentic Spomenka. And as an added bonus, he's a healer who makes house calls." Sinder turned Kyrie so he could see and added, "He knows his stuff."

Timur had dropped to one knee. Smile warm, hands on offer, he said, "Good morning, Kyrie. May I touch?"

Kyrie gave in to instinct and flung himself into Timur's bulk. Here was knowledge and kindness and a sheltering calm.

Timur who understood sadness and sacrifice. Timur who was stronger for it.

"Easy there," Timur soothed. "I'm right here, and I'll stay right here until you're steady. No need to throttle. Or to invest your soul."

"Sorry," he whispered, mortified.

"It's instincts, yeah? You know what you need even if you haven't thought it through. I can guide you, but first ... grab that blanket, Ginkgo?"

"Got it. Hey, should we get him indoors?"

"No. This is fine. We're out of the wind, and we can see the sky."

"We are not out of the wind," said Kyrie. "Anan is warning it off."

"For which I'm grateful," said Timur.

A soft blanket swathed Kyrie, and then Timur's fingers were probing and pressing. Kyrie closed his eyes with a sigh, his tension ebbing.

Sinder said, "I know, right? Best of the best."

"It's all right, Kyrie." There was a reassuring lift to Timur's voice. Like he might be smiling. "I think I know what we're facing, so you can relax. Leave everything to me. It'll be an honor to attend you."

Ginkgo spoke again. "Won't his being a crosser make a difference? When it was my turn, I needed both Dad and Tsumiko."

"Ahhh, to help with your balance? Sinder and I could do it. Or ... well, we *could* fetch Lilya. But I'm assuming Anan would prefer to do it himself. They're already bonded."

Ginkgo said, "Nobody mentioned that it'd gone that far."

"I'd say they're pretty entrenched. Anan's marks shine," said

Sinder. "You've got that whole unassailable alliance thing going on, but I'm betting that an imp's tending packs a wallop. Go easy, Anan Eldermost."

There was some grumbling and some explanations, but Kyrie was mostly focused on feeling safe and surrounded. It was easier to think now. Maybe he should have asked for Lilya, the person who'd always been closest, who'd always be dear to his heart. But their lives were steadily diverging. *These* were the companions on the path at his feet.

Kyrie loved Lilya, but he actually wanted Sibley.

So he called for him.

Not with his voice. Nor was it a thought, like the mind-speak that contributed to a clan's closeness. But the stone beneath their feet resonated with his wish, and that was good. He would keep his promise to this stone. It would anchor an array. It would help him protect his clan.

"What are you doing, Kyrie?" asked Timur. Because of course Timur would notice. He was a ward like Papka.

"I am resonating." He shyly confided, "Sibley says that resonance is a kind of love."

"Yeah, I did say that." And his younger brother marched up and asked, "Where'd you go?"

"Here."

"How come?"

"To be in a place with trees and wind and stars and stone." Until he spoke it aloud, he hadn't realized this was true.

Anan asked, "What of the tides?"

Kyrie considered this. "I have never met a briner."

Sinder snorted. "You're still a kid. Leave yourself a *few* things to grow into."

"One thing at a time," urged Ginkgo. "Can you get a sense of them yet?"

All the words that had been flowing over and around him veered into focus. Kyrie asked, "Is it … wings?"

"Yeah. I think so. You're coming into your own on the early side." Ginkgo asked, "Ready for your attainment?"

"Is it too soon?" He looked to Sinder, who was at least two centuries older than him and who'd only found his own wings the summer before.

"Nope," said Sinder. "There's no such thing as early or late when it comes to this sort of thing. We find what we need when we need it. For you, it's looking like now. Or nearly now."

"Kyrie's got wings?" asked Sibley.

"He will have, yes." Timur sounded completely assured.

"Can I see?" asked Sibley.

Timur let the blanket sag lower, and Sinder gently lifted Kyrie's tunic. "Okay, off," Sinder decreed. "Bear with the cold. Your Uncle Jackie won't thank any of us if you rip your nice shirt."

Kyrie shivered and tried to peer over his shoulder.

Sibley was right there, eyeing him critically.

"What do you see?"

"You've got marks on your back. Here and here." Warm hands pressed firmly against cold skin. "Have you always had them?"

"Yes."

"You might be the only one, then." Sibley's gaze held admiration. "Good for you."

Anan spoke again. "This is what you wanted."

Kyrie thought it over, then admitted, "I did. I do."

"Then take it."

"I do not know how."

"Yes, you do." Anan sat in the snow and beckoned. "Come, little terror."

Timur helped him go, and Gingko crowded so close, he was practically hanging over Anan's shoulder. Then Sinder began to sing, and the woods were tuning, and from somewhere overhead, pure voices added encouragement in gentle cascades.

"Come little terror," Anan repeated. "Do not keep us waiting."

"Winds almost never stay." Kyrie pushed at him with gratitude and love, only to gain a grumble.

"This is no time to be generous, child of trees and stars and stone. Stow your mercy and show a dragon's greed. Take what you need from me. Only from me."

They were weighty words. Binding words.

Anan continued, and his words took on a rolling cadence, a little like a song, one for which Kyrie had always known the lyrics, for they told his story.

"Your mother gave you your name.

"Your father gave you a house.

"Your sire gave you a clan.

"Your tree gave you victory.

"Your siblings give you purpose.

"But I am Anan Eldermost—darkener of lands and harrower of hearts. I am he who was and is and has become music incarnate. And I will give you the sky."

64

WORLD WITHOUT END

Argent supposed he was growing accustomed to having Anjou around. Even though it was the wee hours, his gentleman's gentleman's gentleman smoothly escorted Opal out so Argent could have a private word.

Sinder watched them go with a forlorn expression, then stood with eyes fixed on the carpet, as if contemplating further prostration.

Giving himself time to process this new and unanticipated information, Argent leafed through the papers again. Sinder hadn't tried to hide the enormity of his neglect. Timestamped entries proved just how many years had been lost simply because the information had been filed away.

Kept from him.

But Argent was impressed. With his current resources, he wouldn't have been able to locate any of these children.

Without Sinder, they would have remained lost.

Sinder's fact-finding had been a personal project, done entirely out of curiosity. A sideline to the greater problem, which had been locating the Rogue. Which is why, in the months soon after Kyrie's birth, several more siblings had been located. Other survivors. Orphans without the protection of a clan.

Kyrie had older siblings. A few, anyhow. Assuming they still survived.

It bothered Argent a great deal that the addresses listed were for hospitals, laboratories, and what he suspected were private research facilities. On the bright side, all of them were in the public sector. Breaking in would be so much simpler than locating an uncharted island.

Argent raised his gaze to a fidgeting Sinder. The level of regret radiating from the young dragon was heartening. He'd been mingling with the children long enough to understand what his silence had meant. But Argent was detecting traces of fear, and those needed banishing.

"Well done."

Sinder lifted a startled gaze.

"This information is invaluable. You anticipated my need, and I choose to be grateful."

The dragon winced. "Look, I know I should have—"

Argent held up a hand to forestall any further apologies. "Is this list exhaustive?"

"Not sure. The next step will be to check my findings against Linlu Dimityblest's records. There could be some overlap. Especially if the Hightips were stashing kids in other places."

"Like Inti."

"He sets a precedent, yeah. And expands the search parameters. *Any* crosser that's been culled." He took a step forward and promised, "I can find them. Your kids. I'll look until they're all found."

"And then what?"

Sinder blinked. "This time, we go get them."

"Yes, we will." Argent lifted his brows. "You are used to a certain amount of action."

"Well, sure. All part of the job. Though I'm not sure I *have* a job anymore. Hisoka's retirement or abdication or whatever means he doesn't need a cortege."

"True. How fortuitous that I am in the process of assembling one."

"No kidding?" Sinder brightened. "I don't like to brag, but I know these five other guys. All kinds of elite. Stellar teamwork. Loads of experience. If you're hiring, I could put them in touch."

"That would be a good start."

"Thinking of expanding membership?"

"I am. Some of you have families now. More members in the rotation will mean less time away from bondmates and young. And in your case, the dragon-crossers you will be mentoring alongside Opal."

"Now that I *have* a home, I won't complain if I get to spend time here."

"Are you aware that Fend made your joining my cortege a condition of his acceptance?"

"That little shit. Wait. Are you airing a grievance? You don't actually want me?"

"Not so. Jacques recommended you a few years ago, so you have been under consideration all along. I actually suspect that Fend used the pretense of leverage to alert me to the sudden availability of your team. An effective maneuver. He excels at manipulation."

"You're pretty roundabout yourself." Sinder hesitated, then asked, "Am I in, then?"

"You are in." Argent gestured to Sinder's partial transformation. "Also, thank you for aligning yourself with my son. He has been unusually self-conscious."

"They take some getting used to. Balance and whatnot." Wings with an icy iridescence swept outward in a partial display, but Sinder twitched them back into neat folds along his back. "It's no big deal. Well, it *is* kind of a mess for clothes, but Jacques stepped in. Anjou had this slinky getup with an open back. Timur likes it. The wings, I mean, not the mantraps. Can't keep his hands off them, which is … probably way more than I needed to say. There's nothing weird about it. Just oiling and stretching and … well, shit. Jacques-ish-ness really is catching."

"You can assume that anything you say in here is taken in confidence."

"Thanks for that." With a pained expression, Sinder said, "Timur and me. I swear it's not a romantic thing."

"Timur is a member of the Order of Spomenka. I would be shocked if he did not look after the needs of his dragon."

"He's the best. Him and Fend both. Though that's not his name. Well, it won't be. Assuming he doesn't shut me down again. But if he's pleased, we'll have our bond."

Argent wondered if Hisoka had ever tried to curb Sinder's tongue. "Fend wanted a bond with you?"

"He's been really pushy about it, so yeah. Safe to say he wants it. Or me." Sinder went a little pink. "I keep asking, 'why me?'"

"Does it matter? You do not have to understand why you are happy to know you are happy."

Sinder snorted. "Juuyu spouts crap when he's embarrassed, too."

Argent decided he must *like* being handled with a certain level of irreverence.

His cortege was shaping up nicely.

Timur sat on the low stone wall that safeguarded the drop-off to the sea, even this far along the coast from Stately House. Kicking snow from his boots, he pulled the edges of his cloak around the heavy crystal strapped to his chest. "Do you even feel the cold?" he asked the rock imp.

To his delight, there was a gurgling sort of chuckle.

Sinder was right. Their rock imp liked to chat.

"It was too cold for Gregor, but you're managing well enough, hmm?"

They'd been tromping through the forest surrounding Stately House from sun-up to mid-past, and he was a necessary party member. Because Kyrie was to have his own little house. But one of the conditions that Argent had set was that the boy have good neighbors. More specifically, it had to be someone

Fend would approve.

Fend had immediately put forward *their* names.

Who better to keep an eye on Argent's son than Argent's second-in-command, a Spomenka with parental prowess, and the dragon who'd helped Kyrie gain the sky? Brains, brawn, and beauty.

Decision made.

But vague plans weren't Fend's way, and Kyrie was similarly eager to secure his future. So Kyrie, Ever, Lilya, Fend, and Ginkgo were leading the hunt, with Anan trailing after. And for reasons that weren't entirely clear, both Anjou and Boniface had joined the party. Timur was mostly along for the ride. They'd already decided to build, but he didn't really care where.

Boniface trudged in Timur's direction. His slim figure was slightly overbalanced by the chrysalis he carried. As the man came closer, Timur couldn't help but notice that the Smythe brothers' crystal had been swaddled in cashmere. Only the very top had been left exposed, as if to allow the rock imp to enjoy the scenery.

"Lord, I hope they make up their mind soon. Why did it have to be *today*? Auspicious or not, it's a bitter New Year's Eve."

"The air has teeth, and it's not afraid to bite." It was an old dragon saying, and it definitely applied. "I can understand Kyrie's excitement."

"Can't be helped." Boniface leaned against the wall and hugged his burden. With a nod to Timur's, he blandly asked, "Do you suppose this makes us 'dad friends'?"

"That sounds about right." And because he wasn't sure if Boniface knew him as anything other than the chauffeur's son, he offered, "I'm Timur, but the way."

"Well aware. Suuzu brought me up to speed as far as members of the household and enclave are concerned. I haven't quite sorted out all the wolves, though. The names are tricky. But Boon offered to introduce me to everyone. Another day. When it's less in the way of frigid."

Timur pushed aside his cloak to access the thermos that was slung with his other gear. The action exposed the heavy blade belted at his waist, and he saw Boniface eyeing it warily.

"Expecting trouble from some quarter?"

"I'm a battler. We believe in preparedness." He uncapped the thermos and passed it along.

Boniface sniffed rising steam. "Tea?"

"My own blend. I'm also a healer."

"Doubly reassuring." Boniface sipped, hummed his appreciation, then took a bigger swallow. He lapsed into silence, gazing around the snowy forest with a serene expression. "A healer. That explains why Fend is insisting on space for an herb garden."

"Good of him."

Boniface hummed. "And Kyrie wants someplace near the sea. For Sinder's sake."

"They really are putting a lot of thought into this."

"And you're not?"

"I'll be happy if they're happy."

"You're set then." Boniface stared into the steam still rising from the thermos.

In that moment, Timur thought the man looked terribly lonesome. On impulse, he said, "If you like, after this, why not come by my room. We'll stoke the fires and see you warmed. And

I can give you a packet of that tea."

"Are you just going to ask for embarrassing stories about Jackie?"

"Only if they help us get to know you better." Timur added, "We're dad friends, aren't we?"

That earned him a rueful smile. "And future neighbors. Probably."

"Is that why you're here?"

"Mmm. I've asked Kyrie to make allowances for … well." And completely changing tacks, Boniface announced, "I turned forty this past year. Bloody hell, that sounds older than it feels."

"You're about Papka's age, then."

The smaller man drew himself up. "That can't be right. I'm *not* old enough to be your father."

"I meant … relative age." Timur looked off in the direction of the house, then shrugged. "Papka stopped getting older about a decade ago."

"Ah." And after a lengthy pause, Boniface repeated, "Ah. That sort of thing will happen when you take up with the imps and clans."

Timur dared to ask, "Are you thinking of your brother?"

That earned him a sharp look. "No. My world doesn't revolve around Jackie. But … lord. I suppose I'll never get away from comparisons. First of Smythes? If anyone cared to notice, *I* have the years."

Timur didn't know what to say. He was Jacques' friend. But that didn't mean he couldn't befriend Boniface. They were both good men. And they might be neighbors, though Timur had gotten the vague idea that Boniface's job involved a lot of travel.

"Forever forty," Boniface murmured. "I suppose this *is* meant to be the prime of life."

"Do you mean Papka?"

"What? No. I mean *me*." Boniface gestured with one hand, still hugging the chrysalis with the other. "There's the other route, you know. Dr. Naoki told me about his way. Is it meant to be a secret? I keep running up against them."

"Dr. Noaki. I did meet him briefly. He's Tsumiko's and Akira's father."

"That's the chap. Doesn't look a day over … well, he's thirty-something, isn't he? Started earlier. Can't be helped. But anyway, years plus mobility would be a useful combination."

"You're thinking of taking in a golden seed?"

"Do *not* tell Argent bloody Lord Mettlebright. He's got Jackie on a short leash, but I have plans." His gaze was fierce. "I'm confiding in you. Because we're dad friends. And future neighbors. And … *mon dieu*, I'll probably need help. But I won't ask Jackie. None of his bloody business. And you seem a good sort. Can I rely upon you?"

"You need me?"

"Well, I need *somebody*. I'm on my own in all this."

That put Timur in familiar territory. "In some ways, I'm a single father. Taking sole responsibility for a child is life-changing. Though I'm not alone, and you won't be either. Still, you're facing a big decision. Take your time."

"Bit late for that." Boniface raised the thermos in a toast. "Here's to the queerest New Year's resolution ever made in the history of me."

"It's done?"

"I spoke at length to Dr. Naoki, who chose one of his experimentals. Poor thing can't simply be planted. Has to have a surrogate." Boniface patted his rock imp, who'd begun softly crooning. "Downed my seed on the sly. Early this morning, with cranberry juice. Hajime held my hand. Gave his blessing."

"You're a brave man, Boniface. My invitation stands. Come back with me. Fend will be *delighted* to help you keep your secret. Sinder and I can set up some wards. For secrecy. For safety. We can support you. You won't be alone."

"Knew you were a good sort."

Timur clapped his shoulder and said, "Likewise."

They made an evening of it.

Upon hearing Boniface's well-reasoned yet rebellious decision to keep his choice a secret, Fend fixed Timur with a look of pure adoration. Like he'd brought home a particularly nice treat. After that, Timur was once again along for the ride, because Sinder excelled at drawing people out, and ever since finding speaking form, Fend had been greedy for conversation.

Timur pottered in the background, bringing snacks and brewing tea. He saw to Gregor's bath and tucked him in with Lilya and Vanya. When he returned to his room, the topic had turned to Boniface's courses. He was being mentored on the job by the members of Suuzu's cortege, but he wasn't opposed to a bit of private tutoring.

Fend offered to draw up a syllabus.

Sinder meddled with Boniface's phone, adding all their contact information.

And Timur noted with appreciation that the man had finally relaxed. Boniface's gracious manners had slipped, and it was easier to see how greedy he was for the company of peers.

"You should stay the night," Timur said. He indicated the bed. "Plenty of room."

"That's very generous, I'm sure." Boniface looked as if he wanted to accept.

"You should stay," Sinder echoed, adding a touch of sway.

Timur probably should have called him out, but Boniface looked so relieved. "If you're sure?"

Fend said, "Rest here, among friends. Deepen the bonds of trust."

"Right," said Boniface. "I didn't fancy being alone. Usually, there's Sylphon, you see. Funny how you get used to company …?"

Fend accompanied the man to the onsen, and Sinder checked with Dr. Naoki, who confirmed that a small dose of huddlebud wouldn't go amiss. Within the hour, Boniface was clean and warm and well-warded. And sound asleep.

Timur looked on with satisfaction. More than that, he was happy.

"You *like* having a patient," Sinder accused.

"I like having a dad friend." Timur rested his chin on his palm and considered the man who'd taken refuge with them. "I'm glad he trusted us."

"He has good instincts." Fend warned, "His ambitions may mean we'll foster his child."

Timur wasn't so sure. Still, he said, "Make sure our little house isn't too small, hmm?"

"I can do that."

Fend was nice enough to let Timur think he was in charge once in a while. Probably because they both knew otherwise. And they'd always found the arrangement agreeable. Teamwork. Alliance. It was good for battle, but it was equally good for creating a sheltering space. Timur reflected that he really had taken after Mum, who took great pride in defending her home. And the many people who needed its haven.

While Timur was woolgathering, Sinder dropped to a perch on the arm of his chair. He glanced up, wondering at the impressions he was catching. Sinder was in a simmer of anticipation.

"Two things, okay?" Sinder heaved a breath and announced, "He likes it. So we'll have to get used to calling Fend by his new name."

Timur beckoned to his partner, who came to perch on the other arm of his chair. His eyes were bright with the import of their news.

"So you've come to terms?" Timur asked. "Forged a bond?"

Sinder simply nodded.

Fend began to purr.

Wrapping his arms around both their waists, Timur said, "Well? Which of you is going to tell me?"

His dragon turned his hands palm up and said, "The fathers are strong. Seriously. Both of you have scary-strong dads. And since Fend is a tribute to his sire, I thought he might want to carry forward Deece's name. In part."

Shifting into tones that were both formal and laced with sway, Sinder continued. "Smallest of your litter, you quickly proved your strength. You earned admiration and your first name. Able to fend for yourself, Deece Evernhold named you Fend.

"Since then, you pacted with a reaver, you found speaking form, and you fended for everyone at Stately House. Argent Mettlebright may have handed down your attainment, but you earned it. By your wits and by your cunning.

"You saved my life, you entrusted your partner to me, and you want the bond a name bestows. And so we'll call you Evern. And hold you close."

The feline blinked placidly. "Evern Michaelson. Because I belong to both of you."

Timur reached up to tug his ear. "Is good, yes?"

"Quite satisfactory. But that's only the first thing. Go on, lovely one. Time for the rest."

Sinder leaned away to collect it, then dropped a small stack of folders onto Timur's lap. "Merry Christmas. Belatedly. From us. As promised."

Evern nuzzled Timur's cheek before kissing it. "We've gone past midnight, so we'll call this Happy New Year. Don't be shy, Papka. Have a look. You did well."

He withdrew his arms from around them, touched the stack. Straightened it. Stalled.

"I left out most of their personal information. There's nothing about their parents or where they were born. If they want to talk to you about home, that's up to them." Sinder dropped to the floor, kneeling in order to look up into Timur's face. "This is stuff I thought you'd care about. Some basics. Names, birthdays, early aptitude scores."

Evern interjected, "But there's so much more. He's included

nicknames, favorite colors, family pets, and in several cases, weapon of choice."

"Three of them come from lines with longstanding arrangements with Kith, not unlike your mother. No felines though." Sinder went right on, even though Timur's vision kept blurring. "One young lady has grown up with wolf Kith in the house. Her family was keen on the fact that we have a pack here. I think that swayed them even more than the prestige of our staff."

Timur started. "You spoke to their parents?"

"Not personally, no. Randolla and a few of his lot volunteered to do a bit of touring, as a favor to Argent. They're not official heralds, but they pulled this off like pros. As residents, they were able to talk up the enclave. One unexpected upshot was a couple of applications for colonization. It'll make things easier on the kids if some of their people come along. We'll have to add Russian to our language lessons."

"The battle has turned," said Evern, all superiority. "Those who wanted to take from you, to gain the advantages of pedigree and prestige? They've surrendered. Your children are *ours*."

"Hey, it's not like that," grumbled Sinder. "Don't talk about these kids' folks like they're the enemy. Sure, reavers who add to their families by arrangement are hoping for improved rank, but they don't do it for themselves. It's so the next generation will have more options. Every family Randolla spoke to? They were *thrilled* that their little phenoms are going to get the best possible training."

Timur needed some time to think that through. Later. So he asked, "They're all coming?"

"Every one of them." Evern tapped the folders. "Are you pleased with us?"

"I will be," he promised. "At the moment, I'm too stunned to be anything else."

"There are pictures," prompted Evern. "Have a peek at the future."

Timur carefully flipped open the topmost folder and stared. "She looks just like Lilya."

"She does," agreed Sinder.

That's how it went as he quietly studied the photos.

"He has Papka's green eyes."

"And your smile."

"She has a falcon?"

"She and that Kith have been inseparable since birth."

All twenty-four of the children were between the ages of five and eight. So young to be leaving their mothers, but that was the way of things with reavers. Especially those with dynasty-class pedigrees.

Opening the next file, Timur's voice wobbled a little. "He looks just like me, doesn't he?"

"That one? Sure," said Sinder. "If you were more prone to glaring."

"Is he unhappy?"

"With you? Hardly. Randolla made a point of mentioning that he was the first to accept." Sinder scooted away just long enough to grab the tissue box. "Gather your courage, battler. Ready or not, your wee ickle dragon-slayers will be here by Dichotomy Day next. At midsummer."

"Oh, we'll be ready." Evern licked away some of Timur's tears.

"The fathers are strong, etcetera, etcetera. And we are far from weak."

"Here you are," grumbled Argent.

Tsumiko gently pointed out, "You always know where I am."

"Ah, but this is not where you *usually* are." Arms slipped around her from behind as Argent joined her in contemplating the room Kyrie had finished vacating. It was empty of all but echoes.

She leaned back into Argent, grateful for his support.

"Was I wrong to send him from this place?" he asked.

"No. He was happy to go."

Argent swathed her in the silver softness of his tails, and his hands settled at her waist.

She smiled to herself and pulled them further forward, to rest over her stomach.

Argent huffed. "You spoke with Bethiel for quite some time. Perchance, did the angel have any annunciations for my lady?"

"His message was more along the lines of 'well done, good and faithful,' quickly followed by 'keep up the good work.' Which doesn't sound the least bit angelic, but it's good that he's not lofty or formal. People will quickly come to love and trust him."

"Bethiel will undoubtedly become what Twineshaft was. The Council's guiding star. Our voice." Argent pulled her closer. "Are you pretending not to understand why I sent Kyrie away?"

Since his return from this last rescue mission, Argent had been especially ... attentive. But the natural consequences of his ardor hadn't occurred to her. Until Rhomiko had tugged her arm through theirs and escorted her to Dr. Elara.

After receiving positive test results, Tsumiko hadn't known quite how to break the news to Argent. Yet here he clung, radiating contrition. She almost laughed. "So you knew."

He hummed an affirmative and kissed her jaw. An apology. And something more.

"Why are you embarrassed, of all things?" She turned her head to look up at him.

"Because I have been so careful. Up until now. And I do not like to think of the risks."

"It'll be all right."

"How do you know? Crosser births are difficult enough, but for a beacon ...?"

"O, ye of little faith. I'll be fine." Tsumiko pivoted and pulled Argent down for a light kiss. "*Keep up the good work.* Wouldn't you say that implies many long years in which to prosper?"

"May it be unto me—and thee—as you say."

She laughed.

Argent smiled in a pleased way. His tails took on a much calmer sway. And Tsumiko reflected that this little room wasn't truly empty.

It was ready.

Ready for a future that would be built alongside living stone.

Ready for peaceful days under the shelter of generous trees.

Ready for the songs of ancients and eldermost and oracles and stars.

Ready to be filled with all the things that made Stately House a home.

And she would be ready, too.

"You shine," Argent declared, his voice low with reverence. "Like Soriel of the Dawning, like Auriel of the Golden Seed. Like every tale of the Kindred, the Unbroken, and the Blessed, my lady shines."

Her bondmate rarely spoke of his feelings. Even this reprise of an old confession was oblique in the extreme. But Tsumiko knew that his words were heartfelt, and that for Argent, they amounted to a prayer of thanks. For her, certainly. But also for the future they were building, little by little, life by life, year upon year, together. Onward and evermore, world without end.

And so she kissed his smile and said, "Amen."

*Abundant thanks to all who lend their support by reading, rating, and
reviewing my stories, wherever they may be found. ::twinkle::*

ALSO BY FORTHRIGHT

AMARANTHINE SAGA

Tsumiko and the Enslaved Fox

Kimiko and the Accidental Proposal

Tamiko and the Two Janitors

Mikoto and the Reaver Village

Fumiko and the Finicky Nestmate

Pimiko and the Uncharted Island

Rhomiko and the Confirmed Bachelor

SONGS OF THE AMARANTHINE

Marked by Stars

Followed by Thunder

Dragged through Hedgerows

Governed by Whimsy

Hemmed in Silver

Captured on Film

Bathed in Moonlight

Flattered by Flowers

Scribbled in Margins

Pressed into Service

AMARANTHINE INTERLUDES

Lord Mettlebright's Man

Suuzu and the Nine Nippets of Legend

Coop and the Elderbough Trackers

PATREON EXCLUSIVES

Bard & Barbarian

Kimiko and the Cycle of Moons

never more than
FORTHRIGHT

a teller of tales who began as a fandom ficcer. (Which basically means that no one in RL knows about her anime habit, her manga collection, or her penchant for serial storytelling.) Kinda sorta almost famous for gently-paced, WAFFy adventures that might inadvertently overturn your OTP, forthy will forever adore drabble challenges, surprise fanart, and twinkles (which are rumored to keep well in jars). As always... be nice, play fair, have fun! ::twinkle::

FORTHWRITES.COM

For all those who really wished they could see the *entire* courtship of Kimiko MIyabe and Eloquence Starmark, I have good news! The **serialization is updating now.** All the drama at Kikusawa Shrine (and New Saga High): two roommates, three sisters, twelve kisses, and the long-awaited stirring of a sleeping landmark. Friendship. Courtship.

Become a patron at https://www.patreon.com/forthrightly

Bard & Barbarian

BY FORTHRIGHT

Imber was only a boy when he met the divine beast
who would one day share his adventures.

A serialized fantasy that's currently a Patreon exclusive. Access to the ongoing adventure is available at all tiers of support. Now with bi-weekly audio installments, narrated by Travis Baldree. Become a patron in order to read along.

https://www.patreon.com/forthrightly

She's used to writing headlines.
She's about to become one.

Levity Jones is a local celebrity. As a journalist with the *Perspective*, her reports connect a whole city. Nobody would believe that the one bringing them heartwarming human-interest stories isn't human. Unless she goes public. Which is exactly what the Five are asking her to do. The clans are about to become breaking news, and they need influencers like Levity to cast the Amaranthine people in the best possible light.

WHAT'S NEXT?
COMING IN 2025

A steampunk mystery. An alternate history. Cozy suspense with a paranormal twist.

Get the latest news about upcoming titles by following forthright's blog at **ForthWrites.com**. Even more teasers, reveals, stories, and mailings can be found on Patreon. Support forthright's storyitelling at **patreon.com/forthrightly**.